To Jake

Happy Christmas 2000

The MoonBridge Way Opened

Written by
David G. Sheppard

http://www.themoonbridge.co.uk

Designed and Published By

Jadela Limited

Registered in England and Wales (4059203)
Jadela House, 9 Peak Lane, Fareham
Hampshire PO14 1RP
United Kingdom

http://www.jadela.co.uk

First Published August 2006

ISBN: 0-9552703-0-8
ISBN 13: 978-0-9552703-0-7

Printing & Typesetting

Bishops Printers
Fitzherbert Road
Farlington
Portsmouth
Hampshire
PO6 1RU

www.bishops.co.uk

For Korbyn-George
My first Grandchild,
All my love
Pops

Author's Note

Thank you very much for choosing to purchase my book and welcome to the first, in a series, of exciting adventure stories following Jack Ferns and his friends.

I hope you derive as much enjoyment from reading the story as I've had in writing it. From the first lines, to the final review, I've felt happier than I had for many years. The birth of my grandson and the challenge of his mother, my daughter Elizabeth, to write a book and dedicate it to him, was the inspiration that led to MoonBridge.

Very best regards,

David G. Sheppard

Acknowledgements

Writing a book is a very lengthy and time consuming pastime. I spent many months of commuting from the south coast of England into London five times a week. My I.T. Consultancy commitments meant that my working days were filled with database design and business analysis. However, the three hours per day meant that I could escape instantly into the world of Jack and his friends. The train journey had never flown by so quickly. On so many occasions I couldn't believe that Waterloo or Southampton Parkway Station appeared out of the window and another hour and a half had slipped away.

I could never have completed this book without the dedication and encouragement of my close family and friends. My youngest daughter, Elizabeth, read and re-read the story as it evolved over time. I lost count of the number of times she helped identify possible new threads, glaring mistakes and numerous omissions. My eldest daughter, Laura, proof read the book as well and offered many suggestions; plus James who couldn't wait for the final product. But most of all, my darling wife Ann, who'd, been very poorly during the first few months of my writing. She gave me the conviction to see the task through.

How can I ever thank my dearest friends Rosemary, Billy, Patsy, Hazel, Gladys and last but not least, mum Phyllis Sheppard. All of you generously gave up many hours of your free time to read, review and comment. I'm extremely grateful for your suggestions, error corrections and kind words of support. Even at one of my contractual work places, a colleague suggested his thirteen year old son to act as a sounding board for the viability of the storyline; I gave Jonathan a taster of the first four chapters and was very grateful for his suggestions and comments.

So thank you.

Chapter 1 - We're off again.

The wait was almost over: three long months of disappointment, three missed chances and three frustrating failures; at last, midnight beckoned. Darkness clung to each corner of the bedroom; only the window offered any comfort against the fear of the unknown.

"Can I command the MoonBridge tonight?" Jack Ferns waited nervously - he was desperate to succeed.

Silently, beams of silvery moonlight sliced the room in half; dust danced between the shadows. The contrasting light and dark resembled a finger stabbing blindly across the bedroom floor. Just beyond the safety of his bed; Jack believed mystical hands had opened the narrow gap in his curtains. Subconsciously, he mouthed the first verse of the secret chant.

"When Moon is full and sky is clear, let now a shaft of light appear. Be not afraid; then seize it tight, upon the coming of midnight."

The young man wanted to stay awake but his eyelids refused. Lying fully dressed, on top of his bed, he'd pushed the duvet to one side so only his legs were covered. He yawned quietly, shivering with excitement. "Concentrate. Stay focussed." Jack rubbed his eyes and pinched his nose before sniffing deeply; the cool spring air tickled. Outside, the sky was clear of clouds, he could just glimpse some of the countless stars. "I wonder if they know they're competing with the brightness of the full moon." He mused absentmindedly.

Jack was 'nearly' fifteen years old. Fourteen and a half would've been more accurate but he preferred the sound of fifteen. Desperate to remain alert, he strained to hear the tick of the alarm clock; green luminous hands indicated less than five minutes remaining. Swallowing expectantly; goose bumps ran down the back of his neck. "Time's running slowly tonight," he grumbled. Each passing second seemed longer than the last. His palms were clammy with perspiration; he knew this task was difficult to achieve.

A beautiful girl's face, momentarily, drifted into the boy's thoughts. Focussing on his friend Cathy; his heart ached at the sight of her. During both previous visits he'd enjoyed her company. Firstly, when she was only eleven, and last time when she was fourteen. He still had no idea how it was possible, time moved differently between her world and ours. During the second trip he'd remained, with Cathy, for over three weeks; strangely, on his return, only fifteen minutes had actually ticked away.

"Will she still be there? I hope she isn't too much older." Questions spun through his thoughts in rapid succession; none were answered. Even though he'd managed to open the MoonBridge Way twice before; he knew it wasn't guaranteed. Jack crossed for the first time barely nine months ago.

Disappointingly, the last few full moons were unsuccessful. The failed attempts left a scar of depression hanging over him for days on end. "Your face looks like a wet week." Mum had moaned unsympathetically. "What's the matter with you Jack? Cheer up."

Jack grinned at the memory of his mum's concern. She had no idea why he was miserable and frustrated; no-one had any inkling of his secret. Tonight everything was finally in place again. Directly overhead; the brilliant full moon poured its mystical power over the land. An unexplained energy directed solely towards him; he could already feel tingling electricity running over his skin. Even now, after two successful attempts, he still pinched himself to make sure he wasn't dreaming. "I can hardly believe my luck," he chuckled silently.

Jack yawned again. Despite his best efforts to stay awake, the boy's mind slipped, subconsciously, to that plateau somewhere between wakefulness and sleep. His eyes glazed over as the pulse of the ticking clock overpowered him. Drifting back to when it all started; memories washed through his mind, away to their last family holiday in the West Country. Jack let his recollections surface of that warm summer Sunday. They'd been driving around enjoying the countryside and stumbled upon a bustling car boot sale. Mum and Dad suggested having a look around.

"Must we?" he complained. "I'd rather go to the cliffs."

"Later Jack, I promise," Mum didn't sound convincing.

Jack tutted and dropped his shoulders in disapproval. His elder sister, Christina-Louise, decided to spend the day elsewhere; she'd gone horse riding from their Uncle's holiday home. "I should've gone with Tina-Lu, I knew it."

Uncle Bill always kindly allowed them to spend three or four weeks of the summer holidays enjoying the open space and clean air of the West Country. Most of the time was filled with exploring the wild coastline, finding all sorts of things washed up on the shore and generally having a great adventure.

"Do we have to go in here?" Jack wasn't happy. He knew Mum and Dad could hardly resist a car boot sale.

"You never know what treasures you'll find." Mum tried to convince him.

"Come on son, stop moaning, this'll be fun." Dad was trying his best to sound understanding but was actually getting impatient. They both loved 'bargain hunting'; Jack normally hated it.

"Oh so boring," he remembered grumbling.

With little more than a couple of pounds of pocket money in his hand, he begrudgingly wandered around the rows of stalls. He couldn't have imagined things would've turned out as they did. He still wasn't really sure how he'd managed to find that discarded and gnarled old cane with its silver handle.

"What a worthless piece of junk," Mum said when she saw it for the first time.

Jack certainly didn't believe that; in fact, he was certain it'd been waiting there just for him. Somehow, the wooden staff wanted him to find it; this cane was looking for Jack Ferns.

The morning dragged bitterly. Jack wandered aimlessly around the car boot sale without finding anything of interest. "I should've gone with Tina-Lu," he moaned again. "Anything would be better than this."

He recalled stopping and looking at a couple of stalls selling books and games. One had a lot of football related items he liked nosing around, but generally he was having a torrid time. Then seemingly by chance, of the hundreds of people selling things, somehow Jack managed to be drawn towards that one stall. He could clearly picture the pretty young girl in the pink and blue dress. She'd spotted him rummaging amongst the sticks, staffs and canes. He couldn't explain why, but one particular staff seemed to capture his attention.

"They were my old Grandpa's; he found that one washed up on the shore you know."

Jack looked up at the girl; she spoke with the confidence of someone who 'did' car boots regularly.

"Over there," the girl pointed towards the cliffs about half a kilometre away to his left.

"Um hi, err, how much for this one please?" Jack asked nervously picking up the silver handled cane.

The girl smiled, flicked back her hair flirtingly and gave him 'the once over'. Her grin broadened and she half nodded in approval at what she saw. "One pound to you," she replied.

Jack thought for a couple of seconds before answering. He was busy returning the unspoken compliment by giving her 'the once over' too. "I'll give you fifty pence for it," he answered cheekily; regaining his confidence. He practiced what his Mum and Dad always said; "Barter before you pay, offer them half and see how it goes."

The girl stared intensely for a second and then smiled broadly. "Okay, fifty pence it is. I'm Sally by the way, what's your name?"

Taking the cane he replied, "Hi I'm Jack. Do you live around here? I'm on holiday at my Uncle's house over near the sea." He pointed away to his right in the direction of the coast. He chatted with the girl for a few minutes before another group of people came along wanting other items from her stall.

"Sorry Jack - gotta go," Sally turned her attention to the new customers.

Wandering off feeling very pleased; Jack waved, smiling contentedly. He couldn't resist a glance back over his shoulder. "Wow, she's gorgeous," he thought. "Perhaps it's not so bad here after all."

Jack turned his attention to his purchase. The handle of the cane had a simple engraving of the moon carved into it; it was about an inch across and placed on a raised plate attached to the centre of the silver head. Underneath were inscribed some words in Latin.

'Impero Pons Pontis Abutor Luna'

Jack didn't know they were Latin then; his Uncle, a very knowledgeable man, helped him decipher the words later that day. 'Command the Bridge of the Moon' had been the rough translation, although this seemed to make little sense to anyone at the time.

Eventually, Mum and Dad had walked around the car boot sale enough and they decided to make their way home. Between them they'd bought a few items. Mum showed Jack a smart pair of Jeans for his sister. Dad had found a nice man selling some golfing items; his one true love. Everything else in his life played second fiddle to the great game of golf. They walked to their car. She was an old grey Humber Hawk that seemed to drink as much oil as petrol. Apart from the billowing blue haze of smoke that coughed out of the exhaust when the engine turned over, this beauty was a lovely ride. Inside were two leather bench seats; front and back. In fact; the backseat was wide enough to comfortably sit three adults or four children. Jack loved lying lengthways on the sumptuous bed.

"Come on girl," Dad mumbled, trying to prevent the car juddering as it pulled away. Sometimes the clutch plate stuck until 'she' warmed up and just getting from 'a' to 'b' was an adventure.

On the way back to Uncle Bill's house Jack examined his new bargain. "A very snazzy cane and well worth the fifty pence I paid for it," he congratulated himself.

Light brown in colour, the body was slightly twisted and ornately carved. The silver top really intrigued him; it was a simple design, but attractive. "This must have once belonged to a very distinguished old gentleman," Jack declared studying the construction more closely. He particularly liked the way the handle had a thin rim that ran all the way around the base. "Just right for your hand to grip," he observed.

"Oh that's neat," he said finding a hidden secret button. The maker of this cane had very cunningly disguised the button by tucking it neatly underneath the rim.

A secret it might have been but Jack was a very clever and inquisitive young man. He immediately realised that just pressing the button on its own did nothing. Instead, whilst holding the button in with his thumb nail, he found the face of the engraved moon twisted one quarter turn to the left.

"And if I do this as well," he mumbled thoughtfully whilst rotating the entire head of the cane anticlockwise until it clicked.

"Oops." A soft hiss of escaping air made Jack jump; a concealed spring popped the head open and revealed a hollow tube.

"Hey, there's something hidden inside."

Neatly rolled up in the space was a manuscript of some kind. "How neat is that?" Jack carefully gripped the fragile paper. Slowly removing the scroll; his fingers trembled with excitement - he didn't want to tear it.

"This looks very old." Jack looked cautiously at Mum and Dad to avoid drawing their attention. Thankfully, they were fully occupied chatting away, in the front of the car, discussing the bargains they'd seen.

Almost without breathing, he unrolled the thin material. The paper was really very brittle and he could tell that it would easily crack or tear if he rushed. Jack's pulse was racing. His hands were clammy and quivering uncontrollably as the excitement of the moment took hold of him.

"This might have remained hidden for hundreds of years?" he thought. "That girl said it had been washed up on the beach and found by her granddad."

Jack could already imagine the pirate's map that would lead to some long lost buried treasure. He remembered the stories that Uncle Bill told of the West Country people who had left valuable secret stashes of stolen contraband, like exotic foreign spices or French Brandy, from ages past. He knew there were many secluded coves and beaches used by ancient smugglers. "I bet this will lead to an old cave where one of the smugglers kept his gold." His eyes darted all over the scroll searching for something exciting. "Typical!" he sighed loudly.

Mum turned around at hearing her son's frustration. "What have you got there; Jack?" she asked; twisting her head to look back over the seat.

Jack was bitterly disappointed. The ancient scroll revealed no map, no source of hidden treasure, not even the promise of buried contraband. He was clearly deflated when all he found on the paper were twenty or so lines of neatly scripted text. "Just some stupid old poem written on a piece of parchment; I found it hidden inside this old cane."

Mum reached over and looked more closely at the parchment. "Wow; this is exciting, sure looks old doesn't it? Read it out loud so Dad can hear too."

The rhyming words were all carefully hand scribed in immaculate black ink. Unlike the Latin inscription, on the cane handle, the parchment had been scripted in Old English.

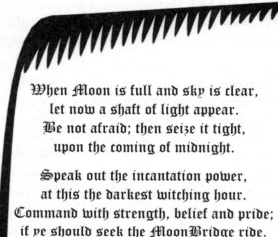

When Moon is full and sky is clear,
let now a shaft of light appear.
Be not afraid; then seize it tight,
upon the coming of midnight.

Speak out the incantation power,
at this the darkest witching hour.
Command with strength, belief and pride;
if ye should seek the MoonBridge ride.

If then ye dare to board the glow,
be not surprised where ye shall go.
For thy return from whence ye came,
let not the cockerel crow again.

Call forth some demons to create,
the daylight powers to rise and wake.
Tis then again MoonBridge ye finds,
to bring ye back as time unwinds.

Afore the dark of this night's gone,
make all good haste; lest fate be long.
Forever lost 'mongst silvery streams,
of countless pale and cold moon beams.

"Sounds like some old pirate's yarn if you ask me," Dad commented. "You should show it to Uncle Bill; he loves all that historical stuff."

"You never know it might be valuable. Well done Jack, perhaps it was a bargain after all? How much did you say you paid for it?" Mum was already calculating the possible profit and dreaming of being rich.

Jack held the staff tightly and rather cautiously replied. "Fifty Pence Mum, I paid fifty pence of my own money."

Mum grinned broadly at him.

"But I'm keeping it!" he said more firmly under his breath.

Over and over again Jack read from the scrolled parchment. For some unexplained reason, he seemed drawn to this verse. A picture painted in his mind making his fingers tingle; he imagined calling this mystical MoonBridge. Mouthing the words caused the hairs on the back of his neck to stand on end; electricity flowed through him. Hidden in this rhyme was magical power and it spun a web of intrigue all around him.

"Command with strength, belief and pride, if ye should seek the MoonBridge ride."

This line, more than any of the others, left him feeling breathless. By the time they had arrived home he'd completely memorised every syllable.

Jack rushed straight to his bedroom, when they arrived back at the holiday home, and dived onto the thick mattress of the large oak bed. Just holding the parchment and feeling its roughened texture sent his mind in a spin. The old, musty smell tickled his nose and seemed to add to the mystery of its meaning. From that moment on and everywhere he went, he carried subliminal messages filtering into his thoughts.

"When the moon is full," rang out in his head and conjured up images of werewolves or ghosts. This was scary stuff and he was getting more excited with every passing moment.

"How can I find out when the next full moon occurs?" he wondered. "I know," he replied to himself, "Uncle Bill's desk diary."

Jack secretly stole down to his uncle's desk and glanced at the open pages of the large book. The leather bound diary, with gold leaf edges, always sat neatly in the middle of the polished wood surface. The page showed one day at a time and on the turn of the page he saw the little moon symbol that identified the phases.

"A full moon in just over one weeks' time and we're staying for another two," Jack could hardly contain himself.

"What would happen next Saturday at midnight?" he wondered. "I can't wait."

***

Jack Ferns is slim and wiry; of average height, for his age, and generally quite cheerful. His fair matted hair is always a mess and looks unwieldy - even at the best of times. He calls it 'natural' looking. The early spring sunshine had already started to tan his face and arms. His family, who weren't at all well off, consisted of Mum and Dad, his older sister Christina-Louise or 'Tina-Lu' as he called her, and of course Brandy, the three year old Golden Retriever. Being nearly sixteen, and just that bit older than him, Tina-Lu is the sort of sister who, much to his annoyance, felt that he somehow needed looking after. Sometimes; he thought that she was okay; but mostly, he thought she was a pain. They lived in a small council estate in the green commuter belt, around sixty miles from London. The small semi-detached house looked out onto two of the fields of the local farm. A footpath led past the front of the house, it headed up towards the railway station and the smarter part of the village. The path divided the two fields; Jack often cycled beneath the huge oaks or walked his dog. Like most boys his age, he played all sports, especially football and cricket. He would regularly hang out with his friends for a kick around. He cycled almost everywhere and kept fit by all of his activities. Up until recently, his life had been very straightforward. He was sort of 'plainly' handsome; not the drop dead gorgeous type, just good looking, fit and healthy. A decidedly average student at school; neither considered a personality nor a disrupter, just someone who was busy getting on with his life. He worked hard to earn his pocket money; he rose early each day to complete two paper rounds before heading off to school. Nothing out of the ordinary ever happened to him, or any member of his family, all that changed the day he bought the cane.

***

As the days followed his discovery, Jack conducted a detailed and careful investigation of the old cane. Uncle Bill looked at the parchment and suggested that Jack take it to the local museum. He felt sure they would be interested in seeing the cane and its contents. Jack completely lost any interest in the holiday; he didn't even bother to go out with the others. Consumed by this mysterious object and its hidden message; he spent most of his time up in the loft above the garage. The dusty, unkempt old room had 'SECRETS' and 'ADVENTURE' written all over it. This was his favourite place and he loved spending his time up there. Everything about this den was exciting: the dust accumulated around the windows from years of neglect, the cobwebs that clung so valiantly to the rafters, even the old oak beams that supported the slate roof.

The carvings on the shaft of the cane scrolled and twisted all around in a clever and intricate fashion.

"What's this?" Jack had borrowed his Uncle's large magnifying glass to look more closely at the pattern.

"I think it's a letter? Yes there's the letter 'n' and that's an 'i'."

Once Jack realised the pattern included cleverly disguised writing, it didn't take long to reveal other hidden letters. In total; he found seven words: 'Night', 'Arise', 'Demon', 'Reveal', 'Bridge', 'Moon' and 'Command'. Rearranging them into several possible combinations; he finally believed he'd found the incantation mentioned in the rhyme. In Old English, the chant would read something like, "Arise ye Night Demon, I Command ye to Reveal the MoonBridge."

He was sure he'd finally solved this riddle. Over the next couple of days Jack thought of nothing else. "There's only two more nights to the full moon…"

Jack shook his head and stretched his arms. Bringing himself out of his dream state, he yawned loudly, forcing his mind back from his holiday. The green glow of the clock hands, on the other side of the room, ticked away slowly - it was still not quite midnight.

"Time's just not running normally tonight," he thought sleepily. "Perhaps that's a good sign."

Without really knowing why, Jack pulled the covers right up to his eyes. His bedroom seemed even darker with a feeling of dread about it. The room was being sliced in half by a single beam of light; brighter than before, it still didn't penetrate the dark corners of the room. To Jack's imagination, shadowy creatures lurked in every hidden space.

"Am I being watched?" he breathlessly contemplated, pulling the covers tighter around his chin. "What will happen? Who will be there on the other side?"

Jack was impatient; the clock had slowed ridiculously.

'Tick' - 'Tock' - 'Tick'. Each movement of the second hand seemed to take an age. The sound became so loud in his mind; it appeared to shake the floor with each strike.

"Will it be safe to travel?" his stomach grumbled and his legs quivered slightly. Jack gripped the covers so tightly; they screwed up into a thick ball around his face. He felt for the MoonBridge cane lying hidden under the bed sheets. Reassuringly; it was still there.

Downstairs, the rickety old Grandfather Clock began striking the first of twelve rings. The moment Jack had been waiting for had finally arrived. He was excited and scared at the same time; he'd no idea where he would end up. The adventure was about to begin, he was sure of it. The moonlight, slipping through the curtains, brightened and widened with each strike of the clock. A crackling filled the air and tingled every nerve in Jack's body.

"Oh wow, this is it." Jack shook with fear and excitement; reaching out from the covers he grasped the widening beam with both hands.

The tips of his fingers took on a mystical silver-blue glow; energy coursed along his arms.

"Now I've got you," Jack exclaimed. The temperature dropped suddenly; seeing his breath condensing, he panted in shock. "Concentrate Jack," he hissed; eager not to lose this opportunity. Barely keeping the beam from slipping away from his grasp; he needed great control and resolve. He started the incantation; quietly at first, just barely under his breath, Jack whispered powerfully. "Arise ye Night Demon, I Command ye to Reveal the MoonBridge."

Jack looked cautiously across his room towards the landing. He was acutely aware he could wake any of the others in the house. He struggled to complete the chant before the final strike of the clock.

"It's working."

To his great delight the curtains slowly pushed apart. As they did, the light grew brighter and wider.

'Swoooshhhh' He blinked at the sudden burst of illumination; the MoonBridge appeared. Over the next few heartbeats it fully formed - he would soon be free to explore. Just as the twelfth chime sounded, the full splendour of the MoonBridge became clear and defined.

"Okay Jack, let's go for it."

Where the empty bedroom floor had been only moments before; now stood a bridge. A shimmering, shining, silver bridge about one metre wide; it had neither sides nor rails, just a smooth rainbow shaped arch that stretched away from the end of the bed. The light streamed out through the open window, up into the sky towards the moon, and disappeared into infinity.

Jack's heart raced with anticipation. "That's the most awesome thing ever."

All he had to do now was to pluck up enough courage to get out from under the covers and slip away to who knows where. The house was completely silent, even the ticking of the clock seemed to have stopped. The only sound Jack could now hear was the pounding of his own heart. "Thump, thump, thump." Jack thought it seemed so loud he was sure it would wake Mum and Dad.

"Come on Jack, let's go," he was desperately trying to drum up his courage.

Thankfully; he had his trusted friend Brandy, lying silently at the foot of his bed. Brandy had been curled up tight with his nose buried under his tail. Jack guessed he'd been busily dreaming of chasing rabbits; his favourite pastime. Brandy realised something unusual was happening. He lifted his head off his paws and briefly opened his eyes. A tiny wag, of his tail, told Jack he was ready too.

The boy finally plucked up enough courage to slip out of the covers. Grabbing his jacket from the unruly pile of clothes on the floor, he tugged at Brandy's collar and they both leapt up onto the bridge. Brandy briefly turned his head back towards the landing and gave a little whimper. The boy just patted his dog gently to reassure him. With the first step onto the bridge they felt the bedroom disappear.

"Yes," Jack exclaimed. Even before he had chance to blink; the house was gone. Not only had the house disappeared: but the trees, the field outside and everything else too. They were on their way.

Brandy barked twice at the bizarre experience. The motion of the bridge was strange, they weren't aware how quickly they were travelling, but it was very fast. All around were the hazy glow of moonbeams; they couldn't see anything as such, just impressions of movement. Only a couple of heartbeats had fluttered, but for Jack it seemed like ages. Time appeared to stand still and the sensation meant he could hardly breathe.

"Oh," Jack screamed. Barely had the thought entered his head, to question how long the journey had taken, than they arrived.

"That is so weird, isn't it boy?" he hugged his dog tightly who was busy wagging his tail furiously in response.

Jack glanced behind. The fading MoonBridge glistened dimly, with a single passing "hiss", it evaporated. The route home was gone. Confusingly; time here was completely unrelated to Jack's world. He gazed, mind racing in wonderment, at the transition from his dark bedroom. In Danthienne; the rising sun revealed a wondrous open landscape. The dawn silhouetted a line of hills stretching away to his left. Rolling grassland, dotted with clumps of trees, meandered ahead until merging into distant pale mist. To his right; a road led down, across the plain, to a small town. Jack remembered, from his second visit, the place was called Brackensham. He didn't want to go there again. The people he'd seen were too scary and dangerous for his liking; all of them looked upon strangers with distrust.

Jack sniffed loudly; the scent of early morning dew wafted though his senses. "I just love that smell Brandy."

Each time the MoonBridge opened in a slightly different location. He thought he was reasonably close to the last exit. Spinning on his heels, Jack spotted a distinctive ruined tower high on 'lookout hill'. His destination lay several kilometres behind that landmark.

"Right, that's where we're heading," he said out loud. "Eastward I think; let's find Cathy." The mention of her name raised a big smile. She previously explained the name Danthienne meant "the land of the Sun and the Moon". He liked that description; a world of mystery powered by the two great forces. "Two opposing forces," he corrected.

Striding off in the direction of lookout hill, Jack recalled his previous visits. He'd discovered the odd way time moved on this side of the Bridge. Strangely; the one month gap, between his first and second trip, had resulted in three years passing in Danthienne. Cathy aged from a petite eleven year old child into a young woman about Jack's height. She kept extremely fit; the kind of fitness that only comes from living in the wilds of the country. He wondered how old she was today. Jack couldn't help grinning; just the thought of Cathy had his heart pumping. "She's probably about the same age as Tina-Lu," he thought fleetingly. "But she's nothing like my sister, yuck." He pictured her hazel eyes, auburn hair and friendly smile. "Yep, I bet she is even more stunning now."

"It's so weird how the time of day and even the month is different. Feel how warm it is."

Back at home, it had been midnight in early April; cool and fresh. The air was far too hot for spring; especially, as it was probably only five or six in the morning. Today felt more like a midsummer's day; warm and really wonderful.

"Late June or early July; what do you think Brandy?"

The dog looked around and gave a little wag of his tail. He was far too busy sniffing for rabbits, or whatever else, to be concerned with his master's ramblings. If he really wanted something important he would whistle.

Jack made good progress. The path was an easy walk of lush grasses and pretty meadow flowers. The air was clean and everything was peacefully tranquil. In less than half an hour he should find the trail that led up between the sides of the steep valley. The route, he was looking for, would take him to the edge of the small lake where Cathy lived with her Aunt Beth. He had to admit she was someone very special and he really fancied her. She'd found him wandering around, completely lost and more than a little scared, on his first trip here.

Their path was blocked by a wide stream; the water moved quickly and seemed too dangerous. "Let's rest a minute," Jack whistled his dog to return and sat in the early sunlight. Watching the water, bubble and tumble over the rocks and boulders, fascinated the boy; everything seemed so alive.

The pair eventually moved on and searched for a suitable place to cross; in several places the stream narrowed. Jack found what he was looking for. A series of very deep pools slowed the flow; each was surrounded by hundreds of large boulders - some as big as houses. Jack paused for a moment before deciding to risk jumping from one to another. He climbed high on top of the first without any problem. Brandy watched his master clambering, precariously, across one rock to the next. He'd no such difficulty or qualms; he jumped straight into the water and quickly "doggy" paddled across. Jack laughed; leaping nimbly onto each boulder.

"Come on slow coach," he teased. His dog splashed madly through the crystal clear pool.

Jack jumped down to the bank; Brandy hauled himself out and bounded alongside. Jack's attention was distracted to an enormous bird flying overhead. Brandy stood still, briefly, and then with a long fast shake of his body; he deftly flicked the water off his coat in all directions. The torrent of rain soaked Jack in the process.

"Stop it you idiot," he screamed. He couldn't help giggling at the situation; he was as wet now as if he'd slipped into the pool and swum across.

Hopping and jumping wildly, he threw his arms out in all directions. Jack chased his dog around playfully trying to catch him. Brandy went mad with delight and barked back at his master. As ever, he was far too quick to be caught but it was great fun anyway. Jack flopped exhausted to the ground and panted heavily.

"Get off me you crazy dog," he pleaded as Brandy mauled him with his soggy tongue. Jack laughed even more and begged for mercy; grabbing his friend by the thick fur around his neck they wrestled playfully. The pair eventually sprawled out on the grass and soaked up the summer sun's warmth. Before long, they were both dried off.

"This is the life eh boy?" Reluctantly, they made their way off again. Jack easily found the trail; he felt he was beginning to know his way around. Soon they were striding below lookout hill. They rounded a dip in the grassland; the bottom end of the lake came into view. Hardly a ripple appeared on its surface; the sky, hills and tree-line reflected perfectly. "You'd think it was made of glass," exclaimed Jack. "Come on boy, another ten minutes and we'll be able to see Cathy's cottage."

The two hurried along the bank for about half a kilometre before heading up again over a ridge.

"Oh no," Jack stopped dead in his tracks.

The sight confronting the boy left him feeling stunned. Instead of the pretty little cottage nestled at the lake's edge; he saw a thin smouldering column of light grey smoke and a jagged blackened area that had once been Cathy's home.

"What's happened? Come on Brandy."

Jack broke in to a run; he sprinted down the slope, across the wide grass clearing and through the trees that lined the edge of the lake. Brandy dashed alongside and then raced ahead barking madly.

"What is it boy?" he panted.

To the side of the smouldering ash was a partly burned body. The stench made Jack heave. Approaching gingerly and realising this person was wearing a uniform; this was a soldier, a dead soldier. All around he saw others lying motionless; they were scattered in little groups of two or three. More than a dozen bodies he counted. Jack looked everywhere; despite his searching, he couldn't find any sign of Cathy or her Aunt. The scene was like something out of a war.

"Perhaps that had happened, could the country have gone to war whilst I've been away? Where was Cathy now?"

The boy charged around frantically looking at this soldier and that. After several minutes of hunting, Jack was completely at a loss.

"What should I do Brandy, where are they?"

He was beginning to panic now and had to bring himself back to his senses.

"Think Jack," he said to himself out loud. "Think."

Suddenly, over to his right he heard a brief groan. Half expecting to fight for his life; he turned, jumping in fright. Instead, a few metres away, a young man of about eighteen or twenty lay dying. The soldier, covered in blood stains, lay twisted painfully on his side.

"Help me," he croaked. Coughing and choking, he gasped for breath. "Please help me."

Jack rushed over and lifted his head a little. Still gripped in the man's hand was a wide sword, it was covered in drying blood and must have been used to inflict some painful injury on another poor soul.

"He probably killed that other soldier just there," Jack thought and felt physically sick in his stomach at the possibility.

"What do you want me to do?" he asked helplessly. He'd never seen anything so horrible in all of his short life. With one final effort, the soldier grabbed Jack's arm and pulled him weakly towards him.

"Take this. She's called Bessie..." the young man choked, thrusting the sword into Jack's hand. "She served me well; you'll need her more than meee..." His voice tailed off. After that final effort his head slipped limply back to the ground. The soldier was dead.

Jack had never seen anyone die before; goose-bumps ran up the back of his neck as he sat down in shock. He stared at the dead soldier; numbed. "I don't even know your name mister?"

Choking back a few tears; the horror of the situation sunk in. He thought he was going to be sick; but instead, he just stared bleary eyed ahead into nothingness. All the while Brandy stood close by; alert and on guard. He couldn't remember how he managed to stumble and stagger to the other end of the lake. Eventually, he looked back along the shoreline to the smouldering cottage in the distance. Brandy took a cooling drink from the edge of the water and that made him realise just how thirsty and hungry he was.

"What's it like boy?" Jack looked, distastefully, at the colour of the water. "Yuck, how can you drink that stinking water Brandy? You'll be ill."

After a quick look around; he found a small trickling brook running over some rocks and into the lake. "Come on boy, this looks cleaner, let's see where it leads to."

Jack was determined to find somewhere nicer to get a drink. The path of the stream was broken by many large boulders and trees. Ahead was a rockier region, a cliff of orangey grey rock blocked their route and they had to follow its base for some distance. Eventually they reached a shallow, crystal clear, rock pool where the water splashed gently from a series of cracks and crevices in the cliff face. Jack knelt down and cautiously lifted a small handful of the refreshingly cool drink. "Ummm, this tastes alright."

"You should've drunk this clean water you silly dog," he scolded his pet.

Brandy sniffed the pool and lapped a few mouthfuls. He looked drearily at Jack grinning back at him. The boy patted him affectionately on the head. His pet turned and walked over to the nearest tree and sniffed at it thoroughly.

Jack thought it would be okay, so he drank his fill. The first few mouthfuls really seemed to invigorate his body. He felt refreshed and strong but the water had a slight tang to it. The bitter taste just made him want to drink even more. After several handfuls he noticed his dog behaving strangely.

"What's up with you boy?"

Brandy looked at him forlorn and lay down panting.

Jack tried to stand up, but within seconds his head started to spin; his body felt tired - something was wrong with the water after all. Brandy dropped down in the shade of the trees and fell asleep. Before he could stop himself, he too, sat and yawned deeply.

"It's poisoned..." he thought; slipping effortlessly into a deep, dreamless sleep.

Chapter 2 - Captured

Away on the other side of the lake, in a small clearing in the trees, an old wizened man stood hunched over. He lent heavily on a long stout staff and groaned quietly at the ache in his old bones. The man was alone except for a solitary inquisitive squirrel that skittered around the base of a tree. Watching in fascination; the old man smiled. The creature hopped and skipped about, foraging for food, oblivious to the harmless person observing him. Life seemed to hang very heavily on the shoulders of Searlan these days; age was finally taking its toll on him. He was considered one of the oldest and wisest Sages of the land; a man of great insight and knowledge. Even he could not remember how many summers he'd seen, but they were many. Some believed he had "special" powers and most thought he was immortal. Despite his frail demeanour few would've dared to cross him, and wisely so, for Searlan was a formidable adversary. At his command was the combined knowledge and wisdom of countless generations of Sages before him. His entire life had been in the pursuit of understanding of the workings of the world around him. Now, in his twilight years, he'd become completely at one with all living and growing things. He could see, deeply, into the natural world and through his influence, he could will creatures, plants and even the earth itself to do his bidding.

With a heavy sigh, Searlan steadied himself and then held his gnarled cane to the sky. "Come forth," he commanded with a strength that seemed impossible from someone so frail looking. Around him, the leaves on the trees quivered, and the air became thicker. Directly in front of him a faint glow grew and a ball of silvery light spun slowly about one metre above the ground. "Open, Open NOW," he demanded, staring straight into the ball of light and pointing his cane towards its centre. Sparks flew briefly around his head and along the cane into the ball. Widening in an instant, the shape expanded to several metres across and darkened to a deep crimson and violet. Inside the ball was bizarrely black; not the black of paint or dark like the night, but a black that made your eyes hurt to look at. Even light didn't reflect back from the blackness, it just fell into a well never to return. The edge of the portal was well defined but at the centre the blackness hid untold secrets from your sight. As soon as the light at the edge stabilised a small child of eleven or twelve years stepped into view.

"Grandfather," the boy greeted Searlan.

"Quickly Jaden, it's not safe here. We must leave now, the Blades are close and they've brought the others I think," the old man said in earnest.

The boy stepped out of the darkness and took his grandfather's arm.

"Close and be gone," Searlan commanded; the ball shrank and faded from view.

"We must hurry back home Jaden, things have become very dangerous since you left. Did you succeed? Did you meet with Tarre-Hare? Has she agreed to intervene?" the old man was impatient for all of the answers.

The boy didn't reply, initially, despite the obvious insistence of his Grandfather. Instead, he thought for a few seconds composing his mind before answering.

"Yes and no Grandfather," he responded cautiously.

Searlan tutted loudly; he expected as much. These goddesses were tricky at the best of times; they were even worse when put on the spot to make a decision.

"Out with it Jaden, tell me everything."

The boy smiled at his grandfather's frustration. He loved him dearly, but he did tend to fluster sometimes. Jaden assumed it was due to his great age and frailty. He squeezed Searlan's hand with much affection and showed how he would do anything at all for him.

"Grandfather, Tarre-Hare did permit me an audience as you had hoped. She listened as we discussed the situation and I explained your concerns. Unfortunately, she would not be drawn on committing her forces to aid us against the Blades. She wasn't convinced the situation demanded her intervention."

The old man rasped in desperation and thumped his staff heavily on the ground.

"Just how bad must it become? Doesn't she know that I would not send you lightly through the portal to do my bidding? Doesn't she understand my frailty?"

"Yes grandfather, she understands. She sends this message to you."

The boy paused again as if switching his mind to that of Tarre-Hare herself.

"Sage of Sages you must seek that which you crave least of all in the place that you dare not delve. Go before the night witch again and take her council. Find and nurture the one who has crossed the boundary of the bridge, he has a very special gift. Maybe he will be able to deliver you."

The old man winced at the thought of facing the moon goddess again. He knew that only pain, heartache and possibly much worse could come from such a meeting.

"You seem terribly agitated grandfather?" the youngster enquired knowledgeably. For Jaden was no ordinary boy, he was the Sageling of choice, a Sage in the making.

"Yes Jaden, this is the worst possible outcome. Tarre-Hare knows full well I haven't the strength to confront Lujnima *(Loon-hee-ma)* again. She's testing me to the limits of my resolve and I don't know if I can do this?"

"I'll help grandfather; let me face the moon goddess for you. I'm not afraid of her, I'm not afraid of either of them."

Searlan looked down affectionately at his grandson. He held his hand happily and knew he'd made the right choice.

"Thank you Jaden, you're a great strength for me. Come on."

They walked at a brisk pace away into the darkened gloom of the woods. They followed a well trodden track across a shallow valley with a bubbling brook running along its course.

As Searlan led them through secret paths that few knew at all, he worried about the encounter that he was going to have to pursue. At his last visit "She" had warned the Sage against returning; to come before her again would seal his own fate.

"Tell me Grandfather, about the ancients you carry with you." Jaden distracted the Sage from his obvious anguish. The boy knew the secret to learning from his grandfather. He knew that he could never resist imparting his knowledge to his only grandson. The boy was destined to take his grandfather's place and needed to learn many secrets that were hidden inside his mentor.

In time, Jaden would become Sage; although, it had not been his original destiny. Unfortunately Searlan's own son, Searlanlay, had been captured many years earlier during a raid by the Blades. Occasionally the old man would insist that, despite their meagre attempts to hide him, he saw his son. Searlanlay was held captive in a very deep dark place. He knew he was in considerable pain and his heart cried out for mercy from the torment and torture he suffered. Searlan was powerless to help his son; he was too well guarded by the enemy. Young Jaden was the only son of Searlan's daughter Searlanelle or Elle as she was known. As was the tradition of the Sageship, only one could be chosen to take forward the accumulated knowledge. Fate had forced Searlan's hand to choose Jaden over Searlanlay; he couldn't afford to risk waiting for his son's return and miss the opportunity to impart the wealth of collective consciousness on to his heir.

As they hurried, Searlan talked of the ancient Sages. He recounted how they had been brought into the fold of natural things and their initial learning of worldly speech. They had each developed the ability to communicate with any living thing and then to pass that knowledge on to a sibling. Over time, this knowledge grew into a wealth of experience and understanding. This included the ability to influence, so called, inanimate objects like rock, fire and water. No-one suggested that a hill or a forest could speak in the normal sense of the word; rather, they could be encouraged or cajoled into doing something out of the ordinary. A stone could be implored to roll, the earth might be asked to move apart, a tree to bend or sway and even a river could be encouraged to stop flowing. The commands were difficult to master, but once accomplished, they made any Sage a formidable enemy and an even stronger ally.

Searlan and Jaden approached a wide clearing in the trees where the land adjoined a tall cliff of orangey grey rock. Many soldiers were gathering. The pair gently lowered to the ground and blended perfectly into their surroundings. They watched, with great interest, and strained to hear some of the soldiers conversations. These were the Resistance fighters that had been gathering to combat the Blades. Searlan knew the fighting was very close and he suspected the marauding enemy had allies. Although these soldiers were essentially on the same side as the Sage, that is to say they were against the Blades; it wasn't wise to assume they were true friends. These freedom fighters often formed into loose alliances and provided resistance to the Blades. Many were undisciplined and were more like a band of mercenaries than a structured force. Searlan knew of a number of more organised groups, but he wasn't sure of these.

"We must be cautious Jaden," the old man advised quietly as they watched from the safety of the undergrowth.

Searlan caught sight of another brief movement; on the far side of the clearing, near the base of the cliff a head appeared above the bushes then dropped quickly down again. He wasn't a soldier, but the Sage felt a brief connection. "There's someone else hiding over there Jaden, we'll have to investigate later. He's important to us."

**

The sun was high in the sky; for more than an hour he'd lay unconscious, slowly he awoke. At first, he thought he was back in his bed. "What a weird dream." Jack puzzled for a second trying to come to his senses. Surely the close sound of voices was just in his imagination. He sat bolt upright, his head hurt, his stomach ached and his body felt like he'd been in a terrible fight. "I feel sick," he thought; realising he'd certainly not been dreaming. Everything had been horribly real; the large sword at his side, still covered in blood stains, confirmed that. Across the clearing, just inside the trees, he saw several soldiers. Jack dived to the ground and slid behind the tree. They didn't seem to have spotted him, he'd been lucky.

Brandy was still soundly asleep; he reached over and tugged at his collar. He refused to wake.

"Come on boy," he said gritting his teeth. "Wake up."

Brandy made a small movement. Jack could tell he was feeling sick too.

"Come on, we've got to get out of here. Quick."

The pair hurried quietly through the undergrowth. They followed the base of the cliff away from the clearing. The ground was higher here and allowed a good view of the surrounding countryside. Down below Jack saw more soldiers arriving. He counted forty men in a long line. All of them were dressed alike, they wore a light grey, brown and green uniform that blended in well with the surroundings. Each one had a large sword and some carried long spears with curved points. These soldiers were different from the ones who had been at Cathy's cottage; they seemed to be quite wary as they were looking in all directions. Even so, the soldiers were completely unaware of being observed.

Jack and Brandy pressed on and left the cliff far behind. The hills steepened in all directions and the lower slopes were covered with short stubby trees and thick undergrowth. Jack heard a voice coming from ahead and dragged Brandy under a large bush.

"Shhhh boy," he said reassuringly to his friend.

The column of soldiers approached. Jack held his breath and pulled Brandy close to his chest. They watched them head off in the direction of the clearing. "That was too close for comfort boy." After a few minutes he felt it was safe to leave their hiding place. "Let's go."

Jack made his way back down towards flatter ground where he saw the other end of the lake to Cathy's house. He walked cautiously back around until he was able to watch the soldiers gathering over on the other side. Jack saw two more groups arriving. They marched in single file and he guessed there must have been another twenty or so. Altogether, a force of about sixty to eighty soldiers seemed to be congregating in this area.

"Surely this means that something big is about to happen?" He wondered rather excitedly. Even though he was quite scared; he was also intrigued.

"Let's keep ourselves out of sight and see if we can watch what's going on."

Jack quietly led Brandy away from the lake shore and up deeper into the tree line. He started to jog to get closer to the soldiers. Carefully, he made his way around the lake until he was in sight of the clearing.

"We'll wait here for a while and watch them Brandy."

Observing the comings and goings; the minutes dragged. This wasn't the excitement he'd expected. All that happened was a few of the soldiers giving orders and others milling around or lying down to rest.

Jack stroked his dog's head, whispering, "What are they up to?" He spent about twenty minutes hiding, watching and waiting for something to happen. Nothing did. "Oh come on boy, this is really boring."

Keeping to the safe cover of bushes and undergrowth, Jack moved out of earshot and sight of the clearing. After a few minutes he jogged quickly to get up to the edge of the cliff again. He felt it was safe enough to slow down to a brisk walk and was less worried about meeting any more of the soldiers.

"Let's go this way."

Jack led his pet down a gully where the trees were much thicker. The bushes and shrubs gave good cover. At the end of the long path was a large stone structure sticking out from the side of the hill. Several enormous pieces of rock formed a simple entranceway that menacingly framed a dark cave. Dry old bones, which had been chewed and gnawed, lay all around.

"Keep your ears open Brandy," Jack was worried the occupant of this lair was either inside or somewhere near by. He certainly didn't want to end up as the main course for dinner.

Brandy pricked up his ears and listened to the sound of some heavy melodic breathing that emanated from the darkness in front of him. Something was sleeping in the depths of this hideaway. He tilted his head and sniffed several times. No matter how hard he tried to identify the owner, the sound and smell were completely new to him. He gave a low growl; this smelt like danger and he wanted to get Jack away from this place.

"What is it boy?" Jack felt the hairs on his neck quiver. The boy swallowed several times and just caught a waft of rotting flesh and a putrid stench that slithered out from the depths of the tunnel, jabbing his nostrils like burning needles. "This was a bad move boy, let's go."

Turning to leave, something glistening in the sunlight caught Jack's eye; he bent down to pick it up. Cautiously, he took a cursory glance at the darkness cut into the hill. He'd found a beautiful golden brooch with some kind of precious stone set in the middle. The red coloured gem was about two centimetres long; oval shaped and looked very valuable.

"Wow, what's this boy? What a find this is."

Brandy briefly sniffed Jack's hand as the boy examined the jewel. He was still concentrating on the sounds drifting out of the cave; something was stirring.

"This looks very expensive I wonder who it belongs to?"

He suddenly realised it was probably the property of one of the meals scattered all around. He gulped at the thought.

Jack explored very quickly and was amazed by the other items that seemed to be randomly scattered everywhere. There were shoes, belts, bits of cloth and a few other nice pieces of jewellery. He picked up several rings, a bracelet, two necklaces and one small dagger that had black stones embedded into the handle. He stuffed the treasure into his jacket pockets and decided against going any nearer to the den, just in case.

Keeping a very watchful eye on the cave; his dog studied the space warily.

"We'd better get out of here Brandy. We don't want to meet anything from in there, do we?"

Brandy growled again, this time more viciously. His hackles were raised and he bared his teeth. A fearsome groan echoed out of the entrance. Jack froze for a second.

"Run boy, let's go." Streaking back along the path; another groan grew into a long drawn out roar. The deep, resonating call made Jack's blood chill. He became very afraid. "Quickly Brandy - run faster."

Jack stumbled and tripped as a third ear-piercing screech leapt up the track; smashing into the centre of his back, it pushed him violently to the ground.

"Thieves..."

Jack couldn't move. The scream drilled into his senses sending his muscles into spasm. He felt trapped; as if an invisible hand pinned him down like an immovable weight. Brandy growled loudly, standing guard over his incapacitated master.

"Kill the thieves... Eat the thieves..."

The voice of the monster, at the entranceway to the cave, left Jack shaking violently. He'd never known such overpowering terror. The loudest crash and earthshaking thump accompanied the obvious sound of terrifying footfalls. Slowly at first, then faster and faster, the creature headed in their direction.

Crunch... crunch... crunch...

Jack felt the rapid approach of something, so incredibly heavy, the ground shook with each step.

"Get up Jack," he ordered his body to comply.

Struggling to his feet; he hardly dared look behind. Brandy growled incessantly. With an immense will to survive, he dragged himself to his knees. The pressure bearing down on his back took an unprecedented effort to overcome. The boy finally grabbed his dog's collar and started running faster than his legs had ever taken him. He sprinted for over a kilometre. Never once did he dare to glance back over his shoulder. Gradually the sound of the pursuing beast subsided.

Jack's lungs burst; he'd no idea what he'd inadvertently stumbled upon and frankly didn't really want to know either.

"We've... escaped... I... think..." he panted. "That... was... close..."

Despite his exhaustion, the boy only slowed to a jog until they'd placed a lot of woodland and hills between themselves and the beast in the cave. Further on, the route became much easier. The undergrowth thinned where larger trees took over. They were tall and had wide, straight trunks coloured light grey. Standing like the gigantic supporting columns of a living cathedral, Jack had never seen such an impressive sight. Far overhead the branches spread out like giant green umbrellas, their broad leaves made the air pale and humid.

His hand slipped inquisitively onto the brooch and he took it out to look at. This was an amazing find, the workmanship was stunning and the quality of the stone looked beautiful. Jack held the gem up to his eye and looked towards the sky through it; everything turned deep crimson. For a brief instant he thought he saw a face looking back at him. He dropped the jewel then chuckled at his vivid imagination. He placed the brooch safely back into his pocket and thought no more of it.

Progress became much slower as the path steepened. They carried on for a few more minutes until the undergrowth became thicker again. Trees, bushes and rocks all seemed to be pushing them further from the direction he'd intended to take. Jack finally found a narrow track cut through the undergrowth. Stepping up to the path cautiously, he looked in both directions to see if the way was clear. For no particular reason, he chose to head to his right.

"This way boy, it seems as good as any. We'll explore up here for a while."

Jack followed Brandy, who'd run off chasing the scent of rabbits. The track meandered, avoiding large rocks and trees, along its route. He rounded a turn and found himself in a very small clearing with several exits.

"Where are you boy?" Jack whistled frustratingly and called to his dog. Brandy had disappeared off in the undergrowth in search of his favourite quarry.

On one side of the clearing was a large flat stone that looked a bit like a bench. He sat down for a brief rest to wait for his pet to return. The seat felt warm and welcoming as it had been heated by the summer sun. Jack lay back stretching out comfortably, he looked up at the white fluffy clouds that dotted the sky and then closed his eyes briefly.

"Ahhh, this feels so good," he exclaimed in utter contentment.

Jack heard the rustle of bushes and opened his eyes expecting to see his pet reappearing.

"Who are you?"

Before Jack could react, two large men had jumped out of the bushes and grabbed him.

"Help…" Jack screamed.

Brandy bounded out from the undergrowth on the other side of the clearing and charged at the man holding the boy. He growled loudly and bared his teeth threateningly in a snarl.

The other man shouted angrily. "Kill the stinking mutt, Jed."

Instinctively, Jed lashed out with his sword and narrowly missed slicing off Brandy's head. The shining blade clattered heavily with a metallic clang as it struck the rocky floor. The dog leapt sideways with a loud yelp and disappeared back behind a bush.

"Run Brandy. Run," Jack screamed desperately.

Greg grabbed Jack by the neck and slapped his other hand around his mouth.

"One more sound from you boy and I'll wring your neck," he hissed into the boy's right ear. The man quickly covered Jack's head, with a black cloth bag, making it impossible to see anything except his feet.

"Watch out for that dog Jed," Greg ordered. "We'll take the boy through here."

A small natural cave had been formed in the slope of the hillside, it seemed to have been carefully concealed from any angle except from directly behind a very large boulder. Greg dragged and pushed Jack through a break in the bushes. He pulled him by the scruff of the neck, forcing the boy into the entrance to the cave where two other soldiers stood guard. They both carried bows and had quivers of arrows slung across their backs.

"There's a vicious dog out there somewhere, kill the mutt if it so much as yelps," he warned.

They both nodded warily as Jack was hauled along. The tunnel twisted a couple of times and headed upwards quite steeply. Jack could hear the sound of running water close by. An underground stream was lower down now and led out to the lake via a series of tributaries; years before it had been responsible for carving out this cave. After a few minutes the tunnel opened out into a wider and higher chamber, not large, maybe only five metres across and just tall enough to easily stand up in. The sound of the water was louder here. One other narrow crevasse opened at the end of the chamber, it was completely dark and the source of the noise. The area was dimly lit by a single small oil burning lantern perched on a ledge.

"Stand still boy," Greg demanded; shoving Jack hard.

Jack was brought to an abrupt standstill directly in front of a man lying on a rug. He looked up with disinterest.

"Seems a bit young for a Blade," he growled. "Show me his face."

Jack's head cover was pulled off. He blinked a couple of times disoriented and afraid.

"What do you want with me?" Jack said terrified.

The man reluctantly stood up; he towered over Jack and grabbed him roughly by the arm. Lieutenant Johnson was a very strong, tall and heavily built soldier. The man's grip was like a vice of iron and it made Jack wince with pain.

"Who the hell are you boy?" he demanded gruffly almost spitting in his face. "Answer quickly or I'll have Jed here, rip your head off."

Quivering with fear, the boy answers, "I'm Jack Ferns Sir, I'm not a Blade. I don't even know what a Blade is."

"Then how do you explain this boy," the Lieutenant pointed, as Jed threw the sword to the ground with a loud clash. "That's a Blade's tool. Where'd you get it then?"

Jack desperately recounted everything about Cathy's cottage, the dying soldier and running away from the other soldiers in the clearing. He didn't, of course, mention anything of the MoonBridge. The big man eased his grip on Jack's arm a little and pressed closely to his face.

"If you're lying, I'll slit your throat myself boy," he snarled.

Jack felt very frightened and spluttered out. "I'm not lying, it's the truth. You can go and check if you want. The cottage is still smouldering and everything."

Lieutenant Johnson pushed Jack harshly to the ground and commanded. "Sit there and don't make a sound."

The three soldiers gathered at the other end of the chamber and spoke in hushed whispers for a few minutes. They occasionally glanced behind and looked at Jack. These men didn't look like they were messing around and Jack started to look for a means of escape. He thought about darting towards the gap at the end of the cavern and trying to get to the stream. His attention was brought back to the

Lieutenant when the whispers stopped and he heard the eager soldier drawl with a pronounced accent, "What we gonna do wiv 'im, boss. Ee can't come wiv us. Let's just do 'im now and be done wiv it. I'll toss 'is body in the river and 'ee'll be 'istory,"

"Shut up Jed, I'll decide who gets done and who doesn't," the big Lieutenant snapped dismissively. He looked menacingly at Jack and contemplated for a few more seconds before he made his decision.

"Right; this is what you'll do Greg. You and Jed take the boy up to camp two and leave him with the other prisoners. They can follow up his story there. Then, I want you to meet me and the rest of the squad when we report back to Captain Connors. Make sure they lock him up with the others before you leave. I expect him to arrive unharmed, mind you, and while you're at it give him something to eat, he looks starving."

Greg looked very dour at the prospect of dragging Jack off to Camp two, which was about half an hour away. He then turned to Jed and nodded before replying begrudgingly.

"Okay boss."

Jack was dragged hastily out of the chamber by the reluctant soldiers.

The Lieutenant tutted gruffly, shaking his head whilst picking up the heavy Blade. He threw it over with the other weapons at the back of the Chamber. Sitting down again, without bothering to glance towards the tunnel, Jack was pushed back down it and out into the air.

"Git a move on boy," Jed snarled.

Jack was brutally hurried forwards with several painful thumps in his back.

The sunlight made him blink blindly as they emerged from the gloom of the cave. The two men dragged him really heavily across the stream and on down towards the path that led to the clearing. They had half walked, half jogged for about five minutes in the general direction of the lake. Grumbling to themselves, they complained about carrying out the orders of the Lieutenant.

"Let's just do 'im anyways," Jed moaned under his breath. "Who's ever gonna know? I ask yer Greg, who's gonna care if I just slit 'im right ere." The soldier lowered the spear he was carrying and aimed it towards Jack's midriff. "Let me run 'im through mate," he pleaded eagerly. "Let me hear this Blade spy squeal like a piggy."

Greg laughed heartily. "Yeh, squeal like a little piggy. Squeak piggy squeak," he teased as they both laughed in Jack's face.

"Get off me," Jack tried his best to push the spear away.

"I'll do 'im now…"

Jed was cut off in mid sentence. Completely without warning; Brandy leapt out from the bushes and up to the man holding the spear. He bit Jed deeply on the leg.

"Look out…" Greg screamed wildly and lashed out with his boot, missing Brandy by a mile.

Grasping the wound on his leg; Jed loosened his grip on Jack's shoulder. Instinctively, the boy spun around and directed a sweeping kick at Jed's other knee. The soldier fell screaming in agony; clutching both legs and rolling around on the grass, he swore loudly.

Jack jumped free and called to his dog. Brandy had other ideas; he rushed at Jed nipping him on his flailing arm.

"Ahhhhh," the man yelped painfully.

Brandy jumped nimbly aside and with a single bound he sunk his teeth deeply into the right arm of Greg.

"Get off me you beast," he complained; striking out at the dog clinging to his arm.

Jack wasted no time. He grabbed the fallen spear, and without even thinking, swung the long weapon around. With all the force he could muster, he sent it crashing heavily against the man's ribcage. The ferocity of the blow made Greg buckle instantly.

"Oooph," the soldier doubled up in agony. He was instantly crippled as the wind was knocked clean out of him. Greg fell to his knees gasping for air as Jack raised the spear high over his head and brought it sweeping down, cracking the soldier across the shoulder blades. Greg dropped hopelessly flat on the ground, incapacitated.

"Run Brandy, let's go," the boy screamed.

Jack threw away the spear and ran until gasping for breath. Brandy galloped happily alongside his freed master and tried to jump up into his arms.

"Good boy, good boy," Jack rasped breathlessly slumping into a heap on the ground. "Very good dog," he hugged his pet tightly praising him continuously for saving the day. Brandy went mad with excitement, trying to lick Jack all over his face. The dog's tail wagged so fast his whole body shook with joy.

Despite needing to rest, Jack forced himself up and kept moving. Heading back towards the lake, he remained alert to the obvious dangers. Soldiers were close by and he slowed to a cautious walk. A few metres away, through the thickets of bushes, the clearing opened. He ducked down, behind one of the many trees, to have a closer look.

"Stay Brandy and don't make a sound."

Several of the soldiers were still sitting on the far side. He looked carefully but couldn't see any sign of the dozens of troops he expected.

"I wonder where they've all disappeared to Brandy."

Just at that moment, a crashing sound of breaking branches came from immediately behind him.

"What on earth..." he spluttered.

Turning, as quickly as he could, Jack barely managed to dive out of the path of a huge machine. Moving quite slowly, but very deliberately as if intelligent, the bright blue, cigar shaped object was unlike anything he'd seen before. Several metres in length by one and half metres wide, it was big. Jack rolled smartly away to the side; the machine floated above him, at about waist height, off the ground.

"That was close," Jack dragged his dog to safety as the thing continued on its course.

An irritating and invasive hum came from deep inside the object. A shimmering glow surrounded its pulsing body.

"What is that stink?" Jack pinched his nose as the back end of the Blue machine slipped towards the clearing. A strong smell of sulphur filled the air.

As the machine moved it left an empty path of grey ash. Trees, bushes and grass were all evaporated as it bulldozed its way onwards. The object rumbled out of the shade, about five metres from Jack, and into the clearing. He waited for the reaction from the soldiers on the other side.

Jack was transfixed. "What would they do now?"

He didn't have to wait long; the first soldier yelled loudly and charged towards the machine - his spear held menacingly towards the foe. The others immediately followed suit. Before they'd reached the middle of the clearing, the incessant hum became louder, and the colour of the machine brightened to a deeper blue. The ground shook in time with the humming and the trees vibrated so violently that leaves flew everywhere. The sound became unbearable. The very last thing Jack remembered was clasping his hands over his ears as searing pain exploded inside his head. He vaguely glimpsed a brilliant blue flash of light as the soldiers dropped. Darkness descended over him; he fell backwards into the grass.

Chapter 3 - Cathy's loss

Cathy stood quietly under the moonlight, staring sadly, at the spot where the MoonBridge had just faded from view. Her new and secretive friend, Jack Ferns, had just returned to his home.

"Wherever that is?" She thought, with a tear in her eye.

This was the second time she'd seen him leave. She wondered if he would ever return; she certainly hoped so. Even though it had only been two visits, Cathy had already grown to like Jack. She thought he was quite sweet, a bit naive perhaps, but certainly very likeable.

"He's nothing like the other young men that live close by," she reflected. "They're only interested in the stupid war; all wanting to join the Resistance, fighting against the Blades. What use is that?"

Jack was different. He was an "outsider" as the locals would say. He wasn't to be trusted, just because, he was from somewhere different. The people in the village would probably have locked him up if they'd suspected. Everyone had heard stories of the MoonBridge and the strangers supposedly travelling across it, but few really believed.

"Just a load of fairy tales for the children," the young men would denounce out of hand.

"How narrow minded they are, and how little they know," Cathy grinned wryly. She thought about the look on their faces if they ever discovered the truth.

The air was fresh and clean here, Cathy loved this time of night when the woods were empty. She would often creep out of her Aunt's cottage and take a stroll amongst the trees. The crispness of the leaf litter, under her feet, seemed like a carpet of feathers. Except for a few foraging creatures, the only movement came from the moonlight as it spilled through the gently swaying branches above. This was the easiest time to open the MoonBridge.

"Am I the only other person who knows the truth?"

Lujnima, the moon goddess, personally granted her the power of the Guardianship.

Standing silently, Cathy glanced down at the bracelet around her slim wrist. The light from the moon danced across its face and cast a mystical glow on her skin. Cathy remembered back to when she was just a little girl, all those years ago. One awful day, held fresh in her memory, as if it were yesterday - the day her mother fell ill. She could still hear the wind rustling the leaves outside her Mother's cottage. Her father had been away fighting in the previous war. Mother had warned he was unlikely to return. Sometimes, she barely remembered what he looked like. As her mother lay desperately clinging to life, she made Cathy sit beside her.

"Wear this, my darling," her mother said; giving her a bracelet of clean crisp silver.

The jewellery was beautifully made, very fine with an ornate decoration of a moon inscribed upon the face. Underneath were written some words, in a language, she didn't understand.

"You must promise you'll always treasure this bracelet. Wear it on your left wrist; never take it off until your time is near an end. Then, you must pass it on to your daughter."

Cathy looked bemused. Her mother continued. "You are my first born daughter. We form a long line of Guardians of the MoonBridge. For many, many generations, the bracelet wearer has guarded a secret that few would ever understand."

She encouraged Cathy to reach inside a little cupboard and take out a pretty old cane with an ornate silver handle.

"Here is the key to calling the MoonBridge."

Over the next few days Cathy's mother gradually explained all about her secret. How to call it? How to find it? How to close it?

"You'll soon be the MoonBridge Guardian my darling." Cathy's mother was very tearful. "You must learn to become its mistress my sweetheart. In time, you'll have to face the moon goddess Lujnima and seek her countenance."

Cathy wasn't sure quite what that meant but it sounded very scary to a seven year old.

Mother explained about her ancestors and how they'd found a way to invoke the powers of the Moon Goddess. Some believed it was a gift, others a curse, depending upon your point of view. Using the MoonBridge, you could safely move between any two points in this land. The danger arose when anyone attempted to cross from this world to the other side. Those travellers were apparently lost forever.

Cathy didn't really grasp the difference even though her mother tried to explain it several times.

"Essentially my darling you can hop from here to Aunt Beth's, if you really needed to, but you couldn't go beyond our world."

The little girl tried her best to understand.

"Be wary of the lure of the MoonBridge Cathy, you could end up being lost for eternity between this life and the next. Many foolish predecessors have met that fate, don't let it be you."

Cathy learned about the good things offered by the MoonBridge but she feared the possible dark and bad things too. Mother warned of a dangerous and invisible person who could also command its power.

"Watch out for this other Guardian my darling. I've felt his presence on several occasions, but have never seen him."

"Him mother, you mean he's a man? I thought you said the Guardian was always a daughter."

"Not always sweetheart, sometimes there has had to be a male Guardian on this side; very occasionally. This Guardian is altogether different though. He's far too powerful and seemingly ancient. Be very careful of him."

Cathy nodded obediently without daring to question any more.

"It's only through his deeds you can trace him. Watch for what he does with the powers of Lujnima, that's the only way to trap him."

Cathy had to swear to search out this other Guardian when she was older and stronger.

"With the grace and help of our dear mistress of the moon, you'll eventually fulfil your destiny to be the only Guardian on this side my darling. My time is fading; I'll never be in her presence again."

A few days later; Mother weakened before slipping painlessly out of this world. Her death left Cathy feeling completely alone; she now had no father, no mother – seemingly no-one. She realised it was impossible for a small child to survive on her own. She couldn't keep this house functioning and her only hope was to leave and head for her Aunt's cottage. The problem was that this wasn't close by; it was a very long walk of several days. She dared not attempt opening the MoonBridge in case she was lost forever; her only option was to find her own way. A lonely journey awaited her; through forest, across the wide savannah and then around the distant hills. Although there were rarely encounters with dangerous animals, they did happen. Not to mention the occasional brush with the Blade scouts who had been seen passing through their lands. None of these possibilities sounded encouraging for the seven year old.

"What if I get lost?" she worried. "What if I never get to Aunt Beth's house?"

She shrugged her shoulders, looked sadly at the familiar surroundings of her comfy little home, and said, "What other choice is there?"

The little girl sat down on the porch and studied the pretty front garden her mother had tendered with such care and devotion. She wondered, once more, if she could ever look after the plants or vegetables.

"What chance do I have of surviving alone?" she thought.

"None Cathy," she agreed with herself. "So let's just go, right now."

The decision had been made. At the tender age of seven and three quarters, Cathy stood up. She gathered a few personal belongings, slipped a small rucksack across her shoulders, and she set out for her

Aunt's home. Thankfully, it was a path she knew quite well. She and her mother had walked the route several times before. Mum liked to see her younger sister at least once each year. She always loved to travel when the summer plants were coming to an end and then return home just as the winter winds set in.

"Never mind all that Cathy, let's get on with this journey." The little girl strode off with confidence.

Years later, she wondered why she never once looked back to her old home. Where, her mother still lay silently in her bedroom - a single clean white sheet draped over her face.

The days were long at this time of year, the air was warm and there were plenty of nice things to eat along the way. Searching for, and finding, different berries, crops and fruit made the journey an enjoyable adventure in itself. Cathy loved eating the freshly picked tasty things nature kindly provided. She hadn't realised, at the time, her mum was busy teaching her the ways of the natural world. These lessons would prove invaluable to her for the forthcoming journey.

"This is where we stopped last time," she recognised a quiet little nook.

Cathy planned to find a number of familiar comfortable resting places: a quiet knoll by a stream, a little round cave set in the side of the sloping hill or under the very large branches of the big oak. One particular tree acted as a good signpost; it stood alone, and proud, in the centre of wide meadow.

On that long journey, Cathy grew from a small child into a young woman. Despite her tender age, she'd matured into a very resolute and clear thinking individual. All the while she felt the responsibility of the MoonBridge Guardianship weighing heavily upon her.

"Am I really the only true Guardian; and what about the other person?"

The questions rolled over and around in her mind.

"What did it all mean? Can I really command the moon powers to do my bidding?" She continued to question her mother's dying explanations.

One evening, she'd looked down at the delicate silver bracelet on her left wrist. She risked removing the cane from its protective cloth sheath; the silver handle glistened. "Now what do I do? Can I command this MoonBridge?" She briefly allowed the moonlight to fall onto the handle of the cane. Electricity flowed along her arms and up around her head. Afraid, she slid the cane back into its cover. The moon powers diminished.

Despite her loss, never once did she cry; Cathy was a naturally strong character. Her situation of losing her father, early on, made her a tough, self sufficient little girl. She already realised that she must stay alert. She must think clearly if she was to reach her aunt's cottage.

As the kilometres slipped by, Cathy became more confident. Every landmark she recognised made her feel better. She felt very proud of herself; she hadn't been lost once. After several days and nights Cathy finally arrived at the end of the lake.

"You've only gone and done it Cathy," she praised herself.

When she reached the water's edge it was late evening. Rather than make the final short trip around to the cottage, she decided to sleep in the safety of the little copse close by. This was one of her favourite special hiding places and she'd spent many secretive nights out here previously. Cathy knew her Aunt liked to lock up early and settle down for a good night's sleep - she always roused around dawn. Cathy found a cosy little den and curled up snug in her warmest clothes. After so many days of effort, she could finally relax.

Completely undisturbed throughout the night, she woke refreshed from her deepest sleep in many days. Cathy stood up and stretched her cramped muscles; how wonderful she felt. Just across the water, she saw the familiar sight of her Aunt's cottage. She guessed that at this early hour, for it was only just after dawn, her Aunt would still be tucked up safely in her bed.

"But, you'll have stoked the stove before long and have the kettle boiling for your regular morning tea soon Aunt Beth, I bet."

Cathy splashed her face with cool water from a stream feeding the lake. "What a surprise she was going to get," she smiled to herself. She skipped along happily, pleased with herself for getting this far all alone. She really looked forward to seeing her aunt's face, when she arrived. Approaching the cottage, she was surprised to see the front door already wide open.

"You're up early today?" Cathy mumbled quietly to herself.

She was shocked to find many of her Aunt's things scattered around the garden. Her joy was quickly extinguished; everything wasn't well. Some of the items were smashed into pieces and others were torn or stamped into the ground. She noticed that plants were snapped and vegetables uprooted. Nearing the front; she saw the door hanging awkwardly on its hinges; the house had been forcibly broken into. Cathy had never heard of such a thing.

"Who would've done this?" Panic took hold of the girl; she rushed in through the broken door not knowing what to expect. Aunt Beth was half sitting, half lying on the floor of the front room; she was sobbing quietly whilst rocking gently backward and forward as if trying to comfort herself. A nasty gash on her forehead was testament to the mistreatment she'd suffered. Drying blood had congealed across her eye and over her cheek; the pain had left her numbed in shock. Her dress was torn at the shoulder and she was badly bruised and obviously very distressed.

"What ever has happened Aunt Beth?" Cathy rushed to her Aunt's aid, adrenalin coursed through her veins. She fought to overcome the horror of her Aunt's condition. "Let me get you something for that cut on your head."

Aunt Beth looked up drearily, unable to gather her thoughts. She was barely able to even focus on the voice in front of her. "Is that you Cathy? Where's mummy?"

Cathy didn't answer directly but busied herself finding bandages, fresh water and some tonic.

"It's me Aunt Beth, I'm going to sort out your cut, just sit still for a moment. It'll be okay." Cathy cleaned and dressed the wound, helped her Aunt up from the floor and guided her back to her bedroom to lie down. Once Aunt Beth was comfortable, she set about firing up the stove and making her Aunt a refreshing cup of tea.

"Thank you my sweetness, now where's mummy?"

"Never mind that now Aunt Beth; you've had a terrible experience and you must rest."

Cathy settled her aunt in her room before she busied herself recovering what she could from the garden. After several hours of effort, the little girl finally sat down in Aunt Beth's favourite comfy chair in the scullery. "Oh my legs ache, I need a break."

Cathy managed to get everything tidied and cleaned up before her Aunt awoke. She started a long list of jobs that needed to be completed.

"I must rush down to the village and get Mr Hodgson to repair the door hinges."

Cathy checked her Aunt was still comfortable and resting before heading off to the village about two kilometres away.

Several weeks came and went before Aunt Beth was strong enough to take over again from Cathy. During that time, her niece had collected water from the well, gathered food for them both and kept the fire stocked with wood, from the shed at the back. In fact, she'd done everything necessary to nurse Aunt Beth back to health.

Only when her Aunt was fully strong enough, did Cathy finally tell her about her mother.

"Oh you poor darling, all that pressure and stress you've been under." Realising the trauma that Cathy must have endured; tears flooded down Aunt Beth's face. She was the bravest, cleverest and most incredibly responsible seven-year old she'd ever imagined. "I love you so much Cathy, thank you for helping me get better, I can never repay you for what you've done," she said sniffing her tears back loudly.

Cathy then started to cry too. For weeks, she'd bottled up everything; first the Guardianship, then her mother dying, her long journey plus the shock of finding her Aunt's cottage all dishevelled, and finally, nursing her sick Aunt back to health. At last she was able to release all of the pent up emotion: sorrow, anger, bitterness and fear, all came flooding out. Both sat, with arms around each other, and they cried together for what seemed like an age.

Over the next few weeks Aunt Beth talked about the raiders. They'd come from somewhere over the hills, she said, and they were looking for anyone hiding Blade insurgents. Even though she had nothing to hide, they were angry and nasty. Someone had accused Aunt Beth of being a Blade sympathiser. One of the raiders had beaten her even though she pleaded her innocence. Aunt Beth was just pleased to be alive; she wouldn't make the mistake of allowing anyone to enter her home again.

Together, they worked hard to reinforce the cottage. Mr. Hodgson fixed the buckled hinges and fitted stout bolts to the top and bottom of the door. As the weeks slipped into months, it seemed the raiders had kept to their word and left Aunt Beth and Cathy alone. Their fear eased into caution and then drifted to a wariness of anything out of the ordinary. Aunt Beth adopted a new routine of double checking every bolt at the end of each day. She called it her "battening down."

"It makes me feel much safer Cathy," she would regularly say.

***

All of these memories had been from such a long time ago; now wandering slowly back from the woods, Cathy thought of her new friend. "I would love to visit your home Jack to meet your family. They all seem lovely, especially your sister Tina-Lu. Your world sounds much more exciting than here. If only I could cross the MoonBridge to your side."

The girl grinned, as droplets of dew tickled her toes. "The air tonight is perfect," she thought aimlessly. On reaching the lake shore, she slipped off her open toed sandals and paddled quietly along the edge - the chill made her giggle. "Mmmm, so clean and refreshing."

The moonlight reflected in the stillness of the lake. Everything was so peaceful and tranquil; she wondered if the war with the Blades would actually reach their home again. She could hardly believe it was over eight years since her aunt had been assaulted. Only in the last few days had their false sense of safety become clear. Fighting had reached the other side of the savannah; barely two days walk away, it was far too close for comfort. One escaping family stopped briefly for water for their horses. They warned that the Blades had a new ally, some kind of mechanical creature called the "Blues". Strange cigar shaped things that moved at about the pace of a running man; they ate everything in their path the stories told. Cathy couldn't even imagine such a creature. The father believed they'd come across the MoonBridge.

"Sent by the devil himself," he whispered, half expecting them to appear at the mention of their name.

"How was this possible, she was the Guardian? She would've known, wouldn't she?"

A shiver shuddered through her body; she realised there could be another Guardian after all. Just as her mother had said, all those years ago, someone else commanded the MoonBridge. Someone Lujnima had kept secret from her. She resolved to seek another audience and try to find out.

The stroll back to the cottage was uneventful. Splashing along the lake shore; she loved feeling the light sandy soil slipping between her toes. The moon provided plenty of light, off the water's surface, to make it easy to see far into the distance. She felt completely refreshed. Reaching the cottage, she carefully opened her bedroom window and climbed back in. Once inside, she silently locked the shutters and secured the window, as her Aunt taught her. Slipping out of her clothes she climbed into bed and fell into a deep, relaxing sleep.

Waking abruptly, Cathy couldn't believe the sun was already brightening the sky with its reds and greens of the dawn twilight. The early morning stillness brought the usual dawn chorus of birds; she could recognise and identify every single one. Unsure of the reason for apprehension she lay back down and gradually drifted between sleep and wakefulness. Subconsciously, her mind wandered outside. The sound of the birds had stopped. She was suddenly alert and sitting bolt upright. Throwing on her dress she dashed out of her room and into the main parlour. Aunt Beth was still asleep. Cathy looked quickly out of the peep-hole in the window shutter. She couldn't see anything out of the ordinary, but something was amiss. The birds never stopped singing at this time of the morning.

Cathy crept into her Aunts room and shook her gently. "Quiet Aunt Beth, something's very wrong outside. I don't know what it is; all the birds have stopped singing."

Aunt Beth jumped out of bed and was instantly alert. "Have you seen anything dear?" she questioned with panic in her voice. "Have you checked all of the windows and doors; are they still secure?"

"I've looked through every window Aunt Beth, I can't see anyone, but there is definitely something happening. I think we should sneak out and hide in the woods."

Aunt Beth considered her niece's suggestion; she agreed hiding was probably safer than assuming their home was secure against marauders. They took another quick look out of each window before unbolting the front door. Gingerly, Aunt Beth poked her head outside.

"The coast seems clear. Let's go now Cathy."

Dashing away from the cottage, they crossed the clearing into the tree line. Both knew every path, marked or otherwise, for many kilometres around. Quickly, they made their way up to the rockier ground where dense undergrowth clung to the sides of the hills. Here it would be easier to hide or escape any marauders.

The sound of trees falling and branches breaking drifted up to their position. In the still airs of dawn Cathy couldn't decide how close they were to the noise.

"Can you hear that humming?" Aunt Beth asked.

"I can smell sulphur," Cathy declared pulling a face.

They huddled quietly together, hardly daring to peep out of their makeshift hideaway.

The strange sounds drifted off towards the east.

"Do you think it's safe yet Aunt Beth?" Cathy answered her own question by continuing. "Listen to the birdcalls, whatever it was must have moved away."

Aunt Beth didn't speak, instead she gestured to Cathy that she thought she could hear someone away to their right. Cupping her hand behind her ear, she tilted her head and pointed wildly away in the direction of the sound.

Cathy nodded, but couldn't help grinning; her Aunt looked so silly. "Who did she think she was some kind of Resistance fighter?"

Her Aunt grinned. She realised how foolish she looked waggling her finger at thin air.

"We must remain silent," she whispered directly into her niece's ear.

"There's someone over there, I'm certain of it; they may have one of those tracker mongrels with them. We mustn't let the animal catch our scent."

They both kept very low as they crept from bush to bush. The sounds were closer again, but they managed to reach a small outcrop of rocks. The position commanded a better view of the trees and bushes below. Cathy held her breath; she watched a long line of soldiers travelling at right angles to them. Most had large heavy packs on their backs; all carried shining swords or long spears. These men were soldiers; that was beyond doubt.

"Are they Blades?" Aunt Beth whispered.

They both watched barely daring to breath. Aunt Beth was becoming more frightened with each passing moment.

"They're definitely Blades Aunt Beth," Cathy announced coldly.

Her aunt trembled; realising the war had finally reached them. They were no longer safe; they must plan an escape.

"I've left it behind?" Realising her stupid oversight; Cathy suddenly stiffened, "I've left my cane in my bedroom cupboard, Aunt Beth. I HAVE to go and get it."

Her Aunt looked at her bemused, "Don't be ridiculous dear; you can't possibly go back to the cottage, it's far too dangerous. You'll get us both killed."

"You don't understand Aunt Beth. I MUST get it; it has been entrusted to me. Mother gave it into my safe keeping on her death bed. What a fool I am?"

Both sat in silence for a few seconds before Cathy continued. "Stay here Aunt Beth, don't leave this place. I'll sneak back, get my cane and return before you know it. I can be fast as a hare and quiet as a mouse when I want to, please trust me."

Cathy could not be persuaded so Aunt Beth reluctantly sat back down. Frustrated at her niece's insistence she said. "Okay dear, I'll hide here but you must be very, very careful. Those soldiers will not hesitate to kill their enemies." She didn't have the heart to tell her niece what else evil soldiers might do to a pretty young woman. The thought made her shudder and shake.

"I can make it back to the cottage in barely ten minutes, if I run, Aunt Beth."

The girl dashed away across the slope. She retraced her steps around the edge of the hill darting in and out of the rocks. Running flat out, she covered the distance quickly. Just before the tree line, surrounding the cottage, she skidded to a halt. Looking warily in all directions, she couldn't see any signs of danger; the cottage seemed untouched. The front door was still firmly closed and the shutters were all drawn tight. One last dash had her crouching by the front door. She opened it cautiously and stepped inside. No-one had been here, she was sure of it. Rushing to the cupboard she found her staff and wrapped it in the sling that let her carry it across her shoulders.

Turning to leave, her heart sank. Voices could be heard coming from across the meadow. They could only be a minute or so from the front door. She paused briefly before making her decision.

"I'm never going to out run a load of soldiers," she cursed. Acting quickly, she looked around desperately trying to think of somewhere to hide. Panic took hold; the only place, she could think of, was to climb up inside the chimney.

"How can I squeeze myself in here?" she moaned bitterly pushing her body up into the dirty, smelly space.

The gap was very tight; Cathy finally managed to force her shoulders about halfway up the inside of the narrow opening. She tried to relax a little, perching, with her feet spread apart. One foot balanced precariously on the stone masonry, the other on a small lump jutting out. Her calf muscles instantly complained about the awkwardness of her stance, making her legs shake. She forced her bottom against the sides of the chimney and pressed her shoulder against another jutting stone. Pain shot through her neck and arms. She felt sure she was going to slip down any moment. Her shoulder disturbed some soot which flew up her nose. Frantically pinching her nostrils; she heard several voices amplified by the chimney.

"Looks like they've already left mate," one of the soldiers declared.

"Check the rest of the rooms, the Captain wants all occupants brought outside. Make sure no-one's hiding anywhere."

Cathy held her breath, squeezed her nose tightly and closed her eyes.

"Ain't nobody ere boss, the place is clear." The soldier's voice was close to the chimney.

Cathy fully expected to be found out any second. Her heart was in her mouth and the time seemed to move impossibly slowly. She involuntarily shifted her position and made a scraping sound.

"Shhh. What was that noise? Came from over there didn't it?" the soldier pointed to the fireplace.

"I didn't here nothing mate," the other soldier replied.

The first soldier moved towards the opening. Placing his hand on the mantle, to allow himself to lean down, he peered into the fireplace and cocked his head to listen for any sounds.

Cathy's heart had stopped beating and she could feel the sweat forming on her forehead. The smell of soot stuck at the back of her throat making her want to cough.

"What is it Archie? Who's up there then?"

The soldier knelt down to look up the chimney. Reaching his head forward, a very loud cooing sound came from above Cathy's head. One of the many local pigeons, which often perched on the chimney stack, announced its presence to the world.

The soldier stood up chuckling. "Just some stupid bird is all Trev; let's go."

The first soldier turned away and called out behind him. "Anyone back there?"

"Nah Rick. Ain't no-one 'ere neither," another soldier shouted. "These back rooms are clear."

"Okay Smithy, we're gone, let's get out of 'ere…" came the answer.

The front door slammed shut, with a loud crash; the last soldier left the building.

"Let's move out you lot, and keep your eyes peeled."

Cathy heard the order echoing down the chimney. This came from outside the cottage, more muffled and distant than before. She strained to hear the clatter of boots and swords as the soldiers up and left. Not daring to move, even though her legs, back and neck were shaking painfully, she waited impatiently. Gingerly, she allowed herself to drop down into the hearth. Completely covered in soot, the girl looked a mess.

"I stink of burnt wood." Cathy never liked to be even slightly grubby, she positively hated being filthy.

The cottage was empty. Cathy glanced at her reflection in the mirror on the far wall. "What I wouldn't give for a hot tub of clean soapy water." With a shake of her head, she focussed on the task at hand. After a quick check through the window shutters, she made her way back across the meadow and into the trees.

Every rustle of leaves, each noise and even a breath of wind had Cathy jumping for fear. Convinced soldiers lay in wait at every turn; she took nearly three quarters of an hour to creep back to the spot where she left her Aunt.

"Aunt Beth," she whispered as loudly as she dared - no reply came. Cathy frantically searched the area but her Aunt was nowhere to be seen.

"Where are you Aunt Beth," she risked being a little louder.

"No," she screamed, seeing fresh blood on one of the rocks. "Is that your blood Aunt Beth?" she cried in horror.

A closer look around identified a few more spots and then again further on. The trail of blood led off around the hill; she would have to track it to find out if it really was her Aunt's. Crawling along almost on her hands and knees, Cathy traced the drips for a few more minutes. Each one seemed to be spaced further and further apart until she was unable to trace any more. They'd been heading off in one general direction; she decided to follow, as best as possible, in the same direction. This was becoming an act of desperation. Cathy had little idea where she was going and didn't even know if the blood had been her Aunt's.

Cathy kept moving forwards until she finally heard her first voices. They were coming from her left and seemed to be very close. She hid under a thick bush and looked across to a group of twenty or so soldiers. Her hand clamped across her mouth again when she saw her poor Aunt, blood all down one side of her face and hands tied behind her back. She was standing, midway, in a line of six other people all tied together. Poor Aunt Beth looked very dejected. The prisoners consisted of another old woman, two younger girls, a small boy and a middle aged woman. They all seemed extremely frightened. As she watched; one very nasty soldier walked up to the old woman and slapped her to the ground. Cathy sat back, shocked at the sight of such cruelty.

"Who were these filthy animals?" she hissed.

"Git up yer scum," ordered the despicable soldier to the woman he'd just slapped to the ground.

"Git up or I'll kick yer," he pulled back his leg as if to strike the desperate woman.

"Leave her alone you sick brute," Aunt Beth said to the man defensively. "She's hurt, can't you see that."

The soldier turned on Cathy's Aunt and slapped her across the face with a very loud crack. "Speak to me again old hag and I'll cut you down right here." He drew his sword and pushed the blade under her throat.

Another soldier walked over. "Alright Digger, don't kill 'em all before the skipper's had chance to see what they knows." With an evil grin and a nod of approval; he continued, "You can do 'em after that."

Digger snorted dismissively. He pulled the injured woman, lying on the ground, up to her feet using the rope that bound her hands. "You'll be the first one I do, scum," he shouted, threateningly, in the poor woman's ear. She shook wildly with fear. "An' you'll be the next," he gestured towards Aunt Beth with his sword handle.

"Git 'em movin'," an order came from the other side of the group.

A taller soldier, in a slightly different uniform, stood up. "Where we off to Cap'n, Sir?" one of the younger soldiers asked him. The younger man, probably only twenty, looked excited at the prospect of more killing.

"Over there, back towards the town. We're heading along the edge of the lake, Charlie. The General wants the place cleared out as quickly as possible so we've got to get back." The Captain waved his arm roughly in the direction of Cathy's cottage.

Charlie rattled his sword in its scabbard expectantly. "More work for you soon, Bessie."

The Captain grinned at the eager young soldier. "These prisoners will be taken with the others for interrogation, and then disposed of."

Cathy nearly screamed again but managed to clamp both hands over her mouth. "I must save my Aunt," she thought desperately.

The group progressed at a slow pace down towards the lake. They walked in single file; a very large man at the front carried an enormous spear, almost twice his height. The prisoners were all tied to each other by strong rope. Painful red welts marked their wrists. Behind them were several gruff looking Blade soldiers carrying swords. The sun reflected off the polished metal.

"Just you wait; I'll get you for this." Cathy threatened.

Ahead, more soldiers gathered. Cathy approached cautiously; keeping at a safe distance, she sneaked from tree to tree. Groups of soldiers congregated near the clearing of Aunt Beth's cottage. Several; forced the prisoners to wait, in a large open space, at the back. She counted thirty people tied up together.

"Is that Mrs Jackson?" she thought. Aunt Beth had known the old lady for many years. She lived peacefully over the other side of the lake and never harmed anyone.

"Git over there you stupid old crow," the nasty soldier struck out again, this time his victim stumbled forwards into the back of the woman in front. Both stayed silent in fear of reprisal. The line of prisoners joined the others. "Stay there and keep quiet," he threatened, prodding one young child with his sword.

Cathy became angry at the sight of this vicious man. She imagined grabbing his sword and sticking it firmly in his back. "See how you'd like it you pig," she cursed. Cathy swiped her arm smartly in a mock thrust.

On reaching the cottage; Cathy hid under the large bush that edged the white painted fence. Peering through the leaves she saw a number of soldiers sitting and standing in the back garden. The cottage had been plundered; some soldiers had stolen Aunt Beth's possessions. Many were eating the contents of the larder and drinking her homemade Elderberry and Sloe wine. They were becoming rowdy as the alcohol took effect. Aunt Beth's wine was well known locally for its flavour and potency. You normally would only drink a few sips of a glass, not the bottles that these men were now downing.

"Ere, punk, that's my tipple," one of the larger, rounder soldiers shouted at another. He grabbed for the bottle and stumbled forwards knocking into the first man. The two immediately started fighting and a mob quickly formed around them.

"Punch 'is lights out 'arry," screamed one, above the din of the cheering and chanting. Another launched out with his heavy boot, kicking the man hard on the shin.

"I'll kill yer…"

The fighter never finished his threat. One of the sergeants pushed through the pack and cracked him over the head with a huge club. The man fell in a heap, blood pouring from the wound. Everyone took a couple of paces backwards, watching the soldier groan.

"Shift you lot, or do you want some of my, Patsy?" he grinned menacingly; stroking the club in mock affection. "I'll pound any one else who steps out of line. The Cap'n said no fightin'."

The other soldiers moved further apart. This sergeant was feared, by all, for his ruthlessness.

Several groups of disgruntled soldiers formed in different areas of the garden. Cathy watched one particular group who were clearly more agitated than the rest. She thought they looked like they were ready to burst at any second. They continued to swig wildly at the bottles of wine and were beginning to feel overconfident due to the effects of the alcohol. The leader of the little bunch, Chas, was obviously the spokesperson. He shouted over to one of the other groups. "Eh

Bazzer, you gonna put up wiv this for much longer? We're sick of that pig orderin' us about. What say's we do 'im and get ourselves back home?"

The other group looked at them as if they were mad.

"You ain't got the bottle for it Chas. All mouth and no trousers I've heard. You wanna start somethin' then go ahead. See how far you get?"

Chas was incensed. He raced across towards Bazzer; lunging at him with his drawn sword. The sharp gleaming blade ran right through the man; he fell to the floor. Chas placed his heavy boot on the man's midriff and pulled the sword from his chest; the man slumped, dead. Stunned silence lasted only for the briefest moment; within seconds the place erupted in violence. The clash and clang of metal swords rang out. Men fell to the floor with blood spurting and bone exposed. In the blink of an eye about ten drunken soldiers lay dead or dying. Cathy covered her mouth to prevent herself from being physically sick.

At the first sign of trouble the sergeant grabbed several other soldiers and rushed over to the carnage. He was very accurate and effective with his own sword. He swept this way and that with power and conviction. Several more lay dead before he finally restored order. He looked down at the now dead Chas and spat on his chest. "Scum!" he cursed. The sergeant looked around, panting heavily at the exertion of the previous few minutes.

"I said no fightin'. Any more and I'll have the Cap'n string all of yer up by yer necks."

He walked past a young man lying twisted and bleeding. The man was still desperately holding his sword, even though he looked near to death. The sergeant kicked him callously in the stomach and the young man let out a low groan.

"Burn this place to the ground," the sergeant ordered.

Several men lit torches and threw them into Aunt Beth's cottage. Cathy could contain her anger no longer, she ran out of her hiding place screaming at the top of her voice.

"STOP…"

She managed to grab one of the burning torches before the soldier could throw it. She punched, kicked and bit the soldier before being overpowered by the nasty 'Digger'.

"What 'ave we 'ere then?" the soldier gripped Cathy tightly by the throat. He wiped some of the soot from her face with his thumb, "You're a pretty little vixen, if ever I saw one?" he drivelled, pulling her towards him. "You'll make a right tasty morsel."

"Get your stinking paws off me you pig," spat Cathy trying her best to scratch, kick or wriggle free.

The man's grip tightened so much, she nearly fainted. Her Aunt looked over in horror and tried to run for her niece. The rope pulled her back and she fell to her knees screaming and shouting for them to stop. This time, the Captain looked up and assessed what was happening.

"Put her down, Digger." The Captain ordered. He then commanded the sergeant to tie Cathy with the other prisoners.

Watching her beautiful cottage blaze; Aunt Beth cried inconsolably.

"Get up you scum, we're movin' out." ordered the lead soldier to the prisoners. Cathy tried to comfort her Aunt as best she could, but she was too overcome by grief.

The pretty little cottage crackled loudly. Red embers spluttered in all directions as the thatched roof ignited. A thick plume of grey smoke rose high into the sky, destroying a lifetime of memories. The soldiers led their prisoners away from the lake; they headed off towards the hills.

"Don't cry Aunt Beth, we'll escape just see if we don't." Cathy tried her best to remain positive, for her Aunt's sake.

Chapter 4 - An audience with Lujnima

"Who is he?" whispered Jaden. "He doesn't look like one of the locals, does he Grandfather?"

Searlan knelt down beside the unconscious boy lying crumpled on the grass. He placed one hand on his forehead and called softly to him. "Come back boy." As he spoke, he made a circular sign across the boy's temple. He waited for a few seconds then continued. "Awake now, you're amongst friends."

The boy opened his eyes slowly, but found it very difficult to focus. "What happened, where are they, who are you?" he blurted out confused.

"Never mind that for now, you and your companion must come with us, it isn't safe here." Searlan gestured towards the wilted animal, still lying in an awkward position.

The dog looked completely limp as if he were dead. The boy managed to struggle to his knees and then to twist himself into a seated position.

Reaching over to the dog, Jaden enquired. "Is he going to be alright Grandfather?"

The Sage placed both hands on the animal's body, one over his head and the other on his stomach. He then commanded. "Awake little one, you are a free spirit here."

The dog raised his head, from the grass, and licked the Sage's hand. Searlan smiled broadly, looking deeply into his wide brown eyes, before turning towards the boy and announcing, "He loves you dearly young Master Jack. Brandy here would willingly give his life for you." Looking now straight at the boy, he said, "That is your name, isn't it, Jack Ferns?"

The boy gulped and nodded silently; this old man seemed both friendly and frightening. "How did he know my name?" he wondered.

Searlan ushered them all to their feet and the four travellers set off along the edge of the lake. The old man was hurrying and it wasn't very long before they reached the burnt out cottage. He was heartbroken to see his friend's home ruined and smouldering. He surveyed the surroundings and examined several dead soldiers.

"These are Blades for sure. Have a quick look around Jaden. See if there are any signs of Beth and Cathy."

"I was here earlier Searlan, I couldn't find them." Jack said.

The Sage nodded in reply but seemed remote and shocked. He knew the two occupants well and had enjoyed the hospitality, of Beth Wilde's supper table, on many happy occasions. He was particularly partial to her home-made wine and always delighted in offering a tale or two of the ancients in repayment. He was ready to take vengeance on the soldiers that did this.

Jaden spent a while searching but found no signs of either Beth or Cathy. Searlan was happier that they didn't appear to be amongst the victims. He walked around to the side of the cottage and looked over by the little white fence. He spotted a long bundle of cloth lying under the bush next to it. "What's this then eh?" he unravelled the cloth and then quickly wrapped it up again ensuring no-one saw his prize. Slinging it over his shoulder, he carried on with his search without a further word.

Jack went briefly over to the soldier who had died. He bent his head in a silent prayer before joining Jaden.

"We've spent enough time here now. Let's move on." Searlan called to the other two.

All four made their way over to the clearing. Something glittering caught Jaden's eye; he paused briefly to bend down and pick it up from the ashes. Dusting it off carefully, on his sleeve, he placed it quietly in his pocket. With a wry grin, he followed on behind the others. They took a pathway that led further down into the woods. The undergrowth made passage difficult. A bramble with spiky thorns grew everywhere; Jack had cuts and scratches all over his Jacket, especially the arms.

"Mum's gonna kill me when I get home," he worried.

Jaden finally took the lead, from his grandfather, and led them deeper into the green gloom. He never once looked back even after so many twists and turns, it was impossible for Jack to know the route they'd taken. Eventually the young boy halted.

"Where are we then?" Jack asked sarcastically. "The middle of nowhere I reckon."

The ground was marginally higher than the surrounding woodland, but nothing else seemed to distinguish it from any other place.

Turning to the Sage; Jaden pleaded. "May I? Please Grandfather?"

Searlan seemed undecided for a moment and then let out a little sigh; he handed the boy his cane. "Remember, all you've been taught," he said. "Tel-Rew-Hay does not lightly take commands from any other keeper. You must use her wisely, she'll know if you don't speak with truth and conviction."

Taking great pride in his grandfather's trust, the boy took the staff; he looked briefly across at Jack and grinned. The wooden cane was large against his small frame; it almost reached up to his shoulder. He knew this gift, from Tarre-Hare, was a powerful tool and capable of many things. In the wrong hands it could easily overwhelm the wielder. Jaden grasped it tightly and pointed ahead, aiming it slightly towards the ground.

"Let us pass." He spoke in a forceful manner.

Jack watched, mildly amused, nothing seemed to happen. The boy waited for a few more seconds, glanced towards his grandfather and frowned.

"Again Jaden," the old man encouraged.

The boy repeated, much louder this time. "Let us pass; by order of this Sageling, I demand that you let us pass."

A slight rumble came from below one of the trees in front of them. Jack blinked a couple of times in disbelief. The trees immediately started to bend backwards. The ground beneath their roots fell away, and an opening into the little hillock appeared. The gap was barely wide enough for one person, but Jaden pushed forward and quietly prayed in a soothing chant. "Hold back old friend as we pass beneath your domain. Let the roots of your soul bathe in the truth of our hearts. We thank you."

With a low gracious bow, nearly to the ground, the boy stood up. Finally, with a long drawn out groan, the ground gave way completely and made an entrance wide enough for two people to walk through. A path appeared leading deep inside the earth. The tunnel was straight as a ruler and led steeply downwards; it continued for many metres.

To his great delight, Jack found himself walking out into a huge cavern. "Wow, this is really great."

The ceiling was so high even the very dim light, coming from hundreds of miniscule glowing points around the walls, failed to light it at all. He could hear the steady dripping of water, there were a number of small puddles on the floor and the space smelt musty and damp.

"Where are we going?" he asked inquisitively. The echo effect of his voice made him giggle.

"You know where we're going young Master Jack – the MoonBridge rider," the old man smiled knowledgeably.

"What, what are you talking about?" Jack flustered unconvincingly.

"Know this young man. Do not be fooled by my frailty. I'm Searlan the ancient one; Sage of Sages, Elder of Elders, Commander of the Natural Order and keeper of the secret knowledge. I know exactly who you are." Searlan pointed his old and bent finger firmly in Jack's chest.

Jack looked at the old man with a renewed sense of awe and finally realised why he'd felt so safe in his presence.

"What I don't know is why you're here?" Searlan mused almost to himself.

Ahead, on a flattened area of the far wall, was a single small ornate carving of the moon about the size of a human head. As they approached, the rock glowed dimly.

"Greetings Sage, do you seek an audience?"

Jack stared at the wall, but couldn't see where the voice had come from. The moon became a little brighter as a faint outline of a face appeared.

"She thinks you're too weak, Sage," the voice taunted.

"Let me do it grandfather, please let me take your place." Jaden interjected.

The voice deepened and sounded far more menacing. "Boy, you are not the Sage; you are yet but a Sageling and have no voice here."

Jack suddenly felt very angry at the tone of this voice. He didn't know why but his blood boiled, "Who is speaking? Show yourself to us."

Searlan and Jaden were amazed to hear the ferocity in Jack's voice and even more so when the moon brightened to blazing silver and the full face of a baby boy appeared.

"Greetings Guardian of the night world, she says you are most welcome. Do YOU seek an audience?"

Jack turned to the other two, pulled a face and shrugged his shoulders. "Yes, yes I do seek an audience, and I expect my friends to attend too."

A disconcerting silent pause, made Jack uncomfortable. Finally, the voice spoke again, "As you wish Guardian, she will see you all now."

The wall around the moon face melted away. Ahead of them glistened, brighter and brighter, until the light was too intense to look at. With a loud whooshing sound, the four were swept forwards into the light. They slid ever faster down into the depths of the earth along a glass-smooth tunnel. All four were then unceremoniously dumped out onto a clean, ice-like, area about ten metres wide. The floor was polished like a mirror, above was a perfect hemisphere. The ceiling sparkled with tiny stars set against a pitch black background.

A mellow female voice, sang, from the very centre of the space, "Guardian, why have you sought my council?"

Searlan placed his hand firmly on Jack's shoulder and answered before he could respond. "We kneel before you majesty of the night. I'm directed to seek your council and to beg once more, for your wisdom, power and generosity."

The old man knelt down slowly, with great difficulty. He ushered Jack to follow suit and Jaden slipped easily into a subservient pose. Brandy just stood there wagging his tail fiercely, as if he'd just met an old friend.

As each of the four remained transfixed before the moon, the voice then addressed each person simultaneously. Although, all of the four believed they were the only one's being spoken to. They all heard different statements and questions. None would ever know or hear the other's words.

Searlan listened to the voice saying.

"So, Sage, you have finally come before me again. Were you not warned that your next audience would be your last? Were you not told your time was at an end and my generosity was not without limit? Were you not ordered to pass your knowledge over to your heir? Speak quickly lest I end your time where you stand."

Jaden believed he heard the statement.

"Young Sageling, you are indeed strong of heart; you will make a good adversary in time, but your moment has not yet come. I let you stand before me now because I see your worth; I hear your truth and I feel your love for the Sage. You will be permitted to leave if you ask the right question."

Believing the voice said only to him; Jack felt overwhelmed with admiration.

"Guardian of the night world, you've taken the path of the bridge. Only those with the soul of truth can command its power. I see you have strength and faith; you'll discover you're capable of so much more than you now realise. Before the cockerel next crows you'll find yourself and will be changed forever. Look to your friends for the guidance you seek; and know this, you carry with you a trinket that may prove very useful in times of indecision. But beware, she can be both helpful and hindering; in the end you must decide."

Brandy wagged his tail even harder as the voice in his head said.

"Friend and protector, your master loves you and needs you more than ever before. Your strength and speed will help him to find his path. Stay close by him at all times and bathe in his love for you. Do not fear if your paths part, you will meet again; this I have foreseen."

All four thought that they spoke in response, but no sound was heard from any one. In their minds they believed they were the only one to answer.

Searlan replied with a very heavy heart.

"Mistress, I'm afraid for the entire world, the balance has shifted and everything is in danger of being undone. The war is on our doorstep and others, outsiders from beyond the bridge I believe, have come to support the Blades. They are now too powerful and I can no longer protect my people. I've sought the Tarre-Hare as an ally but she will not respond. I've no other course but to beg for your help. Guide my hand and deliver me the strength to fulfil my pledge. I fear that I'll not be able to complete my work as my knowledge will soon pass to my Sageling Jaden."

The moon's voice replied with strength and passion.

"You ask much old man. Fear not, the boy will find his own way; he is the Sage by right. I hear your plea for help and accept your honesty in fulfilling your pledge. You will meet your destiny sooner than you know. As you have suspected, you will soon pass over to the Sageling, you will know the time. This force from the other side is closed even to me. They are more dangerous than you dare to imagine and I do not have the power to stop then. You must place your faith in the young Guardian, guide him well whilst you still have time and you will be repaid a thousand times over."

Jaden thought quickly before he answered the moon goddess.

"My grandfather kneels before you and seeks your power and wisdom. Yet you are hidden here in the twilight bowls of the earth afraid of the sun. You live in the darkness alone and are so sad. I'm your light, I'm your hope and I'm your one true voice. Know me; for I'm the new Sage in waiting, and you will learn to fear me. I alone have faced Tarre-Hare and she has shown me my path. Underestimate me at your peril; I'm like my father, my grandfather and all of the ancients before me. My line is strong and my resolve firm."

Drifting across his thoughts; the mellow voice laughed coolly. "Yes my Sageling, I see your truth. You will indeed make an adversary to relish. An age of ages, I've known, since I felt such depth of passion in one so young. You make my heart sing, as it has not, for longer than it deserves. Go forth and return when the moment demands. When next we meet you will have become a man and will be Sage of Sages."

Jack tried to look around him but found he could not move his head or his eyes. Seemingly floating; he mused, "Why am I here Lujnima? Is that your name? Are you the moon goddess or is this all a made up dream? All that I know for sure is that I found that old cane and solved a tricky puzzle. I discovered that MoonBridge of yours and now I'm here. What is it you think I can do? I'm just a stupid kid really. What do I know about wars or fighting or anything?"

As he spoke, he seemed to anticipate the response from her. "So many questions child; I'll answer them as I might, yet I already sense you've perceived their content. Yes, one of my names is Lujnima, but few have ever been so bold to use it directly. In future you will learn to address me as Mistress. Your innocence is refreshing; it has been so long since I felt such tenderness and purity. You are here because you are the chosen night world Guardian. The cane found you and allowed you to attempt the test of the puzzle. Solving this test proved that you are the one it had been waited for. Now you must find your path and seek out your destiny. You do not need any further answers; you already know this to be true."

The visitors knew immediately that Lujnima had completed her audience with them without needing to be told. As she departed; it was as if the room went with her, the space became very hollow and empty. Even breathing seemed to echo and reverberate into the depths. The air chilled and then they felt uneasy as the darkness thickened around them. The walls seemed to swirl and then disappear as if they had never existed at all. Within the twinkle of an eye, they were standing in the bright sunlight and blinking wildly at the sudden change in light levels.

Jack looked around confused. "Where are we now?" he asked Searlan.

"Lujnima has placed us where we would've been, had we not diverted to seek her audience. Such is her way." He answered the boy whilst still trying to get his own bearings. "I think we're many kilometres from the wooded grove where we entered her domain. I don't yet know if it's safe here, we must be careful. Walk quickly; I'll attempt to gain information that may help us."

Jack watched in fascination as Searlan started to chant very quietly to himself. He reached out and let his hands flick branches and leaves. He was careful never to damage any of the plants he touched; just a fleeting caress seemed to leave the tree or bush quivering as if with excitement at meeting the Sage.

"He's asking for help," Jaden explained to the puzzled Jack. "Every time he makes contact, with a living thing, he gains some knowledge of anyone passing. Individually, the information is small, but gradually he will build up a picture of the comings and goings. This will help him decide our safest path."

"How does he do that?" Jack enquired innocently.

Jaden just gave his little grin that said. "Don't ask stupid questions Jack, he's the Sage!"

After about half an hour they came to a crossroads where the narrow rocky path split into three tracks. The Sage stopped and looked in each direction. "The Blades have travelled down there in the last hour," he announced pointing down the slope to the south. "This road here leads up into the hills, but will be too far out of our way." He busily studied the North West route. "Although, I sense the danger in taking this other path, I feel we have no choice. Everywhere is dangerous at the moment, but if we are cautious, we should be able to avoid the worst of it."

Pausing briefly to finalise his decision; the old man thumped his staff into the ground and strode off at a steady pace. "This is the road."

"Come on Jack," said Jaden. "Tell me about yourself. Where are you from? What does it mean being the Guardian of the other world? What's it like in your world?"

The boy skipped along with a beaming smile on his face; he was so happy to be alive. He didn't seem to care about the potential danger of the soldiers or the Blues. He was just grateful to be enjoying the walk. He loved the sun and the beautiful scenery. Most of all he loved gathering knowledge and making new friends. He really liked Jack Ferns and his pet dog Brandy.

Chapter 5 - Journey through the deep

Jack broke the silence of the last half hour. "What did Lujnima mean when she spoke to me Searlan? What do you think my destiny is?"

The old man pondered his questions before answering. "You need to have some background knowledge before you can really understand," he explained. "The audience, you've just witnessed, is a rare and great honour. Few are permitted such an opportunity and rarely are visitors accorded such a welcome."

Mulling over his thoughts, for a few more seconds, he continued. "She is the manifestation of Lujnima, the night goddess, and the twin sister of Tarre-Hare who is the sun goddess. Together they power all nature. Occasionally, you can look into the daylight sky to see that they come together, but mostly they remain separate. Their powers peak when they are furthest apart; they are true opposites, the closer they are, the lesser their influence. Lujnima's powers are always changing, they wax and wane from peak to trough and back again. That's why it's so much easier to command the MoonBridge Way when she is full."

"You mean I can open the bridge at other time besides midnight?" Jack interjected suddenly realising the potential.

"Of course you can," the Sage answered; looking down his nose, sarcastically. "Now don't interrupt."

Jack lowered his gaze.

"Her powers peak, at that time, and have their greatest influence. Beware though; she doesn't ever reveal her true self to any mortal. Some say she is so ugly and hideous that she has to hide away in the shadows to prevent anyone ever actually seeing her face. Even the Guardian or Sage must beware. Some believe the true face of Lujnima would instantly melt you into a gooey pool of blood and cinder. "

Jack gulped and screwed up his lip. "Yuck, now you tell me."

Searlan tutted impatiently, "Her sister, Tarre-Hare; however, has no such qualms about revealing herself. She is so beautiful that your heart melts completely in her presence. If you are ever granted an audience, the radiance of her smile will fall upon you like a waterfall of passionate kisses. The sight of her flowing golden hair will brush over you like the caress of a thousand rose petals. Her large green eyes; those eyes will see through you as if you were made of the purest crystal. Nothing can be hidden from her gaze. You will never love anyone as much, or as intensely, as the love you'll feel for Tarre-Hare." The old man breathed a very deep sigh of painful regret. "That is, of course, if you are ever privileged enough to meet her. But once you do, you'll worship her for the rest of your life."

Jack listened to the Sage intently and was amazed at the transformation of his teacher. Speaking of his adoration for Tarre-Hare; the years seemed to fall from the old man. The very mention of her name brought vitality and life to her worshipper. Her strength, wisdom and power flowed outwards from the soul of her Sage.

"Do you draw your powers from Tarre-Hare or from Lujnima?" Jack enquired further.

Searlan laughed. "Always more questions from you young Master Jack Ferns." He continued with a little shake of his head. "You're worse than my grandson. Between you both, I think I shall never find peace." The old man drifted back into his deep thoughts.

Jack politely stepped away; he eagerly awaited another opportunity to learn from this amazing old man.

"Walk with me," Jaden said to Jack. "Grandfather will not speak again for a while."

Searlan continued to stride along in quiet contemplation. The boys chatted about Jack's home-world and the MoonBridge Way.

As the sun lowered in the sky, they found a very nice spot to rest and eat. A mossy bank climbed up out of a bubbling clear brook. The water tumbled along splashing off the large, football sized, pebbles that filled the bed of its path. Red, yellow and brown lichens and deep green mosses clung precariously to any available space not completely submerged. A refreshing feel to the air ran along the banks of the brook. Just lying there brought vitality back into Jack's aching limbs.

"Try this Jack, one small drink from this stream will send warmth and energy surging though your tired body." Searlan suggested.

"Drink slowly," Jaden cautioned. "Take too much and you'll regret it."

The boy looked questioningly at his young friend.

"The waters in this brook have bubbled up from the depths of the earth further up there in the hills." Jaden pointed vaguely away to their left. "This elixir has been fortified with many minerals and potions that have been given up by the earthly demons. Even though they've been diluted, they are renowned for their powers. When taken, in moderation, they'll benefit the body, drinking too much has the opposite effect."

"Perhaps that's what happened to me before?" Jack mused. He recounted how Brandy and he'd drunk the water from the stream near the lake. "We both fell into a deep sleep then; I thought the water was poisoned."

Jaden agreed, although secretly, he suspected the water may have actually been contaminated by the Blues or even the Blades.

After a short rest they continued on their journey.

"Where are we going Jaden?" enquired Jack. "We seem to have been walking for ages without getting anywhere."

The young boy just looked at him and grinned. "My grandfather knows the way. Trust that he is a great guide and a supreme Sage. He never takes a longer route than is necessary and rarely misses any shortcut that is available."

They walked in silence again for a short distance before Jack asked more insistently. "That still doesn't answer my original question. Where are we actually going?"

The boy smiled again and just shrugged a dismissive answer before skipping ahead to take his grandfather's hand. "Nearly there grandfather?" he smiled broadly, glancing back to Jack, and winking.

They came to a sloping mixture of shingle and slate. Dark, sharp and treacherous; the path ahead stretched down and away across a wide expanse of a valley. Ahead, the hills disappeared into the distance. The trees had thinned considerably in the last few kilometres. All around grew low springy bushes with tiny curled leaves and bright yellow flowers. Directly in front of them stood a small mottled-grey, pyramid shaped obelisk; it was old and heavily weathered. Seemingly growing out of the ground, this strange and ancient artefact was about waist high. Jack examined it as they came closer.

"What's this?" he asked.

"Shush now and don't touch," Jaden warned. "Grandfather must concentrate if we are to take this shortcut; it could save us a great deal of time."

The Sage approached the structure and placed his hand on a well-worn area of stone, about half way up. The position was carefully chosen to force a person to bend over, subserviently. Standing in this bowed position, he concentrated for a few seconds. With his eyes closed, he spoke quietly. "Greetings my old friend, once again I seek your permission to pass through your gate?"

Jack felt a little uneasy as a melodic but mocking reply came from somewhere indistinguishable.

"Why do you seek passage on such a wonderful day old man? Surely the breath of air is preferable to the cold and damp of the under-land."

Searlan paused very briefly before replying with great earnest. "My need is great and my time is short good friend. I have to cross the foothills before darkness comes and my poor aching limbs are too old to make the journey. Would you please grant this small request to one whom has served you so well in the past?"

Again the voice echoed out. "What of these others travelling with you, old man? The small golden creature offers us no concern; the young Sageling we know of old, but this other one, he brings turmoil and danger. This one we do not trust. What of him?"

Searlan was visibly losing his patience but breathed deeply before stating. "Good friend, I've never endangered you or your kin in all our previous encounters, I've always kept to my oath to protect your secrecy and I've proven my worth on too many occasions to count. I ask again. Will you not let us pass?"

Jack watched the conversation taking place with great fascination. He didn't pretend to understand what the voice meant.

"Turmoil and danger," he whispered to Jaden. The boy shrugged his shoulders in answer.

Jack looked at the old Sage affectionately; he seemed like every boy's ideal grandfather: clever, amusing, knowledgeable and generous. He really envied young Jaden to have such a wonderful guide and mentor.

Just as the old man finished his requests, Jack felt a sharp stabbing pain in the middle of his chest. "Ouch, that hurt. What was that?" He gasped in pain as his whole body seemed to go limp –h e felt overpowered. As quickly as it had happened, it became like a forgotten dream.

Jaden looked at him knowingly. "They've just checked you out," he smiled. "Horrible isn't it, feels just like they're crawling around inside you."

Jack nodded slowly feeling a little sick in his stomach.

The voice rang out deeply. "So be it old man, you may pass but do not linger, we will not tolerate this Guardian of the off world for long. If you fail to keep him under control we shall take him."

Jack didn't like the sound of that, but before he could react, the old Sage had answered. "Gracious friend. We thank you for your generosity and I assure you we will honour your requests."

The obelisk structure creaked and groaned as it slid sideways; a set of steps led down into the ground. The way was poorly lit, but you could just about see the route disappearing deep into the earth. Searlan led the others forward, through the entrance, and into the dimly lit interior. A red glow, about the size of a football, floated head high in the darkness ahead. Jack thought it looked like an old fashioned Chinese lantern flickering and swaying. He imagined the owner of the voice carrying it just out of their sight. The Sage pushed them all forwards towards the light and ensured they hurried on at a good pace. Down the steps they travelled, deeper and deeper into the earth.

"Do not tally, do not speak and absolutely do not touch anything in here. My friends have been kind enough to offer us passage but they will not tolerate any intrusion into their well guarded privacy."

The Sage turned to Jack and warned. "You do not want to make these your enemy young Guardian, they can be very dangerous to the un-knowing."

Jack looked sheepish and moved even closer to the old man.

They walked for several minutes in the dim red gloom. As far as Jack was concerned they'd probably travelled about five hundred metres. The steps levelled into a long straight tunnel. This was perfectly smooth and clearly had taken an immense force to cut through the heart of the hill. They continued along the passage for quite a while before reaching more steps, this time heading upwards. They climbed and climbed. For what seemed like an age, they just kept heading upwards into the darkness. Jack became uneasy, the emptiness closed in around him; his palms were wet and clammy and he felt very claustrophobic. He was really glad he'd chosen to wear his jacket; he pulled it closely around himself and shivered involuntarily. Brandy's claws made an eerie - tip-tap - echo on the smooth stone steps. The noise portrayed a much larger creature travelling through the murkiness.

Finally Jack whispered "How is this path a shortcut? All we seem to have done is to walk further down into the bowels of the earth and then up and up, it's taking ages?"

"Quiet I said," Searlan snapped. "No questions."

In the distance, Jack heard a very odd hissing sound. He wasn't able to distinguish what was ahead; it was unlike anything he'd ever heard before. His imagination got the better of him and he believed some powerful, and perhaps nasty, creature waited there to eat them. Maybe it was hiding just around the next corner. He imagined a dragon or a dinosaur. His mind raced as it conjured up something equally hideous. He looked warily at Searlan; the Sage just kept on walking without any apparent fear. He then glanced towards Jaden who'd become visibly excited.

"Perhaps this wasn't something to be afraid of?" he said to convince himself.

The sound grew louder with each passing minute. The hiss became a whoosh and then increased to a roar.

"Whatever it was, it's not far away now surely?"

At long last the steps finished, Jack thought they must have walked up a thousand of them but had lost count around two hundred. The path ahead darkened but at least it was flat again. The walls were very smooth, almost glass like. Jack guessed that someone or something spent their time polishing the stone until it shined. With more light he was convinced he would see his reflection in the rock. The noise was deafening; even if you had wanted to, you couldn't speak above the din.

The air was heavy with moisture; water condensed on Jack's bare skin. He shrugged his shoulders to stop the itch from the water running off his hair and dripping down his neck. The roar was so loud that it shook every part of his body.

Jaden turned back towards Jack; with a huge smile, he shouted as loudly as he could. "We're here. Are you ready for the ride of your life?"

Jack placed his hand to his ear and shook his head, barely able to understand him. Jaden just grinned broadly giving him the thumbs up sign. He then grabbed Jack's hand to hurry him along.

They turned a sharp corner and revealed the source of the noise. A huge underground river raged ahead of them. Terrifyingly, it moved with such a speed it looked as if it was travelling faster than a train. The red glowing light, they'd followed for so long, hovered over a line of strange high walled boats. They were all moored in a large pool stretching away into the darkness.

"How on earth did they get there?" Jack thought to himself.

Jaden leapt straight into the front of the first boat and gestured wildly to Jack to follow. The old Sage carefully sat in the very back and looked nervous for the first time. Jack clambered in, behind Jaden, and followed his example by gripping either side of the craft. Brandy looked a bit hesitant but was coaxed into the boat by the two boys. He nestled himself in the front and rested his head on Jaden's lap. The boat was quite long and very narrow; it seemed to be stable. Jack tried to rock it from side to side to get a feel of it. He'd learned to do that when he went canoeing on a school trip.

Jaden screamed again above the racket. "Hold tight, this is it."

Jack just gestured back; he couldn't understand a word the boy was screaming at him.

Jaden slipped the rope tether and gave a quick shove. At first, the boat moved slowly, edging carefully out of its mooring and into the quiet stillness of the pool. Searlan used a paddle to propel the boat forwards towards the tempest ahead. They travelled a few metres at a snail's pace.

Jack became nervous at the sight of the seething river. "Are you sure this is safe?" Unsure of what was to come; he held his breath. His knees and arms shook involuntarily with fear.

"Hang on Jack…" Jaden was so excited he could barely sit still.

Almost as soon as the boat's nose touched the raging torrent, the river grabbed at the craft and they veered unnervingly to the left. Heaving and twisting violently; the boat was dragged fully into the river by the power of the flow.

Completely unprepared for the sudden change of direction and unexpected jolt of acceleration, the speed took Jack's breath away. He grabbed hopelessly at the sides of the boat and screamed in panic. Jaden; however, was already having the time of his life. Jack flailed around terrified, the blood drained from his face and looked as if he was about to be sick.

"Wooooooh," Jack yelped hopelessly, falling backwards in the boat. Completely losing his grip, he ended up scrambling for control and screamed even louder. He wasn't enjoying this at all. They'd gone from zero to terror in two seconds flat.

Jaden laughed with the utmost delight, screaming at the top of his voice. "Yaa heeeee."

They sped off at break neck speed; Jack thrashed around helplessly in the middle of the boat unable to grasp a firm hold of anything.

"Heeeelp," he cried pitilessly.

Brandy cowered down even lower in the bow and looked completely forlorn; this wasn't to his liking either.

Jaden held tightly to the front of the craft, bobbing up and down with glee. Instantaneously, the boat plunged vertically downwards. The boy swung from side to side, riding the flow, and was clearly relishing every second.

"Grab hold of the sides Jack, like this," the boy tried to show his friend what to do.

Eventually, Jack managed to steady himself, he found a good hand hold, locked his feet into the seat decking and perched once more facing forwards. He nodded to Jaden in thanks.

"Go with the flowwwww," the young boy yelled.

As the boat rocketed down a low tunnel, which barely managed to contain this monstrous raging serpent, the walls streamed past. Every visible part of the passage was polished to a crystal finish by the power and ferocity of the river.

The speeding ride took them racing along very long straights. They crashed around impossibly tight bends. Jack's fingers ached; he'd gripped the wooden sides desperately, maintaining his position. The boat flew through shallow dips and deep, stomach churning, troughs. Each new change of direction sent your body heaving this way and that. After a few minutes of listening to Jaden scream, and realising the boat wasn't going to tip them out, Jack loosened his grip a little, enjoying the experience. They tore around corners barely missing the sides of the tunnel.

"Look out," Jaden warned.

Several times, they had to duck as the ceiling lowered to an alarming level. Jack's stomach came up to his mouth at every dip or violent turn. His head was thrown from side to side and his body felt very heavy one moment and then light as a feather the next. At last, he screamed in unison with Jaden.

"Whoooooooeeeee," he shouted as one particular corner had them tipping so far over they seemed to be touching the ceiling. He hung on for dear life, looking down on the boiling river. The Sage just held tightly in the back, he seemed almost trancelike, keeping his head down and his eyes firmly fixed on his knees.

Barely ten minutes the travellers had been in the boat, but to Jack it felt like a lifetime of rocking and bucking all over the place. As suddenly as it had begun, the raging river spat them out into another tunnel where the water was running far slower.

"Ohhh," The change of pace took Jack by surprise and he fell forwards into Jaden.

"You okay Jack?" the smile on the boy's face was so wide it looked as though his mouth would split.

Jack steadied himself as best he could. His legs quivered uncontrollably and his heart was pounding. Glancing behind, Jack guessed the river continued on its course, sharply off to the right. The boat had skidded to pleasant and easy pace where you could easily see and touch the walls.

"Yes, yes, yessss," shouted Jaden, "That's the best ever."

Ahead, the slower running water opened out into another wide pool. Here, like at the start, there were many boats moored. Again Jack wondered who owned them and how did they get here? Searlan lifted his head, grinned slyly and used the oar to guide the craft into a mooring position at the end of the row. Jaden tied the rope up to the next boat and clambered out with a bounce and a jump.

"That is sooo great," he shouted. "Come on Grandfather, let's go."

Brandy crawled, rather reluctantly, out from the bow. He'd not enjoyed it one bit and was cold wet and very uneasy. Climbing nervously out of the boat; Jack's legs shook.

"That was...wild," he exclaimed without much conviction. "However, did you find that?"

Searlan just looked down his long nose at the boy and shook his head slowly in dismissal. The old Sage led the way out from the pool and up through a passageway. The red glow waited patiently, a few paces ahead of them, and they set off away from the noise and dampness of the air. Steps appeared ahead, carved into the wall on the left. The air was moving quite quickly as if it were flowing up a chimney. The passage was leading up and up.

Once the noise of the river had reduced to a reasonable level the old Sage said. "Remember; do not touch anything down here, under any circumstances. We're not out of my friends' domain yet and they still will not tolerate intrusion."

The journey up the steps was much tougher for Jack. His legs ached within ten minutes and he was starting to lag behind. He couldn't believe how tired he felt. His muscles burned and his head pounded. The river still rang painfully in his ears. He looked ahead to the others, neither seemed to be at all troubled by the effort of heading for the surface.

Brandy stayed close by his master but didn't seem bothered at all now that he was out of the boat. He'd already put the awful ride behind him and could smell the grass and trees wafting down on the breeze. Despite that last episode, this was one of the best walks he'd ever been on

"Come on Jack. Keep up," Jaden called from the darkness ahead.

Jack dropped so far behind that he couldn't see his friends.

"I need to rest for a minute. I'll catch up once I've had a quick sit down. I feel so tired and weary," he called back weakly.

Jack flopped down onto the cold stone step and lay exhausted with his eyes closed. He took several deep breaths, attempting to recover. When he opened his eyes again, he admired the smoothness of the rock. All around him; the polished surface looked as smooth as glass. A glittering luminescence in the walls caught Jack's attention. Before he could stop himself, he reached out and felt the tiny points of sparkling light. On touching the surface; they seemed to slip off the wall, then climb up his hand and all along his arm. He was mesmerised as a rash of coloured dots covered his skin. "Wow, what's happening?" he exclaimed. A low rumble filled the space. Jack quickly withdrew his hand, but it was too late.

The rumble became a moan; the moaning became a wail and the wailing intensified into a scream. "Curse you Guardian you've betrayed our trust, we knew we should never have listened to the old man. Let the bowels of the earth take you…"

A large hole immediately opened beneath Jack's feet. He fell straight down into the darkness; even before he had time to yell for help.

Brandy watched, disbelievingly, as Jack disappeared from view. The hole resealed as if it had never existed. Brandy barked frantically at the empty spot where his master had been lying.

The sound of echoing footfalls preceded Jaden jogging into view.

"What is it Boy? Where's Jack?" he said to the dog. Seeing Brandy sniffing furiously at the step, where Jack had been moments before, Jaden cried out back up the passageway,

"Grandfather they've taken him. I'm sure the ground has swallowed Jack."

Searlan wasn't far behind his Grandson. "What, what's that you say?" replied Searlan, kneeling down to look at the place where Jack had been standing. "What did I just tell the young fool?" he grumbled. "Don't touch anything, that's what I said," the old man threw his arms out in desperation. "I did tell him you know. This is not my doing."

The Sage was so angry, he seemed to light up. "What have you done with my companion?" he demanded.

The sudden silence pressed in on them all.

"Answer me now or I'll bring the full force of Tarre-Hare down upon you. Where is my companion?" The Sage banged his staff, heavily, on the stone floor.

Before any answer came; the three remaining travellers found themselves being pushed along the tunnel at an ever increasing speed. They were thrust, forcibly, onto the side of a hill; the opening slammed shut with a heavy crash. Each tumbled down a mossy bank to the edge of a wide gully. The old man lay still, for a few seconds, trying to regain his composure. Jaden barely moved and Brandy whimpered softly to himself, licking his left front paw.

"This is not good, not good at all," Searlan sighed. "Now we really are in a fix."

Chapter 6 - Interrogation

Cathy's wrists burned. They were red raw from the thick, heavy hemp rope bound tightly around them. She'd been placed at the rear of the line of prisoners. Aunt Beth was three ahead,   she tried to put on a brave face, but these were difficult circumstances. The gash over Aunt Beth's eye oozed; congealed blood clung to her face. The lady directly in front of Cathy was very poorly now. The injuries she'd received from the sadistic soldiers left her barely able to walk. Each time she stumbled she sustained yet more abuse.

"Git movin' you hags." The orders were brutal.

 No-one wanted to be on the receiving end of the ferocity of one particular psychotic soldier. They all realised that Digger was the worst of the bunch of thugs. These men could not be described as soldiers; these were the very worst kind of people imaginable, Digger was the epitome of them all. He was demented.

"What you waitin' for you scum.? I said, git movin'" Digger hit the poor lady once more and then grabbed Cathy's arm tightly. "You'll be mine yet you little beauty."

Cathy wanted to strike out at this animal but thought better of it. "Bide your time Cathy, he'll get what's coming to him," she said quietly to herself.

"Leave her alone you sick pig." Aunt Beth was outraged and stood up for her niece.

Digger was incensed. He turned brutally on Aunt Beth and smashed her across the face again. Falling unconscious on the dirt; fresh blood poured from her wound.

"Now look what your stupid temper's gone and done Digger. We'll have to shove her in the wagon for the rest of the journey." The sergeant, supposedly in charge of this rabble, came over and grabbed Aunt Beth by the arm. She hung limply and looked half dead.

"The Cap'n said he wanted these to be interrogated not killed. I told you that before, didn't I?"

Standing no more than a couple of inches from the madman; he turned to Digger and screwed up his face. "Disobey my orders again and I'll run you through myself," he spat his threat through his clenched teeth.

Digger shook visibly, with rage, but said nothing.

Cathy tried to push forwards to her Aunt. "You callous pigs, you might have killed her. Aunt Beth, can you hear me." She tried, unsuccessfully, to get far enough forward to comfort her Aunt.

"Get the girl and this woman in the wagon. DO IT NOW!" The sergeant screamed at two of the soldiers looking on.

Cathy and her Aunt were removed from the rope and shoved up into the back of a wagon.

"Try to escape and I'll wring your pretty little neck myself and then I'll feed you to Digger." The Sergeant looked evilly at Cathy, threatening her. She nodded quickly in agreement, not daring to say another word.

"Look after your Aunt." The command had a cold finality about it. Cathy shuddered; tears welled up in her eyes.

Aunt Beth slipped in and out of consciousness. Cathy was convinced that she was going to die. She had terrible flash backs of her mother and having to care for Aunt Beth, all those years ago.

"Where are you Jack when I need you most? I need a friend to help me, I miss you so much?"

Tears of frustration ran freely down her face. She'd never felt so alone or hopeless as now. Her Aunt was going to die, she was a prisoner and she'd lost her mother's precious gifts. Both staff and bracelet were gone. She'd left her silver handled cane lying under the large bush by the cottage fence. Her bracelet had come off during the struggle with the soldiers, trying to set fire to the cottage.

"If I ever manage to escape, I promise I'll search for your bracelet Mother, I promise."

This was clearly the worst day she'd ever had, even worse than the time she realised she must fend for herself and set out alone for Aunt Beth's home. Cathy placed her face in her hands and sobbed inconsolably.

"Why aren't you here Jack? Why haven't you come to rescue me, you are all I have in the world. You're my only true friend."

For over an hour Cathy sobbed quietly. Aunt Beth hadn't stirred back to consciousness. Slowly, her mind refocused; somewhere deep inside her soul, a voice called softly to her. "Be brave my child, your friend will come. Take heart, I've not abandoned you." Cathy felt a warming energy seep into her chilled veins. The powers of Lujnima flowed up through the earth and wrapped her in a blanket of love.

The journey across the hills led towards the Blade fortress on the far side of the savannah. Painfully slow, every lump and bump made Aunt Beth wince in pain. Cathy tried to comfort her by stroking her forehead. "Please don't die; Jack is coming for us, I'm certain of it. He's going to rescue us, just hang on a bit longer."

When they eventually arrived at the fortress most of the prisoners were moved below ground and locked into the dungeons. Cathy and her Aunt were separated from the others and taken to a room on the ground floor. The room was large, cold and almost empty. Cathy felt nervous; the long wait compounded her fears. Aunt Beth remained semi-conscious barely able to speak.

"Hold on Aunt Beth, don't leave me. Please," Cathy pleaded.

Eventually, a door at the far end of the room opened slowly and two burly guards stepped through, they walked either side of a very old man. The man seemed impossibly old, he moved at a snails pace.

"Who do we have here then?" The old man asked in a calming and melodic voice. "What's your name my pretty young child?"

Cathy had to shake her head to force her mind back to her immediate concerns. "Sir, my Aunt needs attention; can't you see she's been badly beaten by your vicious guards."

The old man looked deeply into the girl's eyes. He held her gaze for several seconds before replying. "I'll see what can be done for her my dear." The man nodded to one of the guards who immediately disappeared through a door to their right. He returned with a woman who attended to Aunt Beth's wound.

"These are not MY soldiers my dear child; they are the Blade General's. But you have still not told me your name. Mine is Alanthian." He sounded so friendly and caring it was very difficult to grasp his motives.

Cathy found herself actually liking this man even though every fibre of her being screamed at her not to. She couldn't stop herself from replying innocently. "My name is Cathy and this is my Aunt Beth. We've done nothing wrong and we've harmed no-one. Why are we prisoners here?"

"No one has accused you of doing anything wrong my dear child. You are here because the General ordered it. If you swear allegiance to his Blade Army then you'll be able to join their forces and assist in the campaign. If you resist, then you'll be treated accordingly. But that's NOT why you are here, in this room."

Cathy didn't know quite what this strange old man was saying or implying. She tried to look at him and judge him but found that she could not easily look into this man's eyes. He seemed old and frail yet very powerful. He was a lot like Searlan in many ways; he had a great depth to his eyes. To look into them took a lot of effort and then it left you feeling drained. He really seemed to be able to see into and through you. She felt he was reading her every move and response.

"What is it you want from us?" Cathy was trying to be brave and confident but was beginning to quiver in fear.

Alanthian called for a chair and sat down slowly and carefully. He seemed unbelievably old and feeble. "Tell me about yourself Cathy. Tell me ALL about yourself."

Again, Cathy found herself being taken in by this kindly old man. She couldn't resist his enquiries into her life. She told him all about her mother dying and going to live with Aunt Beth. Somehow, she didn't know how, she managed to say something of her bracelet and how it had been torn off in the struggle with the soldiers.

"Tell me about the bracelet child, what did it look like?"

His voice was very mellow and endearing. Cathy fell completely under his spell and had no control of what she was saying. She described, in detail, the moon engraving and the Latin words that were carefully and neatly written into its surface.

Alanthian's face didn't alter; it was still placid and calming. Inside he was already beginning to believe he'd struck gold. He was almost convinced that this was the child he'd been searching for. She was one of the three major pieces of the key that he desired above all else.

"How did you come by the bracelet my dear child? Who gave it to you?" A very slight quiver in Alanthian's voice showed a trace of his excitement.

Cathy found herself telling Alanthian about the story of her Mother and her death bed. She even told him that her mother had made her promise to pass the bracelet on to her daughter.

Alanthian absorbed every word spoken and even more that were not. He watched every slight nuance that came from the pretty young girl before him. His pulse raced at the prospect of finding one of his pieces of the great puzzle. After about half an hour he ordered his guards to take Cathy and her Aunt to another smaller room.

Deeper and darker, underground, they dragged poor Aunt Beth; the air was cold and uninviting. The room was largely empty with only a small chest against one wall and a single small chair. With no bed, Cathy laid her Aunt down on the floor. She made her as comfortable as possible using a cushion from the chair as a makeshift pillow. After a short time, another old woman came in and brought them some food and drink.

"When will we be released? Who will care for my Aunt?" The questions fell on deaf ears.

Cathy was ravenous and couldn't help herself; she tucked into the food with gusto. Her Aunt lay half dazed on the floor, she gave her some fruit and some biscuits but she didn't really eat anything. After taking a little water, her Aunt fell into a deep slumber. She was beginning to get the fever and Cathy didn't know what to do.

"Oh Jack, where are you? Please cross the bridge and find me. Please."

Chapter 7 - Escape from the dark

Jack opened and closed his eyes several times before he realised he was in complete darkness. Not even a glimmer of light, shone, to get his bearings. He was hemmed in tightly and could not move his arms or his legs. The rock, gripping him, was wet and cold. An immovable force squashed his entire body and he felt a panic sweep over him.

"Help me. Help me someone," he frantically screamed at the top of his voice. The plea seemed to be swallowed by the darkness - absorbed like a sponge. Breathing in again, to scream, the rock crushed him even tighter. Another wave of alarm took hold, he struggled helplessly. Pulling and tugging with arms and feet proved useless; his body was completely enclosed. The rock's grip tightened, crushing and suffocating him. His terror increased, out of control, until his body shivered uncontrollably.

"What are you boy?" the darkness hissed.

"What, who said that?" Jack managed to croak.

The voice hissed again sarcastically. "You're not from this world are you boy? You're a poison to this earth; a trouble maker and a trouble seeker. We know you are the night witches hand - aren't you boy? I think I'll just crush you now." The grip of the rock tightened.

Barely able to breathe; he thought he'd soon pass out. Struggling to remain conscious, he rasped. "If I'm the night witches hand, as you say; then you'd better think twice before crushing me. She'll bring great pain and destruction down upon you, if you harm me."

The grip of the rock eased a little.

Jack gasped for breath before feeling a little more confident. "Release me now and I'll not bring her vengeance down upon you."

The rock grip eased further still.

"What vengeance do you think "She" can wreak here boy?" the voice taunted. "What do you think 'She' would do for you? All she ever cared about was her precious moon beams. You are nothing to her."

Jack tried to be strong but was beginning to get very frightened again. He'd been held tightly for some time and was finding it harder and harder to stay conscious. His mind drifted, slipping into a daze. He imagined seeing Cathy sitting on the floor of a room; other people were in the shadows. Her Aunt was laying awkwardly along side her. She looked injured and Cathy was clearly upset and trying her best to comfort her. Focussing on her face; he thought she looked towards him. For an instant; he almost believed, she saw him.

Instinctively smiling, he believed he heard her say, "Jack, is that you?"

Without speaking out loud, he imagined he replied, "Help me Cathy? Help me please if you can?"

She stood up and looked directly at him.

"Can you see me?" he thought rather foolishly.

Her head tilted to one side and her eyes squinted tightly together, "I can sort of see you Jack. You're here, in my head, rather than in front of me." She pointed to her temple. "I can hear your voice but I can't see you properly. Are you closed in somewhere? You seem to be in the dark."

Jack quickly explained about the journey on the river, being trapped in the rock and meeting the Sage and Jaden.

"You've been busy haven't you?" she laughed with joy at hearing her friend. He'd crossed the MoonBridge once again - even if he did need rescuing. "Stay calm Jack, I think I know how to help you, but it may prove to be quite painful so try to relax."

Jack didn't have the slightest idea what she meant; he grew more desperate by the second.

Cathy stood very still to concentrate. She threw her thoughts away from the room. She pressed her mind forwards towards the moon and soon came before the gatekeeper of Lujnima.

"Greetings Guardian, do you seek an audience," the keeper said dryly.

"Yes, yes, yes, and be quick about it, there's no time to waste," she yelled anxiously.

"All in good time Guardian, she doesn't like to be hurried."

Cathy screamed angrily at the gatekeeper. "This is an emergency of the gravest consequences, the off world Guardian is trapped and will be crushed without Lujnima's help."

"Have patience little one," the gatekeeper replied infuriatingly. "I will see if the Mistress will permit your request."

Cathy's mind jumped from the gatekeeper's cavern to the dimly lit room where Lujnima granted her an audience. As usual, she appeared in a different guise. Now she seemed to be a younger woman of about thirty years. Her head was veiled in silvery gossamer and only her eyes could be distinguished. Cathy explained about Jack and how he'd been trapped.

"Strange; that this was hidden from my sight," she mused for a moment and then continued. "I cannot see or feel the Guardian of the off world or his current situation. Wait whilst I search more thoroughly for him."

Lujnima spent some moments seeking Jack, before finally announcing, almost absentmindedly. "Ah yes, there he is. The under-land fools think that they can block me out with their pathetic rock and stone. I think I need to teach them a lesson."

The moon goddess chuckled coldly. "Umm, they should get something worthwhile. Yes, something they will not forget in a hurry."

The low silvery light in the cavern dimmed further as Lujnima gathered information about Jack's predicament. Cathy jumped at a terrifying burst of energy. Multifaceted moonbeams erupted in all directions, bouncing off the walls, ceiling and floor. The moon goddess shouted. "How dare they attempt to smite my Guardian?"

Cathy had never seen or heard Lujnima grow angry before. She became quite alarmed and could sense the wrath that was about to be unleashed. A goddess was a great ally, but Cathy realised that you didn't want to become her enemy.

"What will you do Mistress? What will you do to Jack's captors?" Her voice was laced with fear and apprehension.

Lujnima paused again for several seconds before she replied more calmly. "Fear not little one, the fools who have sought to hide the Guardian from me will be punished but not destroyed. Even they have their purpose in things; they are just mindless creatures and need to be taught some respect. They'll allow the Guardian to go freely once they realise the error of their ways."

Finding herself racing back towards her body; Cathy felt relieved. Travelling away from her audience with Lujnima she sensed a passing message washing over her like leaves fluttering in an autumn breeze.

"Take heart child, your friend will be safe. As I've already said, he'll come for you…"

Blinking rapidly at her change of surroundings, she looked down upon the room in the fortress. She saw herself standing motionless over her aunt. The pain was clearly written on poor Aunt Beth's face, she was very badly injured. Cathy now feared she would die without some immediate help. The fever in her was raging; her head was covered in perspiration and her body thin and limp. In the wink of an eye she entered her body and returned to consciousness. "It's okay Aunt Beth, I'm back again now. Jack's here you know. He's coming to rescue us from this awful place."

Cathy lent down and mopped her Aunt's brow; she guessed her position was hopeless. Looking at the greyness of her skin; anger, bitterness and sorrow raged through her. "Poor Aunt Beth, will you ever be well?"

The room seemed even more menacing. She pleaded, "Jack, where are you? Please come for me, I miss you so much?"

**

Back in his makeshift prison, Jack had now slipped completely into unconsciousness. The rocks had squeezed every last breath of air out of him. His face turned bright purple. All thought had stopped and he was barely moments from death. The under-land creatures could be heard laughing sickeningly in deep melodic tones.

"Meet your doom Guardian we'll have your soul…"

The pressure holding him was released so suddenly that Jack just dropped many metres down through the rock. He bumped and slid along, like a rag doll being dragged by a child, before crashing out into an empty, dark cavern. The floor was lined with a wide shallow pool at its centre. His limp and lifeless body caused a painfully loud thud of flesh meeting rock. The heavy impact threw out the water in all directions.

"Uhhhhh," Jack managed a groan of pain.

The shock of striking the cold rock, and the water rushing back over him, made Jack gasp. His eyes opened widely. Gulping the air, and water, into his lungs; he choked, "What the…" Coughing; he spat out a mouth full of water.

The echo, of his gasping for breath, made a frightful sound. Jack panted uncontrollably, and he breathed so hard, his head spun.

"Ohhh," Jack moved his hand, to rub his scalp, but found it hurt just as much from the fall as it did from the lack of oxygen. "Ohhh my arm…" Regaining consciousness sent his nerves into overdrive; pain messages fired from all over his body. Wet and shocked; he'd badly bruised his right elbow. Jack staggered onto his knees and surveyed the damage. "You're a mess Jack."

Although he could barely stand, and ached from head to toe; with his inimitable sense of humour he thought, "Well, it could have been worse," He laughed mockingly to himself, "At least I'm not dead."

The boy paused for a few seconds before announcing, "Now get out of the water you idiot."

Jack knew what he wanted to do but just didn't have the energy to move. His muscles flatly refused to respond, but his mind raced at seeing Cathy. "How was that possible and was it even real? Where is she now?"

Coming back to his senses, he considered his current predicament. "Well Jack, you're in a right fix. You're sitting in the middle of a cave, waist deep in cold water, it's dark and you haven't a clue where you are. So what are you gonna do about it; eh?" He deliberated for a few seconds, before getting his "practical" head on. "If only I'd a brought my little torch?"

Crawling out of the water, he was numb with cold. "Cathy, can you hear me? I'm free from the rock. Where are you?"

Jack seemed to be looking down on the words as they flew off out of the cave. Away across the hills they travelled; a long way over land he'd never seen. They passed rivers and streams, mountains and valleys. He was amazed at the size of the hill in front of him; it had a huge walled fortress on top of it. An enormous angled tower reached high into the sky. He saw thousands of soldiers and other people milling around. His words plunged over the great wall and down into the ground. Deeper and deeper into the dungeons and tunnels he raced. Along a long corridor with stout, iron-clad doors leading off to the left and right. All were menacing with wide hinges and heavy handles. The third door, from the end, led into a large room. Many people were sitting or lying around. Against one wall sat Cathy with her Aunt lying beside her.

"What have they done to you Cathy? What has happened to your Aunt?"

Before she could answer him, his mind sprung back to the cave. Jack nearly jumped a foot in the air when out of the dark he heard a woman's voice.

"My child, you're safe now, the wretched creatures will not harm you again. They'll be licking their wounds for some time to come. Your way will be clear, but you must hurry to the surface; your companions are searching desperately to find you." Lujnima's voice was as sweet and tender as a loving mother. Jack felt tears welling up in his eyes; he'd never been so relieved in all his life.

"You gave me such a fright," he replied instinctively. Almost immediately he continued much more soberly "oh, and thanks. Thank you so much for freeing me, I thought I was dead for sure."

"You're not dead just yet my child. Now you must find your friends. Together, you must go and help my daughter Guardian. She's in grave danger, a danger that I cannot directly intervene with. The forces that hold her are our mortal enemy, I'm powerless to prevent their current plans."

Jack couldn't imagine anything that would stop Lujnima. Feeling dejected, he listened to his mistress. "I'll offer my support whenever I can. You're her only hope young one. You must save her. If you're successful, I perceive you'll make the transition to the next level; fail and you'll be lost forever." Lujnima's warning made Jack shudder.

"You're too cold and wet to continue." Lujnima concentrated on Jack's clothing for the briefest instant. A pale silvery-blue flash evaporated every drop of water. "There, I've dried your clothes and warmed your body. Now you may proceed."

"Wow, thanks - I was freezing." Jack grinned gratefully.

"I've left you a small gift Guardian, to help you find your way to the surface, use it wisely…"

Jack never had time to tell Lujnima about his vision of Cathy. He wondered if she already knew. "She is, after all, a goddess or something. She probably knows everything?" he thought idly. "But then, how can she be powerless against her enemy? Are there limits to her abilities?"

Glancing down into the darkness, Jack noticed a faint silvery glow coming from his left hand. He stared in disbelief. Looking more closely, his entire hand took on a dim luminescence. "That's weird; really, really weird. Not particularly useful; a bit too dim to see anything."

No sooner had he questioned the level of the light than his hand grew brighter. He pushed it away from his face and rubbed his skin to see if it would come off. The glow didn't rub off, it wasn't hot to touch, and it just seemed to keep on glowing. He held his hand up at arms length and thought positively.

"More light," his hand responded immediately and brightened enough to see the edges of the cavern that he was in. Jack screeched with laughter.

"Wow, that's brilliant," he paused to look around.

"Light off," he commanded giggling at the thought. The light faded quickly and left him in complete darkness again.

"Light on," he ordered; this time more seriously. The light followed his demand literally and was so bright now that it almost hurt his eyes.

"Dimmer," he thought and it responded by shining with just enough light to find his way.

"This is so cool; no one is ever going to believe me at home," the thought of home suddenly made him feel very sad and lonely.

"I don't know how long I've been gone, but I do miss you all. What are you doing right now Sis? You'd never believe me if I told what I was doing?"

After a few moments, Jack stood up. He clambered away from the edge of the shallow pool and explored his surroundings. The space was quite large and it took several minutes to walk carefully all the way around. The light from his hand was great but it did mean you needed to walk with one hand shoved out in front of you, which was a bit awkward.

"This light thing is really amazing." Jack grinned in approval.

At the side of the cavern were a number of passageways, they all seemed to be leading off to the left and downwards. Jack didn't sense any of these led to the surface. He looked further around and found a smaller gap that was very narrow and quite low; the smell of fresh air drifted through. He sniffed loudly before making his decision.

"In here then Jack, let's go for it."

Squeezing tightly through the gap, Jack crawled several metres on his hands and knees. The light on his hand was so useful; he could hardly thank Lujnima enough. The sound of water became louder. He guessed it must be the river he'd ridden on earlier. Drips, made his progress slippery and difficult. Numerous, needle-sharp, stalactites pointed down from the roof, scratching his neck and shoulders. Despite taking considerable care he couldn't avoid them all. The tunnel lowered until he had to slither, on his stomach, like a snake.

"Ouch, that hurt," he snorted as one particularly thick dagger jabbed him sharply in his cheek. A little trickle of blood appeared and he carefully brushed it aside.

Abruptly, the route opened into a wider cavern, he slipped out of the tunnel and slid down to the cave floor. Jack stumbled, trying to stand, stabbing his bruised elbow on a perfectly formed stalagmite. "Arghhhh," he yelled in acute pain. The stone blade pieced his skin deeply, blood gushed from the wound. He reached, frantically, into his pocket and managed to find a dirty old handkerchief. He pressed hard on to the cut, to ease the blood flow.

"That really hurt," he whimpered. The boy scanned the area dejectedly; many passages led away from the cave – he'd no idea which way to go.

"Come on, think Jack. You must think," again he tried to raise his spirits. Somewhere in the back of his mind, a friendly voice called to him. Absentmindedly, he placed his hand into his jacket pocket and held the jewelled brooch he'd found.

The sound of Lujnima's voice echoed far at the back of his consciousness. "In moments of indecision let her help." Jack took out the brooch and let the light of his left hand bathe it in silvery beams. Something stirred inside.

The stone called to him. "Greetings Guardian, I'm Layette the Decider. What is your question?"

Jack stared at the beautiful red crystal and the strange swirling movement inside. He heard the voice but seemed incapable of responding.

"Fear not young Guardian, I mean you no harm. My previous mistress was taken by the great beast of the wood. I was cast aside and left to sink into the depths. You are my master now. What is your question?"

Jack frowned trying to think of some deep and meaningful question to ask. He struggled to think of anything challenging and settled for the obvious. "Well Layette the Decider which way leads to the surface?"

The jewel pulsed briefly in Jack's hand sending out a crimson glow. Layette sang in beautiful clear voice

> *"Your eyes will see, your heart will show.*
> *Your hands will guide, your legs will go.*
> *The route shall be, where feelings grow.*
> *Time to decide, use head and toe.*
> *Let thoughts roam free, be quick not slow.*
> *Trust strength and pride, for these you know."*

The singsong reply was interesting and mildly amusing but fairly meaningless as far as Jack was concerned.

"Can't you just give a straight answer?"

The light in the jewel flashed again briefly before dimming and finally fading. The swirling motion ceased. As the last glimmer of light disappeared Jack heard a final call.

"Trust in yourself Jack Ferns, Guardian of the MoonBridge."

"Well, a lot of use that was?" Jack moaned. He looked again at the dozen or so exits that led off in different directions.

Of all the routes to take, somehow he just felt drawn to one.

"Trust in yourself Jack Ferns - Guardian of the MoonBridge." The message reverberated again in the back of his mind.

Jack doubted his choice was correct, but said, anyway, "Okay Layette the Decider, I'll give it a go. This one is the path to the surface."

The tunnel continued for many metres. Jack grew in confidence as the route led upwards. Eventually, he reached another cavern. This was very large, much wider and higher than the last. Even with the brightest he could make his hand glow; he couldn't see the sides.

"Wow, an underground cathedral."

The brightness of his light allowed Jack to look at himself. He was filthy. His clothes were covered in dirt and mud and his shoes scuffed. His jacket sleeves were in tatters from the stalactites scratching at them.

"What on earth is Mum going to say about this? She'll kill me when I get back home?" He put his hand on his hair and felt the thick mud and rock dust engrained in it. "Yuck, I need a bath. Yes a nice hot bath with lots of soapy bubbles."

The air was moving here and whistled occasionally as it found its way in and around the great underground hall. He saw a crack of light, fairly high up the wall, over to his right and assumed that was the source of the noise.

"Okay Layette the Decider, so you were right after all. I guess there's the surface."

Jack half scrambled and half slithered up a pile of loose shale. The rock had accumulated beneath the opening. High above him, about twenty metres off the floor of the cave, the exit beckoned. With great care he managed to get halfway up. He could clearly see the sky shining through, but no matter how hard he tried, he kept sliding down.

"This is stupid," he exclaimed in frustration.

After a number of exhausting attempts he finally sat down and stared ahead in despair.

"How am I supposed to get out of here?"

The sound of his voice was amplified by the cave and came back to him several times in echo. He laughed at the weirdness of hearing his own voice sounding like some lost ghost or ghoul.

"How, how, how…"

"Am, am, am..."

"I, I, I…"

He shouted, pausing between each word to allow the echo to circle back at him.

"Ho, hoo, hooo…"

Beginning to feel this day was proving to be the most frustrating of his life; he moaned feebly, "Come on Jack Ferns; pull yourself together. Think." Sitting on the floor of the cavern, Jack looked up at the crack of light. A short, tantalising distance it may have been, but it might as well have been on the other side of the planet. "How am I going to get up there?"

He looked closely at the slippery shale that made it impossible to climb. "I need a rope or something?"

Jack got up and hunted around unsuccessfully. He decided that one more try wouldn't hurt. Carefully, he placed one foot ahead of the other, trying, to make headway up the slope. His shoe sank up to his ankle; shale and small stones slipped apart like water. Lifting his other leg, his body weight shifted and he slipped back down almost as far as he'd started. He tried sort of running, but that proved even worse, leaving him gasping for breath. Finally, he plonked himself down on his bottom. Sitting there; he suddenly had a flash of inspiration. He pushed down with both legs and raised his bottom up the shale about half a metre. He then quickly pulled both feet up to his thighs. He sat, leaning backwards, barely daring to breathe in case he slid back again. To his great surprise, he stayed in place. He tried again. Using both feet and legs, to give a big heave, he lifted himself up the slope. Quickly steadying himself, he managed to hold his position. This was working; he hardly dared to look up or down in case he lost his balance and slid to the bottom again. Another few good pushes and he would be there. Half an hour of effort left Jack feeling tired; his back ached and his bottom raw from the splintered shale. Many stones were sharp and dug into his legs. His hands were scratched and the pain in his elbow throbbed continuously where he'd been stabbed by the stalactite.

"One final push Jack," he whispered to encourage himself. "Just one more push."

With an almighty heave, Jack propelled himself upwards and back. Slipping over the ledge, he banged his head painfully on an overhanging rock.

"Ouch," he yelled, rubbing yet another injury.

He looked down, cautiously; he was sitting on a ledge next to the fracture in the side of the cavern wall. The gap looked too narrow to get through now that he was alongside it. He examined it hopefully. "This is barely wide enough to get my arm through, never mind the rest of me." Jack sighed in exasperation. "What a waste of time?"

He could hardly believe his bad luck. All that effort was for nothing, he was still trapped. Jack sat and sobbed helplessly.

"Help me," he spluttered through the narrow opening in desperation. "Can anybody hear me, please?"

Exhausted, Jack lay back against the cavern wall; his arm pounded with stabbing pains. His head throbbed and his hands were scraped with grazes.

"This is hopeless. I'm completely stuck."

Every muscle ached with the effort of the climb. He lay down, precariously, on the narrow ledge and closed his eyes. He sobbed in desperation for a few more minutes.

"Everything's gone horribly wrong. I'm no great Guardian of the MoonBridge, I'm just a stupid kid lost in this stupid cave."

His mind spun so fast that he felt dizzy and sick. "I hate this place and I hate this adventure. Why did I cross that MoonBridge?" Between sobs he groaned pitifully. "I want to go home to my bed."

Jack dozed on the ledge, it may have been seconds or even hours; he couldn't tell. Gradually, his mind wandered far from his body. The grim face of Searlan filled his thoughts, he looked sad and upset. The old man's eyes darted in all directions as if searching for something. The back of Jaden's head came into view. The vision was so powerful; Jack almost believed he was actually looking at the boy.

"Jaden, I need your help," he imagined calling. "I'm trapped and cannot get out. Help me please?"

Jack desperately wanted the boy to turn and look directly at him. He threw his message outwards with increasing effort until his young friend responded.

"Is that you Jack? Where are you?" Jaden's voice called.

Jack sat up alert. He'd hoped to hear the voice in his mind but this sound seemed directed from far above his head.

"Where are you Jaden?" he shouted with renewed hope.

"Up here, can you see us?"

Jack looked upwards through the deep crevice. "I can't see you Jaden, whereabouts are you?"

"Look further up Jack. We're here, I can see you," the boy replied.

Jack strained his neck to see the eye of his friend peering back from far above him.

"There's no way out. I'm trapped; the gap is too narrow Look, I can hardly get my hand through."

"Hold tight Jack, Grandfather will help you."

Jack heard Searlan's mumblings filtering down through the crevice. He felt a great force welling up permeating every part of his body and mind. The rocks oscillated at the sound of the old Sage's voice. His chant became melodic and hypnotic, requesting the gap to open wider. The rock and shale resisted briefly before reluctantly moving apart. In a few minutes the gap was just wide enough for Jack to squeeze into.

Hesitating nervously, the boy looked fearfully at the gap.

"Hurry Jack, Grandfather can't hold this for long."

The rock groaned and shuddered. Jack gulped, shrugged his shoulders in resignation and then wriggling frantically into the rock opening. "If this closes now I'll be squashed flat." He cried.

"That's it Jack, climb; just a bit further," Jaden had his head and shoulders inside the crevice.

Searlan stood motionless. Beads of perspiration formed on his brow giving the only indication of the effort being exerted.

"I've got you Jack." A welcome hand reached inside and grabbed the boy's collar. One good tug and he was sitting beside his young friend. Jack shielded his eyes from the bright sunlight.

"You look awful," Jaden announced with his usual grin. "What've you been doing?"

Jack could do nothing but fall backwards in complete exhaustion and relief. Searlan allowed the rock to return to its original shape. The effort left him drained, he sat down beside the boy.

"Thanks you two, you've saved my life. I thought I was trapped in there forever." Jack rasped. He took a long healing drink from the Sage's water pouch and felt strength slowly return to his aching limbs. The pain subsided in everything except his elbow.

Searlan examined Jack's injuries. "This is a nasty gash, how did it happen?"

The Sage washed and redressed the area in a makeshift bandage. He had some herbs that he mixed with a few drops of water and applied to the wound.

"Ouch, that really stings like hell."

"It's okay Jack, the potion will soon ease the pain and your wound will heal much quicker." Searlan assured him.

"Where's Brandy?" Jack enquired, noticing that his pet wasn't with them.

Jaden explained that his dog had wandered off some hours earlier; they'd not seen him since.

"I shouldn't worry too much about him, he'll turn up, I'm sure of it," the old man suggested.

After about half an hour of welcome rest, they made their way up to the top of the slope. Jack started to tell them about his adventure; including the part about Cathy.

"I've got to rescue her Searlan. Lujnima said she was in grave danger. Can you help me find her?"

The old Sage looked down at the boy affectionately. He was a complete mess. He had a big bruise on his head, his hands were scratched and one arm bandaged. Jack's clothing was in tatters and covered in grime. The earnest look on the boy's face was a picture.

Searlan laughed out loud saying. "Jack Ferns - Guardian of the MoonBridge, of course we'll help you. But first, we need to get you cleaned up a bit. You can hardly rescue your damsel in distress looking like that, now can you?"

Jack looked down at himself and realised the state he was in, he grinned at his friends and then laughed loudly. "You're right, my mum's gonna kill me when I get home."

The three travellers made their way along a ridge path that eventually led down into a grassy valley. A shallow, bubbling brook meandered peacefully between the willows. Jack stopped at a small pool and gave himself a quick refreshing wash. The dirt and grit cleaned off nicely and he felt much better. The old Sage followed the path of the valley for some distance.

"Not far to go now," Searlan said to Jack.

As the day drew to a close, the air temperature dropped noticeably. Jack glanced up at the reddening sky and commented, "Red sky at night shepherd's delight, red sky in the morning shepherd's warning."

The other two look at him quizzically. "What does that mean Jack?" Jaden asked.

"Dunno really, it's just a saying from home. My dad always says it when the sunset's like this."

As they turned a corner, the world opened up in front of them. Jack gasped at the sight, "Now that's breathtaking."

Beams of orange and red stretched across the expanse. Far in the distance, another line of hills merged with the darkening horizon.

"Over there," the old Sage pointed to the twenty or more kilometres of grassy savannah. "That's where Cathy will have been taken; one of the strongholds of the Blades."

"How do we get there?" Jack asked rather foolishly.

"Walk young master Ferns. A good days' walk is how we get there, so you had better rest now. You'll need all of your strength for crossing the grasslands. Judging by the sky this evening I imagine tomorrow is going to be very hot."

Jack didn't need telling twice. He threw himself to the floor, curled up tight and was asleep in no time at all. The excitement of the day finally caught up with him.

Jaden lay down and closed his eyes. "Goodnight Grandfather, I'm so glad we've found Jack. I really like him you know."

"So do I Jaden, so do I. Pleasant dreams..." Searlan rested and let his mind wander. Far across the savannah he searched for Cathy and Beth but his sight was blocked. "Yes, you are close Elder; too close for comfort."

Chapter 8 - New Master

Brandy caught a sniff of rabbits across the other side of the stream. He decided to investigate; rabbits were always good for a chase and some fun.

"Those other two would be safe by themselves for a while and I should try to find my master." Brandy wandered around sniffing every tree, bush or plant for any sign of Jack's scent.

"Had he ever been this way; where's my Jack? Where could he have gone after he sank into the ground without me?"

There were very few scents to follow so Brandy just kept moving. He rambled further and further from Searlan and his grandson, until; he guessed he was unlikely to meet up with them again. At long last he picked up a scent trail, it smelt of the masters, not his Jack, but big people like him. He'd smelt these people before; they were like the ones who were near the lake. These were soldiers.

A band of six Resistance fighters lay in wait, hidden in the undergrowth. The leader had chosen a path leading up a steep slope for their ambush. A Blade patrol was in their vicinity and his orders were clear. "Leave no others alive, bring at least two Blade prisoners in for questioning."

Two scouts had been sent ahead to engage the Blades in a brief skirmish. The ruse worked, ten soldiers gave chase and were led towards the trap.

Brandy could hear the shouts and screams coming from directly ahead. He could smell the men's perspiration, an overpowering odour that told him the men were fighting each other. Two very different scents were detected; soldiers like the ones who were dead at the cottage and others like the people who had captured his Jack. Brandy distrusted them both, but he thought he would investigate anyway. Creeping silently through the brush, he approached the fighting. The skirmish had been short lived and a group gave chase. He kept a discrete distance behind the soldiers; they were crashing through the bushes and shrubs screaming at each other.

"A blind and deaf dog could have tracked this rabble," he scorned.

The soldiers ran towards other men waiting ahead. He'd already registered the scent of a group further up the track.

"Can't they smell them?" he wondered.

The initial confidence, of the chasing soldiers, was broken by a few frantic shouts for support. Lasting only a few moments, the action ceased and was replaced by relative calm.

"Get those two tied up, leave the others." Trevor, the corporal in charge of the ambush, ordered three of his fighters to comply. "We'll take these two Blades over to the Captain. He needs information."

The captured soldiers were bound and gagged before being dragged off. The party headed in the direction of the slope. Eight Resistance fighters and two prisoners made their way along the track followed, unknowingly, by Brandy.

Trevor suspected there would be other Blade patrols in the area and he didn't want to lose the prisoners. His fighters were uninjured; they'd successfully killed four Blades. His band must maintain discipline and stay watchful. The enemy wouldn't be tricked again.

Brandy followed at a sensible distance, he was unsure if he should approach. The men appeared safe enough but he was still wary. As the day progressed he became more confident. One of the men stood out as the leader; he regularly called orders to the others. Brandy edged closer.

Trevor led his men back along the main track towards the hills.

One of his team, 'Smudger', whispered a report. "Don't look behind Trev, but we seem to be being followed."

"I'm going to double back and take a look for myself, keep the men on this path Smudger and stay alert."

Diving quickly out to his left; Trevor took three of his fighters with him. They slipped through the undergrowth in a long arc. The corporal intended to rejoin the path a few hundred metres behind their previous position.

"Quiet now, and keep a good lookout," Trevor ordered.

Carefully surveying the path, he waved his men to follow him.

"I can't see anyone Trev," Nick hissed.

"Perhaps Smudger was getting jittery?" Williams suggested.

"Let's get a bit closer to the others, keep looking." Trevor hurried forwards at a jog. As they approached, close enough to see the rear of the main group, Trevor caught sight of Brandy. He was slipping from one bush to another.

"There look, it's a dog. He's following the group." Nick pointed.

Trevor looked but couldn't see a handler.

"Who's guiding him? There must be someone there, surely." Trevor was perplexed.

"Perhaps he belongs to one of the prisoners; a Blade dog?" Williams suggested.

They followed behind for a few minutes.

"There's no-one else with the dog. I'm sure of it," Trevor approached Brandy cautiously; he kept one hand on his sword handle just in case he had to defend himself. When he was close enough he called. "Come here boy, come on then."

Brandy didn't realise he was being followed; they were down wind of him and he'd concentrated on the group ahead. Spinning smartly, he was ready to fight. He growled deeply in warning.

"It's okay boy. It's okay; I don't want to hurt you…" Trevor loved dogs and this retriever was a beautiful golden colour with two distinctive stripes of darker golden brown sloping from his neck. He put out his hand and crouched down to show his friendly intent.

Brandy growled once more, but knew this man meant him no harm.

"Come on fella, what's your name then?" Trevor used his most persuasive tone.

Brandy edged forwards and sniffed a few times at the outstretched hand. "He seems safe enough," Brandy believed, relaxing a little. This was the leader, the same person he'd been watching. "He's tricky though; sneaking up on me like that."

"Do you want something to eat boy? Here, have a titbit." Trevor reached in his jerkin pocket and pulled out a piece of a sweet biscuit.

Brandy could smell the sweetness of the food and did really want it. He approached slowly, took the morsel and it tasted good. He liked this man after all.

Trevor patted the dog a few times and introduced himself to him. "Are you lost boy? Where is your master then?" he gave Brandy a few more pieces of biscuit and realised the dog was hungry.

"Come on Goldie let's find you some more scraps."

Brandy followed Trevor to rejoin the others. The man found him some scraps of meat and biscuit. He ate heartily.

Trevor guessed Brandy had nothing to do with the captured prisoners. The dog took no interest in them at all. In fact he was a very loving and friendly dog.

Brandy felt comfortable around these men.

"I know that nice lady in the cave said I should guard Jack. But he's gone now. Those other masters are heading in a different direction to me. I'll search for Jack this way and stay with the new master." Brandy decided reluctantly to follow Trevor.

The group of Resistance fighters made their way back towards the camp with the two prisoners securely under guard. The Blades remained gagged and bound by the hands. Corporal Trevor kept the two separate from each other all the time. He was the only member of the local fighters who'd received any formal military training. He was from the far western lands, where they still had a small army. He'd long since moved back to this area. His mother lived here as a child and many of his relations were still in the region. When he'd heard, of the call to arms, he decided to make the journey across the mountains to join up. He would've been granted the rank of Sergeant, except, he was still considered an outsider.

"When we camp later I'll ask the older Blade a few questions of my own Jonno." Trevor spoke to his most trusted fighter. Mr Johnsonby or Jonno as everyone called him; was one of those men you knew you could trust the moment you met him. He was slim and short in stature. He had a long thin face but a huge smile that seemed to stretch fully from one ear to the other. Jonno didn't appear to be the build of a freedom fighter, but he was as agile as a cat. He could climb anything, had no fear of heights and would squeeze into any narrow space. This was perfect for all manner of tasks that they had to conduct. He could get into many places that would be closed to most people.

"Do you think they'll tell us anything but lies Trev?" Jonno wasn't hopeful.

Brandy looked on and watched these two masters talking. He wondered if they would ever take him where he could find his Jack.

Trevor saw Brandy watching him and mistook his interest for a need for another snack. He reached into his pocket and pulled out a small piece of biscuit which he duly threw for Brandy to catch. With a snap of his jaws and a little jump he caught the biscuit and swallowed it whole.

"Good catch Goldie." The man praised with a clap of his hands.

Brandy lay down and placed his head on his paws and continued watching them both.

"Is that his name Trev?" Jonno nodded in the direction of Brandy.

"Dunno really. I've called him Goldie, he seems happy enough with that. At least he seems to come when I call him."

Brandy lifted his head at the name Goldie. He tilted his head one side and thought for a moment.

"Yes, I don't mind being called Goldie. At least whilst I'm with this new master."

Chapter 9 - Rescue

A few remaining stars clung, precariously, to visibility as day-break approached. Jack watched the transforming palette of deep indigo, red and pale blue washing away the night. Ahead, an expanding scene of flat, tawny-brown grassland opened into the far distance. The hills opposite melted indistinguishably into the misty horizon making it difficult to judge their distance.

"How far must we travel today, Jaden?" Jack asked.

His friend shook his head and pointed, "All the way over there, I guess Jack. I've never been to the Blade stronghold either. We'll ask Grandfather later."

Cool night air drifted imperceptibly up the hillside, a hint of dryness suggested the hot summer's day to follow. Peaceful silence was broken only with an occasional distant animal call. Jack enjoyed the spectacle; he'd never imagined anything so breath-taking. He spotted several large birds circling high above the savannah.

"Are they looking for their breakfast?" Jack wondered nervously, hoping they wouldn't consider him their lunch when he reached the centre. "Are there any dangerous creatures out there? You know, like lions or tigers?"

Jaden shrugged his shoulders, "What's a tiger?"

Jaden and the Sage quickly readied themselves. Searlan explained the dangers of travelling by day. Luckily, the plain was very large and offered plenty of cover.

"We need to reach a small lake, near the centre, by midday so we must not dawdle. Keep your wits about you and it should be safe enough. The enemy may patrol the grassland, but I think it unlikely we'll encounter them." Searlan led them down towards the savannah.

The journey down the hill side progressed without incident; an unmarked path of heather and brush gave way to dried grass.

"Travel in silence to conserve energy and body moisture. Try to breath through your nose; you'll lose fewer fluids that way. You'll be surprised how hot it becomes in this great basin. The sun will kill you as readily as any sword if you are reckless out there. Keep your head covered and look where you are treading. I don't want to have to deal with a snake bite or a broken ankle."

Jack was alarmed at the stream of orders from the old Sage. He looked worryingly across to Jaden, who as usual, seemed relaxed. The boy remained as happy and carefree as ever.

"Just follow Grandfather, Jack. Everything will be fine."

Thick scrub covered the ground at the edge of the savannah. One of the predominant grasses was aptly named; "the porcupine plant" with knee high spines, sharp as needles, waiting patiently for any bare flesh. Jack had already been "spiked" a couple of times and didn't relish several more hours of torture. He watched the other two as they deftly side-stepped each clump. Mimicking Jaden, he quickly adopted their style and avoided many potentially painful encounters. Keeping a wary eye on the ground ahead, Jack imagined stumbling upon a venomous snake. He was hopelessly scared of any snake, most especially the poisonous kind.

They made good progress during the first couple of hours of daylight.

Sitting down on a soft grass tuft; Searlan said, "We'll take a break here for a short while."

Everyone had a small drink, from the skin of water carried by the old man. The liquid already tasted warm from the rising heat of the day and didn't seem to refresh Jack at all.

"You must drink even if you think you don't need to," the old man commanded. "The body does not fair well when deprived of moisture. You'll quickly succumb to the heat and then you'll be a burden not an asset."

Jack gulped a few more mouthfuls and tried to imagine he was drinking a tasty sweet strawberry flavoured soft drink.

"Yuk, it didn't work." He was handed a small biscuit made of oats, fruits, nuts and honey. Eating the sweet tasting chewy snack made a surprising difference to Jack's energy levels. He felt revitalised and happier.

"These are made by the villagers," the old man explained. "They are full of nourishment and will help you cope with the walk ahead."

Now refreshed, the old Sage resumed the journey.

An occasional glance back over his shoulder confirmed to Jack they covered the ground quite quickly. The hills behind turned a misty blue and faded into the sky. He was sure they must be nearing the middle; a quizzical look at the Searlan attracted a response.

"Still some distance to go before we reach the lake young Jack. About another hour at least and probably two if we slow our pace."

The boy smiled back but already felt tired. His sore elbow started hurting again; the scratches on his arms itched incessantly and the lump on his head throbbed. "You're a bit of a wreck Jack Ferns," he thought, slipping into a daydream about a relaxing, bubble-bath.

Jack bumped into the back of the Sage. "Oops!" he exclaimed. The old man had stopped dead in his tracks.

Searlan dropped to a crouching position and frantically waved the others to do likewise. "Over there," he whispered cautiously. "There is someone over there," pointing to his left.

The old man peered through the tall grasses, "keep still and listen, I don't think we've been seen yet."

"One move and you're dead," the commanding voice was as cold as it was menacing.

A spear was pushed firmly into the back of the Sage. "Who are you old man and what are you doing here?"

Searlan turned tentatively towards the voice, praying this wasn't a Blade. He eased visibly when he realised the four men were Resistance fighters. The soldiers were quickly joined by six others from all directions.

"Speak quickly old man or I'll drop you right here."

"I am Searlan, Sage of Sages and good friend to all Resistance fighters. We are crossing the savannah to rescue some friends taken by our common enemy. We suspect the Blades have them held in their fortress. We offer you no harm and would welcome your alliance."

The old man steadied himself; he saw his words had some affect. "These two youngsters are in my care, although they may tell it the other way around," he said grinning cautiously. "This is my Sage heir and grandson Jaden and this is our good friend Jack Ferns."

The soldier examined both boys closely. "You look as though you have a few tales to tell young Jack Ferns," the Resistance fighter said to the boy. "Let me take a look at that arm."

The other men relaxed their spears and sat down in several small groups.

"My name is Healworth, Sergeant-at-Arms of the 4th Resistance Group," the soldier said in a friendlier manner.

"I command these volunteers," he gesturing to his men. "There are two other groups out scouting over yonder." Healworth pointed vaguely across the savannah.

"Have you seen any Blade patrols?" Jaden asked.

Healworth shook his head and continued, "I've heard of you Searlan, Sage of Sages. My father once came to you for advice. "

Searlan nodded politely; rapidly searching his memories for any such visitation.

"I'm from the village of Tearwind; over the other side of the hills." Again, Healworth waved his outstretched arm; pointing roughly in a westerly direction. "I don't suppose you would remember him; Charlie Healworth was his name, a tall dark haired farmer, heavily built."

The old Sage screwed up his forehead for a few seconds and then replied. "Yes, I do remember your father, Sergeant. He came to me seeking a solution to your poor soil and weak crops. If I remember correctly, I gave him some advice on how to grow more effectively. I supplied him with a special potion to sprinkle over the soil; he promised to return to me after the next harvest to tell me how things progressed. He never returned." Searlan smiled, knowingly, again at Sergeant Healworth.

The Sergeant was a broad and powerfully built man, just like his father - wide muscular shoulders, thick arms and very strong tree-trunk legs. An imposing character of over six feet, he made a fitting leader of the Resistance. Healworth's face was weathered and tanned from long days spent in the open, and although he had a wide grin, he mostly seemed dour and serious.

"How did you sneak up on us so quietly Mr. Healworth?" Jack asked.

The sergeant laughed loudly. "Practice young Master Jack, plenty of practice." He busied himself redressing the boy's injured arm. Despite the size of his hands, he was adept and quickly cleaned the wound with some spirit. "This may sting a bit," he applied an ointment taken from a little sack on his back.

Jack grimaced as the ointment entered the wound.

"That's a nasty cut, but you should live." Healworth said in a sombre tone. Turning his head, he winked at the old Sage and gave a wry grin.

Jack sat back looking at his arm fearfully without realising the irony in the Sergeant's voice.

Healworth continued soberly, "I'm afraid to say Searlan, but my father was murdered by the Blades. Barely two weeks after returning from meeting you, he was brutally hacked down; the pigs showed no mercy at all. One man against a band of five Blades; father never offered any threat to the murderous rabble. He was just innocently tilling our land. I'll never forget that moment; our whole family witnessed the execution from our front porch. Mother barely helped us escape from their grasp; she rushed us back through the house and away into the wood. We hid for several days, terrified to return. Shortly afterwards, I made a pledge to avenge my father's senseless death; I left to join the Resistance and have never returned. My two younger brothers and older sister were left to care for mother and the farmstead. I'm afraid I've no news regarding the success of the harvest."

The three were speechless, for several minutes they remained silent as the sergeant finished working on Jack's other cuts and grazes.

Searlan eventually said, "That is the bitterest news Sergeant Healworth and a wretched story. I'm afraid it's all too common when innocent, hard-working, people confront the Blade butchers; these are sickening times, and I'm very sorry for your tragic loss."

"How long have you been out here?" Jaden enquired.

"Not long enough, there are still many enemy soldiers around, although, they seem to have reduced of late. Something is brewing, they are preparing for a major assault; I can smell it."

The Sage described their predicament in more detail. He explained about the capture of Cathy and their intention to try to rescue her. His account was thorough but abridged. He missed out many areas that he would not wish to divulge, especially about Lujnima, but was forthcoming none the least. The Sergeant listened intently and went on to voice his concern about their plan. He couldn't believe they would ever be able to gain entry into the fortress.

"It's totally impregnable," he stated adamantly. "An army, greater than the entire Resistance, could lay siege to that fortress for months. Even then, it's unlikely you could force surrender. What you're suggesting is suicide."

Jack looked horrified at the prospect. "How can I save Cathy from such a place?" he thought.

The soldier then questioned. "What chance do you, an old man and two young boys, hope to achieve against such an enemy?"

Searlan's face remained resolute.

Healworth smiled quizzically, puzzling over the strange old man before him. "Or do you possess some other magic potion that would render you invisible? Stories of your powers have reached even my ears Searlan – Sage of Sages, are you secretly an invincible warrior?"

The old Sage shook his head in resignation.

"No sergeant, I'm afraid the tales are just that. I've no magic potion at my disposal."

Searlan agreed with the Sergeant that their task seemed hopeless. Despite the odds, they were determined to carry out the rescue attempt.

"We will not falter in our endeavour to return with Cathy and possibly others too. As impossible as it may seem, we must try."

His resolve impressed the freedom fighter so much that he stood up and took a very low bow to the Sage.

"Well old man, if you do manage to achieve this, your deed will be written into songs and handed down in tales of great courage, audacity and bravery." The Sergeant spoke with utter conviction and respect.

The old man stood up and shook the sergeant's hand.

Jack looked up at the powerful soldier. "Thank you sergeant for helping me, my arm feels better all ready." He shook the man's huge hand and bowed politely.

"We cannot offer you much more than advice and some water, but please take this amulet of mine." He gave the old man a chain of silver with a black and red charm attached. "It does not possess any magic, I'm afraid. But the carrier will be recognised as one whom has the blessings of the Resistance. You are very likely to meet other bands in your travels. This could save you from some who are more ready to strike first before they discover that they might know of you."

Searlan thanked him sincerely and placed the amulet around his neck tucking it, out of sight, into his shirt.

"I suggest that you make for the west end of the fortress, it's safer. Approach from the hills; avoid the wide ditch surrounding most of the walls. The west side is flatter and easier to cross. Quite how you will find your way in is a mystery that I doubt even you can solve Great Sage."

The Sergeant stood up and saluted the three travellers. "Good luck. Maybe we will meet again."

Before taking their leave, they wished the fighters success and good fortune. The three travellers continued their journey for several hours without rest or conversation. Searlan, wrapped privately in deep thought, contemplated many options for entry into the fortress. Healworth's warning hung heavily on his shoulders.

Jack became tired and irritable, this wasn't the adventure he'd hoped for; the savannah was uncomfortably dry, dusty and very hot. His throat rasped with every breath, each step drained his dwindling reserves. Looking up towards the sun, he spotted birds of prey circling effortlessly, great wings outstretched like kites.

"They're called vultures in my world I think," he whispered to Jaden. "They wait until their prey is dead and then eat the carcass. Do you think they're waiting for us to drop?"

"Let's hope not Jack; anyway, Grandfather will stop soon. He's been deep in thought for so long, I guess he's lost track of time. It's best not to disturb him when he's like this but I'm getting tired as well."

As if the old Sage had subconsciously heard his grandson, he turned and waved his hand in the direction of the lowering sun. "We'll not reach the other side before night fall. Better to rest now and make our approach under cover of darkness."

Jack sighed loudly; he was ready to drop where he stood. Both sides of the savannah seemed to be as far away as ever.

They soon found a place to rest; Searlan found an area free from spiky grass. "Watch out for insects and snakes, we don't need to deal with any bites or stings."

Jack took great care to inspect the grass, dusty soil and scrub for any dangers. He flopped exhausted on a large tuft of soft grass.

Searlan's plan to reach the lake had been abandoned after meeting the Resistance fighters. They all stretched out and slept for a couple of uninterrupted hours.

***

"Come on you two, we are still only about half way across." Searlan called.

The boys stretched their stiff limbs as Searlan explained. "We will have to walk for several hours. I want to approach the fortress in darkness. There will be no more rest periods as we have to make up for lost time. Drink some of this water." he offered the half filled skin to Jack.

"Thanks Searlan, I feel much better after that nap, the heat drains your strength."

"The sun is unforgiving to the foolhardy Jack Ferns. Many have perished in the dry regions of the land by underestimating the power of Tarre-Hare.

Searlan led them in the direction of the distant hills. Jack didn't particularly like the fast pace set by the Sage, despite the rest, his feet ached.

"Come on Jack, don't lag behind," Searlan increased the pace; he aimed to reach the foothills before darkness.

Jack hurried but failed to catch Jaden. "How did he walk so fast?"

The soil became noticeably redder in this area; large patches broke the predominant sandy yellow. He bent down and picked up a handful. The granules were quite coarse; a mixture of ochre coloured grains with hundreds of tiny twinkling glass-like fragments.

"Keep up Jack I said, stop daydreaming," the old man scolded.

Jack dropped the sand and rubbed his hands together, most of the dust brushed off but some glistening residue remained. He trotted up alongside the two others and shrugged his shoulders. He looked again at his hands, and sure enough, both were covered with miniscule mirrors reflecting the setting sun. No matter how he tried he didn't seem to be able to clean them off.

Searlan noticed the boy's hands. "You'll never rub those off like that. The harder you try the deeper they'll penetrate your skin; you need to encourage them to leave. Each one is said to be a lost soul; be careful you do not offend them."

Jack looked again at the shining souls he'd unwittingly gathered. "I wonder if they can hear me," he mused.

"We hear you Jack Ferns, Guardian of the MoonBridge. We hear you and know some of your fate. You should beware the under-worlders they are your mortal enemies."

"What! Who said that? I thought Searlan was joking."

"We are the scattered remnants of the lost people of Bellaberry. The Unnamed destroyed our lands after we tried to rise up against his evil forces. He turned us all to ash, with a force so deadly; we were evaporated in a blink of an eye. None lived, but a strange twist of fate meant some of us survived in this form. Our souls are trapped in these gem shards; the winds of time eventually deposited us together. Now fate has brought you to free us and, once more, given Bellaberry a voice."

"What do you want with me?" Jack was surprised, and a little afraid.

"We mean you no harm Guardian of the MoonBridge; we seek only recognition and transportation to our own lands. Many have tried before but we do not know how many have succeeded. Maybe, we can offer you help and assistance on your journey ahead in payment."

Jack relaxed, "Do you have a name? I can hardly call you Bellaberry can I?"

"My name has not been spoken, in your world, since the Unnamed stole my life Jack Ferns. I used to be called Epheron the Younger – Master Creator and Changer, but that was a very long time ago."

"What sort of things did you create Epheron? That's a nice name by the way, I've never heard of one like that before."

"I was best described as a necromancer or perhaps a wizard in your language. I used my knowledge and powers to change one thing into another."

"Wow, can you still do it? I'd love to see some magic."

"Perhaps young Guardian, but I need some mechanism to enable my powers to focus. Your staff perhaps would suffice."

Before the boy could reply, a sharp retort snapped from ahead. "Jack, I told you to stop daydreaming and hurry up. Don't let me tell you again." Searlan sounded quite angry.

"But I..."

"No buts Jack, we need to move quickly and quietly."

Jack threw his mind briefly back to the glistening dust on his hands "We'll talk again when it's safer Epheron. I really would like to see some of your creative magic. Sorry but I've got to go."

The day drew to a close as the three reached the base of the hills. Jack looked back, across the savannah, to the misty blue of the hills on the other side. He was impressed he'd managed to walk so far.

"We must skirt around these hills before reaching the fortress. Be extra vigilant this is Blade territory now, pray we don't meet too many of their troops." Searlan was afraid the enemy would leap out on them at any moment. "Stay alert, both of you."

As they rounded the edge of a broad sweeping slope, Jack caught his first glimpse of the fortress. He just stood and stared in disbelief. The Sergeant had been correct, this massive stone and rock structure looked invincible. Perched high on a hill; dominating the landscape were immense walls, surrounding a central square tower. Each corner had a spire rising up to provide even greater defensive protection. To make matters worse there were hundreds of white tents erected around the base of the fortress. Many thin columns of smoke drifted up into the still air.

"What's all that smoke?" Jack asked.

"Fires used for cooking Jack, an army takes a lot of feeding," answered Searlan.

Frighteningly; soldiers, in dark uniforms, were everywhere. "How can we possibly sneak through all of them; it's hopeless?" Jack was about to continue when the old Sage interrupted.

"They are gathering their forces; that's why we've seen so few. If our chances were slim before, they make them virtually impossible now." He bowed his head and sat down disgruntled.

Jaden, who'd been very quiet for much of the day, finally spoke. "Grandfather, how do they gather water?"

Both turned to him quizzically.

"What do you mean Jaden?" His grandfather asked.

"Do they have wells, or a stream or perhaps barrels of water delivered do you think?"

"Ah I see your idea; you are a clever lad, my boy. If we can find the source of their water we may be able to use it to gain entry; very smart thinking indeed."

The boy's face lit up at his grandfather's praise.

Jack was totally confused. "What does water have to do with getting into the fortress?"

Jaden explained his plan to either find the source of the stream and to follow it in under the walls, or to find the water barrels and use them as ruse to enter the fortress legitimately as water carriers.

"You mean to just walk in the front gate, bold as you like?" Jack questioned sarcastically. "They'll chop our heads off for sure."

"Not necessarily Jack," the old Sage pondered momentarily.

"It's the very last thing anyone one would think of. Look at them down there, they have thousands of soldiers everywhere, why should they fear any form of attack? It's a perfect plan. Audacious I agree; we just need to be confident. No-one will suspect a thing, trust me."

Jack thought long and hard. "How could this possibly work?"

Under cover of darkness; they made their way down the slope, over the ditch and in amongst the first of the tents. A few soldiers milled around but no-one really paid them any attention. They searched for a little while before finding a stockpile of oak barrels of water. Dozens of them were stacked together in a little storage area.

"These would provide enough water for many weeks of siege," Searlan observed.

The old Sage opened the tap on the side of one of them; cool, clean water poured out. "Take a drink and replenish your skins," he ordered.

"We must find the delivery wagon," Jaden whispered; looking hopefully around. "What's that sticking out there?"

On the other side of the area, hidden beneath a heavy tarpaulin, they found a wagon.

"This would require two large shire horses to draw it," Searlan suggested.

"What about this Grandfather?" Jaden uncovered a hand operated cart used for pushing one or two of the barrels. "They probably use this to wheel the barrels into the storerooms."

"Perfect!" Searlan exclaimed. "This is just what I was hoping for." He quietly removed the cart from the covering and then explained his plan. "We'll place one of the empty barrels on this cart and hide you two inside it. Then a part-filled barrel, alongside the first."

"Will you be able to manage both barrels Grandfather? They are heavy." Jaden was concerned he would never be able to push so much weight.

"I only need a little water inside one barrel; it will weigh a lot less than a full one. We can all help to push them up close to the gate before we actually enter the fortress."

Searlan scouted quickly around looking for likely candidates. "We will take these two," he indicated. The three worked together to load the barrels. Searlan then practiced moving the cart up and down to make sure that he was strong enough to push them along. The well greased wheels and lightweight construction made transporting the load an easy task for the old man.

"We will hide under the tarpaulin for the rest of the night and approach the gate at first light. Now help me cover the cart."

They pushed the loaded cart back under the cover. The wagon made a perfect place to sleep. Jack was amazed how quickly he drifted off. His body had finally realised how much effort he'd put in over the last couple of days, he was ready for rest.

***

Jack received a heavy shake from the old Sage.

"What? Ugh, already?"

"Shhh," Searlan warned in a hoarse whisper. "I have heard movement outside."

Jack stretched his cramped limbs but resisted the temptation to yawn loudly. His head throbbed, his arm ached, and he felt stiff, dirty and very uncomfortable.

"Are you okay Jack?" Jaden was bright as a button.

"No I'm not, I don't feel remotely refreshed or rested," complained the boy.

After the old man confirmed the coast was clear, they set out for their rescue attempt. They could hardly believe their luck; most of the tents were closed tightly for the night. Dawn was over an hour away. In the east, you could just discern glimmers of the coming sun.

"It must have been a patrol that I heard," Searlan explained. "Keep a lookout for others."

They pushed the cart slowly, up towards the gate, making as little noise as possible. Just out of sight of the single guard on duty, the two boys squeezed into the empty barrel and Searlan closed the lid over their heads. Once inside, darkness closed around them and Jaden felt afraid. Jack then thought of the light and ordered his hand to glow.

Jaden stared in amazement and said quietly, "How did you learn to do that Jack? That is the neatest trick ever."

Both boys grinned widely and tried to get comfortable in the small space.

"Lujnima gave this to me as a gift when I was stuck in the caves. Neat isn't it. I can make it go much brighter if I need to."

A series of thumps on the outside of the barrel told the boys to be silent. Searlan pushed the cart around the corner and into view of the soldier guarding the gate. He was a thin, gangly sort of man with a heavy sword hanging at his side. The metal helmet on his head was too big and the long spear held in his hand seemed far too large for him to handle effectively.

"What d'you fink your doin' old man?" He challenged Searlan menacingly.

The old Sage never faltered for a moment. "Special water delivery for the officer's mess mate, orders from the Cap'n himself. Guess it's too hot up there for them?" With a wry grin, Searlan gestured with his head towards the centre of the fortress.

"Yeh, alright for some ain't it mate," the guard replied sarcastically. "They don't have to stand around 'alf the night in this drainin' heat, do they?"

"Do you want a quick slurp mate to wet your whistle? What's yer name?" the old man spoke confidently.

"Cheers. Me name's Skimmer. That's right kind of yer, don't mind if I do. What's your name then?"

The Sage opened the tap of the barrel containing the small amount of water and gave the guard a cupful. The guard smiled and nodded his approval at the refreshing drink.

"I'm Jacko mate, see yer later." The old Sage then pushed the barrels through the open gateway as confidently as any normal worker would do. They were in.

Searlan wheeled the cart into the dimly lit square and crossed quickly to the other side. No-one watched him slide behind a stack of hay bales. The boys climbed out of the barrel, relieved to be able to stretch their constrained muscles.

"This way," Searlan abandoned the cart and hurried the boys through a gateway under the inner wall. The opening led to a wide courtyard with many exits. Even at this early hour there were a couple of other people going about their business.

"So far, so good?" Jack mumbled nervously.

"We must find the entrance to the dungeons before everyone wakes up," Searlan urged.

"Look grandfather, it could be that one over there," Jaden pointed to a heavy oak door.

"Okay, let's see." They crossed cautiously. The door wasn't locked; Searlan gingerly pushed it open. "Quietly now, keep close behind me," he whispered.

The three moved inside and pulled the door gently behind them. A wide passage led for a few metres before opening into a large reception room. Three archways were cut into the walls; voices could be heard from one of the corridors. Jack felt uneasy; for some reason the surroundings seemed vaguely familiar; he recognised the high ceiling with its black beams. Searlan searched rapidly for a hiding place. "Quickly, follow me," he ordered, leading them onto a narrowing staircase that wound down into the lower levels.

The air became colder with every passing moment; damp mustiness clung to their clothes, the smell was unpleasant.

"Do you think we are heading in the right direction for the dungeons, Grandfather?" Jaden asked.

"Let's hope so," the old Sage replied, not altogether convincingly.

Jack had moved on ahead. He looked almost hypnotised wandering away from the other two.

"Are you alright Jack?" Jaden questioned, running alongside his friend. He shook him by the hand and Jack snapped out of his daze.

"I've seen this place before," he confessed.

"How could you have, you've never been here?" Jaden asked.

"I saw it in a dream I think, or maybe it was when I spoke with Cathy in my head. Either way, I recognise this place. I knew that room upstairs, I know this passage. We need to head that way. Cathy is down there to the right." He led them onwards waving his hand in the direction he was heading. "Down here," he declared confidently.

Jack was true to his word, the route was already known to him and shortly they came to another stout door. This time it was locked from the inside. Searlan pressed his ear against the wood. "I can hear someone talking in there," he said quietly.

"Cathy's in there; she knows I'm here, I'm certain of it."

Jack drifted into a semi-trance, his mind wandered beyond the door and into Cathy's thoughts.

"Are you really outside the door Jack?"

"Yes Cathy, I'm here with Searlan the Sage of Sages and his grandson and Sageling Jaden. We're here to rescue you but we need to know how many guards are on your side of the door."

Jack stood, rigidly, frozen into a deep trance. Jaden looked directly into his eyes; seeing nothing. He waved his hand in front of his face and called softly to him. "Jack, can you hear me Jack?"

The old Sage came closer and explained that he wasn't present even though his body stood before them.

"He's on another plane of existence beyond my sight. I think his spirit may be on the other side of this door? This may prove very useful."

Jack spoke with Cathy as if he was actually right next to her.

"Can you look around from where you seem to be to me?" she questioned.

"This is really weird Cathy, I'm not sure I believe what I think I'm seeing. Is it true that I'm even talking to you rather than just day-dreaming?

"Look at me Jack, what am I wearing? Tell me what you see?" Cathy asked him earnestly.

"You're wearing a light green blouse and a darker green skirt down to your knees. You have a leather belt with an emerald coloured buckle. Your hair is tucked back behind your ears. Oh, and sorry, but you look filthy dirty." Jack grinned feeling very foolish.

"That is exactly how I look now and there is no way you could have guessed that because these clothes were only made by my Aunt's friend a few weeks ago and you have never seen them. Now look around the room and tell me how many guards you can see?"

Jack looked as if he was just glancing around, it was a little disconcerting and disorienting but he scanned the room from the other side of the door. "Cathy, I don't see any guards, just you, your Aunt lying over there. Where are the other people?"

"You're exactly right again Jack, there's only us here, the others are all locked up in the other dungeons I think. The guards don't waste their time looking after us much. We're only here because my Aunt is too ill to be moved and they don't want to be bothered by her. They come once in while and they were here just as you arrived, they'll not be back again for several hours I should think."

"Perfect, wait here and I'll explain everything to Searlan. It's good to see you again Cathy by the way, I've been worried about you."

Jack slipped back out of the trance and returned to Jaden and Searlan on the other side of the door.

"There aren't any guards, they've left now and will not be back for a couple of hours. Aunt Beth is in a bad way I think; Cathy is very worried about her. All we need to do is find out how to unlock the door and then try to make our getaway."

The other two looked at him in amazement.

"You are full of wonders Jack Ferns, Guardian of the MoonBridge," Jaden gave one of his really huge grins and shook Jack's hand. "How will we get in Grandfather?"

The old Sage walked up to the door and looked long and hard at the heavy metal lock. "Simple, we need to find the key!" He tutted loudly and then grumbled under his breath. "Now, look around and see if it's anywhere at hand."

The three hunted for several minutes without any luck.

"How about using this?" Jack suggested, producing a thin handled knife from a drawer of a chest on the other side of the room.

"We might be able to pick it or prise it open?" His suggestion was logical but not very practical.

Searlan took the knife but didn't seem hopeful. "Keep looking you two, I'll try to open the lock with this."

The others expanded their search whilst the old man fiddled with the key hole. A load snap and clatter rang out as the knife broke into several pieces and fell to the floor. The old man huffed exasperatingly. "It's no use, I'm a hopeless house breaker and even worse lock picker."

Jaden and Jack faired no better despite skirting around all over the place. Suddenly the small boy had an idea; he ran off in the direction of the way they had entered. Jack just continued searching for a few more minutes before giving up in desperation. He returned to the Sage and told him that Jaden had gone off somewhere. Both sat down, trying to come up with a plan, when the boy returned with a big key and an even bigger smile.

"Perhaps this will help," he announced with complete self satisfaction.

Jaden strode up to the door and turned the key in the lock. The mechanism operated as hoped and the door swung back. Cathy came rushing forwards in her dark green skirt and pale green blouse complete with belt and buckle just as Jack had seen her. She rushed straight up to him, threw her arms around his neck and hugged him so tight he almost turned scarlet. The old Sage wondered if it was embarrassment or the strength of the hug that caused his colouring; he guessed it was embarrassment.

"Oh Jack, I'm so glad to see you, I've missed you so much since you last left and seeing you in my mind only made me realise how much I wanted you to be back here."

Jack was even more embarrassed turning nearly bright pink. "It's gggoood to sssee yyyoou too," he stammered, trying to wriggle out of the girls grasp.

Cathy had grown into a very beautiful and shapely fifteen year old. She was even more stunning than Jack had imagined possible and she wasn't letting him get away that easy and gave him a great big kiss before finally releasing her grip. Poor Jack didn't know where to look. Searlan just laughed out loud at the sight of him stepping backwards in fright.

After a few seconds the old Sage said, "Hello Cathy, it's lovely to see you again. Are you alright? Where is your Aunt? Can she travel?"

Searlan was keen to get on with the rescue; the joy of seeing Cathy distracted everyone from their serious predicament.

"Okay, all of you; remember, we still have the small matter of escaping from this impregnable fortress. Cathy, there are thousands of troops camped outside and we must hurry before they all wake up." Cathy led Searlan to her Aunt, he didn't need to examine her closely; he knew she was very sick.

"This is going to be difficult; I don't believe we can move her," Searlan whispered. His assessment suggested the rescue was in jeopardy. "You go and speak to the boys; I'll see what I can do."

Jack and Jaden quickly relayed how they'd managed to reach her; Cathy listened intently.

"The Blades are planning a major assault; possibly even a final war to wipe out the local resistance," Jaden explained.

Cathy nodded solemnly; she had a suggestion but thought it best to discuss it with Searlan. "She is very sick Jaden; I'm so worried about her. Those Blade pigs hurt her badly. Come on through; let's see how Searlan is doing.

As they walked into the dimly lit room the old sage stood up. Taking them all to one side he announced grimly, "I'm truly sorry Cathy but your Aunt is even worse than I feared. I think her wounds have poisoned her blood and I'm unable to help her. I believe she may die, possibly very soon, whether she stays here or we try to move her. I'm not sure it will make much difference."

Cathy looked straight at the old Sage and agreed begrudgingly. "I've been afraid of that, poor Aunt Beth has barely been able to speak for days. We will have to carry her out of here; she has no strength to walk by herself."

The old Sage paused before he answered her. For the first time since Jack met him, he seemed almost lost for words. "You have the most difficult choice to make Cathy. I think you have to consider leaving your Aunt here. She is clearly unable to travel, as you have said, and would hardly survive even if we could carry her."

Jack watch the blood drain from Cathy's face. The Sage coughed apologetically before continuing. "I cannot allow you to be taken; the Guardianship you received is too important. I hate to say this, but you must leave your Aunt to her own fate. You must come with us alone."

The girl just stared at the old Sage in disbelief. "I can't just leave her here Searlan, she's my life; I love her like my own Mother. She has given up everything for me, she must come with us. Even if she dies in the process, at least I'll be with her; at least I'll have tried."

Jaden took his friend's hand caringly; he felt the tremble in her arm.

Tears welled up in Cathy's eyes, "I'll never leave her to these filthy wolves. I would rather stay and take my own chances than give up on her. Please Searlan; don't ask me to do this."

The old man seemed to age as the weight of his decision took hold. He thought briefly, shrugged his shoulders and sighed in resignation. He took Cathy gently in his arms and gave the girl a comforting hug. "Of course my dear, I should never have suggested it. We will have to do the best we can."

Cathy squeezed him tighter in thanks and sniffed her tears away. She wiped her eyes briefly and turned to her Aunt. "We're getting you out of here Aunt Beth; you're going to make it."

Aunt Beth just managed to open her eyes slightly and looked pleased at seeing her niece. She was incapable of focussing on the others and quickly drifted back into unconsciousness.

All four contemplated the task, Jaden offered another interesting idea. "If we could get Cathy's Aunt to that big water wagon, maybe we could hitch up some horses and ride out of here?"

Searlan's face brightened visibly. "Excellent idea Jaden, we do need transportation for her. That is precisely what we need to do. Let's see if we can manage to get Aunt Beth on her feet and at least out of this dungeon. We must try to reach the courtyard."

Aunt Beth was very weak but managed to stand with the aid of Cathy and Jack either side of her. They half carried, half dragged her slowly back through the passageways until stepping out into the courtyard. The sun had risen; daylight was quite bright but not yet shining down into the open space before them. Many more people were busy with their daily business. The hustle and bustle of chores reverberated around the courtyard: a strong smell of fresh vegetables and meat wafted across from the other side. The escapees saw soldiers and workers busily completing their early morning duties.

"That's exactly what we're looking for," Searlan announced excitedly.

On the other side of the courtyard several covered wagons were being unloaded. Men and women emptied food, water and stores. "They probably do this every day; a large fortress needs lots of provisions to run efficiently. We need to sneak into the back of one of those," Searlan directed. "Let's get Aunt Beth a bit closer to the nearest one, that's almost empty. Walk confidently as if we we're just going about our own business, no-one will notice."

They stepped out of the dark shadows and across the courtyard. Just as Searlan had said nobody even turned to look at them. They walked right across to the first wagon and stepped behind it.

"This looks promising." The old sage gestured them all to clamber inside.

In the back were some straw bales, wicker carrying baskets and one large barrel.

The four lifted Aunt Beth in the back and then climbed in after her. Cathy helped her Aunt lay down as far to the front of the wagon as possible. They used some of the bales to hide her from sight by building a little wall of hay in front of her.

"Hide, quickly." Searlan made sure they were not able to be seen.

Cathy crouched down and covered herself with one of the larger wicker baskets. The barrel, standing at the side, was empty and big enough for Jaden and Jack to clamber inside. The old Sage decided it was best to lie down behind the bales of hay alongside Aunt Beth to prevent her from making any unexpected sounds. Looking in from the back of the wagon, no-one would've guessed that five stowaways were hiding there.

"Quiet everyone now, we don't want any mishaps." Searlan held his breath, crossed his fingers and prayed silently for divine intervention.

They didn't have long to wait before they heard the driver returning.

"That's it for this morning Chas," one of the courtyard staff said, near the front of the wagon.

"Okay mate, see yer later. I've got to get another load up to the main camp in an hour or so."

The wagon swayed as the driver climbed aboard, a heavy jolt indicated he'd sat down. Searlan gripped his cane hard and gritted his teeth. Every sinew tightened, fully expecting a rush of guards to descend upon them. He looked down at Aunt Beth, she was still lying silently and barely conscious. "Now is not the time to call out in pain my dear Beth," he thought sympathetically.

Searlan tensed further as the driver made a loud clicking noise with his tongue. The signal encouraged the two great horses to move forwards. They obeyed impeccably; turning the unloaded wagon was easy; the route out of the fortress gate took them over the heavy cobbled surface. The sound of large metal shoes and the wheels of the cart echoed loudly around the walls.

"See yer this afternoon mate." Chas, the driver, nodded to the guard, paying his respects and driving though the entrance.

"Hey, just a minute," the guard ordered. Chas pulled the wagon to a sudden halt.

All five stow-a-ways froze. Searlan's heart sank, they were caught for sure.

"Bring us some extra grub when yer come back will yer Chas?" the guard requested hopefully before waving the wagon to pass.

"You and your stomach 'arry: I'll see what I can do, but I can't promise nothin' though. You know what the boss is like."

The guard nodded to the driver and tutted back at him. "Yeh, I know all right. See yer later."

Without a second glance; Harry the guard turned back to his duties. He never bothered to look up at the fluttering flaps of canvass. He never noticed the two frightened eyes peering intently from behind the hay bale. Searlan bit his lip hardly daring to breath.

Chas drove the wagon cautiously over the final stone cobbles under the archway; once clear, the two powerful drays stepped effortlessly onto the dirt road.

"We're away," Searlan whispered elated at their success. He could hardly believe how lucky they'd been. "If only I knew where we were heading?"

Cathy was the first to come out of hiding; she peeped cautiously out of the back of the wagon. The road ran alongside hundreds of tents, soldiers wandered everywhere. No-one looked at the common sight of the empty delivery wagon leaving the entrance; they might as well have been invisible. "Look how many Blades are here Jack, there must be thousands of them. I've never imagined anything like this, where have all come from?"

The gate to the fortress receded at a steady pace. Jack and Jaden crept clumsily out of the barrel and looked with Cathy. Searlan sat up; pleased they'd managed to get out in one piece. He whispered to them. "We have to be quiet and remain still; we don't want to alert the driver. We'll look for a good moment to get him off. If the driver follows this road we'll come to a wooded area in about half an hour or so. It's winding there; we'll have chance to take over the wagon."

As Searlan suspected, they continued along the road. The cart clattered and clonked violently over the uneven dirt track. Occasionally; one of the horses would whinny complaining at the poor quality of the road. The driver cursed and tugged, unsympathetically, on the reins. "Keep line there White Sock," he ordered impatiently.

After a short time the road turned out of sight of the main camp and away from the fortress. The old Sage relaxed visibly nodding his approval and punching the air in satisfaction. Everyone felt calmer. Even Aunt Beth looked a little less poorly, Cathy thought.

As they reached the first stream, crossing their path, the cart jolted to a halt and they all rolled backwards unexpectedly. Searlan's face darkened visibly, preparing to strike.

"Drink up White Sock. Come on Princess," the driver called to the horses. "We shall not be stopping again this morning."

Searlan seized the moment and slipped out of the back of the wagon. Jaden and Jack jumped beside him not entirely sure of the old man's intentions. Cathy stayed beside Aunt Beth to look after her as best she could. Searlan surprised Jack with his nimbleness and precision; he moved to within striking distance of the fat, balding driver who was busily stuffing his face with a large loaf of bread.

"Shhhh!" he hissed, placing his finger on his lips and looking sternly at the two boys.

Chas had a big floppy hat hanging down the back of his neck, tied by a long leather cord. One hand was holding the bread, the other, a flagon of lukewarm beer. He munched, obliviously, on the tasty crust and looked longingly into the pot in his other hand. The aroma of hops and malt drifted up into his senses. He loved his work.

In one swift fluid movement, Searlan swept his gnarled staff over his shoulder and cracked the man, powerfully, on the side of the head. Chas dropped backwards, the crust of bread still protruding from his mouth and the pot of beer spilled all across the seat beside him. The commotion caused the horses to jolt forwards into the stream.

"Help me get this overweight oaf off our transport," the Sage commanded the boys. He grinned with a good deal of satisfaction at his precision of his blow.

All three splashed through the knee deep stream and leapt briskly up onto the seat. Searlan steered the horses across to the other side and, between them, they managed to roll the fat driver over the edge. He fell painfully in a big crumpled heap on the ground.

"Never mind him you two, we go now," Searlan shook the reins violently to drive the horses onwards. Hurrying them along at almost a trot; they quickly left the ford behind. These were slow weight-carriers; the drays were not used to being driven at speed. They wouldn't continue like this for long, but he needed to put some distance between themselves and the fallen driver.

"Hold tight in the back, it's a bit bumpy ahead." They bounced so violently that Jack nearly fell off the seat. Jaden grabbed him at the last moment and they burst into laughter at the shock and relief.

"Nearly lost you too," Jaden grinned at his friend.

As they reached the next fork in the road the old Sage steered them towards the east. They bounced along over several thick tree roots. Poor Cathy had a terrible journey trying to comfort her Aunt.

"Sorry Cathy, we have to hurry for a few more minutes yet." Searlan was desperate to take full advantage of this opportunity. They continued at a quick pace for about ten minutes before slowing the drays to their usual walking pace.

"Keep a good lookout everyone. This place is far from safe and we are easy targets up here."

Thankfully, nothing out of the ordinary had happened for over an hour; Searlan relaxed, confident they had managed to escape. Again the Sage steered them on an easterly fork and this brought the wagon out onto the fringes of the savannah. They dropped down the gentle slope of the hill and out into the grassland.

"We're well on our way now and, with luck, should reach the central lake within a couple of hours. How is Aunt Beth doing Cathy?" Searlan asked.

A voice came from behind the heavyweight canvas flap. "She's very poorly Searlan. All that jolting and thumping hasn't helped. She has a fever again and is drifting in and out of consciousness. I'm really worried about her, are you sure there is nothing you can do?"

The girl was close to tears again and feeling completely helpless.

"Sorry Cathy, we must keep pushing onwards. We'll stop in another couple of hours; the road should be less bumpy now."

Aunt Beth settled down as the passage became easier. Cathy tended to her as best she could. Some time later she remembered what she had meant to say to earlier. "Oh, by the way Searlan, I need to get back to Aunt Beth's cottage. I've left something of great importance there. Something left to me by my Mother. I'm so afraid that it may have been found and stolen." Her voice had pain and regret running all through it. She had never felt so ashamed of herself for losing these important items.

Searlan slowed the wagon and opened the flap, behind him, to look at Cathy. "You haven't lost THIS by any chance?" the Sage had a twinkle in his eye; he rummaged around by the side of him.

Cathy looked quizzically.

"I think THIS is what you are looking for?" The sage lifted something lying at the edge of the wagon seat. He handed her a cloth wrapped bundle.

"What?... How?... When?..." Cathy could hardly speak to thank the old man enough. She squeezed him tightly; hugging him, she sobbed with joy.

Jaden poked his head around the edge of the flap to see her face. He clambered alongside the overjoyed girl and looked at his smiling grandfather. "Perhaps you'd like this little trinket Cathy - I picked it up on our travels?" He put his hand in his pocket and pulled out the bracelet he'd found, in the dirt, outside the cottage. "You shouldn't be leaving this lying around now should you?" he said with an even wider grin on his face.

Cathy nearly burst; she was completely overcome with joy and gratitude. Jaden was shocked and embarrassed as Cathy reached over and pulled him towards her. Giving him a big kiss; he turned a bright shade of red. "Thank you both. Thank you, I love you both so very much. I thought I'd never see either of these again. You've no idea how important these two things are to me."

"Forgive me child, but I certainly do know their importance to you, and for that matter, to all of us too." Searlan was happier than he'd been in a long time. Things were beginning to turn out for the best.

The two huge drays, with their long thick tails, made light work of cutting across the savannah. Their enormous hooves trampled grass, bush and shrub. The ground was firm and dry and made the passage an easy task. All the while Searlan looked this way and that, never still or content for a single moment, he remained totally alert.

"I almost believe we've made our escape." The old sage declared. "Well done all of you, well done."

Chapter 10 - Battle Plans

General Simian Pen-D'anatè; tall, imposing and ruthless leader of the Blade army, sat with a face like thunder - he didn't suffer failure: absolute obedience was expected, complete devotion required, unquestionable loyalty demanded; accusingly, he stared at the three soldiers in front of his desk. All was silent in the room except for one nerve-wrenching distraction. Pen-D'anatè tapped his fingernails repeatedly on the polished oak surface; a slow, irritating noise designed to intimidate. Systematically, he focussed directly into the eyes of each dungeon-guard in turn - none of the men dared to hold his gaze; fear of death ran though their veins. Not a word had been spoken but one-by-one they shrivelled under the tension; the small man in the centre shook visibly.

"Tell me, you snivelling fool, where is the girl and her sick Aunt? How the hell did you lose this child and an invalid who could barely walk?" Every syllable carried a terrible threat.

The man shook, uncontrollably, unable to answer.

Pen-D'anatè's thick black hair, broad shoulders and immaculate uniform added, significantly, to his fearsome persona. The thin curved scar across his right eye (testament to an early battle encounter) flickered as his face contorted. "Do you have any idea how important this girl was?" The General paused, grinding his teeth menacingly, he continued "and YOU let her escape."

The prisoner gulped trying his best to wet his dry mouth. This General was cold-blooded; many had witnessed first-hand how he disposed of his enemies - or any member of his staff who failed him. Relentlessly cruel: he killed for retribution; he killed for effect, and most of all he killed for pleasure. The man tried to answer but just stammered some gibberish in response.

Pen-D'anatè's patience evaporated. "Take this worthless idiot away!" he screamed, directing his order at one of the five, hand-picked, guards positioned around the room. The Blade snapped to attention before locking the prisoner in a vice-like grip; the fool struggled briefly and, in a final desperate act of madness, begged pitifully for his life. Instinctively, Pen-D'anatè reacted: with one swift, fluid movement he drew his sword; one powerful thrust sent it deep into the prisoner's chest, and one cruel twist finished the act. The man slumped dead in the guard's arms.

No-one dared move. The General wiped the blood from his blade on the dead prisoner's sleeve. Replacing the shining weapon with a deliberate force, he turned to the terrified prisoner on the right, "Well? Where were you when they disappeared?"

The man tried, pathetically, to make up some excuses about locked doors and regular checks on the prisoners - these fell on deaf ears.

"Get them out of my sight," Pen-D'anatè bellowed.

Both were hauled away to a certain death. The General took a deep breath, held it for a second, and then breathed out very slowly and deliberately, "I'm surrounded by incompetents".

Turning to one of his Lieutenants, and with the cold calmness of absolute power, ordered. "Get the men ready, I will address my troops at noon. We will advance tomorrow at first light, and there'd better not be any more slip-ups."

The Lieutenant stamped to attention, saluted smartly. "As you command General, Sir," the soldier turned at right angles, stamped his foot and marched away swiftly.

Pen-D'anatè walked slowly into the planning room. Maps and charts adorned the walls. A large, rectangular, table filled the floor. His six senior officers waited patiently for the final orders.

"I expect this invasion to be swift. The miserable band of Resistance has scattered; they're undisciplined and will pose little threat to my well armed and well trained Blades." The General paced up and down clearly still agitated about the loss of the girl and her Aunt. "The Elder has provided us with a powerful ally; the Blue creatures will assist in ridding me of this pathetic irritation."

Each officer nodded in agreement. Pen-D'anatè clenched his fists tightly, slamming them on the table, "I want them eradicated once and for all."

***

In the courtyard, below the central tower, Captain (Spike) Williams had his small team of elite investigative staff examining the scene of the escape. His nick-name, "Spike", came not from his sticking up hair, but from his indiscriminate use of a needle-sharp implement. The tool was used, to good effect, to extract information from unwilling detainees. His team had already found the key used to open the door and let out the prisoners.

"This was an inside job," he declared authoritatively. "No-one could have achieved this without inside help. We have a traitor or spy amongst us, the General must be informed."

The team nodded in agreement.

"Webb, go and find out who was on the gate duty last night and this morning. I want to interview every one of them. Someone must have seen something."

Captain Williams was the General's most trusted aide. He was short, painfully thin and sickly looking with a hideous permanent smirking grin that made reading his mood impossible. His thick, spiky black hair was greasy and almost shone; bushy black eyebrows met in the middle of his forehead.

"No stone shall remain unturned; I'll find this treacherous spy."

The Captain had successfully served his General for over twenty years; his reputation was even more terrifying than his superior's. All knew his methods were cruel, cold and effective. Every Blade dreaded any possible encounter with Spike; they knew their life was at risk for the least sign of weakness.

"Whoever is responsible for this will pay dearly?"

The two gate guards, of the night before, were hauled before Captain Williams. He stepped uncomfortably close to the first man and spoke coldly into his ear. "You let the girl and her Aunt escape from the fortress last night. Fool."

The man pulled himself up to his fullest height and spoke straight ahead without any eye contact with the Captain. "No Sir Captain Sir, I let no-one escape. I kept a full log of all movements Sir."

Trooper Western nearly spat out the final; Sir. "There were no unofficial entries or exits on MY watch."

The Captain screwed up his nose in disgust; he gave an almost imperceptible nod to one of his staff. At the signal, Jackson, was already checking the log for all movements. The terrified guard went on to give a detailed account of each person, wagon and delivery that moved through the gate. A brief glance in the direction of Jackson confirmed that his story was corroborated by the log entries. Spike then turned his attention to Skimmer; the thin, gangly guard who'd been confronted by Searlan.

"So it was you then."

The finality of the statement made the man visibly shrink. Again, Captain Williams flicked a quick momentary look at one of his staff. This order ensured that Western, the first guard, was quickly removed and returned to his normal duties. The man scurried away without daring to look back. He knew he'd escaped a call too close for comfort.

"Explain to me Skimmer, why did you help these traitors escape?"

Skimmer poured out a minute-by-minute account of every visitor through the gate. Desperate to save his skin; he covered the smallest detail, accurately. Spike sent one of his staff to check whether any special delivery, of water, had been requested by the officer's mess. He repeatedly questioned the blubbering guard about the encounter with Searlan.

"Your story does not hold up, you are lying to me," he accused

The member of staff returned and confirmed that no such request was ever made.

"You failed the General; take him away," the order was final.

Captain Williams appeared nervously before the General to make his report. He never liked to deliver bad news, and this was the worst possible scenario. Explaining all he'd discovered he relayed his assessment; a spy was somewhere amongst them. He concluded, this audacious escape could only have been conducted, successfully, with inside help.

Pen-D'anatè contemplated the report for a few seconds; his face darkened. "I suspected as much Spike. I want this spy and his supporters routed out; they must all be found - I'll not suffer traitors. Whoever dared to help the Resistance scum will be sliced into a hundred pieces and fed to my dogs. Do it quickly, I intend to move my army out tomorrow and I do not want any plans to go astray."

The Captain nodded approvingly. "It will be done General. I'll not rest until the spies are identified." He felt relieved the focus remained on the perpetrators and very excited at the prospect of wheedling out the traitors.

Over three thousand Blades stood rigidly to attention facing the battlements of the fortress. General Pen-D'anatè surveyed his assembled army and rightly felt invincible. Never, in the recent history of this land, had such an army existed. Each man wore a suit of heavy leather. All carried a sharp, gleaming, sword and many held a spear aloft; they were accurately called Blades.

"Now there is a sight to behold." The General lived for these fleeting moments. Pen-D'anatè knew - whether through fear or blind loyalty - they would die for him; his every command would be carried out to the letter.

"Nothing can stand in the way of my army," he derided.

He was destined to become the Supreme Emperor of every square kilometre of Danthienne. He'd already decided to rename this conquered country, Lancaria, in memory of his late mother. Pen-D'anatè harboured an overwhelming desire for power and total domination. He raised himself to his full height and thrust out his chest. Many polished medals and insignia jangled together on his uniform. The sight of his army made him quiver secretly with excitement.

"Today!" he boomed.

"Today, we will finally remove this blight that has distracted us from our task."

The troops cheered in unison.

"Today, we will drive the scum back into the hills."

Another cheer reverberated out, louder this time with whistles and shouts.

"Today, you will be victorious in battle and we will be conquerors of the world."

The eruption of noise, so great, seemed to shake the foundations of the fortress. It was highlighted by hundreds of drawn gleaming Blades glistening in the midday sunshine.

"Today!" he finally bellowed. "We march to glory."

The noise became so great the sound could be heard in every room in the fortress.

"GEN – ER – AL."

"GEN – ER – AL."

"GEN – ER – AL."

The troops emphasised the chant by banging their swords, in time, onto their leather leggings. The atmosphere was electric and made every soldier feel invincible too.

***

High up in the tallest tower of the fortress, a shrivelled and bent old man looked out through a small open window. Dressed from head to toe in a flowing blue gown, the contrast of colour made his heavily lined ashen face seem even starker. Each wrinkle carried a lengthy story highlighting the ravages of great age. At first glance, the wizened individual appeared impossibly frail. He moved slowly, his aching joints never kept pace with his pin-sharp mind these days. Only his eyes gave any indication of the power hidden within his frame. Set deep in his sunken face, two bright green emeralds pierced your soul as easily as an arrow. He grimaced, watching Pen-D'anatè strutting around like a stuffed cockerel.

"All those ridiculous medals shining and clattering on the breast of his uniform; how I despise this fool?" he sneered. "Still; he will achieve my aims and I'll dispose of him when the time is right."

The Elder turned to the blue humming creature, which had just appeared through the MoonBridge and now hovered a few feet away.

"My Lord Tzerach (*Ser-rash*), together we shall wipe this place clean and you shall have the resources you need to build a new homeland. This world will be cleansed and pure."

Tzerach transformed itself into a more plausible human form and spoke slowly to the Elder.

"Alanthian, you have continually proved yourself to be a worthy servant of the Shumiat. The Council have empowered me to deliver a gift for your services; step closer and I will repair your damaged body."

The old man approached the creature, slightly bemused, and a little apprehensive.

"What did he mean – repair my damaged body?"

The Elder stepped closer to the Shumiat. He was bathed in a deep-blue oscillating light emanating from the heart of the creature. His body contorted briefly before straightening; magically, the lines on his face receded. In a few moments the ravages of age faded from his tired old body and he felt completely new and reborn.

The creature hummed softly and then continued. "Your body has been rejuvenated. Time has been unwound and every cell repaired.

You are now approximately eighteen of your years again. Enjoy your new found revitalisation."

The Elder turned to look at the mirror, on the far wall of the small chamber; he couldn't believe the sight that confronted him. "I don't know what to say my Lord. I'm speechless."

The Shumiat waited before speaking again. "Do not trust this General Pen-D'anatè. He has aspirations well above his station and must be treated with great care. Whilst he remains useful to us he should be allowed to function. Maintain caution Elder; he plans to usurp you and will not hesitate to end your life. I'll not be able to repair a completely broken body."

A very much younger man now stood before the Shumiat creature. "Yes my Lord Tzerach, I heed your warnings. Please thank the generosity of the Great Council for their gift. My body was becoming too frail to continue my work." He paused to admire his own reflection. The Elder thoroughly approved the newly rejuvenated Alanthian looking back at him. "You are so young, fit and handsome," he thought approvingly.

The Elder smiled menacingly, "The fool will only remain in place as long as it suits our mutual purpose. I've my closest and most trusted spies in the heart of his order, he suspects nothing. One signal from me and he will be despatched without problem or delay."

The coldness and matter-of-fact attitude was too chilling to contemplate. The Elder had no thought or concern for the miserable lives of the soldiers that would, unwittingly, conduct his bidding.

Lord Tzerach hummed approvingly. "I leave you now Elder to become accustomed to your new body. Ready yourself for our forthcoming invasion, the time approaches."

Alanthian bowed very low to the ground as the Shumiat disappeared back across the MoonBridge. He watched it fade from view and then turned back to the mirror on the wall.

"I'm stronger than I've ever been. None shall stand in my way."

***

The General stepped back from his podium overlooking the battlements. He barked orders to his Lieutenants to make all necessary arrangements for departure at first light tomorrow. He then returned to his chambers to await the inevitable audience with the Elder.

"How I despised that shrivelled old mystic. All that mumbo-jumbo and bowing and scraping to those infernal Shumiat. Doesn't he realise just who runs this army?"

Standing in front of the small window, he looked out over the savannah. "Tomorrow we will sweep across you like a plague of hungry locusts: nothing will remain, and nothing will stand in our way. Once the Resistance are crushed I'll rid myself of that meddlesome Elder once and for all." He grinned evilly rubbing his hands together. From the corner of his eye he caught a glimpse of movement at the door. A very young man, of about eighteen years, stood in the doorway. The General wondered why he was dressed in the garb of the Elder.

"Maybe this was his grandchild – if he had one." Half drawing his sword in readiness, the General growled. "How did you get past my guards? Who the hell are you?" He was taken aback by the ferocity of the response.

"Fool, how dare you draw your sword to me? I'm Alanthian the Elder; rejuvenated!" The Elder waved his hand and the General found himself sitting down involuntarily and replacing his sword into its scabbard. "No guard, or any other fool under your command for that matter, would be able to block my passage."

He released his hand; Pen-D'anatè snapped back to his own control.

The General was genuinely amazed at the transformation before him. "How is this possible? You look like a barely grown child?" He pondered this dreadful development momentarily and realised this complicated matters significantly.

"The mighty Lord Tzerach regenerated my body; a token of appreciation for my years of loyal services to the Shumiat. I'm reborn:

strong and agile as a youth," he looked down his nose at the gaping General. "Rest assured, my mind and resolve are equally fit and prepared, do not make the mistake of underestimating my powers." Alanthian demonstrated his capabilities by flicking his hand again and making the General snap to attention.

Pen-D'anatè couldn't help himself; he swallowed hard at the threat this boy possessed.

The Elder released him and commanded. "Tomorrow you will lead this army across the savannah and will remove all remnants of the Resistance. Make no mistake; I expect this to be swift and efficient. The mighty Lord Tzerach has graciously offered some of his best Blues to assist in the clean up. Neither he, nor I, will tolerate any failure."

The threat only made the General all the more determined. He thought to himself. "Yes, my overconfident young Elder, you'll squirm on the point of my Blade. Mighty Lord Tzerach or no mighty Lord Tzerach, I'll make you pay dearly."

The General's inner thoughts didn't reflect across his placid face. Instead, he said out loud. "Of course Elder, forgive my ignorance; my simple military mind could not possibly conceive that you could be rejuvenated. I bathe in your great good fortune. Tomorrow, my army will sweep aside these pigs and the land will be rid of them forever." He smiled subserviently and bowed his head imperceptibly in deference.

The Elder just stared at him closely before spinning on his heels and leaving the room without a further word.

Chapter 11 - Preparations

The morning sun was especially hot; dust-devils flitted across the dry grassland whipping spiralled vortices several metres into the air. Searlan, weary after the exertion of the rescue, left the boys to drive the wagon. "I must rest a while Cathy, I think I'll have a short nap. Wake me if you have to."

Cathy nodded politely. She loved this old man and understood the toll the previous few hours had taken.

The last audience with Lujnima left Searlan realising the finality of his fate. He would soon have to pass over the Sageship to his grandson and he wondered if the boy was genuinely ready. "No less ready than me," he recalled, drifting into his dreams. The old man fell asleep, snoring in quiet contentment.

Aunt Beth barely stirred for over an hour; Cathy dozed, in the heat, stroking her Aunt's head with a small dampened cloth.

In the front of the wagon, Jack and Jaden took turns at guiding the huge drays. The horses walked, without complaint, for many kilometres; they seemed as strong as ever. Jack thought this was great fun and he quickly forgot the severity of their predicament. He saw the central lake glistening brightly ahead. "We should be there in about ten minutes," he estimated.

Hardly needing to guide the horses; they could smell the water and were heading directly for the lake. The road was a little bumpy; occasionally, they would hit a larger rock and the wheel would clonk over the top before juddering down with a disconcerting crunch. Jaden stood up on the seat and peered ahead; shielding the strong sunlight with his hand he said "we must be careful Jack, we don't know who may be around."

The boy shook himself back to the reality at hand. He remembered the unpleasant encounter with the soldiers and how he only managed to escape because of his brave dog Brandy. Realising it had been more than two days since he'd seen his trusted friend; panic gripped him, "Where've you disappeared to?"

The horses walked straight into the shallows at the edge of the lake. They lowered their mouths into the cool waters and drank thirstily. Jack had never seen large horses quenching their thirst before and was amazed at the huge quantities they consumed.

The sudden halt made Searlan sit up. "What's happened?" he asked; bewildered at the strange surroundings of the hay bail and wagon floor.

Cathy reassured him, "we've reached the lake. The horses are taking a refreshing drink, that's all."

Searlan relaxed and lay back down. His old bones definitely told him his time was near.

Cathy slipped out of the back of the wagon and joined Jack and Jaden. Both were sitting in the refreshing water up to their waists. "What are you two idiots doing?" she laughed at the sight of them.

Jack splashed his hand through the water and sent a huge spray in Cathy's direction. She giggled loudly, slipping off her shoes, and paddled in beside them.

"Oh this feels so good," she said, laying back in the water and wetting her hair. "It's so hot and sticky in there."

The others agreed and moved out a little further to have a quick swim.

"The sun will soon dry us again," Jaden laughed.

The three splashed and played around for about ten minutes without a single care in the world. Finally, Cathy walked back to the shore and gathered up the water skins from the side of the wagon and refilled them.

"I'll take Aunt Beth a wet cloth to cool her down. I think this heat is making her worse but what can we do?"

The horses were removed from their harnesses and allowed to wander off to feed. They didn't walk far; they were both very well trained and extremely placid in nature. The two munched hungrily on the plentiful grass and vegetation surrounding the lake. Searlan had awoken, properly this time, and climbed down from the wagon. He stripped off his shirt and bathed in the refreshing coolness.

"We had better see what we can find to eat," he said.

Scouting around; they found berries and other fruit. The old man added sweet biscuits from his bag. They all sat together and feasted on their meagre fare.

"We'll make for the hills later; let's rest the horses here for a while." Searlan declared, looking up at the scorching sun. "We must try to reach one of the Resistance camps and see if there is any medicine for Aunt Beth."

"How will you find one Searlan?" Cathy asked innocently.

The old Sage looked at the girl and winked with a wry grin. "I have my sources and spies too, my girl. We'll find one okay."

She couldn't help grinning back at the old man. "I do so love him to bits. He's just how I would've loved my Grandpa to have been," she thought longingly.

The drays were rounded up without any problem and reattached to their harnesses. Climbing aboard the wagon; they travelled around the lake for about twenty minutes before heading off towards the tallest of the distant hills.

They had barely left the lake side when Searlan sat bolt upright and looked directly ahead. "Shhh," he pulled the wagon to a halt but it was already too late. Out from the bushes walked fifteen or so well armed soldiers. Searlan wasn't entirely sure they were Resistance as several wore Blade swords.

A voice from behind them called out. "So we meet again Searlan Sage of Sages. Don't tell me YOU actually rescued your young friend from the fortress? I take my hat off to you and your incredibly brave companions."

The familiar face of Sergeant-at-Arms Healworth, and a few more of his brigade, greeted them. Searlan was relieved but accepted the praise offered with a dismissive wave of his hand.

"Sergeant, we must get to your main camp as quickly as possible. I've important information regarding the enemy. And, I've a very sick woman who needs immediate medical attention."

The Sergeant was concerned and offered his services. "My grandfather and uncle were medics." He and Cathy climbed into the back of the wagon and spent some time tending to Aunt Beth. His diagnosis wasn't promising. She's had a nasty blow to the head.

Jack watched with interest. "It's called a concussion isn't it?"

Both Cathy and the Sergeant looked at him in surprise.

"Where did you learn of such a thing Jack?" Cathy asked surprised.

"At school I guess," he answered nonchalantly.

"Do you know the treatment for this condition, as well, young Sir?" The Sergeant enquired, clearly impressed by Jack's knowledge of medicine.

"Not exactly: I seem to remember you had to sit the patient up, keep them awake, give them plenty to drink and make sure they rest - or something like that?"

"Why didn't you say this before Jack?" Cathy asked surprised.

"Dunno," replied Jack with a shrug of his shoulders. "Just didn't think I knew any more than anyone else. That's all."

The Resistance fighters escorted the wagon across the savannah and up into the foot hills; progress was steady and uneventful, they entered the main camp before sundown. Searlan was led away to speak with the senior officers whist Cathy accompanied her Aunt into the field hospital. Two very friendly doctors rushed around examining and assessing Beth's injuries.

"It's alright Miss," one reassured Cathy. "We'll take good care of your Aunt."

Cathy briefly stroked her Aunt's head and kissed her tenderly. "I love you so much," she said; a tear rolling down her cheek. "Please get better; I couldn't bear life without you." She squeezed her Aunt's hand before turning away and walking outside to find Jack and Jaden.

***

Group Captain Smithers welcomed the old Sage into his tent. "You have some news of the Blades I'm told Sir," he said looking intently at the old man before him. He too, had heard tell of this mystical old Sage and the deeds he'd purportedly conducted. The Group Captain was a little in awe of this infamous man.

Searlan relayed the story of the rescue and the number of soldiers camped outside the fortress wall. His detailed account took over an hour. The Group Captain's admiration for the sheer audacity, bravery and unrivalled courage, which this wizened old man had displayed, grew with every word. He signalled to one of his staff to assemble his line officers and prepare for an important briefing.

"This is the bitterest news I've had in a long time. So, they are finally preparing to wipe out any possible resistance to their invasion. What can we hope to do against such overwhelming forces? If the numbers are really as you have described, it would be suicide to face up to them. Let alone, these infernal Blue creatures."

The Group Captain paused in thought for a few seconds, his face glum and darkened. "I suspect they will drive straight across the savannah and overrun our lands. With their exceptional superiority in numbers we will be overpowered; there's little prospect for resistance on our part."

Searlan agreed; he suggested another option would be to disappear into hiding. "You could wait for a better opportunity to continue resisting their invasion. Death and honour now, will win you no battles in the future," he ruminated.

"Exactly," the Group Captain agreed.

The soldiers and old Sage continued their deliberations for several hours.

Cathy found Jack and Jaden sitting by a makeshift fence. The two drays had been penned with the other horses in the corral. They munched contentedly on generous quantities of fresh hay.

"What happens now? Cathy, have you any ideas?" Jack smiled as she approached, he'd grown very fond of this girl and his heart pulsed.

"I think we must wait for Searlan to finish briefing the captain. Then, he may have a plan for us."

"Grandfather can talk the hind legs off a mule when he gets going," Jaden moaned. "We could be hanging around for a while. How's Aunt Beth?"

Cathy explained about the nice doctors in the hospital and how worried she was.

Jaden held her hand and squeezed it gently. "She'll be okay Cathy, just you wait and see. She's made it this far after all."

She didn't know why but she burst into tears and sobbed with her head in her hands. Jack placed his arm around her shoulder. Cathy felt comforted and close to Jack; she loved this young man.

***

The evening had closed in around them and the air became decidedly cooler. Searlan finished briefing the senior officers and sat beside a camp-fire. A couple of pots were suspended above the flames to boil water, and cook a few small animals and root vegetables. The smell of the stew wafted around the tents and had hungry stomachs rumbling.

"That army will not remain at the fortress for long," Searlan surmised. "Within the week, I reckon. The Resistance must make their escape very soon: tonight or tomorrow at the latest; otherwise they'll be caught off guard. I've advised the Group Captain to take his troops into hiding. That way there'll be a Resistance after they have swarmed over these hills. If they don't; this place will be a blood-bath: few will survive."

Searlan's description was grim. He continued. "No-one in this land can stand in the way of that army. We must make plans and preparations to meet them on our terms some time later; not on their terms here in the hills."

All three looked on with fear and dread. "What shall we do Grandfather?" asked Jaden.

"Will we be asked to join the Resistance?" Cathy wondered.

Jack sat silently for a moment and then said. "How can anything stand up to all those soldiers? This Resistance is just a small band of villagers; they don't seem to be armed like the Blade soldiers. What do you think they can do Searlan?"

The old Sage never answered any of the questions being fired at him. Instead, he sat quietly mesmerised by the flickering flames. There was something very intriguing about the two pots being caressed by the deadly touch of the fire. The three children waited patiently until he looked at them and announced. "We must make our own preparations. Jaden, you must assume the Sageship, Cathy you must contact Lujnima for guidance and Jack, you must return across the bridge and return with the other staff."

All three were taken aback by Searlan's bluntness. Each of them tried to speak at the same time.

The old man put up his hand to stop them and smiled weakly. "Your questions will have to wait for the morning. I'm just too exhausted now and I don't think we will be overrun by first light. Let's get some rest and face the new day refreshed."

None could argue with that excellent suggestion and they all retired for the night.

***

Jack woke confused: he thought he could hear Brandy barking. His brain told him he was back in his own bed but his aching limbs gave a different account. Rubbing the sleep from his eyes, he blinked several times before he knew where he was. Lying close by were Searlan,

Jaden and Cathy. The smell of musty army canvas drifted up his nose. A pebble, as big as a house it seemed, poked sharply in his back. Jack groaned; he tried, unsuccessfully, to rub the sore area. He heard a dog barking again.

"That is Brandy, I'm sure of it."

The boy jumped up; dusted himself off and slipped through the flap at the end of the tent. The sun wasn't yet over the horizon but it was already lightening the sky. A dog was definitely barking on the other side of the camp. Jaden awoke and stepped along side. "Sounds like Brandy," he said to his friend. "Let's go see."

Cathy poked her head out of the tent. "Wait for me you two."

The three walked quickly, over dew laden grass, in the direction of the barking. The sounds came from behind a long hedgerow edging a tiny brook. A small group of soldiers laughed and joked at the behaviour of the dog; he'd been barking incessantly at another group of soldiers. They talked closely together, across the small brook, and seemed agitated. Jack immediately recognised Brandy.

"There you are you stupid dog." Jack whistled loudly to his friend. The dog stopped in his tracks at the call. Brandy turned and bounded over to the boy, with such force, he knocked him clean off his feet. Jack wrestled, playfully, with his pet; Bandy's tail wagged so hard his whole body rocked back and forth.

"Where have you been?" Jack scolded, between the laughter, at his dog's attempt to lick every part of his face. Even with both hands covering his eyes and nose, Brandy still managed to nuzzle in between his fingers.

"Stop it, enough Brandy," he pleaded uselessly.

Eventually, they settled down; after many hugs and pats on the head, Brandy stood panting heavily and staring expectantly at Jack.

"I've missed you boy," Jack was relieved to have been rejoined with his friend. "Mum would've killed me if I'd lost you."

Calls from the men caught their attention. One approached; "So you're his owner are you? Trevor's my name, and who might you be?"

Jack gave him a brief introduction but was concerned about the group of men that Brandy had been barking at.

Trevor continued. "Seems this crazy mutt had a run in with old Jed over there; he went mad at the sight of him. Poor old Jed fell over backwards to get away."

Jack looked up in fear at the mention of the name and the blood drained from his face. Jed, the one who had grabbed him, stood large and fearsome. This was the very same soldier he'd hit with the spear; Jack cowered backwards as the man recognised him.

"It's the filthy Blade spy," Jed screamed. He limped towards the boy; his face like thunder and spitting lightning. "I'm gonna snap your stinkin' neck."

The others looked around expecting someone to be behind them.

"He means me," Jack pleaded hurriedly, desperate to find some hole to disappear into.

Trevor stood in front of Jed and told him to wait. He then grabbed Jack by the arm. "I'll get to the bottom of this Jed; before you do any more damage."

Jack was then led away to explain the spy accusation. Cathy and Jaden rushed to find the Sage.

Captain Connors sat, tight lipped, studying Jack. The boy stood in front of the Captain with Jed on one side and Trevor between them. Jed had already blurted out how the boy had been captured whilst wearing a blood-stained Blade. How he'd escaped after Jed had been attacked by the vicious dog and finally beaten by his own spear. He also described how the boy had kicked the legs from under his friend and colleague Greg.

"I'm tellin' yer boss, this kid's an enemy spy; 'e should be strung up." Jed gripped his sword, so tightly, he nearly crushed the handle.

"These are very serious accusations against you boy," the Captain said grimly. "What have you to say in your defence?"

Before Jack could explain; the Sergeant-at-Arms and Searlan stepped through the open tent flap.

"Sir, I can vouch for the integrity of this young man. He is no Blade: in fact he is a very good ally of the Resistance and any accusations of spying laid against him are completely false. Here Sir, is Searlan - Sage of Sages; you have probably heard of him, he also vouches for the boy and calls him friend."

The Captain was impressed. "You have very influential friends; young man."

He dismissed the protesting Jed and ordered him back to his team.

"Thank you Trevor, I'll handle this from here."

"Aye-Aye Sir!" Trevor left the group and returned to his squad as well.

The Captain was told the basic outline of the events, to date, and was equally impressed as all others who had heard the tales. "You are indeed friends of the Resistance," he concluded. "Young Master Ferns; please do not cross Jed or Greg if you can possibly avoid it. They are both well meaning Resistance fighters but are not renowned for their gifts of common sense."

Jack nodded apologetically. "I was frightened; I thought they would kill me."

The Captain accepted Jack's account and dismissed them all. "You are free to go young Sir."

***

Searlan called a meeting. Jack, Jaden, Cathy, and of course, Brandy, who had not left his master's side for a moment since he'd found him the night before, sat together facing the old man. The sun had just risen and the Sage decided to answer the outstanding questions.

Turning first to Jack, Searlan announced, "You must return to your own world; cross the bridge with all haste, find Tel-Vah-Nar and return with her to this land. You'll know what to do when the time is right." He paused briefly then declared solemnly, "we will not meet again young friend."

To Cathy he said, "My time is almost done; I can never seek an audience with Lujnima again. You must confront her about the hidden Guardian; she must know something."

Finally, with a crackle in his voice, he held his grandson's hands and said, "You're nearly ready my child. Soon you will inherit all the knowledge that was passed to me and all that I've gathered too. Fear not little one for I'll always be at your side, you only need to look and you will find me right there with you."

Time wasn't on their side; the enemy, gathered around the fortress across the savannah, was even more terrifying to contemplate.

"You all must act quickly. You cannot afford to dally around, the Blade war is upon us."

Chapter 12 - Sisters

Christina-Louise Ferns heard strange mumblings from the next bedroom. "What's that stupid brother of mine up to now?" she wondered. Her bed-side clock showed the time was close to midnight. "He's been sleep-walking again, I bet."

Tina-Lu quietly crept across the landing; peeping around the door of Jack's bedroom, she saw him holding the cane, chanting the calling incantation and watched the MoonBridge come into view. She could hardly believe her eyes when she saw her brother place the cane under his covers; grab Brandy's collar and step onto the bridge. The dog turned back to her and gave a little whimper.

"It's okay boy," Jack said reassuringly.

The girl's mouth opened and closed, in shock, when the pair disappeared from sight and the MoonBridge faded. She blinked several times and pinched herself, to see if it was her who was sleep-walking. In total disbelief, Tina-Lu double checked the bed to see if her brother was really still in it. He wasn't!

Sitting on the side of the bed, Tina-Lu continuously shook her head. "This is nuts. What on earth is going on? I must be dreaming." Her brain reeled for several minutes unable to grasp the reality of the bizarre experience. Suddenly, the horror of finding her brother's bed empty made Tina-Lu afraid. She took a deep breath, ready to scream. A light, in front of her, glowed; she gulped, as the MoonBridge reformed. Taking two hasty steps backwards, she watched the full glory of the bridge reappear. The girl nearly fainted when Jack and Brandy bundled out from the light.

"What the hell are you doing here Sis?" Jack's face was the picture of shock and surprise. "And, what are you doing in my bedroom?"

"Wh...Where have you just been?" she stammered.

Jack paid little attention to his sister; he was busy looking for the cane. "Where did I leave it?"

"Oh my giddy aunt, what has happened to you?" she said staring at his torn jacket and filthy clothes. "And what has happened to your arm?" she added, hardly able to miss the thick bandage wrapped around his elbow.

Jack just shrugged, frantically scanning the room for clues.

"Mum's gonna kill you when she sees this," Tina-Lu insisted in a hushed whisper. Her insistence spelt out 'listen to me or I'm telling'.

"Okay Sis, I get the message, loud and clear. Now where did I leave it? You haven't taken my silver handled cane have you?"

"What on earth is going on Jack? One second you disappear with Brandy through that light thing. Now you reappear a few moments later. How come you're a wreck and your arm is all bandaged."

Jack shrugged his shoulders again trying his best to ignore her questions and find the cane. He flung dirty washing from one pile to another, chucked books and games off his chest of drawers. He even looked underneath his bed.

"Well little brother, what is that thing?" she pointed at the fading MoonBridge.

Jack put his hand up dismissively. "Can't tell you now, sorry, too much to do…"

He finally lost patience and cursed angrily. "Where the hell did I put it? You sure you haven't taken my cane Sis? This is important!" He pushed her aside roughly in utter frustration.

"You are so stupid brother, I sometimes wonder if we actually come from the same gene pool at all." Tina-Lu lifted the bed covers and pulled the cane out from under them. As any older sister would do, in this situation, she held the cane tantalisingly and said, "Is this what you're looking for?" The sarcasm in her voice was enough to incite Jack's anger.

He grabbed the cane from her hands, with surprising ferocity, and spun on his heels quickly placing his back to his sister. Holding the magical staff, he pointed it at the fading MoonBridge.

"Watch this Sis and then call me stupid." Before the light was able to completely vanish he demanded, "hold, by the power of Lujnima; open for the Guardian."

At his command the MoonBridge immediately brightened and reformed.

Tina-Lu's mouth fell open uncontrollably. She was incapable of speech as the glistening, swirling moonbeams danced all around her body.

"Well Sis: you coming or what?" Jack reached for her arm and gripped it tightly. "I've important work to do and you standing there - mouth wide open like a goldfish - will not help my friends."

Jack pulled Tina-Lu towards him and half dragged her into the light. Brandy instinctively jumped straight after them both. In a flash they were gone.

The transition took his sister's breath away: her mind couldn't register the abrupt change in location. One second she stood in Jack's bedroom; the next, her eyes tried desperately to convince her she had appeared in a wooded clearing. Her ears only vaguely heard Jack speaking excitedly.

"Tina-Lu, this is my friend Cathy, she lives on this side of the MoonBridge. Cathy this is my sister Tina-Lu: remember I told you about her. That was the MoonBridge by the way; our MoonBridge," he grinned at Cathy, and enjoyed his sister's disorientation.

Tina-Lu barely moved a muscle and still had her mouth wide open. "What, where, who…" she panted.

"Cathy's the Guardian of the bridge on this side. Her people, here, need my help; they may all die without it. I had to come back home to collect this staff," he explained, nonchalantly, but with a breathless insistence that time was precious.

"She doesn't know anything about you Cathy," he said turning back to his friend. "She doesn't have a clue about any of this."

Tina-Lu just kept repeating. "What…"

"Unfortunately she was standing right by the bridge when I returned. I just had to bring her with me, it was easier, trust me. How long have we been gone?"

"It's been three days Jack, everything is getting very nasty."

"That long?" Jack was shocked. "I thought it might have been a few hours, but three days, that's weird."

"I think the Blues have increased in numbers, the hidden Guardian is using the bridge again, I'm sure of it. We've got to close them down; and soon. There's some other bad news I'm afraid."

Tina-Lu finally managed to snap out of her obvious shock. Brandy was busily licking her leg and trying to get her attention. "Stop: Stop NOW," she spurted out, interrupting Cathy mid-sentence.

"Stop this nonsense you two; will you. What the hell is going on? Where is this place? Who is this girl? What are you babbling on about? Three days, what do you mean three days, it hasn't even been three minutes?"

Tina-Lu was virtually jumping up and down screaming and waving her arms everywhere. She finally shouted without even drawing another breath. "Who needs your help? Will someone please explain to me what the hell is happening here?"

Bright red in the face, obviously totally out of her depth and extremely confused, Tina-Lu shook angrily.

Jack briefly grabbed his sister in a tight hug. "Sorry Sis," he said, genuinely upset at Tina-Lu's panic attack. "Look, I'll try to explain, but this isn't the time. This place is real, we are not in a dream and Cathy really does exist."

Jack held his sister's hands to show he was telling the truth. He continued, "Cathy is risking a great deal just being here for us. I'll tell you what I can as we walk, but we must hurry, our lives depend on it.

But get this straight, there is a war going on here and we are right in the middle of it. Believe me, this is for real: we could all be killed."

As they made their way through the hidden paths and trails of the countryside, the Guardians did their best to explain. Between them, Cathy and Jack gave a detailed account of their plight. They walked and talked for over an hour, the more they described, the more confused Tina-Lu became. Having crossed the river, they made their way higher into the hills. The journey had brought them to the base of the highest peak around. Their destination was a steep sided hill with a flattened top; an excellent vantage point for defence and observation; Cathy led them up. A wide ditch had been dug all around the rim and a high earth wall constructed behind it. Only one point was open and that was protected by a very stout gate. Soldiers were everywhere; as they approached a shout emanated from above their heads.

"About time too; where have you been?" Jaden carried the bag containing Cathy's Guardian staff, the one that matched the cane in Jack's hand.

The gate slid open allowing them to enter; then slammed shut with a loud thud.

"Sorry we've been so long Jaden, I thought I was only away for a couple of minutes. Anyway, this is..."

"...your elder sister Christina-Louise," Jaden finished the sentence for Jack. "You're exactly as your brother described, I'm very pleased to meet you."

Tina-Lu couldn't fathom Jaden; he seemed about eleven or twelve yet spoke like an adult.

The boy returned his attention to Jack, "I am Sage now. My Grandfather relinquished his hold on this world; his Sageship powers were given freely over to me. We're one with each other and he sends his thanks. Before departing, he said he hoped you would meet him again. He left these words for you: beware the hidden Guardian and trust your instinct. Remember, Lujnima's power is for you to command."

Tina-Lu just shook her head in disbelief. "Where has my stupid little brother brought me to?"

Looking at the staff in Jack's hand; Jaden congratulated his friend. "Well done, you've brought Tel-Vah-Ney's twin - Tel-Vah-Nar; let's see if this is going to be possible?"

Cathy un-wrapped the coverings of her Guardianship cane Tel-Vah-Ney. Looking exactly like Jack's, they were identical in every respect except the engravings were drawn as mirror images of one another. Jack held Tel-Vah-Nar and faced Cathy holding, her staff, Tel-Vah-Ney. Apprehensively, the two canes were brought close to each other until the heads were about half a metre apart. Both staffs shook wildly, refusing to touch.

"It's as I feared," said Jaden. "You can't bring them together. They're like trying to join the same poles of a magnet, they naturally repel each other. Grandfather had been thinking about this possible problem for some time now and we remembered a description of a special connecting conduit that could guide the two powers into one single stream."

Jaden explained about the stories of Tel-Vah-Let the combiner of all forces. "We must find an artefact about thirty centimetres across with an exact imprint of the heads of each of its twins in the indentations. The legends suggest when the staff heads are placed precisely in alignment with the sockets; Tel-Vah-Let will become one with his siblings. Only then can a true Guardian command him to act on their behalf."

Jaden grinned at the looks of bewilderment on his friends faces. "I'm not sure, but I think the Blades may have already managed to capture the conduit. Although, they may not realise that it's within their grasp. I believe it's well disguised and very well hidden. Stories tell of having to find the Lost Room. Apparently; the artefact is hidden in one of the strongest fortresses ever built and there is a real possibility that it may already have been found. We may have to assume the worst and suspect that it has fallen to them."

Jack looked intrigued. "What do you mean a Lost Room? How can a room be lost, it's either there or it's not; surely?"

Jaden shrugged. "The room is not lost in the sense that you once had it and then you somehow lost it. The legends speak of a room of great power. Possibly provided by Tarre-Hare and Lujnima's father; The Unnamed. He is said to have granted the room the ability to disguise itself and to remain lost. Only there, can the key to the MoonBridge be found and unlocked. If the holder of that key is worthy, then he or she will be granted untold and unnamed powers."

The three sat - eyes wide with excitement. Cathy was especially keen to set off to find this Lost Room straight away. Jack was ready and willing to follow Cathy's lead. Tina-Lu just couldn't believe what she was hearing.

"What on earth are you talking about? How could you possibly know about such a thing if it is just an old legend or story? You are barely eleven years old and you expect us to go racing off on some ridiculous wild-goose chase for some imaginary conduit thing, just because you say so? You must think we're completely nuts. Jack what do you mean you'll go off with Cathy here? You're as mad as they are."

They all looked at Tina-Lu and just stared. She had remained quiet for so long that to hear her finally speak, with such passion, was a bit of a shock.

Jaden smiled knowingly at her and put his hand on her arm. "I know I look like an eleven year old to you Tina-Lu. But please try to understand, my Grandfather, Searlan - The Sage of Sages, passed over to me the secrets of many thousands of years of Sages before him. I'm now the combined knowledge of all my forefathers. In me is the ability to see events and stories that have been hidden for more lifetimes than I care to imagine. Sometimes, with contemplation and concentration, I can seek a piece of knowledge that has remained hidden for a very long time. For the past three days, whilst Jack has been gone, I've been seeking such an answer to this difficult question.

Tina-Lu looked long and hard at this small boy. "How...how can that be?" She stammered.

"By spending time quizzing my ancestors, my Grandfather was able to piece together the legend that I've just relayed to you. Please trust me when I say the legend is true and real as it can be. The stories of the Lost Room are well known to many of my forebears."

"I meant, how can you possibly have such knowledge? What do you mean your Grandfather gave you all this knowledge?" Tina-Lu realised this boy was the most amazing person she had ever heard of. "What's it like, having all those thoughts and memories in you head?"

"Not now Tina-Lu, maybe I'll be able to explain when times are less pressing." The young Sage turned to the others, pondering the way forward for them all. "The only course of action is to go and steal the ancient Conduit back. Someone has to sneak into the ancient Blades fortress at Marwearsort, seek out and discover the Lost Room, find the Conduit, gain its confidence and then return here. Please understand; the fortress at Marwearsort is even stronger than the one we managed to break into. This one was built by the early people of this land and had to repel centuries of savage attacks. The Blades took over tenancy a few years ago. They may not even realise the conduit was hidden in the fortress."

Jack was staggered at the audacity of the young boy's plan, he mocked sarcastically. "Can you hear yourself Jaden? What you are describing is totally impossible. You don't know where this Lost Room is? You don't know where to look for it? You don't know if anyone can get into the fortress? An even if they did, you don't know what this conduit really looks like? So please explain to me again, how on earth anybody could do this?"

Cathy jumped in with an equal amount of sarcasm in her voice. "Come off it Jaden, I've heard the tales that say that no prisoner has ever left that place alive. No uninvited person has ever managed to gain entry before. I don't believe we have the combined strength to fight our way in. So how is this to be done, eh?"

Tina-Lu shook her head in disbelief. "This is just the most stupid thing I've ever heard of. What do you lot think you can hope achieve without a clear idea of what you intend to do? We had better start planning seriously rather than just thinking we might pop over to some impregnable fortress, knock on the door and say; please can I come in and find your Lost Room and then steal its secret powerful Conduit. Yeh right, great plan."

The others stopped for a second before bursting into fits of laughter at Tina-Lu's silly accent and keen sense of humour.

"You're right of course Sis," Jack sniffed loudly, drying the tears from his eyes. "Well I guess we had better think of a better way then." This was the Tina-Lu that Jack loved; she was pragmatic, logical and suffered no foolish idea lightly.

They all nodded in agreement and decided that much more thought was needed before agreeing anything. For half an hour everyone, except Tina-Lu, put their minds towards solving this seemingly impossible task. Idea after idea was proposed: most were considered and then immediately rejected for one reason or another.

Eventually, Tina-Lu got fed up with the hair-brained suggestions. "I know I'm new here, but why don't you two just open that MoonBridge of yours in the place you want to go to. Walk over it, grab this conduit thing, and then walk back out across the bridge? Wouldn't that work? It would save a lot of hassle and would solve all of your problems."

The others all turned and looked closely at Tina-Lu; she suddenly felt very self-conscious and embarrassed.

"That's a great suggestion Tina-Lu," Jaden finally replied. "Unfortunately, even if the Guardians could open the bridge and guide it that precisely; which they probably can't, it's impossible to bring the conduit across the bridge. The two powers would annihilate one another if they ever came in contact. You see, the Conduit is the key to the Bridge: it's like an equal and opposite energy; potentially, they would bring instant destruction to us all. Whether that is still true, once the two staffs are brought together, I don't know?

We can't risk taking the Guardian staffs with us, into the fortress, just in case they fall into the enemy's hands. This really is a problem and a most difficult choice." He paused for a few seconds whilst he thought deeply. The three others waited expectantly for something important from the young Sage. "Wait a minute though," he continued. "You could've hit on a good idea after all. We might just be able to get into the fortress using the MoonBridge. Once inside, we could secretly search for the Lost Room. Then, we only need to identify where the conduit is hidden. Getting back out would require some other path."

Jack looked at Cathy and asked. "What do you think? This might just be possible?"

The discussions continued for a short while longer. Tina-Lu felt considerably more comfortable after her idea became the focus of the plans. Everyone agreed the MoonBridge may prove to be one method for gaining access to the fortress. Of course, that all depended upon the two Guardians actually finding a way to control the destination point. Cathy wasn't hopeful; she voiced her concerns.

Tina-Lu pointed out they had described this other, third, Guardian who had opened the bridge to allow the Blues to cross. "Why?" she asked. "Did the bridge go to some other place for that Guardian?"

No one had ever actually thought to question that before. Tina-Lu was already gaining the reputation for good ideas. She felt even more part of this bizarre team and really began to get excited about the whole plan.

They all agreed the best thing was for the two Guardians to join forces and make an attempt to guide and control the bridge. Jack would also spend his time exploring his newly discovered seeing abilities in an attempt to probe the fortresses defences. Jaden and Tina-Lu would make preparations for their eventual departure. Brandy did what all good dogs do in such an emergency and flurry of planning activity; he curled up in the corner, covered his nose with his long bushy tail and snored quietly to himself dreaming of chasing rabbits.

Chapter 13 - Overwhelmed

Cloaked in early morning mist, the pre-dawn calm was shattered as waking horns rang out from the walls of the fortress. Hundreds of soldiers appeared from their tented city; eagerly screaming sergeants called the war machine into action. General Pen-D'anatè watched the unfolding scene far below; the entire surrounding grassland seethed like a busy colony of ants. Every individual had their role to play, some taking down the tents, others gathering stores, many readying the equipment required for the days ahead.

"Let him in," the General called through to the next office.

The guard signalled the Captain to enter. Scurrying nervously, the man stood smartly to attention, "Sir."

"What progress on the spies, Spike?" Pen-D'anatè was in no mood to leave any thread hanging. "I do not want to march into battle and have to watch both my flanks and my back."

The Captain feared reporting his lack of progress; any sign of failure risked immediate retribution. His mouth was dry and his tongue felt twice its normal size. "General, I fear I was mistaken in my original assessment, I've been unable to find any evidence of betrayal. I'm forced to consider the raid was as surreptitious as it was audacious. This infiltrator succeeded with, seemingly, magical efficiency."

The Captain looked decidedly uncomfortable at having to admit, even a minor, mistake to his leader.

The General growled grittily under his breath and then his face lightened. Much to the Captain's relief the reply put him at ease.

"I have already pondered the same outcome myself and have feared this would be the case Spike; the enemy must have a new ally. One who has the ability to breach our defences and to walk in through an entire garrison without even causing an alarm? This new foe is potentially more dangerous than any we have faced before. I want you to double my guard; you will provide complete cover for my safety. Our defences will not be broken again."

The Captain could hardly contain his enthusiasm. This was a stroke of luck indeed: instead of punishment he'd been promoted to the General's personal bodyguard.

"We will not be infiltrated again General. The guard will be trebled and the defences made impregnable. Your safety is guaranteed Sir; I stake my life on it."

The General looked fleetingly at his most trusted Captain and thought to himself. "It would a great loss to me to have to dispose of you Spike. But fail me again and I'll take your blood myself." He then dismissed the Captain with a wave of his hand.

As the Captain left the room, the General turned back to the window and spoke quietly to himself. "So the enemy has a new ally, just as I suspected; and, who might that be eh?" He didn't like to admit it, but for once he felt vulnerable. "An enemy, who can walk into one of my strongest fortresses, pass my guards un-noticed, and then escape with a child and old, sick, woman without being seen. This is a formidable foe indeed. He must possess some form of demonic power; perhaps even invisible." Contemplating his assessment; he found himself looking around the office warily. "Could the perpetrator still be here? How would I know?"

The General grasped the handle of his sword and spoke forcefully. "I'd slice off your head before you could dare touch me, demon." Then drawing his sword, he slashed around the empty space in front of him. With each sweeping strike he fully expected to make contact with some unseen creature. After a few fruitless swipes, the General laughed, "no-one's here but me." Even though he sounded up-beat, the doubts of his own safety were already sown; his confidence dented.

As the rising sun burnt off the fragile mist; the army formed. Long columns of several hundred soldiers stood four abreast; each headed by three officers on horseback. Brightly polished buttons glistened in the morning light, belts of gold and black hung heavily with sheath and sword; each rider wore a spectacular hat of black feathers and tanned leather. Large Blade flags barely fluttered. Along the length of each column, every twenty men or so, stood a sergeant, immaculate and unswerving.

Stepping out onto his balcony, overlooking the savannah, Pen-D'anatè reviewed the scene. "Now, my mighty warriors, onward to victory," the General whispered. Bursting with pride; he signalled his fighting force to set forth. The trumpeted order, to move out, sounded clearly in the early morning stillness.

***

Leaving his high tower behind, Pen-D'anatè descended into the fortress courtyard to mount his favourite horse, Warrior, and rode out with his contingent of guards and trusted captain, Spike. Mist patches still clung precariously to small hollows and dips, another hour and all would be clear; the day promised to be warm and sunny.

"We'll make camp on the other side of the savannah by nightfall Spike. Tomorrow, I'll unleash this war machine on the rabble Resistance." Grinning slyly he added. "When I've swept away those worthless fools I'll turn my attention elsewhere."

Pen-D'anatè's face blackened; he gritted his teeth tightly together and muttered quietly. "Yes, then I'll finish off that meddling Elder."

Plumes of red dust kicked up into an impenetrable smog. Soldiers, horses and wagons trundled, steadily, out towards the grass land. There, the vegetation was sparse and many thousands of boots and hooves soon made it impossible to see both ends of the columns. From a distance, a single hazy snake slithered out from the hills. As the army reached the denser grassland the dust eased and the smog drifted away on the morning breeze.

The beat of drums and marching songs filtered back to the General's position; he smiled broadly. "They are eager and willing Spike. Spirits are high; higher than I can remember for a long time. These soldiers know they are unstoppable." Pen-D'anatè thought for a moment before declaring. "Let any come to face me: the fools, I'll wipe this pathetic Resistance off the face of the earth. Not one will be left standing; it will be as if they had never existed." He rubbed his hands together in expectant glee.

From behind, a persistent low pitched hum emanated; the sound was quiet, but irritating. The General glanced back. He watched fifteen elongated blue creatures form into a 'V' shaped pattern at the fortress gates. They moved slowly but unfalteringly too; absorbing anything that came within their path: trees, shrubs even boulders just seemed to fall apart as they neared. Floating about half a metre from the ground; it was as if they had scraped the floor clean with a knife. The Elder, dressed entirely in blue cloth, seemed to glow in the same manner as the creatures.

Pen-D'anatè sneered, "Who does he think he is?"

The lead Blue had formed a kind of seated throne for the Elder; Lord Tzerach had afforded Alanthian a great honour.

"I'll have to pick my moment carefully to dispatch that one: I don't want to anger those damn Blues when I rid myself of that meddlesome irritation." He thought again for a moment before declaring. "I'll make it seem like a tragic accident. Yes, it'll seem like a great loss to our cause." He chuckled quietly, congratulating himself on his excellent plan.

The Elder sat, eyes closed, comfortably relaxed; his seat mimicked the contours of his body exactly. Gliding smoothly across the surface; the creature below him gave no sensation of movement. Had it not been for the slight breeze blowing across Alanthian's face or the occasional waft of Sulphur, he would never have known they were moving. "So finally, the conquest begins," he mused silently.

Alanthian looked up and surveyed the sight before him, his attention turned towards Pen-D'anatè. "There he is, sitting so confidently on his horse planning his campaign and, of course, plotting my downfall." With a snort he dismissed the idea. "The fool; does he really think his tiny brain and narrow vision is any match for my wisdom and knowledge? Does he really believe I'd permit him to harm me? Once this army has fulfilled its purpose I'll remove this lumbering oaf and install one of my spies as the new General."

The Blues assumed the form of an elongated cigar, when traversing distances. They didn't eat food; but, absorbed special elements, by-products of their disintegration process during movement.

Alanthian took this opportunity to test his regenerated youthfulness. He practiced focussing his mind on every aspect of his accumulated knowledge. Searching his memories, he made himself recall many experiences that had occurred throughout his long life. The mental exercises gave no outward indication of the effort and strain he was applying. However, inside he rushed around seeking out forgotten events and half hidden truths. He traced his life back to his first encounter with the MoonBridge: a very young boy of only seven; he stood with his father and many other men in the sacred temple of the moon. Built at the top of the tallest hill in the area; a ring of high stones, each polished and painted with special rune symbols, invoked the powers of the gods. The air was chilled as it was an early spring night.

"Yes, the winter was just coming to an end," he remembered. A cold breeze blew harshly up the slope of the hillside and he recalled being so cold that his flesh shivered. Each man wore a robe of white with a coloured sash that denoted their status within the sect. Alanthian held a privileged position, but was too young to be ranked; his full initiation would not come for several summers.

"Except it never did come, my destiny lay elsewhere."

Instead, the boy wore a moon shaped brooch pinned to his chest; his father was head of the order and that made Alanthian a special case. As the priests chanted, he watched his father summon the powers of the moon goddess and then open the fabled MoonBridge. He'd been told of its beauty and spectacle, but this had not prepared him for the reality. He was overwhelmed by its simplicity and perfection. The silvery glow seemed to blend with the colour of his skin and its light appeared to penetrate deep behind his eyes. He was drawn towards it, almost hypnotically.

"Come to me Alanthian, Guardian and master of the light," he heard it calling.

No longer aware of any chanting or even the priests standing close by: the bridge called to him and him alone. Walking impossibly slowly towards the light, his world had become blurred and distorted; time ran erratically. He vaguely remembered others trying to intercept his path. Someone shouted; the voice faded into the far reaches of his mind, lost in the mist of confusion. His father pushed forwards, arms outstretched, but it was too late. "Nooooo," was the final sound he ever heard.

Instantaneously, Alanthian was transported away from the cold of the hilltop. Surrounding his body, caressing his thoughts; the most beautiful beams of silvery light reached into his soul and warmed him. His shivering stopped and he felt immersed in the power and strength of the moon beams. This incredible structure possessed a life of its own and he was bathed in its perfection.

"Feed me mighty Lady of the night sky; give me the power I desire."

Alanthian didn't understand why, but he'd already forgotten the people he left behind; they no longer seemed important. He didn't fear for his safety nor care for those he'd previously known and depended upon. The energy of the MoonBridge had somehow made him grow far beyond his years. His mind expanded gifting him the secrets of the universe. He had no idea how long he'd been travelling but it seemed both an instant and an eternity.

"I'm master of the MoonBridge," he screamed in shear exhilaration.

Arriving at his destination, Alanthian fell to his knees. Above, an incomprehensible sight: the sky was so different from its usual star filled blackness, he wasn't even sure if he was still alive. "I have died and risen to heaven," he sighed.

Overhead hung a masterpiece of exquisite colours, all swirling and infused. Reds, yellows, greens and blues; every shade and texture imaginable pierced his consciousness. Alanthian's breathing stopped as his heart pulsed uncontrollably.

"What is this place?"

Where the moon should have been was a sweeping arch filling half the sky. The rings were so breathtaking: a few blazing stars peppered the heavens, everywhere was filled with wispy clouds, each more colourful and beautiful than its neighbour. Some were brightly lit from behind by a hidden source of incandescence.

"I'm dead, I must be," tears rolled down his face, the emotion overwhelming and all encompassing. Alanthian knelt, motionless, for many minutes. His senses gradually took in the indescribable spectacle and he questioned, if he was actually dead.

"What is this place?" he repeated.

Initially unaware of the humming sound coming from somewhere behind him; Alanthian's mind eventually pulled away from the incredible sights, he realised that he wasn't alone. Behind him waited three, perfectly smooth, elongated blue cigar shaped things. He'd been found by the keepers of this place, the Blues. He didn't have time to speak; the sound of humming intensified. Falling to the ground unconscious; he remembered placing his hands over his ears.

***

"Alanthian," Lord Tzerach's voice was insistent and impatient. "Alanthian, are you asleep?"

The Elder forced himself back from his memories and realized that they were almost across the other side of the savannah. "Yes my Lord, I hear you."

"You have been extremely quiet. We will soon reach our first destination." The Shumiat leader hummed melodically - speaking by vibrating the air.

"Forgive me my Lord, I've been testing my powers of memory recall and have been far back in my childhood. I was just remembering the day you found me on your home world and how you took me before the elders of your people. I'm so grateful that you granted me the power to relive these events in such clarity and depth. The gift of youthfulness is a wonder to behold."

Tzerach hummed with approval; he looked upon Alanthian as a well loved pet. "Yes Elder, I clearly remember that day too; a day that changed everything."

The leader recalled how he'd immediately claimed him for his own. He was the first to have revealed the existence of the MoonBridge.

"This portal shall be mine to control," he promised. The ambitious young pretender saw the potential of such a prize.

Even indirect command of the MoonBridge was sufficient to elevate Tzerach to great heights. The title of Lord was granted and the Council bestowed high authority to the young Shumiat. He was the first to learn the language of Alanthian and to discover the existence of other worlds.

The time distortion of the MoonBridge travel permitted Tzerach to dispatch his kind to conquer and destroy tens of thousands of worlds. Each conquest enhanced the Shumiat: like a spreading organism, hungry and demanding; the creatures hopped from system to system stripping all resources and leaving barren wastelands in their wake. Nothing, in the history of the universe, had been so ruthless.

As the Elder listened to his master, he remembered the excitement and challenge of their conquering. "One day you will take me to your home world Alanthian. I'll see it for myself," the Lord Tzerach promised.

A lifetime of successes had brought them to this day; now they were crossing the plain of Alanthian's home world. Here, many centuries had slipped away since the Elder took his first step onto the MoonBridge. Few, if any, could claim to be as ancient as he.

Tzerach still needed Alanthian, but only as his puppet. If it wasn't for the MoonBridge the creature would offer nothing to the Shumiat Lord.

"This world of yours will be cleansed very soon Alanthian and then I'll order the extraction processes. You will be handsomely rewarded for your assistance."

The Elder smiled, he felt like the conqueror of the world: a title he may come to regret.

***

Sergeant-at-Arms Healworth watched the first wave of Blade squadrons march from their camp. He observed the preparatory movements throughout the night; barely chancing any sleep. His eyes were sore and his bones ached. "We pull back now. We must get back to camp and tell the Group Captain; war is upon us."

Healworth's team needed no further instructions; they slipped silently away from the observation point and disappeared into the trees. Not a sound was made, not a twig broken nor a blade of grass crushed under foot. These were the best of the Resistance; elite observers.

Back at the base camp preparations neared completion. The entire Resistance movement readied to escape the army of the Blades. Refuge would be taken in caverns beneath a line of mountains flanking the southern ocean. Few knew of the vast natural hideaway. A march of many days would be needed to cover several hundreds of kilometres.

"This madman Blade General commands an unstoppable army." Group Captain Smithers shook his head submissively knowing they were defeated without raising a sword. He looked at his rag-tag groups of men, women and children. All were keen and resilient, but also, disorganised, poorly trained and hopelessly equipped by comparison to the Blades army. A hint of desperation reflected in his tone. "What chance do we have? They're invincible."

True hearted men followed the Group Captain's lead. Bravery and courage flowed through the veins of all who stood up to the killing machine chasing them. Death was sweeping across this land and he knew Searlan's advice was correct. "We must hide like frightened rabbits. Burrow away from sight in the hope that some may survive long enough to make a stand." He wasn't confident. No leader of men would ever be happy at this course of action. With the heaviest of hearts he finally ordered his troops. "Let's get them moving Captain:

we travel fast and light. I don't want a single person to be caught by these Blade devils."

Captain Connors agreed. "We should be underway within the hour Sir."

"No Sandy; we'll be caught with our pants down. These Blades will be over us like a rash if we don't leave right now. Give the order to the Lieutenants, the war could be lost before we have had chance to regroup and take stock."

Sandy nodded in agreement. The situation was dire and the men knew it. "There's no point deluding ourselves, if we don't get some kind of assistance soon we're doomed." Sandy was sombre.

Neither captain held out much hope for miracles, they were just for fairy stories and not for this war. The entire band of freedom fighters, their families and wagons piled high with possessions, were readied for the long trip south. Connors assessment was accurate; it was about an hour before they finally made their move. The wagon train headed towards the relative safety of the empty southern plains. The journey would be long and arduous, but they had no other option, the choice was simple; hide or die.

Chapter 14 - Desperation

Jaden, Jack, Cathy and Tina-Lu eventually decided the only course of action was to risk opening the MoonBridge within the Blade fortress.

"How else would we gain entry?" Jaden declared. They had contemplated other possibilities but continually returned to this simple solution offered by Tina-Lu. "We must head east to the town of Marwearsort."

Jack and Cathy had discovered they could combine their abilities if they held hands whilst holding a staff in the opposite hand. Cathy's silver bracelet sparkled on her left wrist; the power of the Guardianship seemed to be amplified when they adopted this stance.

"My body tingles with electricity when I grasp your hand Jack. You seem to send an energy surging through me and the bracelet acts like a focal point for your powers."

"Are you sure that's not just his animal magnetism?" teased Tina-Lu: she relished her brother's embarrassment.

Jack coloured up yet again at his older sister's remarks. He tried really hard to pretend he didn't hear her quip, but failed miserably. "Give me a break Sis, we're trying to do something really serious here," Jack pleaded with his older sister, in the hope that she would ease up a little.

Cathy saw the funny side of it though and pulled Jack close to her. "Come on tiger let's show them what we Guardians can do."

The pair concentrated hard on bringing their abilities into synchronisation. As expected, MoonBridge beams were able to be focused even when the moon wasn't shining. The bridge had less potency than at midnight - of the full moon – but, they were only expecting to travel a few hundred kilometres.

"Let's just see if we can open the bridge first," said Cathy. She squeezed Jack's hand tightly and held her staff at shoulder height away from her body. Jack did the opposite and they managed to keep the canes far enough apart to allow them both to function.

Incredibly, they didn't need to speak out loud as they seemed to become almost one person, each sharing the other's thoughts. Jack felt really embarrassed at first, he wondered if Cathy could read his mind, as well as hear what he actually wanted her to hear. Much to his horror, she turned to face him and with a great big grin, she said. "Keep your mind on the task at hand tiger," she winked and gave him a peck on the cheek. "Don't worry; I like you very much too. But this is not the time or the place."

Jack turned the colour of a beetroot and tried his best to be cool and calm, but was completely unconvincing.

"Jack Ferns," Tina-Lu gave her best, shocked-voice, rendition at the sight of her brother's discomfort. "Whatever were you thinking?"

This time they all collapsed in fits of laughter. Poor Jack was the butt of the joke once more; however, even he could see the funny side of it.

"Anyway, she kissed me didn't she?" he secretly congratulated himself.

The four calmed down and returned to the serious task at hand.

"Focus on the bridge Jack and try to see it appearing in your mind. That's it," Cathy declared.

"Make it appear Jack, make it appear before us," encouraged Tina-Lu.

At their command, the bridge formed. Very weak and quite dim by comparison to some days; the vision was a pale shadow of its former night-self.

"We must try to force it to be stronger; somehow, we need to feed it with our energy," Cathy demanded.

"Concentrate Jack; call upon Lujnima's powers to drive the bridge to us: make it stable and strong."

Jack forgot all about his embarrassment and squeezed Cathy's hand. He held his staff aloft; the Guardians of the MoonBridge focussed their minds to enhance their potency. Together, they brightened the apparition.

Jaden watched in admiration as the two Guardians learned to master the opening and closing of the MoonBridge. "Well done you two, you've cracked it."

Tina-Lu also quietly admired her stupid younger brother and wondered how he could actually do such a thing. She reluctantly, had to admit that this was rather spectacular. In fact, she secretly gained a great deal of respect for him, not that she would've ever told him.

After about an hour of practicing, Jack and Cathy became almost like one Guardian. They no longer had to think about opening or closing the bridge, they just willed it to happen; the task became second nature.

"Do you feel ready to control the exit point Jack?" asked Cathy. "Shall we try to place it in the other room first and see if anyone can cross whilst we hold it open?"

Jaden thought that was a great idea. He went into the next room to see if they could focus the exit point in front of him. Several attempts failed, at first. Eventually, the pair managed to imagine the exit point next door and sure enough it appeared. Jaden was the first to hop between the rooms. He stepped back through to join the others waiting for him; this was his first trip across the bridge and found the experience, indescribable, fun.

"Far better than the Portal that Grandfather opened for me to visit Tarre-Hare. That's more like a falling sensation: this feels like sliding along without actually moving your feet." Grinning, he said, "Come on Tina-Lu, let's go back again." Together, they stepped through into the next room; the MoonBridge fade from view.

Tina-Lu shouted through the closed door. "We're here."

Jack and Cathy opened the MoonBridge one more time, lowered their staffs to the floor and then jumped on the bridge before it could close. In a flash they were standing next to Jaden and Tina-Lu.

"We didn't risk bringing the staffs with us," said Jack quickly to the other two. "We thought it might be too risky."

The bridge faded from view with an almost imperceptible hiss.

"Excellent work Jack." Cathy gave her friend a little hug and then continued, "Let's have a break for now, all this concentration has left me feeling famished." She needn't have worried; they were all starving after their efforts. The two Guardians walked next door to collect their staffs and then they all went off to find some tea.

Tina-Lu slid close beside Jack and whispered in his ear, "She fancies you little brother."

Jack tried not to react but coloured up again. "It's not like that," he struggled to answer, without success. "She's just a good mate, that's all?"

Tina-Lu knew she had her brother reeling and continued teasingly. "Oh no, Jack Ferns, I've seen the look in her eyes. She fancies you – a lot."

Jack replied in resignation, "Okay Sis, let it go please. This is serious you know, there are lives at stake here. We're not at home now." Actually inside he was bursting with pride that maybe, just maybe Cathy did fancy him. He certainly fancied her to pieces.

They soon found their way to the kitchens and feasted on fresh baked bread, chicken, cheese and salad.

"I'm so hungry," Jack declared tucking into the fabulous fare.

The daylight faded. "Let's call it a day; we'll continue practicing tomorrow." Jack suggested. They all agreed.

Brandy reappeared from his wanderings; he'd made several new friends amongst the soldiers and they all gave him tasty morsels. Swaggering up to Jack and Tina-Lu; the fat, from the chicken, clung to his whiskers.

"You'll be as fat as a pig if you keep eating all those scraps," scolded Jack; spotting the evidence still stuck to his face.

The dog dropped his ears and his tail and looked completely forlorn. All four laughed so loudly; even the two cooks came over to see what all the fuss was about.

"He's been in here several times sniffing out morsels as well," the head chef confirmed.

Jack wagged his finger at Brandy and ordered, "No more scrapings, titbits or other snacks for you; you'll be sick."

The four thanked the cooks, for the food, before turning-in for the night. The boys and Brandy had one tent and the girls shared another.

Jack closed the flap behind them and climbed into the heavy-weight blankets. "Night Sis," he called and then paused. "Goodnight Cathy," he also half whispered.

In his head he heard a reply that made him turn bright red again. "Goodnight Jack; my dearest off-world Guardian; sleep well. You can never be very far away from me again; never. We are the Guardians and we are a pair, each one half of the other." He knew it to be true and fell asleep with a wide cheesy-grin of contentment all across his face.

"This is the best day of my life – ever," he declared.

***

The new dawn brought a change to the weather. The air had chilled decidedly and the sky was thick with dark, angry, clouds. Until now, Jack had not even thought about the possibility of rain. He just assumed it was always sunny and fun here; the first drops changed all that. Within minutes the air was saturated with billions of droplets the size of peas; everything was soaked. Puddles grew quickly forming into rivulets.

"It's been weeks' since we had any good rain," Cathy noted, sheltering under the flap of the tent. "It's going to get very wild here, hold on to your hats. Let's dash over for breakfast."

By the time the friends made their way back from the kitchen, torrents rushed along every crevice rapidly filling the streams. Thick mud stuck to their shoes; the soil had turned into a reddish-brown sludge. A distant rumble signalled the approaching storm.

"That sounds ominous; I hate thunder." Tina-Lu had never liked the deafening crash of the thunder storm.

The sky lowered: jet-black clouds swirled ominously; heavy rainfall chiselled into the faces of the onlookers. A blinding flash of lightning split the sky in a cascade of jagged fingers. Tina-Lu screamed in panic: instantly, a shattering crack and deep booming rumble echoed around the sky directly overhead. A second, ear-piercing, crash accompanied another fork of brilliant illumination: millions of volts of raw energy struck the ground.

"Wow, that one was close," Jaden said ducking under the shelter of the tent. "I think we'd better get out of the way of this one."

Another flash of lightning struck a tree directly across from their position: splinters of wood blasted in all directions - fire burst through the trunk as easily as if it had melted butter. The thunder was so overpowering it physically shook their bodies and rang loudly in their ears for seconds afterwards.

"We've got to get out of here NOW!" Jaden screamed in fear.

Instead, everyone dived instinctively to the ground for cover and looked around very frightened. Tina-Lu quivered; her hands firmly over her ears and her eyes tightly closed. "I hate it, I hate it, I hate it…" she moaned.

Hail stones started to fall like bullets fired from a machine gun; the noise was deafening. Some were the size of marbles and pointed like a teardrop: they struck the trees, tents and ground with a chilling metallic clatter. In seconds, the floor was white with misshapen lumps of ice.

"Look at that," Jaden had never seen the likes of this before.

Above them, the sky was as black as night. Another flash and crack blasted out of the oppressive structure above them; this time the lightning forked into jagged legs right across the face of the cloud without reaching the ground; an eerie silver light briefly illuminated the tents. Brandy cowered in the corner and looked hopelessly towards Jack for support. The canvas flapped violently as the wind, rain and hail battered it relentlessly.

"Something is happening to me," Jack said to Cathy. He could not explain, but every time a lightning flash struck he felt a surge of energy searing through his body. He felt charged and powerful; Cathy felt it too. She grimaced at him and nodded without the need to explain. She knew he was feeling the power of the conduit reaching out to them.

"It's the strength of the Tarre-Hare, her power is calling us," Cathy whispered.

One particular strike drove deep into Jack's soul: his body snapped rigidly to attention and his muscles locked in painful convulsions. In that moment, his mind expanded dramatically, he knew he was destined to find the Lost Room and that he would meld with the conduit. Jack felt invincible; his powers grew unimaginably.

"I've never felt so completely alive before," he said breathlessly to Cathy pulling her towards him and hugging her tightly.

Cathy could feel Jack shaking as the storm gave up its force to him. He could hardly think straight. "I feel as though I'm being opened up inside and that my senses are stretching outwards."

"This is your storm Jack; Tarre-Hare must have decided to prepare you for the task ahead. I can feel you growing with every breath." Cathy replied.

Jack looked down at his hand and realised that his entire arm was glowing brightly. "I'm changing; I almost believe I could fly at this moment."

Cathy held Jack's glowing hand and looked him in the eyes. "You are becoming more than the Guardian Jack. I don't know what the storm is doing to you; I've felt its power and have seen some of its strength."

Jaden came over to them and looked at Jack. "Do you feel the earth breathing?"

Jack looked down and could hardly believe his eyes; he thought he saw faces in the earth looking back at him. The faces were almost featureless and grey, but they still seemed to be able to convey their message. His mind was drawn closely in towards the underworld beings. They spoke past him to Jaden by his side.

"We warned you Sage this one was trouble; he shouldn't have left the depths of the earth. We foresee great heartache ahead; destruction awaits us all, and he is the cause."

The faces faded from view and Jaden came out of his semi-trance. He realised that only he and Jack had just witnessed the vision. Not even Cathy had seen or heard any of it.

"Are you dangerous Jack?" Jaden thought carefully. "What does their warning mean? What have they foreseen?" He glanced at the Guardian and felt the seeds of doubt growing in his mind. "Are you really our friend or are you, unwittingly, the enemy?"

Over the next hour the storm peaked and slowly subsided. Eventually the blackness of the clouds lightened to a dull grey and lifted a little higher. The rain eased to a drizzle and small breaks in the cloud cover signalled the passing of the storm. Everywhere had changed from the summery sunny landscape into a disaster zone. Several trees were uprooted; mud and debris, driven by the ferocity of the water, lay piled around any stationary object.

Late afternoon arrived before anyone felt safe enough to go out and survey the damage. The little stream, trickling harmlessly alongside the camp, had grown into a raging torrent. The surface boiled dangerously, Jack kept a firm hold of Brandy. "Don't go near there you silly dog," he warned.

The trees - lining the path - hung limply: each seemed sad or punished by the ferocity of storm. "Wow, look at this one." Jack and the others ran over to the site of the lightning bolt strike.

In the middle of the camp stood the blackened remnants of the tree, now broken and twisted; a scar ran down its length, and smelt heavily of smouldering ash. "Lucky we didn't get hit by that one." Jaden whistled, looking closely at the dead tree.

Tina-Lu was still shaken by being so exposed and open to the storm.

"Are you okay?" Jaden affectionately asked his friend. The girl smiled back grateful for his compassion.

They weren't keen on continuing their plans and so decided to sit and chat. "Let's go and find somewhere dry and warm," Cathy suggested eagerly.

The four paired up together. Jack and Cathy wandered off in the direction of the kitchens. Tina-Lu had really hit it off with little Jaden. She was strangely fascinated how he seemed old as the hills, more knowledgeable than an encyclopaedia and yet only a young boy at the same time. She sat and talked endlessly with him about his Grandfather and the stewardship of being a Sage. The boy also found himself feeling very comfortable around Tina-Lu. She was bright, very pretty and exceedingly intelligent. He could sense her wonder and was happy to oblige: for over an hour he described the feeling of having hundreds of ancestors locked up inside his soul.

Jack and Cathy became almost inseparable. They walked and talked for hours about their childhoods and their very different upbringings. Jack was nearly brought to tears when Cathy recounted her loss of her mother and father. He, only then, began to understand how close Cathy was to Aunt Beth. They both looked at each other as if struck by another bolt of lightning.

"Aunt Beth," exclaimed Cathy with a dreadful wail. "Oh the poor dear; she has been left all this time through this dreadful storm. I feel terrible."

The pair rushed off to the hospital tents and found Aunt Beth sitting up in bed.

"Hello Cathy," she said weakly. "That was exciting, wasn't it, all those crashes and bangs going off everywhere. We haven't had a storm like that in ages."

Both grinned in surprise at Aunt Beth's transformation.

"I'm feeling much better; thanks to this lovely man here." Aunt Beth stroked the arm of the kindly doctor who had been caring for her.

"This is Doctor Frank Baker; he has been my life saver. His medicine has eased my fever and I'm now really beginning to feel much better."

The two looked amazed and extremely pleased that Aunt Beth was on the mend. Only a couple of days ago it had been touch and go whether or not she would've survived the journey out of the fortress. Now, here she was sitting up in bed feeling much better. They spent some time chatting before getting back to the others to tell them the good news.

Cathy kissed her Aunt goodbye. Jack gave her a big loving hug too. They waved to her as they left the hospital area.

"I think she fancies him Jack."

"What?" Jack replied.

"I think Aunt Beth fancies that doctor. He is rather handsome."

Jack snorted and tugged at his friends arm. "What do you mean handsome?" he grabbed her in mock jealousy. "You mean he is even more handsome than me?" Jack quizzed scratching for compliments.

Cathy elbowed him playfully in the ribs and ran off towards their tent without answering.

The four met up again and after a short time they all decided that they had better get back to work.

"Shall we have another go with the MoonBridge Cathy?" Jack asked. "I would like to try to get it to reach beyond the trees and up the hill somewhere. I would also like to cross over with our staffs, just to see if we can do so together? What do you think?"

The four practiced again, each time attempting something a little harder than the last.

"You two are damned good at doing this you know," Jaden complimented the Guardians. "What do you think Tina-Lu?"

Tina-Lu nodded in agreement. She couldn't help herself, but wondered if this was all actually a dream and that she would wake up any minute in her nice warm snug bed at home.

Jack caught her sombre moment and read her thoughts; he stepped close up beside her. "This is no dream Sis; you are here just as I am. The MoonBridge is real enough and the enemy is as deadly as Jaden described."

"I know Jack, but how can all this be true? It doesn't make any sense."

Jack reached absentmindedly inside his jacket pocket and twiddled with the jewelled brooch he'd found when he first arrived. Taking it out, he showed it to his sister.

"Where did you get that Jack, it's beautiful."

"Take it Sis, it's yours; I found it when I was walking. Lujnima told me about a spirit who lives inside the jewel; she helped me in the caves. Have a look and if you can hear her, she's called Layette the Decider. Anyway, the brooch looks better pinned on a girl."

Jack thrust the gem into his sister's hand and left her transfixed by the huge size and beauty of the precious stone at its centre.

Cathy noticed Jack pass something to Tina-Lu and went over to see the gift. Jack had walked off and joined Jaden in some deep discussion.

"What's that Tina-Lu? Wow it's beautiful," Cathy said.

Tina-Lu handed Cathy the brooch for a closer look. Immediately, the bracelet around the girl's wrist reacted. Bathing the jewel in a silvery beam, the mystical light fell onto the brooch causing an explosion of the brightest red light. Everywhere burst into a brilliant luminescence; Cathy nearly dropped the gemstone in surprise. Out from the miniature prison formed a transparent, and apparently naked, outline of a woman. Jack and Jaden's eyes nearly popped out of their heads as they turned to see the beautiful spirit dancing before them.

"Greetings Guardian, long have I sought your presence. I'm Layette the Decider and I'm your servant. What is your question?"

The light from Layette bathed the room in a warm, crimson glow. Cathy seemed to take on an older and wiser look under the intensity of the beams.

"How do you know who I am Layette?" Cathy asked inquisitively, missing entirely the gaping mouths of the two boys.

"I belong to your blood line Guardian. Many generations ago my spirit was locked in the deep dark places of the world by the evil that is Lutharim. The Guardian found my soul and battled valiantly on my behalf. Unfortunately, she was overwhelmed by the dreadful spirit. I initially escaped before Lutharim locked me inside this jewel as a punishment. I was placed in a golden crown and had to endure my silence for generations. Eventually, a thief stole me and I was traded many times. One time I was a chain, another time a bangle and now a brooch. However, I managed to swear an undying oath to your forebears. Only the touch of the Guardian child would allow me to reach out from the confines of my prison home. Only the female Guardian has the power to permit me to step free; even briefly. Here I am, and at your service I shall be. What is your question?"

Cathy was amazed and extremely excited; she winked at Jack before asking cleverly. "How do we find the Lost Room Layette?"

The spirit's eyes opened wide with fear, her crimson light dimmed noticeably and the air around them all chilled to the point of making each shiver involuntarily. Layette became even thinner and an, almost invisible, wraith spinning and swirling as if dancing in the beams of her own glow. Hissing the answer; her voice sounded tortured.

"A question that you should not ask,
a place that never should be found.
A beast in there is hidden fast,
a world of death beneath the ground..."

Layette's voice reduced to a wounded screech; the light in the brooch extinguished.

"Oops, guess that was the wrong question to ask," Cathy cringed apologetically before handing the brooch back to Tina-Lu. "Thanks, but this belongs to you."

Tina-Lu looked closely at the brooch, then at her brother and finally at Cathy. "No Cathy, this is definitely yours. Sorry Jack, but we all heard what Layette said, this belongs to the bloodline of the Guardians." Tina-Lu opened the clasp, at the back of the brooch, and pinned it on the lapel of Cathy's blouse.

The girl coloured up at her kindness and honesty. "Thanks Tina-Lu, you are a real friend." She hugged the girl tightly and felt a really strong bond forming between them.

Jack and Jaden barely managed to wipe the grins from their faces. At last, Jaden commented sensibly, "well at least she gave us a clue to the location of the Lost Room. Now let's get back to the task at hand."

As the afternoon progressed their experiments went very well. Guiding the MoonBridge proved easier than either of the Guardians realised; they only needed to concentrate upon creating a mental picture of where they wanted to exit. Jack also found, since the effect of the storm, his ability to picture things from afar had grown stronger.

"I think I can actually see things out of my sight Cathy," he explained. "Just like in the cave or behind the door in the dungeons; it's like I'm really there. I now seem to be able to drive my mind out of my body and rush off in any direction. With a bit of practice I should be able to find my way over to this fortress. I may even be able to find the Lost Room."

Jack and Cathy guided the MoonBridge to the top of the nearby hills: they all successfully stepped through. "How clever is that?" Jack exclaimed. "Let's see if we can get back again?" The route was reversed; everyone agreed the trials had been a resounding success.

Jaden linked arms with Tina-Lu; he stretched up and said, in his best posh voice, "Ladies and Gentlemen, may I proudly present the Guardians of the MoonBridge; Jack and Cathy, our very own master and mistress of Lujnima's secret power." He bowed low to the ground clapping loudly as Tina-Lu joined him in a mocking curtsey.

"Yes my lord and lady, very nicely done, I must say." Tina-Lu mimicked the 'posh' voice too.

"Oh shut up you two," Jack retaliated.

The four laughed together and thought about the way ahead. After a short discussion the final plan was agreed.

"This is what we'll do." Jaden declared. "All of us will head towards the fortress by transiting the MoonBridge. You two Guardians will open and close the bridge to allow us all to hop across the countryside. When we come within sight of the place, Jack must attempt to find an exit point for the bridge. Your new projection abilities will really be put to the test then. Whilst you two are gone; Tina-Lu, Brandy and I will remain behind guarding the staffs and wait for the pair of you to return with the conduit." His plan sounded straightforward, but the others doubted it would be that easy.

"How are we going to get back Jaden?" Tina-Lu's question was on all of their lips.

"I think we'll have to take things as they come until we know what we are up against. We might have to walk home."

The look on Tina-Lu's face was a picture. She certainly didn't fancy that very much.

"Let's get some things together and just get on with it, shall we?" Cathy was ready for the off and so was Jack.

They all went away to gather food, water and other supplies. They carefully packed small rucksacks and slung them confidently on their backs.

"Let's do it!" Jack said excitedly.

The two Guardians opened the bridge and set the exit point, on the peak of a distant hilltop, about ten kilometres away. All five stepped onto the bridge and were instantly transported to their first destination.

"That is so weird," Tina-Lu laughed. She looked back to the camp nestled in amongst the distant trees. The misty tree line spread continuously along the contours of the hills. "That saved about a day's walk. Look, you can hardly see the camp at all."

Jack stood alongside his sister and agreed. "No-one would ever believe this at home, Sis."

Jaden stared over to the east and saw another vantage point far on the horizon. "Over there," He pointed to the Guardians.

The bridge opened for a second time; again, all five scurried across the opening.

"Where now Jaden?" Cathy was enjoying herself; she had never felt so in control of the MoonBridge. Combining her abilities with Jack's made a huge difference.

Jaden pointed towards a flattened ridge standing above the distant horizon. "That hill is easily thirty-five kilometres away," he warned.

All was going well; they stepped out onto their destination and surveyed the landscape. Ahead, a wide barren area stretched farther than the eye could see.

Jack squinted looking into the distance. "It looks pretty bleak out there."

"These are called, the unnamed lands," Jaden whispered mysteriously. "Few enter here willingly."

A shiver ran down Tina-Lu's back at the warning. "Is it safe?"

"And why is it called Unnamed?" Jack finished the sentence for his sister.

"Do you remember, I explained before about the Unnamed, he is the father of Lujnima and Tarre-Hare? Legends say that he is Unnamed because his actual name is so sacred that by even just thinking it would be enough to cause a person to burst into flames and evaporate right where he stood."

"What, just from mentioning his name?" Jack wasn't convinced at all.

"That place down there is where many thousands of ancients perished in a great war. The citizens were destroyed by the Unnamed because they decided to rise up against the elders and took His name in vain. Legends tell that He wreaked his wrath against them all, and they all died. The land remains barren because nothing can ever grow on its scorched earth." Jaden's explanation left them cold and afraid.

Tina-Lu screwed her nose up in horror at the story. "You mean there are dead bodies down there. What right now?" She looked sick to the stomach.

"No silly, every person was turned instantly to ash. All that remains is dust and the barren soil."

"How come the Unnamed was so cruel and dreadful and yet his daughter Lujnima is so helpful and kind?" Jack wondered.

"He wasn't dreadful Jack; it was just that he would not permit the people to rise up against him. The stories tell that he could not help himself and he destroyed everything in a flash."

"You talk about him as if he no longer exists, what has happened to him? Where is he now?"

"That is not known for certain Jack. Some legends tell that one day he just decided to leave and only his two daughters remained. They will never be drawn on the subject of their father even though many have enquired. Some say the two daughters colluded to remove him from power and to divide his world into the two halves we now see. Others claim that after he destroyed the armies he fell into a great depression of guilt and then left this place to go into self imposed isolation. Either way, he no longer seems to be in existence."

They all decided it was best to pass this awful place as quickly as possible and Jaden directed them to the far distance over to the south east.

"There is a small oasis, over there, right on the horizon," he said pointing with his finger out into the heat haze.

Cathy couldn't see anything in the direction that Jaden indicated.

"I might as well try to project my mind over there, as a test." Jack stood quietly for a second with his arms hanging limply at his sides.

He felt his mind leave his body and he raced across the barren lands at phenomenal speed. Flying about 50 feet off the ground; he looked down and had visions of hundreds of men and women dressed in armour and uniforms being evaporated by a single blinding light. The vision left a chill in his blood. Speeding across the barren plain, he reached the oasis just as Jaden had described. A clear blue pool, about thirty feet across and very deep was surrounded by a few trees and bushes clinging precariously to life in this desolate place.

"That water looks very inviting," Jack sighed.

As quickly as he'd travelled, he returned. Jack blinked a few times adjusting to his body and stance. Of course, to the others he'd only stood in a semi-trance for a few seconds.

"I reached the oasis Cathy," he announced. "Follow my thoughts and help me direct the bridge to the edge of the pool."

Cathy joined with Jack and looked through his mind's eye at the water's edge. The MoonBridge was opened again and the exit point placed alongside the clear blue pool.

"Well done Cathy you were perfect," Jack smiled encouragingly.

"You both did brilliantly." Tina-Lu praised the Guardians.

Jack took the compliment from his sister and secretly felt very proud. She rarely gave him any genuine credit.

"I'm going for a swim when we get back," Jack stated adamantly.

"Me too," giggled Tina-Lu; contemplating jumping in.

Brandy didn't need any encouragement; one bound saw him splashing around, barking with excitement. He really couldn't understand what the rest were waiting for.

"Get out you crazy dog," Jack ordered.

Brandy ignored the command and paddled madly to the other side. Clambering out, he shook most of the water from his coat. Nonchalantly, he sniffed his way back checking out each bush and plant.

"Come here I said." Jack's voice was harsh.

Brandy sat beside his master. He looked upwards with his deep brown eyes and dropped his ears subserviently.

Jack huffed before patting the dog. "That's better."

"Where to next Jaden, we'll have to get beyond these trees to see our route ahead?" Cathy mused.

Jaden agreed and wandered off for a few minutes, he looked over to the north east. A place on the distant horizon caught his attention; although, mostly the land seemed to melt into the sky with the haze and rising heat.

"If I remember correctly, there is a line of hills over there overlooking the fortress town of Marwearsort. Just aim for the horizon," Jaden pointed roughly in the direction he needed to go.

Cathy and Jack held hands again and prepared to open the MoonBridge. They concentrated and imagined the bridge appearing. Nothing happened.

"Did you..." Jack looked quizzically at Cathy. She in return shrugged her shoulders. They tried again; still no bridge appeared.

"What's wrong you two?" Tina-Lu asked them both.

"The bridge doesn't respond to our call," Jack looked extremely puzzled.

Jaden walked around for a few seconds thinking deeply and then said. "I suppose it's possible you have a limited number of opportunities to open the bridge in any one day? Or maybe you are both tired by the previous openings?"

Neither had any answer. They had one more attempt and then sat down by the water.

"It's no good; we can't make the bridge appear. I think it's actually missing somehow. Cathy, did you feel that way too?"

Cathy thought carefully before she replied to Jack's question. "I definitely felt we called exactly as before but I didn't sense any response whatsoever. So, yes, I guess it did feel like it was no longer there."

Jaden was very concerned. "If what you describe is true, then there is a possibility that something has happened to Lujnima. She, after all, powers the bridge when you command it to appear. If something had happened to her then it wouldn't appear, would it?"

"How can you find out?" asked Tina-Lu. She now felt uncomfortable. They'd travelled a very long way and the dead lands were probably twenty five to thirty kilometres across. Water was in plentiful supply; food was the problem. She suddenly realised they hadn't brought nearly enough supplies. Each wore a small back pack with some basic provisions but barely enough food to last more than a couple of days.

"If you cannot re-open the bridge we are going to have to choose to either turn back or to carry on across the dead lands." Tina-Lu exclaimed with more than a little panic in her voice.

"All is not lost Tina-Lu," Jaden soothed his friend. "We must see if it's possible to contact Lujnima first. Then we'll know whether we have to worry or not."

Jack and Cathy had slipped back into a semi-trance as they tried to make contact with Lujnima. The look on there faces gave nothing away. They both seemed to be half asleep as they stood there staring blankly into the space in front of them.

Brandy had already lain down and fallen fast asleep in the shade of one of the bushes near the water. Tina-Lu paced restlessly up and down looking more concerned and frightened with every passing moment.

"Come and sit down Tina-Lu, for goodness sake, you are making me dizzy pacing up and down like that."

Jaden was trying his best to calm her down, but it wasn't working.

Jack and Cathy merged their minds and called to Lujnima. Jack even tried to lead Cathy out of her body and over towards the entry point where he'd been taken on his first visit. All around them seemed like a thick grey impenetrable fog.

"She isn't here Jack. I can't sense her at all?" Cathy was correct; neither could sense Lujnima's presence.

"Is it possible for us to contact Tarre-Hare; Cathy?" Jack was desperately grasping for any answer.

"I don't think so, perhaps we should ask Jaden?"

They agreed this was the only other course of action open to them. Slipping out of their trance, the two reported to the others and suggested that Jaden attempt to seek an audience with Tarre-Hare.

Jaden wasn't keen, "you don't pop in on someone like Tarre-Hare. She might fry us all. We should seek help from her sister, as she ordered."

Slipping off her shoes, Tina-Lu looked at the others and shouted. "Oh, what the hell," she ran a couple paces towards the inviting water and swallow dived perfectly into the cool and refreshing blue pool. Barely a few ripples spread out from her dive; she swam underwater all the way to the middle, before rising up gasping for breath.

"What are you wimps waiting for? If we are going to be stuck here for a while we might as well cool off first."

None of the others needed any further encouragement. They instantly forgot their troubles and plunged into the pool. Brandy opened an eye and looked at the four as they screamed with joy at the coolness of the water. "Now they decide to go for a swim," he closed his eye again and drifted back into his dreams of chasing rabbits.

With no-one for miles around they screamed, shouted and laughed at the tops of their voices. The four played for ages having the best fun and enjoyment imaginable; not one of them acted as if they had a care in the world. For over an hour they relaxed, everyone was exhausted by the time they clambered out; Jack went straight over and lay on the warm rocks to dry off. Tina-Lu lay down beside her brother and stared up at the sky. The sun rose high and very hot; she basked in the refreshing warmth and remembered some of the things Jaden had spoken of earlier.

Barely a breath of air moved, the sun baked the ground and dried everyone. Tina-Lu closed her eyes and drifted silently off to sleep.

"Child, your brother will bring destruction to us all. He must be stopped."

Tina-Lu heard the voice in her dream, she looked around to see the speaker; no-one could be seen.

"You carry a heavy burden, child. You must learn to see your brother in for what he is. The death of us all – he must be stopped."

"Who said that?" Tina-Lu's dream state couldn't find this person.

"Who I am is not important child. My warning must be heeded or we will all perish, even the Crechy, oldest of all living beings – hidden from sight. You must take your brother back, never to return."

Tina-Lu knew this to be correct without having to question. She didn't ask for anything further – the truth in the statement was clear for her to see. Her ten minute nap came to an abrupt end with Jaden tugging at her arm.

"Are you asleep?"

"Not any more!"

The young Sage shrugged his shoulders. "Come on, we've work to do."

"I was just wondering; perhaps Lujnima cannot be contacted because of where we are. I mean, if this place is called the unnamed lands, because the father of Lujnima and Tarre-Hare, maybe you can't call them from here. Maybe it's cursed or something, like you can't call anyone from these dead-lands?"

Jaden looked down with great admiration at his friend lying dripping wet on the rocks He realised that she was probably right. "Of course: this place is preventing any signals, or whatever they are, from getting through. Maybe the fog resulted from the destruction caused by the Unnamed."

"That's all very well Jaden, but that still means that we will have to walk out of here." Jack wasn't relishing a long journey in the heat and the dust.

"The road looks very long either to the fortress or back the way we came." Tina-Lu agreed with her brother.

"It is easily a days' walk in either direction, maybe a little more," Jaden pointed out guardedly.

"We could choose to walk back the way we came and then hope to use the bridge to leap right across the dead lands to the other side. Or just accept that we must walk over to the hills in the distance. Neither seems to be ideal." Cathy wasn't happy at either prospect.

"I say head for the fortress," Tina-Lu offered. "We came to find the conduit and that is really our only hope."

"Yes, but if we get there and find that Lujnima really is gone, we are even farther away from the Resistance and our friends. We'll have to walk all the way back again," Jack grumbled with considerable doubt in his voice.

"Is there really no other way? What about your portal Jaden, can't you use that?" Tina-Lu was trying hard to avoid having to walk across the desert.

"Sorry Tina-Lu, but my portal doesn't work like the MoonBridge. As far as I know, the exit only points to Tarre-Hare and nowhere else."

Despite much discussion, the only realistic option was to continue with their original plan and head for the fortress. "We must try to find the Lost Room and hunt for the conduit," Jaden declared reluctantly. "These are the only genuine hopes for our future survival and that means we walk."

"Let's wait until the tomorrow morning before we set off. We could use the cool of the morning to cross as much as possible," Jack suggested.

"No Jack, we should set off now. The heat will ease as the afternoon progresses and we have plenty of water. I don't like the idea of spending a night here, this place feels wrong to me some how. Anyway, we will hopefully arrive before dark."

The early afternoon sun beat down from a cloudless sky. The scorched earth was compacted hard as concrete and covered with scatterings of jagged rocks and dark red sand. Ahead, the blistering heat haze shimmered and flowed like a river of imaginary water melting the horizon. Each of the four looked solemn and apprehensive.

Jaden did his best to cheer them all up. "Come on you lot, think of all those times you have wanted to strip off and enjoy the sun. Well here there's plenty of sun for you to enjoy."

The team pulled their small packs onto their backs, and carrying as much water as their skins could hold, they set off.

After about an hour, they were all hot, tired and fed up. Jack saw visions and flashbacks of people being instantly thrust out of this existence and into a limbo. His arms itched and twitched painfully; the waking dream consumed his thoughts. Lagging behind the others, Jack heard voices calling, "Help us Guardian, take our souls and free our pain."

Echoes, of memories long dead, spilled through Jack's semi-conscious mind. He saw the faces of thousands and thousands of men all with a frozen look of horror etched deeply into their terrified stares. Jack felt the blast of the irrepressible heat that evaporated each and every one of them in the blink of an eye. He heard the screams reverberating only in the spirit world of lost souls.

One voice rose above all others. "Why have you brought us back to this unholy place Guardian? Only pain and death reside here; we are all cursed because of this terrible hell." Epheron's plea dug deeply into Jack's heart and he was surprised to find tears welling up in his eyes.

The spirit voice continued "We are all doomed because of our foolish notion that we were better than our cousins from across the great divide. We have all paid a terrible price for our vanity and none of us know peace. You must free us from our torment Guardian. You must find a way to set us free."

Jack glanced down at his arm; thousands of tiny mirrors twinkled and glistened in the sun. With every step he attracted more lost souls; the weight of their grief bore down on his shoulders, the voices in his mind became a deafening melee. He slapped his hands on his ears, collapsed to his knees exhausted and screamed, "shut-up: all of you!"

Cathy turned back to see her friend falling to the ground. She struggled to hurry to help him. Jaden and Tina-Lu were further ahead and oblivious to Jack's plight. "What's happened to you Jack?"

The boy's eyes rolled in pain; he could barely understand anything Cathy was saying.

"Here, drink this." Cathy put the skin of water to Jacks lips and poured a few drops into his mouth. "What's that all over your arm?"

The boy blinked several times as the refreshing drink brought him back to reality. "Lost souls," he croaked. "They're lost souls from the war."

Cathy took Jack's hand and joined her thoughts with his. She couldn't hear any voices or sense anything. Smiling sympathetically, she assumed Jack was suffering from heatstroke and hallucinating. "Have some more water Jack, you're dehydrated. You'll feel better in a moment."

Chapter 15 - The Lost Room

"This place is cursed," Tina-Lu moaned loudly; her feet ached and her nose itched from the choking dust. The last six hours had been very boring. She was tired and extremely grubby. "I never want to do that again."

Finally, they made their way up into the foothills and reached the first greenery they'd seen since leaving the refreshing pool at the oasis.

"At last, something living to walk on," Throwing herself down onto the grass and taking off her shoes; Tina-Lu declared with a sigh, "My poor feet are killing me. What we need now is another pool or stream, to cool off and freshen up. I'm filthy and I hate it."

They all agreed how inviting that sounded and after a brief rest made their way around the hill. Unfortunately, there were no streams or pools to splash in here. The hill just led to an even higher hill that seemed to block their path.

"I think we're still some distance from Marwearsort." They all groaned in disapproval at Jaden's assessment. "We need to be further up to the north I think. Perhaps we should just sleep here for the night and try again tomorrow. We're all too tired anyway."

None of them needed to be asked twice; the exertion of previous few hours left them all exhausted. They threw themselves down onto the grass and fell straight to sleep.

***

A cool and pleasant breeze signalled the early dawn; Cathy was the first to wake and roused the others.

Tina-Lu woke grumpily: her bones ached; her muscles were stiff and despite the night's sleep, she still felt tired. "What did I listen to you for Jack, I should've stayed at home in my nice warm bed."

Jaden awoke and was instantly happy and upbeat as ever; he bounced around making a simple breakfast of food they'd brought with them. Brandy just looked out of one eye and barely moved.

Jack was quiet and looked pensively around him. "Something's really not right here," he announced, looking up and down the hillside. "I'm getting a very strange feeling running down my neck; I think it's a sign of some kind. Maybe we're being watched."

Cathy looked over at Jack and replied. "Yes, I'm feeling it too. Just like something is pressing down on my head; I think we should move from here now."

Tina-Lu suddenly remembered her dream voice at the oasis. The grass called to her deep in her mind. "You must take him away my child; before he destroys us all." She shook her head and tried to pretend she had heard nothing. "All in my imagination," she convinced herself.

They moved off in a northerly direction. Their journey took them over the first hill and around the second. The five travellers made slow, but steady, progress. After a short while they reached the peak of a hill; they could finally see their destination for the first time. The fortress stood about five kilometres from them and looked impregnable even from this distance. Perched high above a small town spreading out from its gates; the fortress was a single wide round tower surrounded by an even larger round wall. The whole structure was built upon a tall rock base making it seem twice its real height. The stone walls were formed of a shiny blackish rock that reflected the sun in a beautiful, but menacing manner. The town of Marwearsort had many scattered buildings dotted apart from one another. Roads stretched away from the town in all directions and it was clear that a lot of people lived there.

"I think we are now far enough away from the dead lands to attempt to open the bridge again," Jaden suggested hopefully. "But first Jack, you should try to find an exit point, over there, inside the fortress walls."

Jack stared across the space towards Marwearsort and the fortress. He felt himself rush across the distance in the blink of an eye. Looking down; the outskirts of the town was filled with soldiers. The centre was bustling with activity; a glance up at the walls, of the fortress, made him realise just how imposing this great structure was. The ancients had carved a spiralling roadway that wound its way up the sides of the rock foundation. Below the imposing surrounding wall was a huge cliff face of the same gleaming rock. Jack drove his mind over the barrier and into the fortress itself. The area was empty except for a few tents and soldiers patrolling. The outer wall formed a perfect circle and was wide enough for ten to fifteen men to easily walk side-by-side. The central tower was even larger than he imagined. Also circular in shape, it was as wide as it was tall.

"Hundreds of rooms and possibly thousands of soldiers could be hidden inside there?" Even though they couldn't see him, he feared his spirit-self might rouse the hidden armies below.

Jack focussed upon the central tower and thrust his mind towards the shining black marble. Rushing forwards, he was brought, painfully, to an abrupt halt; the change of speed was so sudden his physical body, back on the hill, lurched backwards and fell down. Almost instantly, Jack was thrown out of his semi-trance and found himself sitting on the grass with the others.

"Whatever happened to you Jack?" asked Cathy; helping him to his feet.

"I hit some kind of barrier I think. I'd no problem reaching the town or the outer wall. But the tower stopped me from entering. I think I hit an invisible wall; it really shook me up." He rubbed his nose as if he'd actually crashed into something. "The really weird part though is that I felt as though it was someone rather than something. An ancient power stopped me, I'm sure of it."

Jaden looked worried. "I have no knowledge of such a force. This is worse than I imagined."

"Perhaps you have just found the Lost Room Jack?" Tina-Lu suggested with a shrug of her shoulders; taking a closer look at Jack's face. He wasn't physically hurt.

The suggestion was greeted with surprise but it seemed possible; after all a Lost Room would surely be invisible.

"But this was outside the walls of the tower," Jack said. "And, didn't Layette say something about under the ground?"

"Yes, but it would be a perfect place to hide a room I'd say. No-one would ever think of looking outside the walls of the tower," Tina-Lu suggested. "I reckon it's exactly where you would put it if you could."

"I'm going back for another look," he said, preparing himself for another trip. "But, I'll be more cautious this time."

Before his sister could protest, the walls of the fortress stood before him. He decided to slowly walk towards the tower rather than rushing like before. To his great surprise he walked right up to, and through, the great black walls. He found himself inside an empty outer room.

"Weird!" he mumbled. "This is so weird."

Turning around, he walked back through the wall and out into the sunlight. Now he was really confused. He thought for a moment, "I'll get back to the same position when I hit the barrier and have another go."

The idea was sound, but left Jack struggling; the tower and fortress were round, every point looked almost identical to every other point. After a few attempts, he identified the right spot and then travelled straight towards the tower. Once again, he sped straight through the walls and into one of the rooms on the inside. The wall presented no barrier to his path nor caused any collision. The Lost Room, if that is what it had been before; wasn't there any more.

"I see you Guardian."

Jack spun towards the fleeting sound of the voice behind him; nothing was visible. "Who said that?" he demanded. A cold shiver ran down the boy's back, he felt the invisible eyes watching him but saw no-one.

"Leave now, or die..." the ethereal voice drifted out of the polished rock surface to his left.

"What? Show yourself, who is that?" Jack panicked, his skin wrinkled into thousands of goose-bumps. Before he could react again, his mind rushed back across the landscape and retuned to the hill-top. The changing look on Jack's face showed that he was coming out of his semi-trance.

"Did you succeed Jack?" Cathy asked impatiently.

Jack didn't answer immediately; his mind raced in fear.

"What about the Lost Room Jack?" Tina-Lu pressed. "Have you found the Lost Room?"

Still Jack stood silently. His mind replayed the warning: 'leave now, or die'. "Um, not exactly," he stuttered. "Yes, I've discovered something; um, something very odd."

"He's found it, I knew you would Jack."

"You may be right Tina-Lu. But it may also be something more sinister. I fear he may have accidentally bumped into one of the ancient Vinkef." Jaden warned, his voice lowering to a whisper and his eyes darting around expectantly.

The girls moved closer to learn of this new peril.

"Something weird happened, um, I think there is some spirit in there; I heard voices." Jack continued confusingly.

"What voices Jack, what did you hear?" Jaden demanded; ignoring the girls.

Jack relayed his encounter.

"This is just as I feared." Jaden ushered them closer to him; he continued in a frantic tone. "Whilst Jack has been away I've been searching my memories for anything that could also do this. The ancient elders reportedly had invisible allies that prevented any enemy from entering the castle. These Vinkef were only ever described as the Invisible Protectors in my memories, but they were very effective because no-one who had encountered them were ever seen again. Rumours quickly spread and the fortress became even more impenetrable. That might also explain the strange feeling that he and Cathy had when they woke up this morning."

Tina-Lu no longer looked smug, her faced changed to fear. "You mean these things, if they exist, are invisible. They'll probably kill us or something, and you want to send my brother back in there." she became more animated with each sentence.

Jaden didn't answer because Jack stood up to his sister. "Look Sis, I know your motives are sound, but you have to stop thinking of me as your little kid brother. I'm quite capable of making my own choices here, and anyway, I'll be careful. If things get too hairy, I'll just leave."

"You're getting too cocky little brother. This entire Guardianship thing is really going to your head and I KNOW that mum and dad would never forgive me if something serious actually happened to you. I don't think you have the slightest idea what you might be getting in to. That place down there is surrounded and filled with soldiers, not to mention these Vinkef things. Get it in your head that they will mean business if you get caught, I can't bear to think what they might do to you."

Jack saw the tears forming in his sister's eyes; she'd become very upset and frightened. He guessed she was just beginning to realise they were a very long way from home and this adventure wasn't a game. He put his arm around her and said comfortingly, "It's okay Sis; I know all you've described is true - we should be worried. But I've changed; honestly, I've changed more than I can describe. I've grown somehow; Lujnima and Tarre-Hare have given me abilities that I never would've dreamed of. I really am the Guardian; you've seen me command the MoonBridge on many occasions. I even have the power to leave my body and travel across the land to other places."

Pausing for a moment; Jack held up his left arm and concentrated. The generated light shone as brightly as the sun for a few seconds.

"Do you think I could have done that back home? I don't think so. Please trust me and believe me when I tell you that it will be okay. We are going to find the Lost Room and the conduit and then we're going to find out what the three together can achieve as the key. Cathy and I will look out for each other. I realise now that this is my destiny and she and I are the Guardians. We will call on all of the strengths that Lujnima and Tarre-Hare offer and will use their powers as wisely as we can."

Tina-Lu had tears streaming down her cheeks. She looked at her brother in a completely different light. "I never understood, until right now, just how different you are Jack. I feel I hardly know you. I don't think I'll ever consider you my little brother again, if anything, I feel like your lowly sister."

"Don't feel that way Sis. You are part of the team, we need to stick together. Each brings out the best in all of us. You are full of great ideas and plans; we all know how much help you've been so far. You'll always be my big sister and I'm proud you are. I'm not sure I ever knew just how much I appreciate you being here." Hugging his sister tightly; she sniffed loudly several times.

Tina-Lu wiped away her tears and turned to Jaden. "Right, let's see if we can get them into this place," she choked.

Jack and Cathy looked at each other and held hands. They both lifted their staffs aloft and commanded the bridge to open. Thankfully, after a few seconds the light formed.

"That's a relief," exclaimed Jaden. "Well done you two."

Tina-Lu had been correct again; the Dead Lands had prevented the bridge from being called.

"We'll place the exit point right inside the room on the other side of the round tower Cathy. That way we will avoid being seen by the guards and soldiers," Jack concentrated upon the room he'd briefly entered.

The two Guardians guided the MoonBridge. Quickly saying their goodbyes, they placed the pair of staffs on the ground and stepped through. The bridge faded from view taking Jack and Cathy with it - Tina-Lu, Jaden and Brandy watched solemnly.

"Well, now we wait." Jaden sounded nervous and apprehensive.

***

Jack led Cathy, by the hand, out of the moonbeams. The room they entered was quite large and completely empty; the walls followed the contours of the outer wall making the shape roughly like a slightly rounded square. On the outside wall was one small window, letting in very little light, and opposite, a single door led, presumably, into the tower. They guessed it must have been a store room as it had no furnishings or fittings. The door was firmly locked; the window was only a very thin crossed slit that arrows could have been fired through, at an enemy below.

"Now what mastermind?" Cathy teased. "You've managed to place us in the only locked room in the tower, I bet," she was being really sarcastic and sounded a bit fed up.

Jack grinned at her and said wryly. "Don't give up on me yet Cathy. I may be able to get us out of here." He opened his little back pack and pulled out a set of keys. "Jaden thought I might need these," he grinned cunningly.

The third key he tried made a reassuring click as it threw the bolt in the mechanism. The door was unlocked.

Cathy gave him a playful slap and shook her head in disbelief. "Alright smarty pants; you are my hero and a mastermind too."

Quietly and slowly they opened the door. A wide passageway wound around the outer edge of the tower.

"I can hear someone down there," Jack pointed cautiously.

Faint voices murmured from their left. Cathy looked in both directions before stepping through the door into the tower. "Let's go this way," she said.

217

Cautiously following the corridor to their right, they opened several doors before finding a staircase. Cathy looked up and down. "Which way?" she whispered.

Jack shrugged his shoulders and then pointed down for no particular reason.

They walked down, about thirty stairs, spiralling along in-line with the curve of the tower walls. Another doorway opened out onto the floor below. Again, they could choose to continue down the stairs or to explore this floor.

Cathy whispered in Jack's ear. "Why don't you just whip around this place first and then lead us to the room we need to be in?"

Jack laughed quietly. "Of course, what an idiot I am. Mastermind, I don't think I can claim to be any kind of mastermind."

They crossed the passageway and sneaked into the nearest room. This one was filled with large wooden cases with symbols stamped on the outside. They moved behind a pile, stacked high to the ceiling, and sat on the floor.

"You get off and see what you can find. I'll keep watch," Cathy said; holding his hands tightly. "It's okay, I'm not afraid. Not with you here."

Once again, Cathy managed to make Jack colour up like a beetroot. He grinned back at her, sheepishly, feeling really proud she felt that way.

***

Back at the hilltop Tina-Lu paced backwards and forwards making Jaden dizzy.

"How long has it been Jaden? How long have they been gone? They should be back by now shouldn't they?"

"Lu, will you please sit down, you're driving me nuts. They've only been gone about ten minutes. They might not be back for ages so stop worrying." Jaden had never called Tina-Lu just Lu before, he was pleased that she didn't complain. Even though he was only eleven years of bodily age he'd formed a very strong bond with this older girl.

Tina-Lu didn't sit down. Instead, she walked further away, somehow she felt closer to her brother and Cathy. Raising her hand to shield her eyes, she looked intently across the distance. "Where are you little brother? Are you alright?"

"Wow!" She jumped a foot in the air hearing her brother's voice as clear as if he was stood right next to her.

"It's alright Sis, we're in the tower. Cathy is keeping watch whilst I search the place with my mind. I heard your call and felt your concern. I didn't realise I could also talk to you the same way I've called Jaden and Cathy before. Relax and stop worrying, I'll keep you up to date with events as they unfold. By the way Sis, I love you very much. You're the best sister I could ever have wished for."

Tina-Lu flopped down on the ground right where she stood. She opened and closed her mouth several times, without being able to make any sense, whilst pointing aimlessly towards the fortress.

Jaden looked at her bemused, before finally laughing out loud, "So, the Guardians have been in contact have they? I wondered how long it would take Jack to realise he could let us know what was happening. Everything okay is it?" He laughed at the gaping face of Tina-Lu coming to terms with the shock.

"It's okay Lu; the first time is always a bit scary. You just can't believe he isn't there; it really spooks you out."

She nodded in agreement before starting to calm down and then thought to herself. "This is the weirdest place I've ever imagined. Perhaps I should've just stayed in bed after all. That'll teach me for spying on my brother. So he loves me does he, I don't ever remember him telling me that before; still it's quite nice. I guess I love him too, the stupid idiot."

***

Jack searched every room, on every floor, at a speed that made him feel giddy. He was really getting the hang of flying through the walls without even slowing down. He noted all the soldiers and workers; they were everywhere. He found store rooms, kitchens, sleeping quarters, living rooms and every other kind of room imaginable; but he didn't find any Lost Room. He returned to Cathy.

"It's hopeless Cathy. I've been everywhere at least twice; I haven't got a clue what I'm supposed to be looking for. How do you find a Lost Room? And what on earth would one look like?"

She smiled at him and said. "I haven't any idea either; I thought that you knew what to look for, and somehow you would just know?" She squeezed his hands again and said. "Let's just try to not think of the answer; instead, let's just imagine we already know the answer and then see what happens. I sometimes find the harder you try the harder it gets. So just relax and let our minds do the work for us."

Jack didn't have any idea what Cathy was going on about, but he smiled and went along with her anyway.

The two sat quietly with their eyes closed, holding hands loosely. Their backs rested against the pile of large boxes. Jack was certain nothing was going to happen. Cathy relaxed; she fell into a deep trance hovering on the edge of sleep. Although she had her eyes firmly closed, she could clearly see Jack and the room, perfectly. From a vantage point several feet above the floor, she looked closer and realised she could also see herself, sitting cross-legged with her head bent slightly forwards. She thought that her hair was all over the place and said to herself. "Yuck, what a terrible sight I look."

Jack realised Cathy had slipped fully into a trance and wondered if she was having any more luck than he was. He thought about letting go of Cathy's hand, but guessed she needed to feel he was still there for her.

Cathy could hear herself breathing slowly but didn't have any sense it was her body. She slipped away from the room, or rather; the room seemed to be slipping away from her. The whole place gradually disappeared. A grey mistiness filled her mind and then it deepened to blackness.

"Hello my child. I've been expecting you."

The voice wasn't really in her head, nor was it exactly anywhere she could pinpoint.

"I know you can hear me; I also know you're seeking something that shouldn't be found."

The voice seemed to come from a very young child but felt ancient at the same time.

"Your friend is dangerously powerful you know. He'll bring destruction to us all before his time is done if he is not stopped. He wants that which is hidden even though he doesn't know why yet. I'm afraid, I cannot let either of you find it; neither of you are yet ready."

"Who are you?" Cathy said in her mind.

"You know who I am. Search your heart my darling and you'll know; I'm your father. You know this to be true Cathy."

"What? What are you talking about? My Father is dead; he died in the wars long ago."

"Yes, that's one truth Cathy. I did die as you would describe, but I was also reborn at the same time. My physical body was left to rot, along with many other captured soldiers, in the dungeons of this awful place - many years ago. My flesh has long since gone and my bones are now just dust. But instead of going on, I ended up here. I've been waiting for you ever since."

"What do you mean, waiting? How could you be waiting, I didn't even know that I was coming here until a couple of days ago."

"Oh no my sweet child, you've been coming here, to this very moment, all of your life. The Vinkef knew and kept my soul here just so we could meet. Listen carefully daughter, it's now most important that you do exactly as I say. The entire world will depend upon the choices, you and your friends, make over the coming days. To falter or fail will spell doom for us all; dead or alive, it will make no odds. The Unnamed is unwilling to strike out again, even though there are few who can stand up to his anger. You and your friend must find a different path and lead the rebellion. Even the mighty Vinkef cannot stand against the deadly power that threatens. You must save us all Cathy."

The voice faded away; the mistiness, in her head, cleared. She realised she was back in her own body and tears were running down her face. She sobbed and Jack tried his best to comfort her.

"Cathy, can you hear me. Whatever has happened to you?" he sounded really concerned and unable to help.

Her eyes opened and she wiped the tears away. "It's my father Jack. He's here somewhere. He spoke to me." She waved her hands around and pulled a face of pain and anguish.

"What, I thought you told me he was dead?"

"He is, or rather, he isn't. Oh I don't know. But he did speak to me. He said he'd been waiting for me to come here. He also said we wouldn't be permitted to find what we seek."

"You're not making any sense. Are you sure you haven't just been dreaming?"

Cathy relayed all she'd heard and what she'd felt. They both wondered what all of it meant. Jack again had to ask himself. "Why was this being, saying, I'd bring destruction? That's what the underworld creatures said too."

"If your father is really here somewhere, perhaps, I should meet him to. You said he was kept here by the Vinkef. What does it, or they, have to do with this affair?"

Jack felt the hairs on his neck rise and a chill run down his spine. The air around them cooled and they could clearly see their breath. Mistiness formed in front of them and started to take the shape of a face, a baby's face.

"Hello Jack; Cathy." The face spoke in a soft, high pitched infantile voice.

"This is very difficult for me. I'm not used to becoming visible. My name is Korbynithus and I'm the embodiment of the Vinkef. I know you have many questions but there is no time for answers now. You must listen to what I've to say. You must then leave this place and never return. Your presence here signals the commencement of a chain of events that have been expected and waited for. The Unnamed foresaw this day and has been preparing for its arrival for many generations of your people."

The image of the Vinkef faded and then reappeared. The child seemed to be struggling to maintain the form.

"The world was still young when the Vinkef were brought across the bridge by the Unnamed one. He needed our assistance to guard this sacred place against a foe, so powerful, that even the mighty Unnamed could not defend it alone. He created the thing, you seek, and then the place where it's securely kept. He made it impossible for anyone to find it or to steal it."

Again the image faded; it was several seconds before it was able to reform.

"No-one has ever managed to unlock its secrets, not even the Vinkef who are sworn to protect it. Eons ago we made a very powerful pact with the Unnamed one and we've kept to our word ever since."

Jack and Cathy were drawn to the eyes of Korbynithus; they were a beautiful bright blue. His features were round and very welcoming. The child gave off an air of friendliness and love, hardly expected of a creature said to have mercilessly destroyed any intruders.

"Yes Jack, I do not look as dangerous as I've been portrayed. However, all of the stories you've been told are true. The Vinkef have destroyed every intruder who has ever foolishly come seeking that which must remain hidden. You're the first and only ones, who'll leave this place who've come to find the Unnamed's prize. You will carry with you a burden even greater than that which the Vinkef undertook all those ages ago. Our pact was to guard this place for all eternity and in return our society was freed from the curse of the Blues."

Jack and Cathy couldn't comprehend what possible burden could be harder than spending eternity guarding this place.

"Your task, and indeed your destiny, is to seek out the Blue menace. You must send them back from whence they came."

They didn't think this task was as hard as Korbynithus had described. But before either could speak, he continued. "When this evil is banished from this place; then you must destroy the MoonBridge."

Cathy just gasped at the notion.

Jack jumped up and felt himself screaming in disbelief. "What? Destroy the MoonBridge; never! Anyway, I doubt that's even possible. That would mean we'd have to kill Lujnima first and possibly Tarre-Hare too."

The child's face before them blinked in silent agreement.

Cathy slapped her hand across her mouth in revulsion at the thought.

"Please understand; the Blues are merciless creatures from a dimension far beyond your comprehension. They lure, unsuspecting, individuals into helping them and then take over the entire world before stripping it clean of every living thing. They leave a dead empty shell behind that can never be used by anyone. They must never again be given the chance to reach out and destroy any other worlds. The MoonBridge MUST be destroyed and it's you that must do it."

"I can't; I won't. Cathy and I would never do such a thing. Never," Jack became angry. "There must be another way. I'll NEVER do this."

"I'm sorry but I can no longer maintain this vision, I must leave you now and you must rejoin your friends. Please do not try to return to this place. Our pact with the Unnamed only permits this one offering of truce. Next time you will have to face the full and terrible might of the Vinkef. The Invisible Protectors do not wish to destroy you Jack Ferns. Good luck Guardians..."

The vision faded and Jack and Cathy were instantly transported back to the hill top where Jaden and Tina-Lu were lying in the shade with Brandy.

Chapter 16 - Rekindled Love

"Sister – speak to me?" Lujnima had not called her sister in an age of ages. Not since they had chosen to banish their father for his indiscretion. Only silence greeted her, a silence she'd never become accustomed to. "Sister – you MUST hear me. Put aside your pain and speak to me. Events are unfolding that threaten us both. We must speak."

Tarre-Hare hadn't wanted to confront this moment. She knew it was inevitable, but preferred the Guardians to solve this growing problem. Ever since Searlan had sent the boy; she knew this moment was approaching.

"The boy Guardian is strong; I've felt his power and witnessed his potential. You must make him resolve this problem and guide him towards his rightful destiny. I don't wish to speak with you," Tarre-Hare was still angry even after eons of time.

"No sister – neither of us can hide from this, we must join together again and confront the foe as one. My young Guardian does have great potential, as you've surmised, but you must also know that I cannot grant him his destiny, only he can find that," Lujnima couldn't mask her sarcasm.

Tarre-Hare left her twin sister, all those lifetimes ago, and resolved never to directly deal with her again. Lujnima's insistence was a violation of that pact and she felt trapped by the possibility of having to speak with her.

"Enough of this hatred sister; let us finally put aside our differences. Let us rekindle our friendship we enjoyed as children. Let us be as one again and put all these wrongs to right."

Tarre-Hare chose not to respond initially, but eventually weakened. "This is all you're doing sister, you and your ridiculous gateway. Why did you have to let father bring those things across the bridge in the first place? All this pain is your fault."

Hearing the voice of reason, coming from her twin; Lujnima felt a great weight lift from her shoulders. "Yes sister, I know I'm to blame. I've regretted my part for so long it's difficult to remember a time before my pain. I've hidden in the shadows, afraid to be seen, but do you really believe guilt and sorrow will resolve anything. I've prepared for this day, almost as long as I've grieved. I need your help desperately; I can't defeat these terrible creatures alone - they were beyond father's ability to destroy them and they are beyond mine. My Guardians are indeed strong, but I fear not strong enough. The enemy; however, is fully grown; these Shumiat will destroy us all."

Tarre-Hare listened, not entirely convinced; she hated Lujnima. "You created that infernal bridge out of sheer petulance," the anger spilled out. "You allowed father to bring in the enemy and then forced his hand to attempt to right the wrong. All those lives lost." Tarre-Hare couldn't hide the abhorrence any longer. "You alone encouraged father to undertake his desperate action. I never wanted to banish him; you made me conspire against him when he became unstable." Tarre-Hare hated her sister, so much; she could hardly bear to hear her voice again. Even though it had been an unimaginably long time; for her it had felt only a few moments.

"How do you expect me to forgive you sister, for all the wrongs you've done to father and to me? How can you ever be trusted again? Destroy that bridge of yours and maybe I'll believe you."

Lujnima expected as much. Her sister would never relent and would always distrust her. "You know full well that I cannot destroy the bridge. The bridge is me and I'm the bridge. To destroy one would be to destroy the other. Father knew this when he forged Tel-Vah-Let to control access. He didn't anticipate the effect of creating the key. That wasn't my mistake it was his. I never unleashed this evil; I only provided the mechanism for its movement. Father found them and brought them here. He allowed the Elders to traverse the bridge and to return with this evil."

Tarre-Hare couldn't admit her twin sister had only been a young innocent fool. Even if it wasn't her fault, everything was because of her.

"Tarre-Hare, enough is enough. I'm pleading with you to help right these wrongs. I need you to help me bring us all back from the brink of disaster. I need you to help me turn father around and bring him back to us."

Lujnima's sister stopped in her tracks; she never suspected this of her troubled twin.

"Please sister, please help me to correct all the bad times between us. Please let me restore the balance, but please don't ask me to destroy the bridge - I can never do that."

"You want to help father?"

"Yes, yes I do; he is the key to this. Only he can undo the wrongs; only he can send them back."

"And you will promise to help me free father from the curse you created."

"WE CREATED, Tarre-Hare I couldn't have created it alone."

"As you say, sister; but we will free him, won't we?"

"We will and I promise you'll be the one to take the credit. Father always loved you more than me anyway. I'll take all the blame, if you like, but I need your help."

The darkness surrounding Lujnima suddenly lightened. She cowered, hugging the little shadow remaining in her inner sanctuary, afraid of the power of her sister's light. Tarre-Hare gradually appeared. The 'Day' had finally come to meet the 'Night'.

"I've missed you so much sister, even though you believe I have not." Tarre-Hare was greeted by her cowering twin.

"I'm so sorry for all I've done. I promise I'll make things better between us. We will free father and we'll help him recover his pride and dignity."

"You're a fool sister; you've always been a jealous fool. You created your bridge to be better than me; just to impress father. You wrongly thought he loved me more than you; actually, he loved us equally. You chose to see things differently."

The two sisters faced each other for the first time in an age. They didn't look any different of course, such was their way. But they had endured an age of hatred, distrust and mutual disgust.

"How do you intend to put things right sister? What's your plan?" Tarre-Hare asked sceptically. "I've come before you as you requested, even though it's against my better judgement. Prove yourself or pay the consequences."

"We must help the Guardians grow. They must reach their full potential and then they'll be strong enough to help us free father. The Vinkef must be defeated; we'll never break their oath. They're the key that must be unlocked. My Guardians MUST break into the Lost Room to free father."

Tarre-Hare pondered the plan for a moment and replied. "Only then can we hope to repair the damage caused to father. This will not be easy? He's still very angry with us, I'm certain of it. How do you intend to stop him destroying us all?"

"My Guardians will have to do this. Jack Ferns is the only one who can convince father to help us. I've been waiting for his arrival for so long I almost believed he would never be born. Many others have promised much, but he alone has this destiny. If he doesn't succeed we'll all pass over; that much I've foreseen. Nothing will be left for any of us."

Tarre-Hare listened carefully to her twin. She wanted to hurt her for all the pain she'd caused, but now she finally saw her again, she pitied her.

"He's potentially very dangerous sister, this Guardian of yours. I've watched him you know, he doesn't have any idea how close he is to becoming the most dangerous creature ever to have lived. Are you sure of this path? I fear that once the waters are released there'll be no turning back. Not even Father will be able to undo this."

The twin sisters sat and looked at each other for the first time since they were children. Not since the dawn of time had they shared a moment like this.

"Take my hand Sister, join with me and feel the truth in me." Lujnima held out her shrouded hand.

Reluctantly, Tarre-Hare took her sister's hand and their powers combined once again. Not since the day they colluded to entrap their father had this happened.

"It's time; bring the boy here now. He must face us both." Lujnima relished her sister's company.

Tarre-Hare accepted the proposal and without any outward sign, her demand was met. Jack appeared instantaneously before the twins; he had to shade his eyes, from the brightness of the light of the day goddess. She studied the boy; before her stood this ordinary young man, neither good looking nor ugly; this simple man-child who harboured an extraordinary gift.

"He doesn't look like much does he sister?" Tarre-Hare mocked.

Jack stared at the two goddesses, completely bewildered. He'd not been permitted to speak by the Tarre-Hare. His body was frozen in time and only his eyes had the ability to move.

"Do you think he realises his fate sister?"

Lujnima took pity on Jack and, with a wag of her finger, gave him freedom to move and speak for himself.

"I take it you are Tarre-Hare," Jack said brashly to the glowing being before him. She was just as Searlan had described; unimaginably beautiful: sleek, powerful and very, very dangerous.

"Why have you brought me here?"

"You've been seeking something that should remain hidden boy. Why?" Tarre-Hare didn't yet trust this Guardian, even though she feared what he may become.

Jack placed his head on one side and considered the being before him. "You are very beautiful indeed Tarre-Hare; I think even more beautiful than Searlan described. He adored you, did you know that. I'll not suffer the same fate."

Tarre-Hare was actually taken aback. "And you are brash boy. Who gave you permission to speak my name? I should strike you down where you stand you impudent youth."

Lujnima looked on amused. Even she'd not suspected her Guardian would be so bold - not yet anyway.

Jack couldn't explain why, but he didn't feel threatened anymore. If this was some kind of a test, then he was about to pass with flying colours. "As I said, you are truly more beautiful than anyone I've ever seen. Beautiful and deadly no doubt, but you will not strike me down. Will you Tarre-Hare? If you'd wanted to do that, you wouldn't have brought me here. I doubt that you could anyway. I'm told I'm dangerous, more dangerous than anyone can imagine. Is that true? Is that what you believe also?"

Jack watched for any sign of a reaction. The beauty before him didn't even flinch. "No Tarre-Hare, I don't think you'll strike me down. What is it you want of me?"

Lujnima was positively enjoying her Guardian being so head-strong. He was quite right of course, even if her sister had wanted to, she couldn't destroy this off-world Guardian. "Could it be true?" she wondered. Had she found the one she sought at long last? Was he their only hope?

Jack continued unperturbed. "The Vinkef have already warned me about you two. I know you imprisoned your father. I know you colluded to trick him somehow, and now he is angrier than ever. I believe he will destroy everyone if I don't, apparently, get involved. Is this why I'm here?"

"You see sister, it's true. My Guardian is the one I've sought for so long. He is the one to wield the key; he is." Lujnima hadn't been this excited or happy for longer than she cared to remember.

"Sit down boy, you are not master here - yet."

Jack sat down on a comfortable chair that appeared magically behind him. Tarre-Hare walked close up beside him. Jack could smell her alluring perfume. His head swam in the subtlety of its overpowering attraction. He fought against his mind to remain aloof, but could easily see why anyone would instantly fall in love with this unbelievably powerful being.

"So the Vinkef have broken their time-honoured promise have they and told you of their view of history? I will deal with their indiscretion later." She then explained about the circumstances leading up to their father being imprisoned.

"So he is in the Lost Room?" Jack said in amazement. "I thought the conduit was in the room?"

"Father is the conduit fool. Just as I'm the left hand and my sister is the right. Each is one with the other," Tarre-Hare could scarcely hide her distain.

"But none of us can ever be the whole key Jack Ferns. We are the pieces but we can never be the key. Father saw to that, he forged the conduit to make it impossible for any one of us to assume absolute control. He made it impossible for anyone to dominate any other."

"But you two joined forces against your father; you imprisoned him."

"Yes, but at a great price. One you can never imagine Jack Ferns." Lujnima was as close to tears as an omnipotent being could ever be.

"We lost ourselves for eternity; we lost our love, our hope and even our family. All we have known since that day is continuous pain. Believe me Jack Ferns; I've forever regretted my stupid mistake."

Tarre-Hare could hardly believe how much weight lifted from her shoulders. This simple boy sitting here, actually made her feel young again. Was it true? Was he really the one to right all these ages of wrongs? The questions flew around her in a swathe of unimaginable grief and unquenchable hope.

"You must find and open the Lost Room Jack Ferns. Defeat the Vinkef and face our father; only you can convince him to rejoin us. You must become the hidden conduit and form the one key. Only then will you rid us all of the evil that it has brought."

Jack sat open mouthed. "Oh I see? You want me to face your father. You want me to right your wrongs; and, what I pray do I get out of this? Don't tell me, if I fail, I'll be disintegrated by the Vinkef, smitten by you two or evaporated by your father. Great idea, even greater choice, thanks a million." Jack hopped around waving his hands in anger and disbelief.

Lujnima enjoyed every moment of her Guardian's outburst. She smiled broadly but responded solemnly. "Yes Jack, you may have to face, and possibly overcome, the Vinkef first. However, nothing of this is certain. This particular future is not fully written which is why you alone are so dangerous. Nothing but chaos can be seen for your future. You Jack Ferns cannot be entirely fathomed and your fate cannot be accurately foretold. We know the Vinkef will never knowingly break their oath. They'll never deliberately allow you to find the Lost Room. Their destiny is to guard the entrance against any intruder."

Jack laughed so loudly that even Tarre-Hare was taken aback.

"I see nothing funny in anything we have stated boy." She seemed oblivious to the sarcasm Jack was portraying.

"Funny, of course it isn't funny. Suicide is what it is, not funny. Only it's me that's going to die NOT YOU TWO," Jack was on his feet again, bright red in the face and screaming at the two beings.

"You are right sister." Tarre-Hare said dismissively. "He has a refreshing spirit, perhaps he is the one you have sought." She smiled turning back to the boy.

Jack opened his mouth to continue but froze instantly. "Silence boy. You are the one that my sister has been waiting for, I believe this now.

You must find a way to achieve this task as only you can. You must learn to see your own path; this is your only possible destiny."

Jack didn't really understand what she was saying. He was still too busy thinking about the threat of death from the Vinkef.

"You will succeed young Jack Ferns and you will become the key-master. My dearest Guardian I'm so happy." Lujnima was almost motherly in her tone.

Tarre-Hare was much more abrupt and menacing. "Enough of this now, speak nothing of what you have seen or heard Guardian. You have never been here - leave now."

Without a further word Jack was gone.

"Well done sister, I think you may have, at last, found a solution to this problem." Tarre-Hare embraced her sister for the first time in an age of ages. They both cried tears of joy, sadness and regret.

Chapter 17 - Pursuit

The front-line had crossed the hills and was at the edge of the plain; soldiers stretched out towards the south and east. General Pen-D'anatè wasn't happy; he sat astride his favourite horse, Warrior, seething with anger. News filtered back to his ears, but not the news he expected to hear. No Resistance fighter had been found or killed despite the size of his magnificent Blade army.

"Not even one Spike," he raved at his Captain sitting motionless and pan faced.

"Where are they all? How did they know? You told me there were no spies Spike; you told me there were no leaks?"

"They could easily see us crossing the savannah General. Maybe the fools fled in terror at the sight of your mighty army." Captain Williams was clutching at straws and he knew it.

"No Spike; not fled, the Resistance have retreated. That is something altogether different. These soldiers are regrouping or in hiding; track my enemy before any surprise attacks are mounted. I want them all destroyed, once and for all. Find them Spike; find them soon, my patience wears very thin; very thin indeed."

Captain Williams left his General and issued fresh orders to the remaining officers. "The land must be searched," he demanded. "Scour every centimetre, find these cowards." He knew his fate hung by a tenuous thread. The General wasn't satisfied and he was the focus of his anger. Spike knew it was his life that would be taken in payment for this failure. "I want no stone unturned; these vermin have hidden away, somewhere - they must be found. I want every man out looking. Spread as far and wide as you need, but find their trail. The General will have all your heads if this is not wrapped up soon"

Spike was in no mood for discussions, he barked his orders venomously. Not one of the officers doubted his threat; the General would never accept failure of his plans. Thousands of soldiers commenced searching. As minutes stretched to hours, Spike became increasingly worried. If word didn't reach him soon, his punishment would be swift and unpleasant.

At long last, a young Lieutenant reported back. Covered in red dust and clearly fatigued, he'd travelled a great distance to bring his message.

"Captain Williams Sir," he panted. "We have found their trail heading towards the southern ocean."

"They escaped over the hills whilst we crossed the savannah," Williams agreed. "That would place them more than a day ahead."

"There were many wagons and horses in the column Sir. Dozens of them, I would estimate, possibly hundreds. "

"Well done Jenkins, now get back outside and sound the recall, we need to reassemble our forces to begin our pursuit."

Spike dismissed the Lieutenant and made his way to the General's office. Crossley, the General's personal orderly, sat stony-faced outside the door. "You had better have good news to tell Captain; I've never known him so grumpy."

Spike nodded gratefully, "Thank you Crossley; my news will cheer the General up. Is he alone?"

Crossley tapped gently on the door and slipped inside. Moments later he returned, "He will see you now Captain."

Pen-D'anatè stood behind his desk: the scar across his eye twitched annoyingly; his patience was spent and his mood barely contained.

"Good news General, Sir. The Resistance have been traced." Captain Williams made his report with enthusiasm. "The army is being reformed, as we speak; we should be ready to move within the hour."

The General's face transformed. "Good work Spike and about time too. Hunt them down; I want their heads on poles for all to see. I want every last one of them dead. Get a raiding party of cavalry after them now and let the rest of the army follow on, do not let the trail go cold."

Spike left and made the arrangements. Two hundred cavalry troops were despatched under the command of young Lieutenant Jenkins.

"Pursue these worthless fool; the General demands their trail is followed with all haste. Do this right and you'll make Captain before the week is out."

Jenkins led his troops across the hills; he drove them forwards relentlessly. Their horses were the finest black stallions; large and powerful. The men were fit and well trained soldiers; by nightfall, they'd covered many tens of kilometres. He permitted them a few hours sleep before resuming the chase. Ahead lay the enemy, the prospect of battle excited the young Lieutenant. He would be promoted Captain before the week was out, he would be the General's new hero.

*****

Captain Williams took charge of the recall; he continually barked orders to ready the column for its pursuit of the Resistance. The soldiers returned from their search and reformed over the next few days. Eventually, Pen-D'anatè's army was ready to march.

"Leave a token force behind Spike; three-hundred should do it. I don't want any surprises - especially anyone sneaking up behind us." The General may have been very confident but he was no fool. He considered this may have been a trap. He suspected the Resistance were trying to lure them into a position of disadvantage.

The main army column assembled; orders rang out and they progressed, slowly, towards the southerly ocean. General Pen-D'anatè grew impatient for his final conquering battle.

*****

Lieutenant Jenkins permitted another short rest as dawn approached. The men and horses recovered quickly and they readied themselves for the continuing pursuit. Mid-morning approached when one of the scouts galloped back

"Lieutenant Jenkins Sir, I've seen the dust trail of the enemy. They're barely two or three hours ahead of your current position."

"Excellent news Cartwright; I want you to take a couple of outriders and make your way back to the General. Report what you have seen and then rejoin the main column."

"Aye, aye Sir," Cartwright replied.

News spread through the troops; the enemy was close, this spurred them on even faster. The young Lieutenant was impressed by the speed and enthusiasm of his soldiers. They would attack the Resistance and win the battle before the main army arrived. The General would promote him for sure.

***

Group Captain Smithers sat in the front of one of the wagons, his first lieutenant sat along side him. "This is the best position in the column Jon. From here I'm able to see as many of my Resistance fighters as possible, just by turning around." The Group Captain spun on his seat to demonstrate.

From this vantage point he was able to receive reports quickly from the front or rear. A scout rode up to his side.

"As you expected Sir, we've caught sight of the approaching Blade enemy."

"How many are there Charlie?"

"About two to three hundred horse: a good sized force I'd say, a raiding party, but nothing close to the numbers that will follow in the main column. They're pushing forward hard and fast."

"Well done Charlie, would you call forward Captain Connors, I think it's time to face the enemy head on." The Group Captain grinned at the prospect of dealing a blow to this evil enemy. Who were these fools who thought they could send a scouting party out to face the combined bands of the Resistance?

The Group Captain briefed his officers of his plan. The whole column would make haste to reach the higher ground, only a couple of kilometres ahead. He was planning a little welcoming party for these Blades.

***

The distance between the two forces fell away; Jenkins no longer needed to push his men as they were all hungry for battle. Each wanted the glory of destroying the escaping Resistance. Cowards all of them, they thought, running from the fight. Lieutenant Jenkins could now see the enemy on the horizon. Huge clouds of dust were thrown up by the many wagons in that train.

"A very nice trail that makes it easy to follow," he smiled with a wicked and fearsome grin. "In another hour we should be able to see their eyes."

***

Captain Connors took charge of one hundred of his best men, all well armed with stout bows and quivers full of arrows. They rode ahead of the column to find a suitable vantage point amongst the hills. As hoped, the terrain steepened - it wasn't difficult to find the valley he was looking for; one of the many paths led them through a narrowing pass. His men would lie in wait above the route, ready for the ambush.

***

Jenkins screamed excitedly from the front of the pursuing cavalry, "come on men, we have these worthless cowards in sight. Hack them down."

The men cheered finding renewed strength; their pace was amazing considering the distance they'd covered. Formed into a long line, they galloped towards the Resistance.

"They're heading for the hills." Jenkins expected to reach the tail-enders as they slowed on the up-slopes. "We have them now. Follow me Blades; take your revenge." Racing ahead, he was desperate to be first to strike with his great sword.

***

The Resistance hurried into the pass prepared by Captain Connors. The first wagons drove forwards to the end of the valley and formed into a barrier. The occupants jumped down and readied themselves with bows and swords.

Group Captain Smithers shouted to his troops, "None of these dogs will leave." The last of the wagons rushed into the valley pursued by the fastest of the Blades. His men desperately fired their arrows and barely held them off.

Connors kept his troops hidden; he didn't want to spring the trap too early. Dust blew everywhere and it was actually quite hard to see their enemy. "NOWWWWW!" he screamed at the top of his voice and one hundred bow men fired several arrows in quick succession. The Blades were caught completely off guard. In seconds most had fallen from their horses. Others turned aside and were rounded on by dozens of charging Resistance fighters.

"Get that one there," screamed Group Captain Smithers. "He's their leader."

Ten Resistance fighters swept down upon the luckless Lieutenant and pounded him to the ground.

The entire skirmish took barely five minutes. Every Blade was dead except for one; Jenkins had been captured. He was bound and gagged, dragged into one of the wagons and chained to a stout metal eye.

The Group Captain caught his breath and directed his orders. "Get their horses if you can. Check there are none alive Connors. We cannot afford to have any of them telling of this. You know what you must do."

Connors led ten of his best men through the soldiers lying all over the valley. He thrust one of their own spears into the heart of each man lying on the ground. The Captain knew that this was necessary for the protection of them all, but it still made him feel sick to his stomach. These men had come here to destroy them all but he still couldn't forget they were perhaps fathers, brothers or sons. He wondered if any of them would've felt the same; he doubted it.

"How many did we lose?" The Group Captain was prepared for the worst, but hoped for the best.

"Six dead and nine wounded Sir." The soldier reporting was injured himself; he'd been struck across the shoulder and it was clearly still bleeding.

"Get yourself seen to Corporal, and well done, very well done indeed." The Group Captain could hardly contain his relief. "It could have been so much worse," he thought thankfully. "But we have one of them alive. That is a stroke of luck."

As Connors completed his grizzly task, the wagons were readied for the onward journey. Smithers hastened everyone, "Bring our fallen; we'll not bury them in the same ground made filthy by the blood of our enemy." He glanced back at the destruction; nearly two hundred dead soldiers would provide rich pickings for the carrion and prowling beasts. But even more so, a clear message to the pursuing enemy – the Resistance would not die lightly without a fight.

Chapter 18 - Tough decisions

"How long have I been away?" Jack sounded disoriented after his audience with Lujnima and Tarre-Hare.

The others looked at Jack even more bewildered than he was.

"What Jack?" Jaden wasn't even sure he heard his friend correctly.

"HOW long have I been away?" Jack repeated; he was more animated and clearly agitated.

"You haven't been anywhere Jack. You've been standing right there the whole time." Cathy didn't understand the question.

Tina-Lu came across to her brother and looked into his eyes. "Do you think something happened to you Jack? None of us saw anything."

"I've just been to..." Jack paused, blinked his eyes rapidly and shook his head. "I think I was just with..." he couldn't quite bring himself to say.

Jack looked drawn and unsure of himself. He read the reaction of his friends, they'd not seen him leave or return.

Jaden wondered, "Perhaps you've had a daydream or your mind is just playing tricks on you?"

"No Jaden, I've just been taken for an..." he still couldn't finish the sentence. No matter how hard he tried he couldn't describe his visit to anyone else.

Jaden tried to fill in the gaps for his friend, "you think you've been somewhere else Jack?"

The boy nodded.

"But you cannot tell us where you've been?"

Jack shook his head slowly.

"Even though you want to tell us?"

Trying to nod again; a blinding pain pierced Jack's head. Screwing up his face in agony, he clutched both temples with the palms of his hands.

"Are you okay Jack?" Jaden held his friend's arm and continued, "your memories are being blocked, be careful Jack this might be dangerous."

Cathy rubbed Jack's neck sympathetically.

"Have you been before THEM Jack?" Jaden whispered quietly to his friend deliberately not using Lujnima and Tarre-Hare's names.

Jack bent forwards and then crouched down still holding his head. He wasn't entirely sure Jaden had truly guessed what had happened.

"Were they both together?" The Sage pressed.

Jack fell forwards as excruciating pain seared all down one side of his body.

"You are being prevented from speaking about this meeting, aren't you Jack."

The question might as well have been rhetorical, because, Jack had no ability to respond. His subconscious mind worked against his consciousness. He wanted to answer and discuss his meeting with the two beings, but he was no longer in control of his actions. The boy froze, staring straight ahead.

Tina-Lu became very worried. "What's going on Jack? Are you alright? What have you done to him Jaden?"

Jaden was unsure whether to be concerned or amused. Poor Jack looked like he was fighting a battle within his own body. His face contorted, trying to win back his ability to speak.

Tina-Lu shook him gently and then a little harder. "Jack, what are you doing? Speak to us, what has happened to you?"

Cathy stared right into Jack's eyes and tried to make him see her. "I think he's slipped into some kind of unconscious state. He doesn't appear to be here anymore. I can't feel him inside my head the way I did before."

Now Jaden was genuinely worried. "What do you mean Cathy? What do you feel when you look at Jack; has he faded, is that what you are saying?"

Jack had frozen rigid as a board. His entire body was locked in an internal battle that threatened to overwhelm him.

Jaden walked away deep in thought. "Searlan would've known what to do. Grandfather was truly a Sage; I'm just a kid who pretends to be a Sage." He scolded himself for his lack of foresight. "What would you have done Grandfather? How would you have helped Jack?" From the depths of his soul a voice struggled for recognition. Extremely quiet at first and barely even a whisper, it seemed more like a shrouded idea. But it did steadily grow until Jaden could recognise it.

"I passed on my Sageship to you Jaden because you are the Sage by rights. You are not just a child; you are the Sage." The boy listened to the familiar and friendly voice of his Grandfather. "You have it within you to seek the answers to more questions than can be listed in a dozen lifetimes. You must learn to recognise the advice and guidance of the ancients and elders who have given up their accumulated knowledge to you. My small contribution is insignificant beside the wealth at your command. I'm just one voice in an ocean of voices. During my lifetime I learned to use the knowledge within; mentors guided me through the myriad of potential help."

"But Grandfather, I never imagined it would be so difficult. Whom should I turn to? Why can't you guide me, they would listen to you."

"Later maybe Jaden, now we should concentrate upon our friend Jack. I perceive he has been called before Tarre-Hare and Lujnima. Wheels are turning my boy; the two goddesses haven't met for eons. One or both have blocked Jack's ability to speak of this. They are afraid of the consequences of people learning of the rejoining of the twins. If you are to save our Guardian, you must enter his mind and guide him back. You are the Sage NOW my child; only you can do this."

Jaden had never felt so feeble: all of these voices, all this knowledge and he didn't have the presence to command any of them. Despite the encouragement of Searlan, he wasn't confident of helping his friend.

The girls turned from the frozen body of Jack and recognised the look of indecision on Jaden's face.

Tina-Lu held the young boy's hand and bent down to be close to his face. "Jaden you are the most special and amazing person I've ever met. You have a gift beyond our comprehension. Your Grandfather entrusted you with this great responsibility because he believed you alone should take this task forward. You ARE the Sage of Sages now and you're the only person who can help my brother."

Tears welled up in his eyes; his heart melted at the sight of this sixteen year old girl, telling him he was so special. He wasn't the Sage of Sages, Searlan was; he was too young to be able to handle this huge responsibility. "Lu, I'm no great Sage, I'll never fill Grandfather's shoes."

"Look at me Jaden. Look straight at me," Tina-Lu held him tightly by both arms.

"You can do this; only you can do this. You have to help Jack; draw on whatever is inside you and help him. You must."

Worrying about the faith this older girl had in him; Jaden swallowed several times, his mouth felt dry and his heart beat faster. He liked Tina-Lu very much and he didn't want to let her down. "I'll do this for you Tina-Lu, I'll find a way," he thought unconvincingly. Smiling, he declared. "It's okay Lu; I know what I'm to do. Grandfather has helped me to understand. You're right; I'm the Sage of Sages now. Or rather, I should be. I'll help your brother; I'll do it for you, for all of us."

Jaden walked back over to the frozen body of Jack. He placed his hand on his forehead, just as Searlan had done to others in need of help, and closed his eyes tightly shut. He imagined himself being part of his friend; his mind slipped easily alongside Jack's.

"Where are you Jack?" his question fell into a deep abyss and disappeared. "Where are you Jack?" he shouted, more insistent this time.

***

Deep inside a dark mistiness Jack wandered around hopelessly lost. He wasn't sure why, but he felt like he was imprisoned; trapped by some external force. He was sure he'd forgotten to do something, but no matter how hard he tried he couldn't remember what it was.

"Where am I?" his voice was weak and the sound seemed to be absorbed before it even left his mouth.

"HELLO…" he tried to shout. His words fell silently, at his feet, without making any impression on the fog surrounding him.

"What am I doing here?" Jack was sure he should've known the answer. Like an irritating itch, in the middle of his back, no matter how hard he tried he just could not quite reach it.

"WHERE AM I?" he shouted again but still his voice just seemed to fall directly ahead of him. His world had turned into a curdled soup without any hope of seeing his hand in front of his face. There seemed to be no light nor sign indicating any direction. He wandered aimlessly with no idea if he covered any ground or just walked in circles. He was lost, completely lost.

"What was it I should remember?" Jack became really frustrated. "I know I should remember something, something important, and something I shouldn't have forgotten?"

An almost imperceptibly small voice called. "Jack – where are you?" The voice was so quiet and far away he almost dismissed it; moments later he heard it again. "Jack – answer me."

"I should know that voice," he thought it was somewhat familiar.

"Jack – follow my voice, it's your friend Jaden. Come back."

"Jaden; of course, I thought I knew that voice." The answer to the question helped him pull back from the veil thrown over his mind.

"I'M HERE JADEN," his voice still didn't penetrate the fog, but he felt he should try to join his friend. "KEEP CALLING SO I CAN FIND YOU."

Jaden didn't hear Jack's response at all but knew he needed a voice to follow. "Come this way Jack. Come towards my voice if you can hear me. You're lost and you must come towards my voice."

Jack heard the boy again. Every direction seemed as similar as the next; this fog just muffled any sense of bearing. "Which way did the voice come from?" He was disorientated. "Concentrate, think now; which way should I go?" Hearing Jaden call again Jack realised his voice was coming slightly from his left. He turned and walked hopefully through the thinning fog.

***

Tina-Lu and Cathy looked on helplessly as the two boys stood transfixed; neither moved a muscle or even blinked. They both looked as though they had faded out of reality and into another world.

"Come on Jack, you can do this. Listen to Jaden; he's there to help you." Cathy had taken Jack's cold and clammy hand.

"What about that brooch Cathy? Can Layette help us with this problem do you think?"

Cathy nodded enthusiastically and took the brooch firmly in her hands. Instantly, the girls were bathed in a bright red glow as Layette's silhouette shimmered in amongst the radiance.

"Greetings Guardian, what's your question?" Layette the Decider sounded less than enthusiastic after the pain and anguish of Cathy's last offering.

"I'm really sorry about last time Layette; I didn't mean to cause you any grief. How was I to know that you couldn't answer my question? Anyway, our friend Jack here seems to be trapped inside his own body. How can we help him?"

Layette's facial features relaxed visibly at the apology and the simplicity of this question posed by the Guardian. The light of her glowing luminescence shone brilliantly all around the two girls. She danced happily over and through the stationary Jack and Jaden before she delivered her sing-song reply.

> *"Hold a hand and send your love,*
> *look on down from far above.*
> *Join together, more is best,*
> *one alone would never rest.*
> *Think of things that both would choose,*
> *never again, a friend to lose.*
> *Know his soul and stay so true,*
> *this is how he will find you..."*

Layette laughed cheerily disappearing back into the brooch jewel.

"Did you understand that one Tina-Lu? At least she wasn't upset by the question this time. I guess we must send our thoughts into Jack somehow. Perhaps if we all hold hands, you take Jaden's and I'll take Jack's. Think about finding your brother and leading him back to us."

Tina-Lu was a little self conscious and sceptical, but held Jaden's hand anyway.

"Just imagine you're guiding him; like a search-light stretching across the sea or a beacon of hope. Think about standing next to your brother and drawing him to you."

***

Deep inside Jack's misty world, Jaden was surprised to see the faint outline of Cathy and Tina-Lu. "What are you two doing here?"

"We're here to help," Cathy announced. "Layette suggested how to bring Jack home. We must picture him in our minds and he will follow our thoughts."

Jaden smiled, nodding his approval and gratitude. They all called several more times unsuccessfully before finally hearing a weak response. "Come this way Jack. We can hear you; come this way."

Jack found his way through the fog; he approached and was confused to see the face of Searlan not his grandson Jaden. The old man stood before him. When he looked again he realised it wasn't exactly Searlan, rather it was like a much younger version of him. The voice of Jaden came from the mouth of the Sage.

"Hello Jack. You had us all worried there for a moment. We thought we'd lost you. You need to follow us back; we'll guide you out of the fog."

Jack didn't look convinced; his face was drawn and haggard - the weight of the entire world appeared to be hanging on his shoulders.

Jaden turned to the girls and said, "Thanks, girls, I can bring Jack out from here. You go back now; we'll be along in shortly." He needed to spend a couple of minutes alone with his friend and didn't want to make the situation worse.

The girls waved goodbye and faded from view as they returned to the world outside.

"Listen Jaden or is it Searlan. I must speak with you urgently."

The boy seemed surprised; "It's me Jaden, not Searlan. Are you okay Jack?" He didn't think he looked anything like his grandfather.

"Just listen." Jack became frustrated and didn't fully understand his anger. He knew he was supposed to remember something; something really important. He tried, as best he could, to explain how desperate he was to remember something. "I need your help. I need you to look inside me and to read my thoughts. I need to find out what has been hidden in my head."

Jaden smiled at his friend. "Jack, I'm already inside your head. This is where we are? I'm talking to you inside your mind; you're lost in your own memory, which is why I need you to follow me. You must come with me."

Jack thought for a moment trying to grasp the concept, he knew he'd been somewhere he just couldn't remember.

"Earlier, I asked you if you'd seen Lujnima and Tarre-Hare together Jack. Do you remember? You then tried to answer but something happened to you. The more you tried the harder it became. Then your mind collapsed in on itself and you became locked in your own memories. Something, or more likely someone, prevented you from discussing anything about your encounter. Think Jack, what happened to you, can you remember?"

The puzzled look on his face was answer enough for Jaden. "You asked us how long you'd been gone. To us you'd never left. Clearly something did happen it's just that we were not meant to be aware of it. Did you swear to keep it a secret or were you ordered never to speak of it? Is that the problem?"

Still Jack seemed unable to remember or even speak of the events. He just screwed up his nose and shrugged his shoulders.

"I need you to find out for me Jaden. I know there's something important I should do. I'm certain it's just out of reach; if I could just find the start of the thread I could follow it to the hidden memories. There's something I've been told to do - something amazing."

"Okay Jack I'll try to find your hidden orders, but first you must come back out with me. I can't do anything whilst we are both in here."

Jack wasn't entirely convinced; however, he held Jaden's hand to walk away from the fog and into the light of day. Jaden disappeared and he became aware of Tina-Lu, Cathy and Brandy. He was back with the others; Jaden still had his eyes closed and looked as if he was in a very deep sleep.

Jack was confronted by a hundred questions all at once. He saw the girl's mouths opening and closing but it all seemed to be in slow motion and he didn't hear a word of what they were asking. He placed his head in his hands shaking it slowly in denial.

Jaden awoke from his contemplations after several anxious minutes. "Good to see you Jack." The boy could tell all wasn't well with his friend, but at least he was here again.

"He's not said a word to us," Tina-Lu whispered. "I think he is still in shock or something."

"Do you know what I think has happened?" Cathy busily comforted her friend; she turned to Jaden. "He's being prevented from speaking to us Jaden; he's had his memory blocked."

"That's exactly what has happened Cathy. Jack has been altered by..." He gestured to two girls to come out of earshot of Jack. Then he spoke in a hushed voice. "He's been called before Tarre-Hare and Lujnima and ordered by them to not discuss the meeting. They've taken him outside of time itself and returned him to the exact moment of his departure. I had to call upon all of my Sageship powers to discover this event in his mind. I don't think he'll ever be able to remember this, they've blocked it so deeply."

"How much do you know? What did they want that was so important?" Tina-Lu was intrigued that Jaden could do this.

"I believe Jack has been ordered to do something, so terrible, his mind hasn't been able to contemplate it. I think he's been ordered to destroy the MoonBridge. In doing so, he'll probably kill Tarre-Hare and Lujnima in the process."

The two girls gasped in disbelief. Cathy sat down; shocked at the revelation.

"What can we do Jaden? We can't possibly let Jack do such a thing?" Cathy looked across at her friend, someone she was beginning to believe she loved, "What would I do if he did this terrible thing?" She questioned.

"I'm sorry Lu; I'm beginning to think Jack is more dangerous than any of us can imagine. Everywhere we turn we're being warned about him. Now this has happened, I'm not sure he can be trusted. What if he really did do this?"

Tina-Lu tried to jump to her brother's defence when Cathy placed her hand on her arm. "He can NEVER be allowed to do this Jaden. We must do whatever is necessary to prevent it from happening. The

MoonBridge can't be allowed to be destroyed. No matter what else happens this can never be permitted."

Jaden had never seen Cathy so cold or calculating. He read the desperation in her voice and realised that she meant every word, "Would she consider something as drastic as taking Jack's life?" he agonised. This was the worst situation he could've imagined.

Tina-Lu stood open mouthed. Hearing her friends speaking in this way; she suddenly felt very alone. "What is it you intend to do? I'll never let you harm my Brother, you do know that don't you?" Tina-Lu stood up to her tallest height and towered down on young Jaden. She clenched her fists in readiness.

"We don't want to harm Jack, believe me Lu. But we can't allow him to do this thing either. We must find a solution and find it fast." Jaden struggled to think of any possible course of action that could divert them from the approaching disaster.

"Can't we lock him away somewhere or even banish him from controlling the MoonBridge? Maybe Tina-Lu and Jack could go back home without his staff. Surely that would prevent him from ever opening the MoonBridge again." Cathy was also clutching at any possible option that didn't actually harm her dearest friend.

The standoff between the three had eased a little, but Tina-Lu was unsure of their true intentions. She looked across at her brother who seemed to be coming out of his imposed silence.

"What are you three up to? What's all this whispering going on?" Jack was as bright as a button and showed no signs of the earlier troubles. To him, nothing had ever happened.

All three felt like they had already betrayed their close friend. Tina-Lu nearly burst into tears and Cathy hung her head in shame.

"It's okay Jack; we wondered where we were going from here?" Jaden could barely look his friend in the eyes. He didn't know this person at all. In fact, he was positively afraid of him. All those warnings had finally had their effect.

"We were just thinking maybe you and Tina-Lu should return across the MoonBridge for a while. What do you think?" Jaden was totally unconvincing and the reticence in his voice betrayed his distrust of Jack.

"Why on earth would I want to do that Jaden? I thought we had important work to do for the Resistance. Aren't we supposed to be helping them out?"

"This isn't really your fight is it Jack? We must take responsibility for ourselves; we can't always rely on others to help us now can we?" Cathy didn't sound in the least bit convincing either.

"Have I missed something here? What are you talking about; you're not making any sense? Do you know what they're going on about Tina-Lu?"

His sister couldn't bring herself to answer. She just stood, looking at the ground, unable to respond; she mumbled something about agreeing with them and Jack became incensed.

"You want Tina-Lu and me to go home? What right now; right here and now?" He just couldn't understand it. "What has happened? Tell me?"

"We can't tell you Jack. You have to trust us, you must leave now. You must leave and never return; what's more, you can never ever ask anyone why. Believe me."

Jack didn't understand and he didn't like the tone his, supposed, friends were taking. He grabbed his sister's arm and pulled her away from the other two.

"Tell me Sis; are you in with them on this?" Jack was amazed when his sister looked at him and nodded silently.

"Fine; we're leaving - we're leaving right now, I know when I'm not wanted. I've just realised that I'm sick of this place, and I'm sick of those two as well. Come on Brandy we're off."

He stood for a moment composing his thoughts. Without even uttering a word the MoonBridge formed right in front of him. Never before had it been so bright; the silvery light burst like a million burning suns. The power driving the bridge seemed to have been amplified many times. His anger fired the apparition as his command over its use charged to new levels of control. He pulled Brandy by the collar and led Tina-Lu across the bridge without a word or a glance behind. The bridge closed immediately and they were gone.

Cathy was left stunned at the sudden disappearance of her best friend and started sobbing inconsolably. Jaden waited, unable to speak. He'd never felt so dreadful and realised he'd let his friend down. He believed he would regret this decision for the rest of his life.

***

The darkness was shattered as a brightly shining glow formed into the MoonBridge. Jack led his sister and Brandy across the threshold as the light dimmed and faded from view behind them. Each remained motionless, for a few seconds, as they adjusted to the return to Jack's bedroom. The transition from day to night was a shock and their eyes took a while to adjust to the dim silvery moonlight. The green glow of the clock's hands indicated 12:35.

Tina-Lu looked at her brother and whispered. "What day is it Jack? We've been gone for weeks. What will mum and dad say when we turn up, they'll have been worried sick."

Jack shrugged his shoulders, but he suspected it was only about half an hour since they actually left their own world. The house was still in silence, except for the pounding of their hearts, and the faint reverberation of dad snoring in the next bedroom.

"I think it's the same night as we left, look at the time, we've only been away for a few minutes. The bridge can do that; Cathy suggested there isn't any correlation between the time here and the time in her world. Sometimes this one moves faster and sometimes it moves slower, I'm not sure how it works." He pulled back the curtains and the full moon was still overhead, the air was decidedly cooler and the breeze made him shiver. He immediately regretted rushing off from his friends. He was still angry with them but he already missed Cathy and Jaden.

Tina-Lu fixed her eyes on her brother, he'd grown up so much in her opinion, and he was like a completely new person. Mum and dad wouldn't recognise him. "Are you sure you did the right thing Jack, leaving them like that? They were scared you know, scared of what you might become. You really put the wind up us all with that 'disappearing inside yourself' thing. When Jaden read your mind he found out you were supposed to destroy the MoonBridge - what did you expect them to think?"

Jack had never seen his sister looking at him as she did right then. This was the first time he didn't feel like her little brother. She actually treated him as her equal and even her friend too.

"What do you mean destroy the MoonBridge? I would never do that, you know me better than that Sis, surely? What did Jaden say to you? I wouldn't have destroyed anything." Jack felt a sudden and overpowering wave of guilt sweep through him. He came to his senses and knew they had to go back.

"Perhaps we should go back to them?" Tina-Lu suggested.

"You're right Sis. I'm opening the bridge right now. This situation needs to be resolved and the sooner the better."

Jack turned to call the bridge and then realised he'd not brought the cane back with him. He commanded the bridge to open anyway but nothing happened. He tried to compose himself and call again; still nothing happened. His, so called, powers had either deserted him or they only worked on the other side; not here. He felt desperate and panicky. "What if I can never return? I might never see Cathy again, ever."

Tina-Lu saw the look of horror on her brother's face and realised that without his staff he was powerless.

"Make your arm and hand glow," she asked hopefully.

He held out his hand and commanded it to glow. Nothing happened, not even a flicker.

"Try again Jack. Concentrate as hard as you can."

Jack's heart sank; he knew straight away it was hopeless. The Guardian powers had deserted him. "It's no use Sis, we're stuffed."

Both sat down heavily on the edge of Jack's bed. Tina-Lu put her arm around her brother's shoulder and pulled him closer to her. "It's okay Jack, something will happen, something will turn up. Just you wait and see..."

Chapter 19 - Risks and chances

Cathy had never felt so depressed with life: her hair was matted, her face blotchy and her clothes tatty. Rolling over and over again in her mind she wrangled with mixed emotions: one moment she was angry, the next bitter and almost continually riddled with tearful upset. Part of her tried to argue it wasn't really Jaden's fault, but he'd revealed Jack's intention to destroy the MoonBridge.

"I should never have listened; he wouldn't have done it. He couldn't have done it." After leaving Jaden to his own fate, she strayed far from his company. "This is your fault Jaden; why did you meddle inside Jack's mind?"

Every night, since they left, Cathy cried herself to sleep. She couldn't accept how readily she'd followed Jaden's viewpoint and betrayed Jack. Despite feeling terribly guilty, she was also cross with her friends, "You shouldn't have left us like that; you shouldn't."

Walking aimlessly across the open countryside, she didn't care if she was captured or killed by the Blades; her life, without Jack, was meaningless. Hours slipped into days and the days melted into three long weeks. Time, in this instance, wasn't proving to be a healer; turmoil consumed her every waking moment and sorrow filled her dreams. Having wandered for many kilometres; she eventually found herself standing in front of a small overgrown building. Cathy tentatively touched the broken gate hanging precariously by one rusty hinge. Her mind struggled to recognise her surroundings. The structure was covered in enormous vines. The once proud, front door looked sad and neglected; a pitiful reflection of the happiness that previously beckoned any approaching visitor. Hidden deep in recesses of her memories, a distant thought tried to surface; a vague recollection of some long forgotten comfort.

"How did I end-up here?" she said, knowing full well no-one would answer.

"This will always be your home."

The voice made Cathy jump a foot in the air. She spun around to find Jaden leaning against the trunk of a large oak tree.

"You must have taken the long road to get here. I've been waiting for over a week."

Cathy was dumbstruck. "How did you know I would come here? I don't even know where here is?"

"Look around you Cathy, this is the home of your mother, you've walked back to your roots. You've come back to the one person who loved you more than any other. This is the only place where you could face yourself and find comfort for your hurt and pain."

The poor girl was already crying. Seeing Jaden, waiting patiently for her, was such a relief and comfort. She did love Jaden; he was just like the little brother she never been able to have. He was, of course, now the Sage but that didn't stop Cathy seeing him as her dearest friend.

"I've learned so much since we parted Cathy. I've finally had time to speak with many of my inner memories and found great comfort and knowledge in their council. Please forgive me for bringing this terrible burden to you. I know you love Jack; it's so plain to see. I know he loves you too and that I must find a way to right this terrible wrong."

Cathy barely heard her friend; her eyes were drawn to the little house. She saw through the overgrown plants and vines; beyond the years of neglect and disrepair – memories flooded back to a lovely spring morning where the sun warmed her heart. Rays of sunlight shimmered through the newly grown leaves of the oak; speckles and shadows danced across the grass and along the white painted fence. Her mother hummed softly whilst pegging out their washing. The world seemed to smile as she walked around the garden; an angelic apparition that swept away any cares or worries. Cathy felt the tears slipping down her cheeks again. "Can she see me?" She sobbed. "Would she know how much I miss her and love her? Will she ever know how much I've wanted to have a daughter of my own?" The questions only made matters worse; she flopped down on the long grass and saw the beautiful spring morning melt back into history. The summer evening returned and the overgrown house stood before her. Cathy looked at Jaden who had crouched beside her.

"We must call for Jack to return Cathy. We must get him back here to be with you; above all, we must let him meet his destiny, whatever that may be. My guides and mentors have explained he would never knowingly destroy the MoonBridge, even if Tarre-Hare ordered it. I was wrong Cathy, I was so very wrong."

Cathy knew Jaden was heartbroken too; he'd faced his elders, consulted the ancients and sought guidance from his forebears. He'd taken this opportunity to examine himself and to question the meanings of his existence. Jaden had grown from a small boy into a young Sage and wasn't afraid to admit his error. She wiped the tears from her face, she looked down at her clothes finally realising how filthy dirty and dishevelled she had become. "What do you think we should do Jaden? We have no way of contacting Jack and it's impossible for us to cross to his side."

"I was hoping we would be able to open either the bridge or the portal and find some way to call to them. Perhaps if we joined our thoughts, maybe we could drive across the barrier, what do you think?"

Cathy thought for a moment and considered Jaden's idea. She dismissed her pain and misery, of the last three weeks, to focus upon her Jack again. If it was possible she would find a way.

"When I open the MoonBridge Jaden, I've no way to guide it outside of this world; I certainly can't make it reach Jack. How would you suggest we do this?"

They both agreed; it just didn't seem likely, after all these ages of previous Sages and Guardians, that either one of them could make this happen.

"I know when I call my portal it automatically leads to Tarre-Hare. I just wondered if it could be guided in some way; like you and Jack did with the MoonBridge. I also wondered what would happen if I projected the portal though an open bridge - I don't think anyone has ever tried that before."

Their initial enthusiasm was quickly extinguished; after three unsuccessful attempts they realised this idea was never likely to work. The bridge cancelled out the portal and the portal did the same to the bridge. They couldn't ever be called together.

Cathy sat for a long time considering her options, which seemed fewer by the minute. She walked over to the house and pulled the vines away from the dirt covered window behind it; inside was dark and covered in dust and cobwebs. The house looked like no-one had set foot in there since she left all those years ago.

"Help me mother? Please guide my hand now, I need your help."

Cathy half expected to see her mother again walking out of the front door to come to her aid, but only silence confronted her. She walked away from the old house and away from her long lost past.

"Perhaps Layette can help us?" Jaden suggested hopefully.

Cathy held the beautiful ruby red gemstone in her hands and waited for the stunning figure of Layette to materialise in her shimmering red beams of light.

"Greetings Guardian, what is your question?"

"Layette, Jaden and I have a terrible dilemma; how do we contact Jack?"

Layette pulled a face of disgust before spinning high in the air. Beams of crimson shot in all directions, her voice rang out grim and cold.

Foolish girl for this you ask,
the most impossible of tasks.
Not from here, will thy thoughts drive,
for none can see the other side,
Across the bridge you must depart,
to seek your one true lover's heart.
Remember though, pursue your dreams,
lest you'll be lost 'mongst cold moon-beams.

Layette never waited for any response; she spiralled instantly down into the depths of her jewelled home and extinguished her light.

Cathy huffed dejectedly; Jaden waited patiently to ponder the meaning of the suggestion. They both wondered if there were any other choices.

"What do you think she meant by 'pursue your dreams' Jaden? Is that a clue how to cross the MoonBridge divide?" Her voice was understandably nervous.

"I've been thinking about it myself and believe Layette meant for you to be completely focussed upon Jack. Only then would you be able to traverse the barrier. I guess it would be the strength of your love and your belief in him that would overcome the prophecy."

"I don't know if I can do this Jaden, I'm scared I'll never return. My mother warned me against trying to cross; so many others have been lost, she said."

"Your right to worry, but why did Layette tell you to cross? Do you think she would deliberately put you in danger?"

Neither could make a decision. Jaden suggested they take a stroll across the meadows towards the low hills at the edge of the woodland. "We'll think clearer with a good view of the countryside."

They set off and chatted about their many journeys over the last few weeks. When they reached the top of the hill the view was as refreshing as Jaden had suggested. The sun cast long shadows as it prepared to set; the three-quarter moon had already risen and hung low in the sky.

"I know what I must do Jaden, I must take Layette's advice. I'll cross the bridge and find Jack for myself." Cathy sounded confident and determined.

"I must admit Cathy it seems this is the only course open to you. But if it is, then I'm coming too; if we are to be lost forever, let's be lost together. I could never live with myself if you disappeared and were never heard of again."

Holding her friend's hand; Cathy smiled brightly for the first time in weeks. She finally accepted this was her destiny and hers alone. She could never permit Jaden to risk being lost too.

"No Jaden, you're far too important. You must stay here and grow into the Sage of Sages as you are meant to be. I must take this trip and make my own path. I believe I'll find my Jack. My heart will guide me safely, I'm certain of it."

Jaden couldn't convince her to change her mind. He conceded defeat, she was determined to throw her soul to the wind and hope it blew in the right direction. Hugging her tightly he said his final goodbye.

"It's okay," she said comfortingly. "I'll be okay Jaden, I promise."

Cathy raised her staff and opened the bridge one more time. The glow didn't seem as bright or convincing as before and this worried Jaden. "Is it powerful enough to transport you?"

"Don't worry dear Jaden. I'll find my Jack and we will return. I love you..."

Cathy stepped forward towards the light of the MoonBridge. She paused briefly turning back to her friend, with a little wave she took the tiny step necessary to be consumed by the moonbeams.

Jaden gave a short gasp and gulped back a tear as his friend and her MoonBridge faded from view - he'd never felt so completely alone.

Chapter 20 - Crossing the line

For nearly ten minutes; Sister and Brother sat in silence on the edge of Jack's bed. They both stared, into the darkness, each recalling the amazing adventures across the MoonBridge. Tina-Lu finally stood up and said, "I'm going to my own room."

Jack hardly acknowledged her statement.

Squeezing her brother's hand Tina-Lu said comfortingly. "As mum always says Jack, things will look different in the morning." She paused to gain his attention. "Try to sleep. Hey, you did really well you know. You are the true MoonBridge Guardian."

Jack attempted a smile for his sister. He didn't want to sleep; his mind was still racing. Tina-Lu closed the bedroom door quietly behind her. Darkness hugged him like an invisible cloak. Throwing off his dirty clothes, he climbed into bed – the covers were still ruffled and untouched. Brandy had already curled up in his favourite spot and snored contentedly. The fresh smell of the sheets felt very comforting. He normally felt safe here but his heart and mind where on the other side of the MoonBridge.

"I've really screwed it up this time, what an idiot I am."

Jack didn't think it would be possible to sleep, however, within a few minutes his weary body allowed him to drift into a troubled state of sub-consciousness. Memories floated in and out of his mind – visions unravelled the events that had transpired. Questions without answers, answers without questions, "What does it all mean?" One thread permeated the jostling recollections – the stabilising influence of Cathy.

"You are the true love of my life Cathy; I've never felt like this before." The pain in his heart tore his soul apart. Every bone in his body complained; even his fingernails seemed to be aching. Jack was in love for the first time and he was completely unprepared for the sensation.

***

Tina-Lu crept back into her bedroom and closed the door quietly behind her. Here was a lovely tidy and neatly laid out room; nothing like her brother's. She had many 'girly' trinkets all around. A few teddy bears and fluffy toys lined a shelf on the wall and looked over her for protection. Three, colour coordinated cushions were neatly arranged at the end of the bed. Her sheets were still carefully turned back from where she had left them all those weeks ago. She mentally corrected herself, realising in this world, only about an hour had transpired.

"That's so weird," she said quietly under her breath. "I must be three weeks older."

Slipping out of her filthy clothes, she sighed with relief; she'd never spent so long in the same outfit. Standing there before her full-length mirror she looked at herself as if looking at someone else. She didn't recognise the image before her. Her waist was thinner and she seemed fitter, her muscles were more defined. Mostly, she liked what she saw, except for her hair, which was a terrible mess; it made her look like a street vagabond all dishevelled and unkempt.

"I so need a long hot soak in some gorgeous bubbles and scent," she declared.

The clothes she'd thrown off were ruined and only fit for the bin; she kicked them into a pile in the corner of the room. She wrapped herself in a large towelling robe and crept across the landing to the bathroom. Without putting on the light she closed the door, silently, and as quietly as possible, ran a hot bath with loads of bubbles, oils and scents.

"Ecstasy!" she exclaimed sliding full length into the cleansing waters. She hadn't felt so good since swimming in the pool at the oasis. The hot water surrounded her aching body and held her suspended, almost weightless. She could feel the stress slipping away as the

264

calming aroma of lavender wafted around the bathroom. Tina-Lu closed her eyes and allowed the soothing water to help her slip into a relaxing sleep.

Troubles, seemingly so real only moments before, drifted away.

"This is just the most perfect way to relax," she hummed contentedly. Tina-Lu imagined invisible hands massaging each aching muscle releasing the tension from her body. For perhaps an hour she was completely at peace in the sanctuary of this perfect place.

"Lu, can you hear me Lu?"

Tina-Lu sat up with a splash, bubbles flying everywhere and a wave of water crashing over the bathroom floor. She blushed instantly; grabbing the towel she sank deeply back down again. "Jaden, is that you?" His voice sounded deeper, she thought.

A crackling sound echoed around the walls.

"I'm in the bath; you can't come in here," she flustered.

A small ball of light appeared about one metre above the floor of the bathroom; it grew to the size of a football.

"Oh shut-up Lu and listen. I can't see you; I don't know how long I can hold the portal open."

Something heavy hit the tiled floor with a very loud clonk. Tina-Lu jumped and thought it was going to wake the entire house.

"What the hell was that?"

"SHUT-UP and listen." Jaden demanded. "I've been trying for the last two years, since you left, to be able to control the portal. This is the first time I've been successful in all that time. Cathy left to find you and Jack by crossing the bridge a few weeks after…" His voice faded as the ball crackled and disappeared in a spluttering of lightning. She was alone again in the privacy of her bathroom - she swallowed hard regaining her composure.

"Jaden was in my bathroom and I was in the bath. Oh my god, I'll never live this down, never."

Tina-Lu stayed firmly in the bath for about another fifteen minutes hardly daring to breathe. She made sure the water and bubbles reached right up to her neck. With each passing second she fully expected Jaden's portal to reappear and the boy to step through.

"I'll never feel safe in here again, EVER," she hissed angrily.

As the minutes ticked by she guessed he was unlikely to return.

"What did he mean; he'd been trying for two years? TWO YEARS, how could it have been two years? And what has happened to Cathy?"

Tina-Lu jumped up, quickly dried herself, and wrapped a towel firmly around her body completely covering her modesty. She gingerly stepped across the wet floor towards the door and stubbed her toe on a heavy object lying on the floor.

"Ouch, what's that?" she cursed. Reaching down, she picked up something long and fairly heavy wrapped in cloth.

Tina-Lu finally risked turning on the bathroom light and saw to her amazement the silver handled staff. Jaden had found a way to transport Jack's staff across to them.

In an instant, Tina-Lu swept out of the bathroom. She rushed to her own room and dressed quickly. The thoughts of Jaden being in her bathroom and everything else raced around her head like a swarm of hungry bees. She opened her bedroom door slowly and breathed a sigh of relief as silence confronted her.

"No-one heard anything," she thought gratefully, tiptoeing over to her brother's room.

Jack snored quietly; he would've said he was breathing heavily. Tina-Lu couldn't help herself; she watched him for a few moments, grinning.

"Jack," she whispered; shaking his shoulder gently. Then placing her hand across his mouth, she made sure he didn't make too much noise. "Shhhh."

"What's the matter Sis?" he asked hoarsely. Still full of sleep, he'd just managed to drift into the dream world and his body took some moments to readjust.

"You're never going to believe this?" Tina-Lu replied excitedly. "You're never going to guess who I've just spoken to."

Jack glanced at the clock – almost two in the morning.

"What? Tell me for goodness sake," a rasp of desperation rattled from Jack's frustration. His mind was groggy with the disorientation of having been woken so suddenly.

Tina-Lu raised the silver handled cane as if she had just won an Olympic Gold medal. Jack was stunned. He checked it out several times before he could speak.

"How on earth did you get this?" he couldn't imagine how his sister did this but here it was, his staff, right here in his hand.

Tina-Lu excitedly relayed most of what had happened. She just neglected to mention anything at all about subjects including thoughts of NAKED, BATH or EMBARRASSMENT

Jack was still stunned. "How had Jaden opened the portal into this world? I thought that was impossible."

His sister reiterated Jaden's own words.

Jack couldn't grasp that he'd spent two years attempting the portal opening.

"That would make him nearly as old as you Jack, do you realise that?"

No longer listening to his sister; Jack was far too busy contemplating their next move. Tina-Lu, however, absorbed that obvious, but very interesting, piece of deduction.

"Yes it would, wouldn't it? I wonder what he's like now." Tina-Lu's curiosity was aroused; she felt her pulse racing at the prospect of returning and finding an older Jaden much nearer to her own age.

Jack came to his senses again. "What did he say about Cathy? Surely she didn't cross the MoonBridge to our side – she could be lost forever."

They were both horror struck that Cathy had done such a foolhardy thing; despite all the warnings against it.

"What are we going to do Jack?"

"I think I should try and find Cathy first?"

"Perhaps it would be better to meet up with Jaden, hear the full story, and then set off from their side to look for her." Tina-Lu had her fingers firmly crossed behind her back hoping that Jack would take up her suggestion. She was concerned for Cathy but she also really wanted to meet this older Jaden.

Jack quickly dressed, thinking about the right thing to do.

"Your right Sis; I need to hear what Jaden has to say. Do you think we should take Brandy with us this time? He looks pretty comfortable where he is."

At the mention of his name, Brandy opened his eyes a little and pricked up his ears. He'd been sound asleep nestled in the warmth and comfort of the covers. He could hardly believe they were talking about going out again already. He put his head down on his paws and went straight back to sleep.

Jack smiled, looking at his dog. "So much for our 'killer' guard dog Sis; we'll leave him behind then."

Tina-Lu nodded as Jack summoned the MoonBridge. This was the first time he'd called the MoonBridge, from this side, when the time wasn't exactly midnight. He wasn't sure how easy it was going to be.

Tina-Lu interrupted his concentration. "Don't forget we need to find Jaden so open the bridge close to him."

Jack's thoughts were side tracked and the bridge faded. He huffed and then started the process once again.

Tina-Lu grasped him by the shoulders. "Concentrate Jack, this is more difficult than last time isn't it? I'm right behind you."

Jack tutted loudly, this time, and mumbled under his breath. "I'M trying to concentrate, if you would stop interrupting." He shook his head and began for the third time; the MoonBridge glowed.

"You will place us close to Jaden..."

Jack cringed and exploded. "Give me a chance Sis; I'm trying my best here."

"Shhh, you'll wake mum and dad." Tina-Lu looked totally dejected, "Anyway, there's no need to moan. I'm only trying to help."

The young guardian held the staff tightly in both hands and thought briefly of wringing his sister's neck. Then he grinned quietly to himself before he pointed it at the spot where the MoonBridge had originally formed. He let his thoughts wander back to the other side and called to his friend.

"Jaden – where are you? I'm opening the bridge and need you to guide me. Show me where you are." Over and over in his mind he repeated the call.

Tina-Lu grew edgy, as nothing much seemed to be happening. She bit her lip two or three times before bursting. "Come-on Jack; I thought you were the master of this thing? I could do better my self."

Jack snapped; this was the last straw and he completely flipped. "Shut-up will you Sis. YOU cannot do this; I'm the Guardian, not you. Believe it or not, I'm trying to concentrate on a very difficult task and all you do is continually interrupt. I think it would be better if you cleared off and let me get on with it."

Tina-Lu looked so upset. She didn't mean to wind her brother up, but he took a very long time. She sat down on his bed and put her hand across her mouth. Jack couldn't help but laugh at her.

"That's better," he said with a giggle. "Pity you aren't like that more often." He jumped quickly out of the way of the low, swinging, kick aimed at a very delicate part of his anatomy. Tina-Lu would only be pushed so far.

Jack settled back down and thought about calling the MoonBridge. He imagined the powers of Lujnima coalescing; he saw the bridge form in his mind. Tina-Lu gave out a little "Yes" as the MoonBridge formed before them.

"Do you know if the exit has appeared near to Jaden?"

Jack shrugged his shoulders. "I think so Sis, but I cannot guarantee it. I can't seem to 'see' across the divide to make sure of its position.

The two held hands as they leapt up onto the bridge. Brandy barely even registered they'd gone; he only half noticed the light fading and the bridge closing. The house was back in silence again, perfect for sleeping and dreaming of chasing rabbits.

Chapter 21 - Moonbeams and Dreams

Nothing could have prepared Cathy for the overwhelming feelings she was experiencing. For all the times she had entered the MoonBridge, never before had the true depth or strength been exposed to her. Tears welled up in her eyes; the exhilaration took her breath away. Her heart pounded: this was more frightening than any war with the Blues, more beautiful than any summer sunset, and even more intense than any love she could imagine.

"Forgive me Lujnima, I had no idea..." her voice trailed off, lost amongst the myriad of silvery streamers.

Cathy stood motionless, but travelled faster than anything she'd ever imagined. This was nothing like the short instantaneous flits across the bridge she had taken with the others. She rode the moonbeams and seemed to be accelerating faster with every beat of her pounding heart. Her view of the 'outside', if that is what it could be called, was stretched and distorted. She thought she saw faces of people; perhaps, endless elongated shapes representing places along her route. Looking down at her feet, they were lost in a mist of denser moonbeams. Reaching her arms outwards, she sliced through the silvery beams forming swirling patterns of eddies and currents.

"Now Jack, think of me." Cathy gathered her thoughts picturing his face. "Where are you Jack? Help me cross to you."

The visions just kept streaming without showing any sign of slowing.

"How will I know when to get off?" Cathy worried.

Slowly, a thin veil of fear grew. Jack and Tina-Lu described the crossing lasting for a few seconds at the most - one or two breaths Jack had said.

"How long is a heart beat or two?" Cathy felt uncomfortable. "Okay, I've been here for more than two breaths. There should be some sign of arriving."

Panic nipped at her throat, she gulped back the fear welling in her stomach. She wanted to step to the side and get off the bridge. Despite every effort she couldn't make herself reach the edge. The moonbeams twisted each time she turned; they always streamed directly into her face. Desperation took hold sapping the girl's energy, claustrophobic fears surfaced as the realisation flooded her mind.

"Oh you stupid fool. You and your over confidence, now you really are in trouble."

Reluctantly, she accepted she was trapped. The warning from her mother had become a reality; she could be here forever just as the ancestors had prophesised.

"I must get off, NOW," she screamed.

As if in answer to her demands her journey ended. As quickly as it had started; she thrust forwards and tumbled to her knees. The MoonBridge was gone and she was, apparently, nowhere. All around her was white light: no floor or ceiling, no sky nor land, not even a plant or visible creature.

Cathy stood up and looked around. "Hello - can anybody hear me?" She wasn't sure if her voice carried. Without any reference point to guide her and no sensation of movement, she didn't know if she was standing, floating or flying.

"Hello." She shouted again, as loudly as she could. "JACK CAN YOU HEAR ME?" Nothing happened.

Her voice didn't seem to leave her mouth. Her lips moved but her words only seemed to be inside her head, if she did make any sound it didn't reach her ears.

Cathy wondered if she was asleep, she couldn't tell if she was dreaming or really 'seeing' this nothingness that surrounded her.

"How long has it been since I left Jaden?" she tried to calm herself and to make some sense of this place.

"It can't have been more than a few minutes, surely." Cathy was trying to be sensible and analytical. Her attempts weren't working;

she was very frightened and could just imagine that she might be trapped in here, wherever here was, for the rest of her days. She started to cry again. This time it was more of a pitiful sob; even though her body shook and her lips moved, no sound could be heard. All around her was utter silence; a world of pure whiteness and total silence. Inside she was sobbing and feeling desperate - outside was deathly still.

Cathy wondered if time was passing. She wiped the tears from her face, sniffed hard several times and rubbed her forearm across her nose in a defiant gesture.

"I'll try and walk somewhere else," she thought adamantly. She'd stopped trying to make any sounds. "I'll not give up, I'm better than that."

Setting off, she headed in the only direction she could be sure of - straight ahead. She walked in what she imagined was a straight line, but in this place everything looked identical in all directions.

"How can I tell where I'm headed when there are no points of reference?" she continued for what she judged to be a few more minutes, nothing looked any different. She broke into a run; faster and faster she ran until her chest hurt and her lungs were bursting. Still everywhere was unchanged.

"This is impossible," she gasped.

Once she had her breath back, Cathy started to question a few oddities about her predicament.

"If everywhere is exactly the same then what am I standing on?"

She placed her hand down to where the floor should be. Instead of stopping at ground level, her hand just kept on going. She reached downwards right past her feet; nothing was there at all. She even waved her hand right under the sole of her shoe. Cathy wasn't standing on anything.

"So how am I standing then?" This puzzle had her mind racing.

"If I'm not standing on anything then how can I have been running or walking? I must be locked in exactly the same spot. I haven't moved anywhere. This must be an illusion; my mind is playing tricks on me."

She tried to reach, stretching outwards; but, found nothing to touch.

"Think Cathy, what were you doing before you ended up here? What exactly were you doing?"

She thought for a while and tried to remember the exact circumstances that led to her being trapped in this non-place.

"I was looking out and screamed for the bridge to stop," Cathy remembered. "Then I fell to my knees and ended up here."

The conundrum only deepened.

"I wonder if this is what it's like to be in a Lost Room." She was trying anything to keep her mind focussed on solving the mystery rather than panicking and losing control again.

She recounted everything that she could remember about her journey on the bridge. Nothing gave her any clue about where she had ended up.

"I must be either in a moonbeam or trapped between my world and Jack's, some kind of limbo."

Not that knowing, actually helped her, but she did feel better having made a decision.

"I must remain calm. What did Layette say - follow my dreams to find Jack?" She was feeling more positive now. "Layette, of course; maybe she can help."

Cathy held the crimson gem stone tightly and called to the spirit within. Nothing happened: no light swelled, no being appeared and no help arrived.

"I'm NOT going to be trapped in here for eternity, and that's all there is to it." She was resolute; shrugging her shoulders, she brushed back her hair in defiance.

"Jack; can you hear me Jack? Think Jack, listen to my voice," Cathy tried desperately to connect with her love but all she received was utter silence. Over and over again she tried dozens and dozens of thoughts and wishes directed at her friend.

"This is hopeless," she rasped, distraughtly.

Tired and frustrated; her mental state deteriorated and it took her ages before she felt strong enough to repeat the exercise. She called and called to Lujnima this time, the outcome was exactly the same; nothing.

"I'm as good as dead," she declared helplessly. All of her inner strength was drained and she couldn't see any possible way out of this place. Just as her mother had said, she was trapped forever.

Cathy stood or drifted, she couldn't tell which, for what felt like an eternity.

"I'm going to starve to death in this horrible place." Her inner fears overwhelmed her. "I'll die and no-one will ever find me or know what happened?"

Chapter 22 - Coming of Age

Jaden sat, cross-legged, on a rough stone floor; the room was in the lower basement of Searlan's house. Positioned high in the hills and overlooking the southern plains, this was a quiet and remote spot. The old Sage chose this location carefully as it was many days walk from the nearest neighbour. Seclusion provided security; the peace and quiet were perfect for contemplation, reflection and meditation.

"Clear your mind to make room for useful knowledge," he reminded the young Sage on many occasions.

After many months perfecting the manipulation of the portal; Jaden finally managed to open it across the great divide. The intense effort left him mentally drained; never before had he felt so utterly exhausted. Immediately after delivering the staff he'd lost the strength to hold the connection, the sudden release threw him backwards to where he now lay.

More than two years had slipped away since he'd watched Cathy take that fateful step; his heart sank as she faded from his sight. He knew, instinctively, she'd be lost, and yet, he couldn't bring himself to stop her, she needed to find her own path. His destiny was to master the portal; no other Sage, in the long history of Sages, had ever done so. Since confronting Tarre-Hare, he'd known he was special; perhaps more than any Sage before him. Even his Grandfather had never fully managed to control the exit point of the portal. In the time since Cathy disappeared he'd thought of little else.

"Except for Lu," he grinned. Jaden had missed her more than anyone else. "You must come back Lu; I need you here with me." His heart ached.

Jaden had grown; he'd suddenly started to shoot up about eight months ago. Now about thirty centimetres taller, he was broader across the shoulders, his voice had deepened and his facial hair darkened. Jaden had moved from a boy into a young man.

Throughout the period of study, he'd expanded his understanding of the Sageship. Mastering his gift of great knowledge he'd managed to instil order into his memories. His Grandfather's ideas were employed to encourage his mind to categorise the wealth of ancient information. Usefully, this process dramatically improved his ability to recall detailed accounts from his forebears. Ideas and reflections from his past lives intermingled with the present; he couldn't tell the difference between his own memories and the ancients.

"Come on Lu, give Jack the cane and follow my thoughts."

The room was barely lit by the single flickering candle; he preferred as few distractions as possible whilst he meditated. Sitting in relaxed contemplation; he waited for his friends to appear. Then, closing his eyes for a few seconds, breathing very slowly and deliberately; he focussed his thoughts. Picturing Tina-Lu passing the staff to her brother; he imagined him raising it to summon the bridge. "Follow my thoughts Jack. Follow my calling and you'll find your exit point. I'm here my friend, hear my call."

Jaden repeated his guiding message over and over for many minutes. Each time, he expectantly believed the bridge would appear.

"You can do this Jack. You are the Guardian of the off world, hear my voice."

Summoning every fibre of his being he thrust his mind out across the universe. Farther and faster he travelled. "Jack, Lu - Hear me."

A sudden blinding silvery-light shattered the darkened cellar. Jaden shielded his eyes; for this was the brightest, strongest and widest he'd ever seen the MoonBridge. Without moving, he watched Lu and Jack step from the beautifully formed apparition. They stared at each other for a second.

"Well done you two; great to see you again - you heard my call."

Jack couldn't believe his eyes, the young man sitting on the floor was Jaden, and yet it wasn't. They'd only left a couple of hours ago, at the most, and here was Jaden more than two years older.

Tina-Lu stood and grinned at her friend, she was excited and pleased to see him. As he stood up, she nearly gasped; her little friend was almost her height. Her heart melted, her knees went weak and she felt her pulse beating faster by the second. He was gorgeous; Jaden had changed beyond all recognition, he wasn't just taller, he looked wiser, much older and very much the Sage of Sages. She giggled girlishly.

"Hello Lu, I've missed you so much."

Tina-Lu couldn't speak; her friend had turned into this incredibly handsome young man and she was lost for words.

"What's happened to Cathy?" Jack was extremely worried about his lost friend and didn't want to waste time whilst his sister flirted, so blatantly, with Jaden.

The Sage quickly filled them in on the days that followed their departure and the events leading to Cathy's decision.

"The moment she set foot on the bridge I knew it was a mistake Jack. She was determined to find you though, you know Cathy. I was powerless to stop her."

"And, you've never heard anything from her in all that time.

"Not a word Jack, you have to find her; you're the only one who can. Somehow, you have to bring her home."

Jack nodded but wasn't convinced. "She could be trapped inside the bridge itself - the rhyme describes being lost amongst endless cold moonbeams. I fear she may be in limbo, neither one side nor the other. I've no idea how to communicate with her."

"I feared this too. Open the bridge Jack, and then let's project our thoughts into the opening; hopefully we can guide her back."

"You may be right Jaden and it's certainly worth a try. Let's get started right away; we'll give it a go now?"

"Not in here Jack, we'll try later. I think we should walk up to the top of the hill and wait for dark. We should use the power of the full moon. Did you realise it was full tonight? I purposely called you on this day to allow us the best chance of focussing and harnessing

Lujnima's powers. I hope to bring the power of Tarre-Hare too. Between us we might just make this happen."

Jack was impressed; Jaden even sounded like the Sage. He was clearly more knowledgeable and had a distinct air of authority about him.

Yes; let's go up into the air anyway?" Tina-Lu was keen to see her friend in the full light of day.

They stepped out into the dipping afternoon sun; the late autumn greeted them with a chilly blast. The trees, edging the side of the hills, presented a mixed palette of red, brown and orange. Jack and Tina-Lu could hardly adjust to the difference in the landscape. For them, it had been the height of summer only a few hours ago, then a cool spring night at home and now the leaves rustled around their feet.

"Where are we Jaden?" Jack asked.

"This is my home Jack; Searlan built this house for me." As they strolled, the young Sage talked continuously. He described how he'd grown to understand his destiny. He even tried to explain the reasons behind his misinterpretation of Jack's inner thoughts.

"I don't believe you're destined to destroy the MoonBridge after all Jack. I think this idea was planted in your brain by Tarre-Hare to stop you from fulfilling your true destiny. I now believe you must find the Lost Room and that you must learn its secrets."

Jack tried to listen to his friend but found his mind swirling at the very mention of the Lost Room. The two witches had manipulated him so completely; he could barely grasp Jaden's suggestion. "How was he to find the Lost Room?" He felt he could barely find himself.

Tina-Lu, however, absorbed every word. She didn't quite know how or where she fitted into this strange world, but somehow she knew that HER destiny was caught up in this Lost Room. A subconscious message filtered through to her thoughts; the words grew in stature and forced their way out of her mouth "You are the key Jack, the key to the lock that opens the Lost Room. Jaden, you are the light that illuminates the dark places hiding the prize and Cathy is the hand that reaches out to the life lost forever in there. I'm the voice; my destiny is to speak on the Unnamed's behalf?"

The other two stared at Tina-Lu surprised at her revelations.

"Where did that little gem spring from sis? Who told you that I'm the key, and how do you know that you're the voice of the Unnamed?"

Tina-Lu shrugged her shoulders and looked bewildered. She wasn't sure how she knew this information. "I just felt the words forming in my head and said them. What do you think it all means?"

Jaden held Tina-Lu's hand and sent his mind deeply into her subconscious thoughts. He looked and searched for any clue to her insight; Tina-Lu grinned at Jaden's concern. He was sweet and comforting she thought.

The day came to a cold and windy close. The three friends talked for hours learning all about Jaden's time alone. They caught up on the state of the war - the Blades controlled all areas in the vicinity. Many homes were razed to the ground; families fled into the hills finding whatever shelter and safety they could. Few were taken as prisoners; most captured people were killed outright.

"The place is like a ghost town; houses and villages are empty or destroyed. I've had to be fully alert to protect this home from the enemy. All of my newly found Sage powers have been necessary to keep this place secret." Jaden seemed more serious than Jack had ever seen.

"How have you kept them away Jaden?" Tina-Lu was intrigued.

"I've formed a mental perimeter fence that part of my mind manages. Any person reaching the barrier alerts me to their presence. I can probe their minds to discourage them from coming in this direction."

"That's a neat trick; who taught you to do that?" Jack was even more impressed.

"I remembered something the ancients had learned; all people are open to suggestion. With the right leverage it's possible to make anyone do almost anything. All I've done is manage this knowledge in a way that allows, me, to concentrate on my task at hand. I employ some of my hidden memories and personalities to complete the monitoring for me. I guess you could think of it as a bit like having a separate Guardian looking after me." Explaining his newly learned skills; Jaden seemed remote and strange.

"What was that noise?" Jack hissed to his friends urgently; he'd heard a strange rumbling from across the valley.

Jaden stared in the direction of the sound and looked very puzzled.

Tina-Lu grabbed both the boys, "get down. The enemy's over there, they've found us."

Jack scanned the direction that Tina-Lu frantically pointed to, "Why didn't you sense anyone coming Jaden?"

The Sage shook his head whilst probing the mistiness surrounding the area of hillside opposite.

"I can't feel anything; it's as if nothing exists there." Jaden had never experienced anything like this before.

"Look, look there," Tina-Lu pointed to the 'v' shaped line of deep blue objects melting their way across the side of the hill and down towards the valley floor.

"They are heading straight for us Jaden. What's that at the front, it looks like someone sitting on top of one of them?"

"Not 'what' Jaden, it's a person. Who is that?" Jack was beginning to panic at the sight of the strange blue creatures. He remembered the burning pain piercing his head and instinctively put both hands across his ears. "We've got to get out of here, now."

The three ran down the other side of the hill away from the fast approaching enemy.

"Which way now?" Jack gasped.

"Follow me…" Jaden took the lead. He rushed down to the next valley and into the thick trees that lined a small stream. "There's a cave up ahead, the river dives down into it, and we'll hide there."

A blinding silver blue flash shattered the dimly lit tree cover. Jack fell to one side. Tina-Lu tripped over his leg and crumpled heavily; she'd banged her head, painfully, on a root sticking up from the ground. Jaden collapsed instantly unconscious and unmoving.

"What was that?" Jack could barely speak, no-one answered.

An even louder blast exploded a few metres away; a tree disintegrated into jagged splinters.

"Aaarghhh," Searing pain shocked Jaden back into consciousness and made him scream in agony. A half-metre spike, as thick as your thumb, pierced his leg and embedded itself into the ground.

Jack pulled himself up again as a third massive explosion destroyed several more trees over to their right. This time he managed to see the blue streak of light that accompanied the destruction. The enemy fired some kind of energy beam or ray.

"We're being blasted by the Blues," he screamed to the others. "How do they know where we are?"

Jack hauled himself across the ground to Jaden. Blood poured from the wound and needed immediate treatment if his friend was to survive. He tore the sleeve from his shirt and tied it around Jaden's leg to stem the flow of blood.

"Pull it out Jack; get this thing out of my leg." Jaden pleaded barely able to stay focussed.

Jack looked at his friend and across to his sister; he felt sick and hopeless.

"Pull it out Jack, now." Jaden grabbed at the spike passing through the fleshy part of his lower leg muscle.

Jack grabbed the boy's leg and gave one almighty tug to free the flesh from the wooden spike. A horrible squelching sound accompanied the removal. He was amazed how easily it came out; unsurprisingly, blood gushed from the open wound.

"Hold still, I'll see if I can stop the blood." Both hands were needed to tighten the tourniquet, thankfully the blood flow eased immediately. Jack felt terrified his friend would die.

"We must get you to the hospital Jaden, this wound needs stitches."

Tina-Lu had barely raised her head before the next explosion rocked the area. This time four simultaneous blasts covered a wide area over to their left. The shockwave battered their bodies but it had travelled far enough to lose some of its potency, none of them were damaged.

"We need to jump the bridge or portal; if we don't escape soon we'll all be dead." Jack sweated fearfully. "Come on, I'll try to call the MoonBridge."

"Urgggh, what's happening?" Tina-Lu groaned in a daze. Blood tricking from several splinter wounds in her face and arm. "Where are we Jack?"

Jack took up his cane and pointed it at the sky. He commanded the bridge to appear and thought of the only place he could picture clearly, Aunt Beth's burnt out cottage. The bridge barely appeared as a spluttering dull mist.

Another series of blasts exploded all around as the bridge disappeared from view. Jack looked worried and afraid. A deep rumble filled the air, trees started to shake and the earth vibrated violently.

"They are on us. We've got to get out of here," Jack was frantic; he couldn't concentrate and could hardly focus his mind on anything let alone the MoonBridge.

The vibrations increased dramatically as their bodies shook painfully. Jack pressed his hands over his ears and felt the pain searing through his head again. He expected the blue creatures to appear at any second.

"Don't give up Jack, you can do it. Call the bridge." Tina-Lu saw the pain in her brother; his memories of the previous encounter resurfaced. "Think Jack, think of the bridge."

Jack took heart from his sister's encouragement. He grabbed his cane again and pointed it to the sky once more. Gritting his teeth he commanded the bridge to appear. Again, a spluttering mistiness appeared before them - this wasn't the bright shining MoonBridge they expected to see.

"I think it's being blocked somehow. The bridge is not able to form properly." Jack couldn't understand why it didn't open.

"Concentrate Jack…" Tina-Lu was thrown heavily to the ground as another huge blast cleared several trees from immediately behind them.

Jack fell awkwardly dropping his staff; the pain in his head was bursting his brain. Intense humming increased dramatically to an intolerable scream, he was sure this was the end.

"Try again Jack, concentrate or we're all dead." Tina-Lu rasped; struggling to raise her battered body.

Jack picked up his cane and gripped it tightly. Seeing the first signs of blue through a gap in the trees; he forced himself to ignore the violent shaking of his body. Sitting on top of one of the Blue creatures was a man; dressed from head to toe in a brilliant blue robe, he wore a face of pure hatred. He was staring straight at Jack and pointing towards him.

Jack gulped, demanding the bridge to form. The air combined into a dull, fully formed, MoonBridge.

"Get up Tina-Lu, come on Jaden. This is our only chance; let's go." He helped his friend to stand and tugged at his sister's sleeve.

The three linked arms and staggered half a step towards the bridge. A huge blue and white flash exploded directly behind them. The heat of the blast smashed them headlong into the bridge. All three screamed in pain as the brilliant electric flame swept them across the MoonBridge; silence collapsed around them.

Jack barely had the strength to lift his head; hisses, bells and rings reverberated around his skull. He clasped his head as if to stop it shacking. "I've dropped it Tina-Lu, I've lost the staff."

Tina-Lu could hardly offer her brother any comfort for loosing his guardian cane. "Where are we Jack?" She asked, still half dazed.

Jack stopped scolding himself and looked first at his injured friend and then at his sister.

"We're in the MoonBridge, I guess, we don't appear to have arrived anywhere. That last blast seems to have closed it down around us." Jack looked all about but could only see silvery moonbeams streaking in all directions.

Jaden lay awkwardly; he was unconscious and in a very poor condition. Jack tried to shake him gently; the boy didn't move. A large blood stain coved his trouser leg - the wound worsened.

"This might be where Cathy is Jack." Tina-Lu suggested coming to her senses. "What has happened to Jaden's leg?" She finally focussed on her friend for the first time since he was injured. "He needs a doctor." She knelt down beside the boy.

"I know sis, I was trying to get us away from those Blues so that we could find the hospital where Aunt Beth stayed."

"But that was two years ago Jack, everything has changed here don't forget."

"Oh of course, I'd forgotten in the midst of it all. What shall we do?"

"What about trying to call Cathy and see if she can hear you, she might be near by, or something?"

Jack thought about his sister's idea for a few seconds and then tried to focus his mind. He pictured Cathy in his head, and then transmitted his thoughts, in all directions.

"You must help me recall the bridge Cathy." Jack sent the message several times.

"Answer me Cathy it's Jack."

***

No matter how far Cathy walked she found only white nothingness. "This is hopeless; I'm never going to get out of here. Where are you Jack, why can't you find me?"

A faint breath of air brushed Cathy's hair; she thought she heard a high pitched whistle. Goose-bumps ran down her neck – someone was close beside her. Spinning quickly around, no-one was visible. "Who's there?" she demanded.

Cathy jumped, a hand touched her leg. She spun again; still no-one could be seen.

"Wwwhat..." she stammered. The goose-bumps spread to her forearms; Cathy swallowed nervously. "Show yourself."

Nothing but emptiness could be seen in any direction. "Ouch!" Cathy jumped again in panic; something had pinched the back of her arm. "Who are you? Show yourself."

All around the light faded, a dull grey fog lifted to replace the emptiness. Cathy shivered uncontrollably – the temperature dropped suddenly revealing her breath.

"What is it doing here – I wonder?" the voice came from everywhere.

Cathy fell backwards from a painful prod in the stomach. "That hurt, stop it," she complained – still unable to see who was doing this.

"Is it from the other side, it doesn't seem dangerous," a second voice asked. The fog thickened until it was almost solid.

"Who are you? I'm not an 'it' I'm a girl; my name's Cathy."

"How did it get here? Can I keep it – please?" The second voice pleaded.

Cathy gasped, feeling a huge hand squeeze her body and lift her; the pressure was excruciating.

"Yes, but don't kill it my dear - hold it gently. They are not like us, they break easily."

The pressure immediately eased and Cathy struggled, ineffectively, to free herself from the invisible grip. "Ahhhh stop," she screamed in agony. Her whole body, both inside and out, felt as though it had been probed and prodded by a thousand needles.

"Careful now – you're hurting it."

"I only wanted to know what it's made of. It's a mixture of lots of squishy things, very odd."

The pressure, squeezing the girl, released as suddenly as it started. The sensation of other 'beings' close by, vanished. "Who was that, in here?" Cathy sighed.

"You must call the bridge; use your mind to call the bridge," came the unexpected reply.

"WHAT?" Cathy jumped around on hearing another person's voice.

"Who said that?" she couldn't tell if the voice was only in her head.

"Listen Cathy, hear my call."

The voice definitely seemed to come from behind her, Cathy spun again but found no-one.

"Think about the MoonBridge, help me, only together can we call the bridge."

Again, the voice came from behind Cathy. She looked behind but couldn't see anything except white.

"Jack is that you? Is it really you or am I dreaming?"

The look of relief on Jack's face told Tina-Lu he'd found her.

"Yes, yes it's me. Call the bridge; we are all trapped without an exit. We must think of the same place, think of Aunt Beth's cottage, right in front of the gate."

"Yes, of course, I'll call the bridge. Why didn't I think of that before?"

A great swirling and stirring of moonbeams entombed them all as the bridge reformed. With a loud hiss and single pop the MoonBridge opened. The blackened soil, where the front gate had once stood, was now covered in lush grass. Four people were spat out onto the ground as the bridge closed with a loud slurping sound.

Cathy picked herself up and threw her arms around Jack's neck. "I thought I was stuck in there for ever. Oh my god what's happened to Jaden?" She looked more closely at Jack and Tina-Lu. "Are you okay, you look like you've been in a war?"

Jack quickly explained everything, including losing his cane. He hugged her, saying, "You gave us real fright; we thought we'd lost you too. What was it like in there?"

Cathy shook her head and didn't answer.

"Never mind that now we need to get Jaden to a doctor; his wound looks very serious." Cathy was distraught at the sight of the blood covering Jaden's lower leg. "And how did he get so big?" She continued in amazement realising he was half as tall again.

Jack tried to tell Cathy about the previous two years; she wouldn't believe it.

"Don't be ridiculous Jack I've only been gone a couple of hours at the most."

"Do you think I'll still be able to call the bridge without having my cane?" Jack wasn't altogether sure about his ability.

Tina-Lu's impatience boiled over. "Come on you two, let's find out shall we. Get that bridge open again and get us to the hospital. Jaden will die before you two stop yakking."

The Guardians came back to their senses and grinned at each other. Jack shrugged his shoulders and said, "What the heck. Let's try."

Holding hands and focussing their minds, Jack and Cathy pictured the only person they could think of who might be able to help them - Doctor Frank Baker.

Jack and Tina-Lu's concerns were answered immediately. Cathy was stunned at the brightness of the MoonBridge. "I've never seen it like this before, how's it possible?"

"Jaden said the same thing when we first came back. It's something to do with Jack he said. He's amplifying it somehow and now it seems he doesn't even need his cane." Tina-Lu spoke with a real pride in her voice about her younger brother's powers.

"Help me get Jaden up." Jack said; trying his best to gloss over the comment but happy none the least.

He and the girls lifted Jaden from the ground and crossed the MoonBridge again.

***

Doctor Frank Baker stood in front of a large chart covering the entire side wall of the small room. He studied various parts of the body, depicted in clearly drawn sections. With great care, he drew an extra diagram. The accumulation of his medical knowledge was stored in this work of art. The room contained a wooden bench used as a makeshift operating table; his instruments were all neatly laid out on another smaller table covered with a clean white cloth. The room was dimly lit by two oil burning lanterns.

"It won't be long now Frank; the war is upon us and soldiers will be coming in thick and fast over the next few days. Your skills have never been so necessary." The doctor readied himself for the frantic period ahead.

Suddenly Frank jumped, "What the..." he exclaimed. The brightest light, he'd ever imagined, burned behind him. Turning instantly, he gasped, open-mouthed, as three youths stepped from the MoonBridge supporting the injured Jaden. The three laid the youth down on the bench as the MoonBridge disappeared.

"What... What was that?" The doctor stammered. "Where did you lot come from?"

"No time for that now Doc; Jaden needs your help, he's dying." Jack explained.

The doctor responded instinctively. "Beth, get in here quick," he shouted. Without a word the nursing assistant rushed to his side.

The three youths could hardly believe their eyes - Aunt Beth stopped dead in her tracks.

"Cathy, oh Cathy my darling, I thought you were dead. You've been gone so long. I thought I'd lost you forever." She swept her niece up in her arms and hugged her tightly - the pair burst into tears.

The doctor had already cut away Jaden's trouser leg to reveal the wound. "Right you lot, clear out, I've work to do if you want me to help your friend."

Aunt Beth slipped into action ushering the others into a small reception area at the end of a short darkened tunnel.

"Wait here; I'll return as soon as I can." She kissed her niece and hurried back to assist the doctor.

Chapter 23 - Alanthian gains the edge

Alanthian screamed, "Get them..." The MoonBridge closed before he could capture his prey. Cursing loudly, he watched the three slip from his grasp. "You were supposed to stop them."

The surrounding area had been obliterated: trees were smashed, boulders shattered and even the ground smouldered from the energy beam weapons.

"How did you miss? How could they have escaped? All that power and they still managed to get away."

The Blue creature gave no response.

"We must find them again; the Lord Tzerach will not be happy. That boy's definitely the other Guardian and he was carrying..." Alanthian's outburst halted mid-sentence. He'd spotted a silvery handle lying half buried in the smouldering ash.

"Look there Master Protector, what's that?" The Elder jumped down, from the top of the Blue, to examine the object. Grasping the cane firmly in both hands Alanthian pulled it free and waved it around his head several times. Dusting the cinders from the ornate carvings; fury gave way to exhilaration, "Ha, it's here – look! It's mine at last." This was the prize he'd coveted for longer than he dared to remember. "I take it all back Master Protector; well done, you did get them after all. He must have dropped this during the final attack."

The Blue hummed quietly without giving any indication he acknowledged the Elder.

Alanthian stepped away to consider his next move. Lovingly caressing the cane, he thought about his options. "Should I seek the remainder of the great key or should I return to placate the Shumiat?" The Elder returned and said, "Protector Beharim, we'll return to The Lord Tzerach to brief him and then I'll continue to search for the enemy."

The humming momentarily paused; Alanthian took the response as confirmation. "So be it. Now let's see what this can do?" Holding aloft the Guardian Cane, he commanded, "Open for your new master." Brilliant sparks of silver and blue leapt from the metallic end. The energy pierced the sky and the MoonBridge appeared. "Come Master Protector, we return." The Blues followed Alanthian back to their fortress. Confidently, he stepped from the moonbeams to confront the waiting Shumiat Leader.

"So Alanthian you managed to lose the enemy despite my Protector's best efforts." Lord Tzerach spoke coldly. "Beharim suggests the youngsters opened the bridge despite your meagre attempt to prevent them and then they slipped from your fingers."

The Elder seethed inside. He puzzled, "How does he know when we've only just arrived. They must be able to communicate across great distances." He calmed his thoughts and spoke in a flat, unflustered voice. "It wasn't exactly as you heard my Lord. The Protectors failed to halt the three; they should be dead by now. As for preventing the opening of the bridge, I now have the Guardian's cane and the source of his power."

The Shumiat Lord growled disapprovingly.

Alanthian hated this infernal creature. "I'll soon command the great key," he thought silently. "Then I'll wipe your kind from my world. You'll learn to fear me Tzerach, I'll be master..." The Elder smiled wryly, leaving the Lord of the Shumiat.

Returning to his sanctuary atop the northern tower; Alanthian continued his grumbling. "You'll all learn to fear me."

From the narrow window, the world seemed peaceful – a cool refreshing breeze calmed the Elder's pent-up anger. Turning his mind to more important things; he heard the power of the Guardianship calling seductively, it emanated from the cane and directed his thoughts. "I'm the one true Guardian, the one true keeper. I should command the MoonBridge again and search for the great key."

Alanthian paced around his chamber, rarely had he felt so indecisive. "What about the Lord Tzerach, he won't take kindly to my leaving. Do I care though, I'll find the great key and then I'll be master." The questions and answers spun around his head. Gradually he reached agreement and his excitement grew. "Let's just go, I'll worry about Tzerach afterwards." Pointing the Guardianship cane to the space above; he ordered. "Come forth and serve your new master."

Never before had the Elder seen the MoonBridge appear so vividly. The power from this staff was greater than his wildest imaginings. Alanthian stood transfixed as beams washed over him - he could feel the energy coursing through his veins.

"Grant me the strength I desire." Alanthian glowed silvery-blue; moonbeams swirled over his body, galvanising his muscles. "I am invincible," he declared. "This is my true destiny. I'm the master of the MoonBridge and I'll fulfil my pledge. I shall become the key." Alanthian screamed loudly and the walls of his tower shook.

Projecting his mind out across the lands, he desperately sought his exit point; hidden secrets from the beginning of time unveiled themselves to his call. Mystical truths and magical enchantments carved pathways through his memories. None uncovered the prize. "Come forth; reveal your hiding place. I command it by all the powers of the MoonBridge. Show yourself to the master of the secret forces." Pulses of light flooded from the windows – the Elder's life blood drained as each attempt drove farther and deeper into the abyss. Alanthian fell exhausted to the floor - he crawled slowly onto his chair; frustrated at his lack of success. "I need the matching cane. I must find Tel-Vah-Ney and use the power of both sisters to reveal the Lost Room."

The power faded. "Close now," he grunted pitifully. The MoonBridge disappeared instantly leaving the room dark and foreboding. "I must sleep." Silence engulfed the Elder.

**

The three friends paced restlessly across the small chamber. None could settle; they all waited impatiently for news of Jaden's leg wound.

"This is taking ages, how long does it take to sew a few stitches?" Tina-Lu's patience was wearing very thin.

Aunt Beth came scurrying out from the tunnel and briefly updated them. "Calm down all of you. You'll be able to see him very soon." She rushed away on her errand and they all sat back down.

"Tell us about being lost Cathy, what was it like in there." Jack managed to divert their attention away from their present concerns.

Cathy gulped before answering. "I was so afraid; I really believed I'd be lost forever. Then there was a voice, well two voices actually, scary and powerful. Something lives in there you know - something huge."

Brother and Sister leant closer as Cathy told of her desperate encounter.

"A massive hand squeezed my entire body and nearly crushed me to pieces. Then you called Jack, and they faded. I've no idea who they were, but I sensed they were very old."

"Come on you three, Doctor Baker says you can come through to see Jaden now." Aunt Beth had a beaming smile on her face. "He's going to be okay. His wound has been treated."

***

The East facing window beamed the early morning sun rays across the face of the Elder. Ten hours had slipped by in the twinkling of an eye. Alanthian groaned - his body had been strained to its limit: every bone ached; every muscle felt stiff and every movement caused a wince. Despite hours of undisturbed sleep he didn't feel at all refreshed. He stood up gingerly and tried to stretch his complaining body.

"I'll be more cautious next time." He exercised his arms, legs and torso. "I must find the second staff. I need their combined powers to reach my goal."

Alanthian bathed in the early morning sunlight as it streamed though his window. The air was cold and crisp. Autumn was fully upon them and the trees were beautiful in their myriad of colours. He held out both arms as if to embrace the beauty of the sight before him.

"I'll seek out that other Guardian. The girl will hand her staff over to me or I'll destroy her and take it."

Alanthian's mind cleared as a vision of Cathy formed. She stood alongside a boy; others were with her just beyond his sight. The boy was badly injured.

"So I did catch you Sage." Alanthian correctly identified Jaden lying semi-conscious on the hospital bed. "My Shumiat burned you after all. Now where's my other cane? The girl doesn't have it with her."

The Elder cast his mind, unsuccessfully, around the room; he couldn't see his prize. "Where've you hidden it girl?"

He spread his thoughts wider and came to the small reception room. Spotting something lying beside the small bench; his heart raced, "Ah, there you are my beauty; and you've been left all alone, how careless." The Elder rubbed his hands together in glee.

Alanthian took up Jack's cane and opened the MoonBridge. He thrust the exit point alongside Cathy's staff. With a single bound he was looking down at it. Hearing a voice, he turned briskly.

"What's that light?" Jack screamed. "Who's in there?"

Alanthian heard the footsteps running towards him - they were far too late. Grabbing his prize, he jumped back across the MoonBridge. The light was already dimming behind him. He never bothered about the commotion happening so far away. He couldn't care less about Cathy screaming as she realised her staff had been stolen, from right under her nose. He certainly didn't give a second thought to the two Guardians shouting hopelessly at the fading bridge or their pathetic attempts to keep it open. Alanthian only cared that he was safely returned to his tower and now had both his coveted ancient artefacts. The MoonBridge closed with a resounding pop.

"The Guardianship will belong to me alone; just as I've foreseen it." The Elder laughed heartily at the ease of his success. He held both staffs aloft and felt more powerful than ever.

"Now I'll find the rest of the key…"

Chapter 24 - Key Quest

Cathy cried inconsolably. "I've lost it again, my mother entrusted the Guardianship cane to me and now I've lost it for a third time."

Aunt Beth put her arm around her niece to try to comfort her. She remembered how determined she'd been, to return to the cottage, to retrieve it before the soldiers came. She hurt more than anyone else could realise. "Your friends will help you get it back darling. As soon as Jaden is better he'll help you. What about Jack, he's one of the Guardians isn't he, surely he can get it back?"

Jack remained unusually quiet since the MoonBridge disappeared. Sitting pensively, in the shadows, he thought about the presence of the other Guardian. He'd felt his power. Now this person was able to seek the rest of the key. "He's looking for the Lost Room," he deduced. "What else could he want both canes for?"

Tina-Lu heard her brother's mumblings - she slid alongside him and put her arm around his shoulder.

"Searlan would've known what to do Sis. We're all just stupid kids, what do we know of such things? This is crazy, only a couple of months ago I didn't even know what a MoonBridge was. Now look at us, we're expected to save the world or something."

"Jack, I've told you before, you're the chosen Guardian. Lujnima knew what she was doing when she picked you. You've something within you that sets you apart from everyone else. You don't need the cane, nor does Cathy I bet. You control the MoonBridge, not the cane. That was just a means to show you the way. You need to be strong, for us all."

Yet again, Jack was struck dumb by his sister's faith in him. Never, in all his short life, had he imagined his sister actually praising him or offering any kind of support. But, here she was doing just that. He lifted his head and looked deep into her eyes. There were no signs of sarcasm; none of her usual teasing. Tina-Lu meant every word. "Thanks Sis, you don't know how much that means to me. I'm really scared though. What are we supposed to do? Can we really make a difference here? And, what are we to do about that other Guardian? I'm scared; now he has both canes, we're all as good as dead."

Tina-Lu grabbed Jack's arm tightly in a vicious pinch. "Listen to me little brother. If you ever talk like that again I'll wring your scrawny neck myself. Pull yourself together and stop feeling so sorry for yourself."

Jack didn't know whether to laugh or cry. His sister's pinch hurt but her words made great sense. He decided to laugh - they both decided to laugh and hug each other.

"You're right Sis. Let's get this geezer and sort him out once and for all. I want my cane back."

Jack jumped up and went straight over to Cathy; holding her firmly by both arms he put his face very close to hers and said. "Tina-Lu is right; we don't need the canes to control the MoonBridge. We're the Guardians, you and me. Together we're unstoppable: one mind, one force and one soul. Stop crying and help me get our canes back; then we'll find this Lost Room."

Cathy sniffed and grinned. She tilted her head on one side and couldn't pass up the opportunity, it was just too tempting. She looked deeply into Jack's eyes. "I love you so much Jack Ferns. Don't ever lose me again." She kissed him tenderly on the lips as tears of joy rolled down her face.

Aunt Beth hugged the two youngsters and joined her niece in some well deserved joyful tears.

"With all this excitement and panic..." Aunt Beth sobbed between sniffs. "I almost forgot to tell you; I've married the good doctor, I'm Mrs Frank Baker now."

Cathy took two steps back, her mouth wide open. "What?" She said with a huge grin. "When did this all happen? I thought you looked at him oddly when we saw you in the hospital."

"I know, isn't it wonderful. I think I fell in love with him the moment I opened my eyes. Over the next few months he nursed me back to health and we learned a lot about each other. I couldn't believe how much in common we shared. He asked me to work with him, when I was well enough, and popped the question only two weeks ago. I said yes, of course, and we married that very day."

Everyone congratulated Aunt Beth. Jack was pleased someone had found happiness amongst all this war and destruction. Doctor Baker came through to see them and suggested they have a celebration.

"It would be nice if Jaden could share in it too." Tina-Lu wasn't about to let them forget about their other friend.

"Of course my dear, he's going to be fine; the wound is healing nicely. He was lucky the wood pierced where it did, a few centimetres either way would've been much more difficult. Anyway; young Jack saved his life by using the tourniquet. Well done my boy, you'll make a doctor yet." Doctor Baker slapped Jack on the back and made him turn bright red with embarrassment.

Everyone laughed and congratulated Jack as well.

"Let's settle for some supper then - until Jaden is strong enough for a proper celebration. I'm famished." Frank winked at Aunt Beth.

The Doctor's suggestion was greeted with unanimous approval and Aunt Beth led them all down to the cook house. The smell of fresh baked bread and stew wafted down the passageways, far from the actual chamber, where the kitchens had been set up. They were all starving. Jack's stomach churned and his mouth salivated at the loaded plates of meat stew and thick cut bread. No-one said another word before the first course was cleaned away. Every plate had been wiped clean and every drop of delicious juice had been mopped up with the fluffy light bread.

Mrs Hadley, the head cook, was delighted at their appreciation of her culinary skills. She particularly warmed to Jack.

"The most delicious dish I've ever eaten Mrs H." he'd said

"Seconds for all of you, I insist." Mrs Hadley nearly burst with pride; she filled their plates again and cut extra thick slices off her freshest loaf.

"This is my very special recipe young Jack. Eat well." She scurried back into her kitchen as they all sat back down to seconds.

The friends sat and chatted for the next hour catching up on all of Aunt Beth's news. When they'd finished their seconds, and cleared away the dishes, they walked outside into the late evening air. Darkness had descended over the plateau. Nothing moved in the emptiness that stretched for several days walk to the north. From the entrance to the cave system the friends saw the cloudless sky filled with thousands of bright stars. The autumn air had a crisp freshness that contrasted with the stuffy caverns. Everyone felt rejuvenated and content.

"I know we've got to find the key but do we wait until Jaden is better?" Cathy was unsure of Jack's plans.

"No Cathy, we must leave soon. Tomorrow I think. The other Guardian has both canes now and will waste no time seeking the Lost Room. If he finds it we're all lost, not just the room." Jack was solemn despite his poor attempt at humour.

"I'm staying with Jaden." Tina-Lu announced adamantly. "He needs a friend and I want to wait with him."

"Okay Sis. That's a good idea. We'll look for the Lost Room and try to beat this other Guardian to the key. You help Jaden recover and then join us. Jaden will be able to use the portal or perhaps I'll try to contact you like before."

They sat for some time watching the full moon rising. The thick autumn airs magnified the face to twice its usual size and altered the colour to a straw yellow.

"This is our moon Jack." Cathy held her friend's hand tightly and felt him squeeze her fingers in response.

They all admired the huge face of the moon smiling down at them.

"Lujnima will guide us Jack. She'll give you the strength to fulfil your destiny."

Cathy's faith heartened Jack, but secretly; he was afraid and didn't believe he possessed the strength or courage to do this task. He held Cathy's hand even tighter. "Let's go and find somewhere to sleep. I don't know about you lot; I'm suddenly feeling exhausted. Today has been a really long day."

Tina-Lu yawned deeply and set the others off as well. They all laughed as they agreed they needed to rest. Aunt Beth led them through the caves to the sleeping areas. Bedding was borrowed and they snuggled down to a well deserved nights sleep.

In the caves, night and day had no meaning at all, everywhere was the same. The dull glow of oil lamps made little difference to the overall levels of light. Tina-Lu sat up from her warm covers and looked around. "Are you awake, Jack? What time is it?"

Jack didn't stir. Many people busily went about their business; most were soldiers, Resistance Fighters who'd fled from the tyranny of the Blues and the Blades. They'd remained hidden here for over two years in relative safety, few heard of the oppressor's whereabouts. Aunt Beth had described the regular patrols and expeditions sent out to spy on the enemy. Thankfully, none had ever crossed the northern plateau.

"Cathy, wake up; it's morning." Tina-Lu was having no success rousing the two Guardians. She'd just groaned and pulled the covers tighter around her head. Leaving her sleepy friends, she set out to find Jaden. The cave system was a maze of passages; hundreds of tunnels and caverns disappeared in all directions. "Which way now?" she wondered. A few junctions were marked with make-shift signs pointing to the main areas; following them allowed her to find her way to the infirmary.

"Hello, I'm Tina-Lu, a friend of Jaden. How's he doing please?"

The staff-nurse looked up at Tina-Lu and smiled sweetly. "He's slept all night long, I'm pleased to say, a very good sign. The doctor will see him later this morning and I expect he'll be allowed to hobble around. You can go in and see him if you like; he's just having some breakfast."

Jaden was sitting up in bed eating a delicious breakfast of eggs and toasted bread. The smell made Tina-Lu's stomach grumble.

"Hello Lu, thanks for coming to see me. Where's everyone else, I was just beginning to worry. Anyway, how did we get here?"

Tina-Lu brought Jaden up to date whilst he tucked into his breakfast. Jaden was horror struck when she recounted the loss of the second staff – he choked on his toast. "You mean BOTH staffs have been taken? This is disastrous, I must get up immediately." He attempted to throw back the covers and jump into action.

"Sit back down you idiot. You're not going anywhere; at least, not until the doctor says you're fit enough. You're very lucky to be alive he said yesterday. So don't even think of racing off after some missing Guardian staffs."

Jaden grinned at his friend's insistence. "Yes mummy," he answered cheekily, sitting back down.

Tina-Lu slapped him coyly on the arm. "Anyway, it's already decided. Jack and Cathy are going after the other Guardian and looking for the Lost Room whilst I stay here to look after you." Tina-Lu was adamant her patient would do as he was told.

Jaden thought for a few moments about the plan. "I need to talk to Jack before he goes off and does something he may come to regret Lu. This other Guardian has already demonstrated just how dangerous he is. Now he has both staffs I fear he's even more deadly. Your brother must not take on this person lightly."

Seeing the concern on Jaden's face, she felt afraid for her brother. "I'll make sure they both come to see you before they do anything. Anyway, they were still soundly asleep when I left them so they aren't rushing off anywhere yet."

The pair chatted for about another half an hour before Doctor Baker arrived.

"How's my patient doing then?" The doctor greeted them both with a cheerful smile.

They talked for a few minutes before Tina-Lu decided to take her leave and find the others. She knew the doctor wanted to examine his patient alone.

"I'll be back to see you later," she said to Jaden; leaving with a smile and a wave of her hand. "Take good care of him Doctor Baker; he's my best friend in the whole wide world and very special to me."

Jaden's grin nearly split his face it was so wide. "Wow…" he thought.

Jack and Cathy were still tucked up soundly in their beds when Tina-Lu returned. "Come on you lazy pair, the day is old and it's time you were up. We've a lot to do today."

Jack opened an eye and looked at his sister. "Leave us alone Lu," he said grumpily.

"That's Tina-Lu to you; little brother. I'll find a jug of water in a minute and that'll wake you up; if you don't get a move on."

The pair begrudgingly climbed out of their beds and refreshed themselves with a wash in some cool clear water. They made their way to the cook house, for breakfast, and were amazed at the numbers of people eating, talking and working.

Aunt Beth bumped into the three.

"Morning Aunt Beth." Jack greeted her like one of his own.

Cathy hugged her tightly and gave her a peck on the cheek.

"Look after Jaden for me Aunt Beth please." Tina-Lu wasn't about to be left out of adopting a new Aunt.

Beth grinned broadly at her new siblings. "A bit of a lie in this morning was it? We rise early here you know," she teased. "Of course I'll look after him for you my dear. A handsome lad isn't he," She winked knowingly at Tina-Lu who blushed at the insinuation.

"Are all of these people Resistance fighters?" Jack enquired.

"Mostly; we also have some villagers and individuals who joined along the way. The last count was over four hundred soldiers and their families. They take a lot of feeding."

The clamour of voices, from the cook house, was bewildering. Mrs Hadley flittered around like the queen bee. She seemed to be everywhere tending her flock and fussing over every morsel left on a plate. "Eat up my dears. You can't go to war on an empty stomach now can you." Her rosy red cheeks and beaming smile warmed all who came in contact with her.

The three friends ate a hearty breakfast before Tina-Lu guided them back to the infirmary. Jaden was half asleep.

"He lost a lot of blood yesterday and needs to have as much rest as possible. Don't go over exciting him. I've given him a sedative so he may be a little drowsy." Doctor Baker warned.

"We'll not stay long." Tina-Lu replied. "Jack and Cathy just need to see him before they leave."

They'd had never seen their friend looking so drawn and frail. His skin looked grey and lifeless. His leg was raised up on a support and heavily bandaged.

"The Doctor gave me something to help me sleep." Jaden yawned. "You mustn't go rushing off looking for the other Guardian; he's very dangerous, I'm sure of it. Look what he is capable of." He nodded towards his injured leg. "He was trying to kill us all, you do realise that don't you?"

Jack and Cathy nodded solemnly in reply.

"You should wait for me to get better. Have you forgotten the Vinkef warning Jack? You were told never to return," he continued.

After a short conversation it was agreed that Jack and Cathy should attempt to open the MoonBridge to secretly observe the area of the fortress. They were to look for signs of the other Guardian, not to confront him or the Vinkef. If a safe opportunity arose, they would try to regain their canes.

The Guardians and Tina-Lu hugged their friend farewell. They headed back to get some provisions for the journey before stepping outside. The sky had darkened with angry looking black clouds. Rain was expected today and they were glad of their jackets. Tina-Lu decided to accompany them as they made their way to the top of the hill behind the cave entrance. The climb was difficult and quite tiring. All three panted hard when they reached the top. Jack flopped down exhausted until his heart stopped beating so fast.

"Shall we try to open the MoonBridge Jack?" Cathy had recovered from the exertion and was impatient to get on with things.

"Not yet. I think I'll first try to throw my mind forwards to the fortress and see if I can find anything out before we go charging in there." Jack sat up, concentrating his thoughts. He steadied his breathing; it took a few minutes to settle his thoughts. Suddenly his mind left his body and flew along the ground to the north. He travelled faster and faster passing a few places he recognised. The lake by Cathy's cottage looked grey and unwelcoming as it reflected the miserable looking sky. He whizzed over the hills that skirted the dead-lands. Even the oasis looked forlorn in the autumn weather. He stopped on the hilltop that overlooked the fortress in the distance.

"This is where we were before," he reflected. "Just one more hop."

Jack crossed the plain aiming for the outer wall of the fortress. He'd travelled about half way when he noticed a shimmer surrounding the entire area; the light was distorted and made the fortress appear out of focus. Instead of rushing right into the barrier he slowed and tentatively reached its boundary. He peered at it in fascination. The distortion made the air flow turbulent and hypnotic in appearance, a bit like looking at a bubble. He was hesitant, but believed he should attempt to touch the obstruction. Jack reached out his hand, instantly the glistening region grabbed him and he was trapped. He struggled to retract his hand but only managed to be sucked even deeper into the distortion. This strange light held him rigidly in its grasp. With each attempt to resist he became even more entangled.

Tina-Lu and Cathy became alarmed when Jack sprang rigidly to attention, his gaze froze and his eyes stared widely without blinking. His body was as stiff as a board and perfectly straight. Slowly, Jack's face darkened as his trance led him into a deep coma. The two shook him harshly and screamed at him. Nothing could rouse him from his entrapment.

Jack couldn't move at all now. The shimmering air around him held him tightly; he could neither retract his mind nor move in any other direction. His soul was caught in an unrelenting web.

"You were warned, young Guardian, never to return to this place." The voice was cold with deadly malice.

A shiver of fear flushed through Jack's entire body and mind. He felt overwhelmed by the finality of the declaration. "Who ssssaid that?" He stammered a fearful reply.

"You know who I am, and you know what I must do. Death is your only destiny." The voice deepened to a terrifying resonance grasping Jack's heart and quashing any sense of hope. "Do you have any final proclamation you would wish to make, foolish young Guardian?" A hint of sarcasm grated from the offer.

Jack struggled to think of something meaningful to say; instead, he just froze unable to respond. Subconsciously, his thoughts tunnelled deeper into his soul and listened to a diminutive voice whispering to him.

"Fear not young master Jack. You're the Guardian by right and you'll know what to do. Speak now; speak your innermost thoughts. We'll meet sooner than you know." The encouraging voice of Searlan warmed and revitalised Jack's frozen heart.

With a greater strength than he imagined possible, Jack responded. "I heard your warning and I knew the danger of coming back here. But you've looked in the wrong direction; it's not me you should fear. Look again Korbynithus and you'll find there's a hidden Guardian who's stolen both canes. His cunning and deviousness has fooled all of you. He craves the Lost Room and its hidden secrets. They'll soon be found and he'll steal the key from under your noses." Jack sensed his words having an effect and continued. "Once the other Guardian has the key no-one will be safe, not even the mighty Vinkef."

***

Far away on the hill top Cathy shook Jack's rigid body furiously. She knelt beside him trying her best to communicate with him. "Wake up Jack. Come back to us." Everything was going wrong again.

Tina-Lu asked, "What's happened Cathy? What should we do?"

"You must go and get help; bring Jaden. He's the only one who can bring him back."

Tina-Lu didn't need asking twice, she set off down the hill at a blistering pace.

Cathy held Jack's head in her hands. "Come back to me Jack. Break this spell and come back."

***

Jack felt the Vinkef oppressively close beside him.

"We hear your words Guardian and will deal with this other threat in our own time. You however, were warned of the punishment for disobeying the invisible protectors. None may cross the Vinkef and live. This is how it's always been and shall be into eternity."

This power, confronting him, was immeasurably greater than anything he could conjure up or even imagine. Jack couldn't escape; the Vinkef were about to destroy him and he was incapable of reacting. Korbynithus reached out with deadly accuracy and pieced Jack's heart.

"Arhhhh," the pain seared though him; a million burning needles stabbed every centimetre of his skin. Power ebbed from his weary mind; Jack grasped desperately for anything other than the agonising onslaught. Deeper and deeper, he plunged, flailing wildly against defeat.

A faint voice spoke, "Look to Cathy for your strength, young Guardian. Remember her gift; it's not just to show the way. Now fight for your life." The voice of Searlan filtered up from the depths of despair.

With one final monumental effort, Jack managed to grapple back from the brink of destruction, "Get away from me." The force of his passion thrust the deadly creature away.

Jack struggled to escape again but could not break free. The bonds of the entangling web tightened further strangling him. "I… am… the… one… true… Guardian…" He grated each word with teeth firmly clenched. "You… will… release… me."

The Vinkef moved further away from the power emanating from the desperate Guardian.

"By the power of Lujnima, I command you to free me," Jack summoned up every ounce of his inner strength to overcome the Vinkef. He remembered his gift from Lujnima and thought of the illumination in his hand and arm. He imagined it brightening until it was like the sun on a hot summer's day. All of a sudden he projected a terrifying bolt of silvery light that streaked out from his hands and smashed into the invisible foe.

"Eeeeeee." The screech of a wounded banshee made Jack cringe. Despite the pain and pressure from his bonds, Jack became more confident. "I said free me or feel the full power of the chosen Guardian." Jack shone silvery-white; his hand, arm and then entire body illuminated the area all around.

"Take that." Another massive solid beam arced directly into the invisible tormenter outlining its form. "I see you Vinkef. Release me now." He sent a third blinding flash of incandescent magnitude driving into the belly of the Vinkef. Every fibre of his being thrust the blow deep into the enemy. He felt sure it would be enough to finish the Vinkef off. "Get away from me…"

Instead of destroying the monster, the energy had the opposite effect. Korbynithus absorbed every drop, his outline doubled in size.

Jack finally learned the terrible secret of this creature's success. He rapidly adapted his existence to drink the full force of his opposition, Korbynithus consumed Jack's anger. The Vinkef truly were invincible.

"You are indeed a formidable adversary Guardian. The night sister chose well when she sought her new emissary. But the Vinkef cannot be destroyed by any mortal soul; however, powerful you become. Even the Unnamed couldn't defeat the eternal protectors."

A brief pause allowed Jack to digest the truth in the words. Korbynithus calmly concluded with a definitive cruel finality. "Now we will fulfil our oath."

A screeching howl, of ear-shattering intensity, smashed every atom in Jack's body. He recoiled physically at the overpowering decisiveness of this killer blow. Every ounce of anger, courage or determination, Jack had shown, was amplified one hundred times and delivered back at him with unmatched ferocity. The young Guardian couldn't offer any form of resistance to the concentrated onslaught. The invisible protectors, of the Lost Room, had won. In an instant; every last breath was extinguished. Jack's world darkened immediately to total blackness. He plunged far into a dimension without light, sound or sense of time. His form faded from the web of entangling light. The spirit of Jack was totally lost.

Back on the hilltop, Cathy held her dearest friend tightly, he lay unmoving. Suddenly his body fell limp and lifeless in her hands. He stopped breathing and turned an ashen grey. Jack's life ebbed away as he slipped through her fingers and out this world. The truth struck like a hammer, she looked skywards and screamed, as loud as her lungs would permit. "Noooooooooo..."

Chapter 25 - Unleashed

Silvery beams swirled silently beside the immense outer wall of the fortress. A vision of pure blue stepped quickly from the centre of the apparition. The hooded figure clutched a silver tipped staff in each hand. "Be gone," Alanthian ordered powerfully - the MoonBridge disappeared silently.

The Elder stood poised and alert ready to do battle; he relaxed visibly when nothing came to attack. Away to his left he observed a strange light flickering. Beams fired in all directions; powerful blinding beams like great searchlights switching on and off. Alanthian projected his vision towards the commotion. A battle raged between two mighty adversaries and the Elder knew better than to intervene. He chose to watch, listen and learn.

"So the invisible protectors really do exist, they're not just a terrifying legend. I must be cautious here."

Alanthian surreptitiously observed the battle from his distant vantage point. A shimmering form battered an invisible force. Bolts of silvery lightning pieced the air. He caught sight of the outline of the Vinkef but couldn't distinguish who was projecting the beams of power. He recoiled instinctively as the Vinkef grew to twice its size and delivered the final blow.

"This adversary is even more potent than the legends suggest."

The shimmering form faded; almost immediately the invisible protector disappeared. Alanthian turned away, still pondering the outcome, and continued his search for the hidden conduit. He ran towards one of the doorways and entered. Inside was gloomy; the chilled air carried a mustiness that caught the back of his throat.

"Where should I start?" Alanthian searched frantically for a sign. Each room or passageway was as bleak as the last. The entire area was deserted now, all of the occupants had moved across the savannah to help with the search for the resistance. The place was cold and desolate.

Several floors above, and at the end of a long straight corridor, stood an immense archway filled by an equally impressive oak door. Alanthian gingerly tried to open it. To his surprise, the great weight moved with barely any effort. As the door swung back it revealed a vast hall. The ornately decorated marble flooring was covered in dust. Enormous high walls, peppered with stained-glass windows, created an immediate impression of wealth and power. Each window depicted a scene from a long forgotten age; kings and queens, warriors and gods, all frozen in time. A large dome perched above the centre of the room, filling the space with mystical light. The Elder stepped nervously inside; the sound of his shoes echoed fearfully. Approaching the middle, his blood froze.

"Welcome Elder Alanthian, master of the secret powers. I've been expecting you." The voice boomed around the walls and seemed to emanate from the open space below the great dome.

The Elder stepped backwards and spun around at the sound of the enormous door slamming closed. Heavy, unseen, bolts clanked loudly as they locked it tight.

"Come forth and approach me." The voice was very powerful and persuasive.

Alanthian moved cautiously towards the centre of the hall but couldn't see anyone.

"Who are you and how is it you have been expecting me?" The Elder looked, unsuccessfully, for the owner of the voice.

"Step into the light where I may see you." The voice commanded.

Alanthian became increasingly cautious. Stepping into the wide open space, at the centre of the great hall, a single beam of light shone down onto his face. Instinctively, he shielded his eyes and looked above; the dome was so large, and so high, it was impossible to distinguish any of its structure.

"Long have I expected this moment Elder." The voice of the Vinkef shrank to that of a small child. "The world was much younger when you took your first steps; and yet, here you are barely aged beyond your twenties. A conundrum I would say."

The Elder turned to the voice and beheld an infant child floating about head height away to his left. "What are you?"

"I'm called Korbynithus and I'm the voice of the Vinkef, the eternal protectors."

"How could you have been expecting me?" Alanthian asked more forcibly.

"You've been destined to stand before me ever since you took your first daring step across the night witch's bridge"

"You know why I've come then." Alanthian held the two staffs aloft in a threatening manner. "You must also know that I'll not permit you to prevent me finding the prize."

"Strong is your heart Elder and powerful your gift. But these trinkets do not belong to any of the Ancients. They were crafted long after you departed your world. How did you come by them?"

Alanthian held the staffs firmly and pointed them towards the child. "How I came by them is my business alone. But you'll feel the full force of them if you attempt to interfere in my search."

"You've grown powerful indeed if you believe you're able to wield both Tel-Vah-Nar and Tel-Vah-Ney. Few have such ability and none have ever dared threaten the invisible protectors."

Alanthian closed his eyes briefly and imagined a great white and silvery light swirling around his body. He called the energy and sent it streaming upwards filling the great dome with brilliance. "Behold Vinkef, the light of the sisters. I'm the master of the secret powers and the key shall be mine. Show the hidden doorway to me or die protecting it."

Korbynithus tilted his head and grinned wryly. "Impressive is your control Alanthian but foolish and impulsive. Do you really believe your idle threats can influence the Vinkef?" The child blinked, nodding towards the staffs. The light was instantly extinguished and the canes clattered to the floor. They were ripped effortlessly from the hands of the Elder and thrown to the far sides of the great hall.

"Never underestimate your enemy Elder. You're only permitted to speak, at all, because it amuses me to understand you." Korbynithus nodded again and the Elder slumped heavily to the marble floor. "I could crush you without a second thought fool. Now explain your youthfulness before I destroy you where you lie."

The Vinkef paused briefly; his voice deepened into a terrifying thunderous boom and shook the foundations of the fortress. "Speak NOW!"

Alanthian couldn't resist the demands of the mighty protector. Despite his every effort to prevent it, he poured out a lengthy explanation about the Blues and their plans.

The Vinkef listened with great interest and then pondered the tale revealed by the Elder. "So you've been touched by the Shumiat. They're very dangerous allies; I doubt you've any idea of their true plans for you. I believe it would be wise to steer clear of these creatures."

Alanthian was permitted to stand again.

Korbynithus read the Elder's thoughts and concluded, "So Elder, you believe the hidden key will make you a match for these Blues as you call them. Know this Alanthian, not even the great Unnamed could defeat the ancestors of these creatures. He unwittingly brought them into this dimension and regretted it ever since, what possible hope do you have?"

Alanthian closely observed this strange child floating before him; he noted the briefest loss of control that accompanied the creature's meanderings. A plan of attack hatched in his mind - he just needed the Vinkef to relax its grip a little more and when the opportunity arose, he would strike. "You are correct; I'm certain the key will empower me to deal with the Shumiat. What you haven't guessed is my plans didn't include trying to destroy them. I merely intended to transport them away from here via the bridge – back the way they came, far from this dimension." Alanthian engaged the Vinkef in conversation and gave him more than enough to consider. He waited for just the right moment.

"An interesting strategy Elder, and how did you think you could lure them into the bridge?"

Alanthian smiled at the child. He'd achieved his aim to lure the creature into discussion and to open a window of opportunity.

"Tell me about the Lost Room; how would I find it?" The Elder changed tack again.

"Do you truly think I'd actually tell you anything of this? But then, to know the answer to such questions, wouldn't solve the paradox of the hidden place. Those who've sought this before have all died trying. Is that a fate you seek also?"

"My fate is already written it would seem, why else would you have been awaiting my arrival? If I'm to die anyway, what harm would come from speaking of the Lost Room?" Alanthian felt ever more in control.

The Vinkef thought about the question. He enjoyed this battle of wits and was perplexed at the simplicity of the request.

Korbynithus smiled. "Your logic amuses me Elder. The Lost Room cannot be found by merely looking; the place isn't actually lost or hidden, but could be described as residing outside of here. No-one from your plane of existence could ever find this ethereal space. The Vinkef believe the Lost Room may find the seeker. Bizarre though it may seem to you, it's all a matter of perspective - the room has to want to be found."

Alanthian followed the signs of the Vinkef's mood. He'd waited for any slight advantage when the creature was distracted. This was the moment; this was what he'd been waiting for. The Elder grabbed both canes and fired an immeasurably brilliant bolt of silvery-blue light into the face of the Vinkef. The entire hall flashed and crackled with the blinding intensity. Every molecule, in the Elder's body, drove the full force of the twin sisters at the protector. Brighter and more intense with each passing second - the beam ploughed straight into the heart of the Vinkef.

As he'd observed earlier, the Vinkef grew with the power of the unrelenting onslaught; Alanthian's plan unravelled. The unfathomable being doubled and then trebled in size; still the Elder didn't relent. Sweat poured from his forehead, the veins on his arms stood proud with the effort. He focussed, increased and re-directed a light so strong, none had ever witnessed anything to approach it.

Korbynithus had been caught off guard. The influx of energy wounded him acutely; he wailed a deep throated painful moan. For over a minute Alanthian accurately directed the full force of these two mighty sisters. The sun darkened significantly, the moon aligning with her sister until they became one.

The Vinkef's moans reached a scream of realisation; here was something entirely unexpected. The Elder had tricked them, for the first time in an eternity the Vinkef met a worthy adversary. Alanthian's cunning was even smarter than the Unnamed one. He wasn't attempting to defeat these creatures; he was making them impossibly powerful. Just as a balloon can be stretched to a limit and then bursts; the Elder filled the Vinkef with unrelenting power. The moaning became a scream of panic; at last; the Vinkef met their match.

"Noooo…" Korbynithus erupted releasing all of the Elder's energy. The domed roof, of the central tower, blasted high into the sky. The top floors shattered in all directions; even the massive outer protective walls shook like a jelly. The blinding conflagration expanded, instantly, engulfing everything for kilometres. A smouldering wasteland was left in its wake.

At the very moment the creature screamed; the Elder redirected his energy beam, around his body, forming an impenetrable barrier against the destruction. He ducked, instinctively, down onto his knees and covered his head with his arms. He needn't have been afraid; the veil of force cloaked him completely. Not a single hair on his head had moved. Alanthian felt a great rush of triumphant elation, his heart pounded and his muscles seethed. He jumped up shutting off the energy from the canes and shouted. "Yes!" He punched the air over and over again. "I'm the key keeper by rights."

The Elder surveyed the devastation, as far as the eye could see, was blasted. He took a sharp intake of breath and let out one long whistle. "I've defeated the invisible protectors."

Pausing only to take in the revelation; he continued, "The Lost Room will now reveal itself to me and I shall claim my prize. I'm master of both Guardian staffs."

Alanthian lay flat on the ground, his arms stretched outwards. He stared up to the sky and noted a slight darkening. He blinked to make sure he was really seeing the change in colour. The sky turned from blue to a pinkish red just like a sunset, but the sun was still high in the sky.

The very brief moments of calm, following the enormous destruction, were interrupted by a new sound - a strange sound not heard since the world was young. A whistling accompanied a swirling whirlwind. A bizarre shape formed above Alanthian's head, all of the debris from the explosion disappeared into the vortex. The surrounding landscape was sucked clean by a gigantic vacuum cleaner. All that is, except for Alanthian; he remained unmoved at the centre of the chaos just watching the vision settling above his head. The whistling stopped and a painful silence fell over the lands. In the middle of the vortex, a plain white door materialised.

"Well now, there's something you don't see everyday; the Lost Room has found me."

Chapter 26 - The Sage of Sages

The sound of Cathy's voice coursed far across the lands chilling the souls of all who heard her pain. The message of Jack's death penetrated the caves below, flooding into the infirmary. Attempting to stand; Jaden felt a body blow thump into him. "Urghhhh," he complained bitterly. The outpouring of grief signalled his friend was gone. Blank emptiness filled his vision and he wondered, "What's happened to you Jack?"

Tina-Lu mouthed something frantically, but Jaden couldn't hear her words. "Perhaps she's calling for the doctor?" he thought. "Your brother is gone and nothing I could've done would've prevented his passing?" Jaden cast his mind away to the hilltop where Cathy sat weeping.

Tina-Lu shook the young man eagerly, "Are you alright Jaden?" She pulled him to his feet. "I'm to get you to the hilltop, something awful has happened to Jack."

Jaden reluctantly explained his feeling of empty blackness and the sense that Jack was no longer with them.

"What does that mean? Are you saying he's dead?" Tina-Lu shook with shock. "I don't believe you, I won't believe you. This can't be true."

Jaden comforted his friend, hobbling out of the caves. Progress was slow; his leg was well bandaged, but felt very painful. He lent heavily on Tina-Lu's arm until they eventually reached Cathy. She sat motionless, holding Jack's limp body.

As they approached; Cathy looked up and said. "He's gone Tina-Lu; they've taken him."

Jaden reached down and placed his hand on Jack's forehead. He pressed hard and spoke an incantation quietly. "Hear my calling Jack Ferns. Return to us." Jaden dug deeply into his Sageship knowledge to seek out one particular memory. He remembered an encounter with the Vinkef from ages past. A great Sage, of old, witnessed a Guardian being driven out of this plane and into the next. His body remained lifeless and grey in colour and seemed almost dead. He looked exactly like Jack did now.

"You're in a deep dark place and you may think you're dead – Jack, come back to my voice."

Cathy and Tina-Lu were amazed.

"Jaden - Jack's dead. Look he's not breathing." Cathy sobbed.

"No Cathy, I first thought he was dead too. But, seeing him, I'm not so sure. I think he's been cast out by the Vinkef. My ancestors witnessed this once before, many generations ago. I believe he has been plunged into a deep and dark place; so far away his body thinks he's dead. Believe me when I tell you; he's not."

"So how do we get him back?" Tina-Lu knelt beside her brother.

"I don't know Lu; we wait and pray I guess. I'll keep calling to him in the hope he hears me."

"Can we find him like he came to me inside the MoonBridge?" Cathy's mind raced; for the past half hour she thought Jack was gone forever. Now she had a glimmer of hope.

"What about your portal Jaden? Can we all focus our minds together to find him?" Cathy clutched at any straw possible.

Jaden doubted but agreed it was worth a try. He had no idea where the portal would take them if they tried to collectively control it. This had never been done before. The three held hands in a small circle. Jaden tried desperately to imagine the portal opening next to his friend Jack. He wanted to see him. "You must think of his face and imagine you're stood alongside him. Believe he's talking to you and that he can see you."

Jaden focussed his thoughts, to a single point, right alongside his friend. "Concentrate girls; focus only on Jack."

A small light formed into a ball of beautiful multicoloured turbulence.

"Help me girls, think harder. Drive your thoughts into the black centre of the portal. Make it see Jack. Make it find him in his dark place."

Squeezing their hands tightly together they made the portal grow to the size of a football; the strange apparition spun rapidly.

"Jack," Jaden called. "Jack, hear us. We're coming for you."

The girls screwed up their eyes to help them concentrate and focus on Jack's face.

The portal expanded to the size of a man. "Come on girls, let's go. Follow me." Jaden pulled the two girls through the open portal. With one step they fell into the void. The pitch black opening swallowed them without a sound and then flicked silently out of existence. The portal closed.

Tina-Lu couldn't imagine a weirder experience; she thought the MoonBridge was bizarre but this was worse. You were left with a disconcerting sensation of falling – a mixture of sea sickness and dropping quickly in a lift, as if you had jumped off a high cliff, but then never quite reached the bottom.

Suddenly; the three found themselves standing in a space formed of spiralling colours and sweeping sounds.

"Where are we Jaden?" Cathy felt sick at the oscillating surroundings.

"I'm not sure? We certainly haven't appeared alongside Jack."

"You are wrong my friend. You have found me just as you suspected."

All three spun around to the sound of the voice behind them. Nothing was visible.

"Where are you Jack?" Tina-Lu became frustrated at this awful place.

"I'm right here. Look." The strange surroundings dissolved like water washing away paint from a brush. A perfectly circular room of brilliant white replaced the swirling colours. Jack floated in the middle about two metres from the floor. He sat cross legged and looked different; he seemed larger and more powerful somehow.

"Jack; is that you?" Tina-Lu wasn't convinced.

Her brother held a new staff that seemed to shift shape and rarely occupied the same space for more than a few seconds.

Jaden and Cathy stared confused and amazed.

"Welcome to the Lost Room. Welcome to the eternal prison." Jack's lips didn't move but his voice spoke loudly.

"We're inside the Lost Room - I thought that was impossible?" Jaden was puzzled.

"Unwittingly, the Vinkef sent me here when they tried to destroy me. I don't know why or how you found this place. That's supposed to be impossible." Jack still didn't move his lips to speak.

"Oh, of course," said Jaden. "The off-world Guardian couldn't be destroyed directly; the only avenue was to drive you out of normal existence. Hence you ended up here." Jaden was surprised he hadn't considered this possibility before. "The reason I saw you in a dark black place was that I couldn't penetrate the Lost Room with my mind."

"Precisely, but that still doesn't explain how you managed to end up here. The Vinkef are supposed to prevent anyone finding this Lost Room." Jack smiled.

"If we're in the Lost Room; where's the… um…. Unnamed?" Tina-Lu half spoke and half whispered as if she didn't want anyone else to hear. She looked in all directions expectantly.

"He's here somewhere Sis, I feel his presence. He's very close by." Jack shimmered; his entire body glowed in a pulsing beauty.

"Why are you glowing like that Jack and what are you holding?" Tina-Lu was still not sure about this.

"Don't worry Sis, you're not in any danger, in fact, I've never felt so wonderfully alive. As soon as I arrived, this staff materialised in my hands. Electricity, or something, is feeding me and strengthening my powers. Look at this…"

The three ducked down as Jack spread his arms and lightning bolts shot out in all directions. He grinned broadly, shining as bright as the sun. "I'm growing into something new; I just don't know what it is yet. But this power is flowing through me and around me. I feel like I could run faster than the wind or jump higher than the sky." He grew so bright; the others couldn't look at him.

"Stop it Jack, you're hurting us." Tina-Lu screamed at her brother.

He realised he'd gone a little too far with his demonstration. "Sorry Sis, I didn't mean to get so bright; I'll have to practice a bit more." Returning to normal, he looked embarrassed he'd not been able to control this new power. He jumped alongside his sister and grabbed her arm. "Come on then – let's get out of here."

"Not so fast Guardian. You have something of mine." Alanthian appeared from nowhere and stood right in front of the boy. He pointed the two staffs at Jack's face and looked very threatening.

"Sit!" The Elder commanded; over his shoulder. Tina-Lu and Cathy obeyed without resistance. Jaden remained standing, but felt a great compulsion to obey also.

"SIT." He delivered an even stronger order. Jaden fell to the floor unable to resist a second time.

"DO NOT MOVE." The authority of the Elder's demand was more than the three could ignore. They all sat perfectly still.

Alanthian returned his attention to Jack. "YOU have something of MINE." He conjured every nuance of power into his demand, but Jack just looked at him in puzzlement.

"So, you're the hidden Guardian are you? I wondered when you'd show up here. Strange, somehow I imagined you would be older." Jack paused and tilted his head to one side. The Elder opened his mouth to speak, but Jack interrupted.

"SILENCE FOOL; I think you'll find YOU have something of MINE," Jack spat the retort back into the face of Alanthian. The demand was delivered with such venom the Elder recoiled against its potency. "That staff belongs to me. Give it up NOW." Jack thrust out his hand and the cane jumped from the grasp of the Elder and straight to him. He clasped it tightly as the Elder screeched.

"And that one belongs to my friend." He called the second staff away from the Elder.

This time Alanthian was prepared; he held on with both hands and resisted valiantly. Gathering all his strength; he dived at Jack. In one swift, smooth movement, he lifted the cane above his head and swung it like a club bringing it down in a great sweeping arc. The cane smashed into the staff Jack was holding. He'd instinctively held up his arm and parried the heavy blow.

"Give me back my cane." Alanthian tried hard to wrestle the staff from Jack's grasp.

Whilst Jack and Alanthian grappled in combat; Jaden and the girls were released from the Elder's grip, they leapt up from the floor. Jaden ran to Jack's aid; he grabbed the Elder by one arm and shouted to the girls. "Get him you two."

The girls piled into the affray and all four attempted to overpower the Elder.

Alanthian wasn't only very strong he was also very cunning. He easily threw Tina-Lu over one shoulder knocking Cathy to the floor in the same movement. He then grabbed Jaden by the arm and spun him effortlessly down to his knees. With one flowing action he punched Jack hard in the stomach and snatched the cane from his hands.

"Grab him…" Jaden pleaded. He thought his arm was about to break as the Elder twisted it painfully.

Alanthian jumped backwards with both canes held aloft. Sneering gruffly, he recalled the MoonBridge and dived into the opening to escape.

All four sat staring at the space where the Elder disappeared.

Jaden spoke first, "This is not good; he now knows what he's up against - we'll not be so fortunate next time. The Elder will return with the full force of the Blues and Blades, of that we can be sure."

"We must leave this place and pursue him. A wounded animal is a dangerous beast; he'll seek out his allies, as you've said, and we'll be his prey. None will be safe until he's removed." Jack sounded desperate and afraid.

"Are you both okay?" Jaden helped the girls to their feet. "We're in grave danger now. This madman is never going to allow us to live. He wants the great key and has the forces, at his disposal, to take it."

"He's quite good looking though," Tina-Lu grinned to Cathy who agreed with her. "I always imagined an Elder would be like Searlan, not some young fit dishy guy."

The two boys sneered at the girls.

"Typical," Jack thought of his sister's reaction. "What do we do now Jaden?"

A small, brightly coloured, shimmering light appeared between Jaden and Jack at about head height. Growing slowly at first; the four stood back, fearfully, watching in fascination as the light became wide and tall. Surprisingly; out from the light stepped a very old man. He was tall and broad with long silver hair and an authoritative looking face. He lent heavily on a gold headed stick that looked very similar to the silver headed Guardian canes.

"The Vinkef have been defeated; you're lucky to still be alive." The man smiled at Jaden and held out his hand to him. "Keeper of the secret knowledge you're injured - let me help." The old man squinted whilst examining the boy's bandaged leg. "Ummm... You've a nasty gash there." Humming quietly, the old man rubbed his hand over Jaden's wound. "There, I've fixed the damage for you; remove the bindings."

Jaden felt down his leg and found no trace of the injury; the tissue was perfectly healed.

"Who are you?" Tina-Lu asked nervously. "Are you the um… the Unnamed?"

The old man's face burst into a huge smile, he laughed heartily. "Unnamed? Goodness me no. That's just an old wives tale of foolish gossips. No my dear child I'm not Unnamed. I've been given many names, over the ages, and have been afforded even more faces." He laughed again and rapidly took the form of dozens of colours, creeds and religious deities.

"Those are a few of the faces I'm known by," he reached out and took Tina-Lu's hand. "Know me for who I really am daughter child. You're the voice of the off world and you've a great gift; call me, Allfather." He lent down and kissed her on the cheek.

Tina-Lu flushed bright red.

The Allfather turned to the others and said with a big grin. "Yes, you may each know me as the Allfather; for that's what I am, to you at least. You would know me as the father of all things, the father of all creation."

"Are you God?" Tina-Lu felt closer to this old man than anyone she'd ever known.

The Allfather smiled at her and replied. "That's perhaps one of my many names, child. But it all gets very complicated you know."

"If you really are God; and therefore, I suppose all powerful, why have you remained locked in here? Why didn't you just leave?" Jaden was puzzled by this apparent conundrum.

The old man faced Jaden and took on a very quizzical look. "There is nowhere, in all of my creation, that I can be prevented from going or from seeing young Sage. If that's what you ask. Why I choose to remain here is outside of your ability to understand. Suffice to say; it's suited my purpose to seem to be confined within the constraints of this Lost Room."

Jaden didn't pretend to understand. How could he?

The Allfather continued. "My children needed room to grow and time to find their own paths. This place made that easier to achieve."

"What of your key Allfather? Is that an old wives tale as well?" Jack was overcome by admiration for this beguiling man.

"Ah, off world Guardian. You've a great weight upon such tender and young shoulders. My daughters have been very remiss to lay such a burden at your feet. The answer to your question is itself a conundrum. The answer is both Yes and No depending upon your point of view."

Jack grinned broadly. How could anyone help but love this old man? He was like one hundred Sages all rolled into one. Somehow, he just knew the answer would be complicated.

The Allfather continued, "The conundrum exists because the key you seek is hidden. Yes, it's hidden even more so than the Lost Room. Does it still exist? Who can tell? When I removed it from existence I made sure it would never be found by anyone in all eternity, not even myself. My daughters never believed that to be the case and always hoped one day a Soothsayer would come along. One who could undo the undoable; they believe that person is you Jack Ferns. They believe you can reach out beyond all creation and retrieve the irretrievable. If that's the case then it's beyond even my sight."

"What is this then Allfather?" Jack held his multi-coloured staff up above his head. A bright flash of golden sunshine illuminated all of their faces for the briefest instant. "Is this not the conduit that we seek?"

"No my young impatient Guardian, it's not. This is my gift to you; and you'll need it before too long. My daughter's staffs are coming to an end; the fool doesn't realise, of course. When he defeated the Vinkef, he also relinquished much of their potency; they'll not recover as he believes. In a very short time they'll revert to being just walking canes and he's going to be very disappointed." The old man smiled again as if laughing at his own private joke. "You have in your hands a new conduit of sorts. One I created to help you grow to your full potential, if that's to be your destiny. Take time to learn some of her secrets Jack Ferns. She'll help you in many more ways than you can yet fathom. As you grow, so shall she."

"Does she have a name Allfather?" Jack asked expecting some strange name like the two lost staffs.

"What name do you think young Guardian; she shares the name of your true love?"

Jack looked a little bewildered and shrugged his shoulders.

Turning to speak; the old man had a glint in his eye, "Why, her name is Cathy of course."

Cathy and Jack both blushed instantly. Trying to gloss over the insinuation, Jack looked at the Allfather and hurriedly said. "I don't know why, but when I arrived here a strange poem formed in my mind. Can you explain it to me?"

"A poem you say? That's a surprising development and completely unforeseen. I do so enjoy the unexpected you know."

Cathy and Jaden were enthusiastic to hear what had popped into Jack's head but his sister had a different opinion.

"Poetry from you Jack, oh come on."

The Allfather smiled again and sat down comfortably on a huge chair made of pure light that formed around him.

"Let's hear his rendition and then make up our minds shall we." He cast a sideways glance at Jack's sister.

The boy stood quietly for a moment and then looked skywards. He imagined the great swathe of stars that twinkled against the inky blackness.

> *"The stars I see at night, far out across the void.*
> *They seem so small and yet I'm told their size is great.*
> *Huge suns of boiling burning mass,*
> *that warm and feed the life that grows*
> *on endless cold and silent worlds.*
> *Each giving birth, in many ways,*
> *to creatures that I'll never know.*

Unseen
Unheard
So far away they almost seem unreal.
But with my mind, I reach on out.
At speed of thought,
no need to look with eyes that see the light so slow.
I touch the infinite wondrous place
where energies unfurl themselves.
For mighty is this Universe,
but within my mind, I view it all,
A glowing orb that spreads itself,
across the emptiness that waits,
For man to reach of himself,
To feel and know,
that he is truly great..."

Jaden couldn't stop himself from continuing as Jack paused for a breath.

"Beyond infinity I sit and gaze upon my Universe,
For now I walk beyond the stars,
No longer tied to anything, I'm free at last.
The bonds that held me to the Earth are now released.
For I have solved the paradox of life and death.
Goodbye mankind, I'll wait for you to grow as I have grown."

Jack looked at his friend Jaden and nodded solemnly.

Tina-Lu stood aghast that her brother would speak such meaningful and potent poetry. "Where did you say those words came from Jack? And, how did you know the ending Jaden?"

Cathy slid closer to Jack and gave him a little hug. "That was lovely; the words really sum you and Jaden up, don't they? You both sit beyond infinity, don't you?"

"These are the hallowed words of the ancients Jack. They've not been uttered to any uninitiated Sageling since they were devised countless generations ago. Passed secretly from father to son, they've been handed down across the centuries. These are the words of the keeper of the secret power and are never uttered lightly. I mistakenly believed I was the only remaining custodian of this declaration. Quite why you would've come by them, on entry here, I cannot guess, but maybe the Allfather can explain."

They all turned to the old man who sat daydreaming. "Quite beautifully recited young Guardian, I'm moved by your passion and conviction. My daughters were right, it would seem; you are very exceptional indeed. These words are a special bequest for you, a hidden and secret gift afforded only the very few that have the depth of foresight and Searship. When I created those words and handed them to Belandron, an ancient ancestor of Jaden's, I wondered if they would survive. I now see they have. Thank you; my heart is lightened and my soul lifted at hearing you speak them." Drifting again within his own thoughts; he paused for several seconds, "As to their meaning; that's simple. You are, who you are, and you'll be what you will be; these words just confirm that."

Jack shook his head in complete confusion, he thought better of saying out loud. "What exactly does that mean?"

Jaden shrugged and grinned sympathetically at his friend.

"Well I think that's about as clear as mud Allfather. What on earth did you mean by that?" Tina-Lu was having none of it. She didn't understand a word of what had been said and wasn't about to pretend she did.

Everyone else laughed loudly. Jack put his arm around his sister's waist and hugged her tightly. "I'm so pleased you're here Sis; life would be so boring without you."

"Well! You are what you are, and you'll be, what you will be," She mocked him and laughed even louder. "He doesn't know what he will be Allfather. This is Jack we're talking about here; my LITTLE brother."

"Daughter-child; haven't you guessed? Do you genuinely believe I need to tell you who Jack Ferns really is?" The Allfather held Tina-Lu's gaze and lifted his eyebrows quizzically.

Jaden stood up and walked over to Jack and bowed his head before dropping down on one knee.

"I see it now Lu, Jack is the Sage of Sages; a Soothsayer who will walk beyond infinity and become the true Master Guardian of the Bridge. Your little brother is growing into something very special, something the world has never seen before. I kneel before you Jack Ferns, you're the true keeper of the secret knowledge and I salute you."

Jack grabbed his friend and pulled him up. "Don't be so ridiculous Jaden. You're the Sage of Sages, just as your Grandfather before you. Me; I'm just a stupid kid really, not much more than that. You certainly don't kneel before me."

Cathy took Jaden's other arm and held him tightly. "You're the best and dearest friend anyone could ever hope for Jaden. We all know you're the one true Sage and that you've taken your Grandfather's place. Jack will be whatever he is going to be. You though, are already the keeper of the secret knowledge and no-one is ever going to take that from you. We should all kneel before you, not the other way around." She kissed him lightly on the cheek and squeezed him so tightly he flushed bright red.

Tina-Lu and the Allfather watched in mild amusement at the discussions taking place.

"Please Allfather, tell them the truth about Jack, and put us all out of our misery." Tina-Lu pleaded.

"Try to understand little ones; never has it been my way to directly tell people anything. Life is such a great adventure Daughter-child and the discovery of knowledge is the secret of all success. Fulfilment and enjoyment go hand in glove; to be given an answer is to spoil the question. Seek and ye shall find; one of my better quotes I always thought."

The Allfather stepped back and floated higher into the air away from them.

"Now my children it's time for us to depart, we'll not meet here again, but you can always find me if you really need to. You'll know how."

He pointed to his head and then to his heart. Smiling sweetly at all four before him, he bowed slowly. "You'll all realize your destiny in time. I know, for I've already set you on your path of enlightenment. Stay true to one another."

With that profound statement the Allfather gave a slight wave and the four friends disappeared from the Lost Room. The light around them faded and they reappeared high on a hilltop overlooking the cave system used by the Resistance fighters. Each held the other and grinned.

"Well, what did you make of that then? Did you hear him; he called me Daughter-Child? No-one is ever going to believe this at home." Tina-Lu was, as ever, the first and often the last to speak.

Chapter 27 - Trials and Tribulations

Alanthian tumbled out of the MoonBridge, panting, and rolled onto the grass. "You'll pay for this," he fumed; cursing the Guardians. "You'll pay dearly." The fading exit deposited him on the inside of the old fortress wall – sitting up, he found his bearings. Except for a few birds flying around, the place was empty. Soldiers had abandoned the area, over two years earlier, to march with General Pen-D'anatè to war - none had returned.

Alanthian considered returning to his chambers. "How will I overcome the other Guardians now? I need some kind of lure to trap them; something to get them out of the Lost Room and into the open. Maybe I'll have the Shumiat eradicate them for me. Yes, then I'd be free to deal with the Unnamed and find his infernal hidden key."

The Elder paced back and forth becoming more agitated at the humiliation he'd just endured. "I'll crush them where they stand. They'll all pay for this insult; I'm the true Guardian and will have my revenge. Lord Tzerach will help me for sure, I may even get that fool Pen-D'anatè to assist."

***

The Lord Tzerach, of the Shumiat, gathered his thirteen Blue protectors around him. He'd been informed, by his spies; Alanthian was no longer in the fortress. "We may have been betrayed, my friends; I know the Elder has other agendas, but this time he's gone too far. His reckless pursuit of this key has left us unsupported. We need his Guardianship to ensure access to the MoonBridge. He must be found and returned to me."

The humming intensified as the loyal protectors acknowledged their leader.

"I must find a replacement Guardian; one who can control the opening of the MoonBridge without having ideas above his station?"

Tzerach paused in contemplation. "The Elder has become a liability; perhaps it was a mistake to grant him regeneration after all."

Each of the Blues stood patiently awaiting orders. The Lord Tzerach didn't tolerate insubordination from any Shumiat; a great leader afforded the highest honour by the most privileged of their order, his word was law.

"You must travel quickly and widely; return with this snivelling fool or find another Guardian, don't fail me my trusted friends."

Before the Blues could depart, a bright light formed; the MoonBridge opened in front of them. Lord Tzerach prepared his protectors to fight any enemy appearing across the divide.

"My Lords," Alanthian was surprised to find all of the Shumiat gathered together. "My Lords, I've barely escaped with my life – in service of your great plan. You must come at once if we're to secure victory; the Unnamed must be destroyed to unlock the secret of the Lost Room. Only with the hidden key can I serve you fully."

Looking subserviently at the leader of the Blues; Alanthian became concerned at the lack of response from the Shumiat. "Lord Tzerach, I've attempted to gain the great key and have narrowly failed. The combined efforts of two Guardians, a Sage and another unknown witch have forced me to withdraw. Although I didn't actually see the key, they were clearly protecting it from me. With your support I could return and overcome them." He knelt down, pleading with his masters.

The Lord Tzerach finally spoke. "Fool, did you think the all powerful Tzerach would permit you to take this key and use it against me. You've attempted to betray me and failed; now you return and dare to seek my assistance - I should destroy you where you stand."

Alanthian froze; this time the Shumiat Lord wasn't going to be coerced. He thought rapidly as the other creatures crowded closer around him. "You're mistaken my great and mighty Lord. I would never betray the Shumiat; least of all you Lord Tzerach. Ever have I served you and assisted you in all your plans. Have I not delivered these lands to you as I promised? Have I not opened the MoonBridge and transported you wherever and whenever you required."

The Shumiat hummed menacingly and pushed even closer to the fearful Elder.

"Look at my wonderful body my Lord; before your miracle it was frail. My old weakness is gone; you've graciously afforded me this magnificent gift of youth. Why would I turn against such generosity? I merely sought to achieve this task alone as I believed it was within my ability to do so. This great key has always been my goal, of that you are aware. The power it will bestow is no match for the Shumiat, we both know that. Why then, do you believe I would betray you? I throw myself before you and beg you believe this fool for his naivety." Alanthian fell flat on his face half expecting to be fried by the death-ray of the Shumiat. Nothing happened for a few seconds except the humming of the creatures.

"So be it fool; I'm convinced, for now. You're more use to me alive than dead; you've been reprieved only because it suits my purpose to do so. Rest assured, no such warning will be offered again. Cross me once more and death will seem like fresh summer's morning compared to the pain and hurt I'll bestow upon you."

The Elder gingerly stood up as the other Shumiat backed away. The humming lowered considerably as the majority of the creatures left the room.

Alanthian looked directly at the great Lord Tzerach and bowed very slowly. "Thank you my Lord. I'll never make such a rash and foolish mistake again. Your generosity and kindness humble this poor fool." Even as he spoke the words, Alanthian plotted how to banish these dreadful creatures to the places between this world and the next. He would send them out into the voids across the MoonBridge. They would be lost forever.

Tzerach growled deeply.

"Soon I will be free to rule." The Elder thought surreptitiously. "Yes, you'll pay dearly for this Tzerach. I've already overcome and defeated the supposed eternal protectors. Even the mighty Vinkef couldn't stand before me. Know this, once I possess the key, you'll pay dearly." His face never betrayed his anger.

Alanthian bowed once more and backed away from the Shumiat Lord to seek refuge in his tower. This campaign hadn't gone entirely as he'd planned. He'd been remiss in failing to anticipate the combined strength of his enemies. Even with both staffs he'd still not been able to overcome them. He wouldn't make that mistake again. The Elder lay down on his bed attempting to relax and meditate. "I mustn't rush again into the unknown. I must plan even more meticulously and use these staffs to help me see far across the lands to my enemies." He grasped both staffs tightly and laid them across his chest forming an 'X'.

"You'll bring a prize so powerful and terrible that I'll destroy every enemy before me." He closed his eyes. "That was too close for comfort. They'll never have that opportunity again; next time it'll be me doing the threatening, not Tzerach."

Subconsciously, his mind drifted away; he approached sleep. Without realising why, his thoughts moved to focus on a person's face. The pretty face of girl, a very beautiful girl he'd seen that day. He'd never seen anyone so intriguing or dangerous in a lifetime of ages. "And who was that other girl? Lu, the Sage had called her. She was strangely powerful despite my ability to control her. Umm, also very beautiful; I'd certainly not expected that?" Alanthian hadn't imagined his change in body would also spark a seed of yearning forgotten so long ago. The beguiling scent of her hair drifted into his vision. As he'd thrown her over his shoulder he'd not consciously recognised that smell. But now, his memory recalled the sweetness of some unknown perfume. The Elder liked this feeling; he liked it very much indeed.

Hours later, Alanthian awoke with a start. Outside was dark and overcast, the air was heavy. He wiped the beads of sweat from his forehead and cursed the oppressive atmosphere. A brilliant flash, of pure silver, filled his room quickly followed by a deafening clap of thunder. "So this is what woke me." He mumbled.

"No my foolish Elder, it was I that woke you."

The darkened shadow, of a hooded being, lurked menacingly across the other side of the room. Alanthian sprang out of bed and reached for his two staffs.

"What," he yelled. "Where are they?"

The hideous creature slithered silently back into the darkest recess of the room. "You're careless Elder. I now possess that which you have sought so desperately."

"Thief, show yourself to me. "

"Your threats mean nothing to me Elder. I'd sooner see you destroyed than permit any further interference. Unfortunately, my masters demand you meet with them, and I'm here to collect you."

"What have you done with my canes thief? Speak now or you'll never leave this room." Alanthian forced every ounce of his powers into the threat and knew the blow would break a hundred men.

The creature fell backwards, against the wall, and dropped to the floor writhing in agony. The power of the Elder's voice smashed deep into the being's soul.

"I was warned you had power Elder, although I doubted my colleagues' assessment of you. That was a mighty attempt to break me and I salute you for your efforts, but know this I still stand." The creature rose slowly and became twice its original size. The dark hood reached almost to the ceiling of the great tower room.

"Lesser mortals would've buckled under such a command. Who are you thief? What do you want with me?" Alanthian was intrigued. This creature was strong; he wouldn't be given a second chance to destroy him so it was better to gain his confidence. "Why have you come to my side and stolen my possessions? If your leaders genuinely required an audience with me, why come sneaking into my private chambers to do it?"

"You've brought an enemy here capable of destroying us all. If you think you're in league with them then you're very much mistaken.

The one you call Lord Tzerach is already planning to bring tens of thousands of his kind across the gateway. He intends to destroy you once you've opened the path and to take another Guardian as his slave. "

"How do you know this and why are you telling me? What is your name; anyway, I can hardly keep addressing you as thief, even if you are?"

"So many questions Elder; I know this because, we, the underworld peoples make it our business to know. We have endless passages and tunnels honeycombing the four corners of the lands. We listen and we watch, but we're rarely seen. Why I'm telling you; is because we need to seek your council. As to whom I am, you may address me as Chaos."

"You still haven't told me where my canes are. I want them before I go anywhere or do anything for you Chaos."

"The trinkets you seek are hidden from you. I no longer possess them; they've been taken from this place and held safely as means to ensure your cooperation."

"You have them on your person thief; you cannot possibly have hidden them. You lie."

The creature wearied of the questioning and threw back his hooded cape. A disgustingly twisted and hideously contorted creature appeared before the Elder.

"Search if you must fool. That is, if your stomach can take the sight of my hidden form." Chaos laughed at the repulsive reaction of the Elder.

"Foul beast, cover yourself before I vomit all over you." Alanthian's stomach reached several times before he could take control of his actions. He'd never witnessed anything so foul in all his long years.

"Why do you think we live in the bowels of the earth fool? We know we're not wanted by the surface folk. Most have forgotten we even exist."

Alanthian gasped for breath at the stench emanating from the rotting flesh of this foul creature.

"Enough of this, fool, it's time for us to leave. You'll receive your precious trinkets after you've met with the council. Come, we leave now."

The creature grabbed Alanthian by the arm and melted into the solid rock of the tower. An archway opened; as they entered, the wall closed in behind them.

"The Council of Speakers," the creature growled.

Instantly, the room obeyed, Alanthian was thrown against the side of the perfectly smooth rock and then slid upwards until he was squashed flat against the ceiling. The space they occupied sped through solid rock, just as a pebble, dropped into a pool, passes through the water. Faster and faster they flew before plummeting into the bowels of the earth.

"What's happening?" Alanthian pleaded breathlessly.

Deep into the foundations of the world the room rocketed. The air temperature rose alarmingly to an unbearable level.

"I can't breathe," the Elder rasped; his face contorted with the unyielding acceleration.

Chaos stood, unmoved, by the forces being exerted. He neither swayed nor buckled; his body altered in form and seemed to grow into a living part of the surrounding rock.

"We're arriving," the creature's monotone, and matter-of-fact, statement in no way prepared the Elder for the abrupt end of the journey.

Alanthian was hurled headlong into the side of the creature. He screamed in agony as the journey ended; a loud crack accompanied his head hitting the creature's heavy bony elbow. To top it all, the Elder smashed heavily to the floor and lay unconscious for several seconds. His body shuddered uncontrollably. Twisting his neck; his head came to rest on the contorted, and foul smelling, foot of the underworld creature.

"Arghh, yughh." Alanthian spat and coughed at both the pain in his neck and the stench from the layers of rotting flesh under his nose. His stomach reached again and he choked out a mouthful of vomit all over the creature's leg. The liquid hissed and boiled as soon as it touched the hideous flesh.

"Get up fool. We've arrived at the meeting of the Council of Speakers." Chaos grabbed the Elder's arm and hauled him to his feet.

"Wake up and look before you. Few outsiders have ever been permitted to visit this place; fewer still have left in one piece."

Alanthian swallowed hard and tried to stop the painful ringing in his ears. Every part of his body hurt and he could still taste the stench from the creature's foot.

"My Lords, here is the Elder you seek." Chaos threw Alanthian onto the smooth rock surface. He came to rest at the feet of the three creatures sitting on thrones of living rock.

Alanthian managed to stagger into a standing position. "Who are you? Why've you brought me here? And, where are my stolen canes?"

The three underworld Lords looked on dispassionately at the obviously injured overworlder. Just like Chaos, these creatures were shrouded in large cloaks with enormous hoods hung over their heads. As one, they slowly lifted back their shrouds and revealed their distorted and twisted faces. Each one was horribly ugly to Alanthian's eyes.

The Lord in the centre raised his heavy eyebrows and spoke in a deep, guttural tone. "Elder, we have watched you for a very long time and have seen this Blue enemy grow in confidence under your guidance. Whilst we've little interest in the overworld, when the actions of the surfacers causes danger to the depths we must take note. Time is rapidly running out for us to act; we fear these Blue monsters are about to overrun this world. Many underworlders have called for your immediate destruction; their hands are stayed only through respect for this council. You're only permitted to exist at all whilst we decide your fate."

Alanthian felt very claustrophobic, the air was hot and stifling, and he could see no means of escape. These revolting creatures would surely kill him with little more thought than stepping on an ant.

The underworld Lord continued. "You may address me as Lord Shadenor if you must. This is Lord Granstone to my left and Lord Shalewort to my right. Together, we form the Council of Speakers, we're the Underworld leaders. You've been brought before us to give yourself one final opportunity to redeem your wrongdoings. The evil Blue creatures, you brought across the MoonBridge, will soon number in their thousands. Already they're stripping the lands bare. Stone and rock are disappearing in their quest for complete domination; they're absorbing our very lifeblood. They must be stopped and the MoonBridge closed, permanently, before all life is extinguished, yours included. As for your staffs, they'll act as collateral, for the time being, and help to ensure your co-operation and closest attention."

Alanthian looked dejected; he was a prisoner in all but name. These creatures could destroy him within a blink of an eye, and he was in great pain from the knock to the side of his head. He struggled to think clearly. "What would you have me do Lord Shadenor of the Council of Speakers? It seems you already hold all of the cards. You say my life is forfeited; so what point is there in my helping you? Without my staffs how do you expect me to control the MoonBridge on your behalf?"

The Lords huddled closely as they conversed together in a deep rumbling incomprehensible speech. Lord Shadenor looked across to Alanthian. "These trinkets will be released to you in good time Elder. First, you must explain about the Blue creatures and their powers. What weaknesses do they have? Can they be destroyed? How do we stop them? Answer these questions, to our satisfaction, and you'll be viewed as a co-operator. Only then will your life be considered safe."

Alanthian realised co-operation with these underworlders was his only option. "I agree Lord Shadenor, you'll have all of the information I can provide. Then I'll need to have my staffs to enable the closing of the MoonBridge."

He smiled at the Underworld Lords and thought. "Yes, and then I'll escape from here and you will also pay for this."

Chapter 28 - Showdown

Studying Jaden's leg; Doctor Frank Baker looked bewildered, "I've never seen anything like this in my whole life Beth - the wound is completely healed. Look, there's no sign of any scar or the stitches. You would've thought nothing had ever happened." He looked at Jaden and asked, "Who did you say did this?"

The Sage grinned, "You'd never believe me if I told you Doc. Suffice to say I've been gifted a great miracle and will be eternally grateful for the honour. I'm humbled that I've been treated in such a manner and could never forget the experience. The kindness bestowed upon me leaves me feeling insignificant."

The Doctor and Aunt Beth shook their heads in amazement. "I'll have to document this Jaden; no-one has ever recorded any event like this, in any book I've ever read. You'll become even more famous than your Grandfather I believe. The Miracle Sage they'll call you; healed by the very hand of God."

Jaden took his leave and escaped the dreaded prospect of being known by such a thing. He went searching for his friends and found them sitting, at one of the tables, in the restaurant area. Jack had been brought a huge loaf of bread, a mass of cheese and some fresh sliced ham. He'd obviously been sweet-talking Mrs Hadley, the cook.

"Tuck in Jaden, there's plenty for everyone." Tina-Lu gave her friend a huge, doorstep size, sandwich.

"Am I supposed to eat this or sit on it?"

The friends burst out laughing.

Speaking with a mouth full of fresh bread and thick sliced ham; Jack almost choked, "Have we heard any news of the Group Captain's plans to move against the Blades yet?"

"I've only been to see the Doctor and Aunt Beth; I'll visit the Group Captain later. For now, we should plan our next move. I think we're going to have to return to the fortress and face Alanthian the Elder. He's never going to give up on the great key and the Allfather isn't going to prevent him, it's clearly not his way."

"Do you think the Elder will bring his Blue creatures with him?" Cathy was agitated at the prospect of meeting these dangerous off-worlders.

"What chance do we have against their kind of power? We've already seen what they can do, and could easily be killed." Tina-Lu was also frightened.

"I simply don't know, but maybe, Jack could project across to the fortress to find out if the Elder is actually there. If not, can we set up some kind of a search to find him? I don't like this situation where we're completely in the dark."

Jaden munched on his sandwich. "Mmmm. This bread is as delicious as it smells. No wonder my stomach churned when I entered this hall, fresh baked bread really sets my taste buds off."

They all agreed and called out compliments and thanks to Mrs Hadley, in the kitchens behind them.

"You're welcome my dears..." came the reply.

The friends sat and finished their food. They set off in search of the Group Captain; as they approached his Head Quarters area, one of the Officers came along.

"Lieutenant Johnson is that you?" Jack enquired.

"I'm Captain Johnson now young Jack. I've been promoted since we last met. How are you all? Why, you hardly seemed to have aged a day and who's this? Is that you Jaden? You've certainly grown."

They exchanged pleasantries and brought the Captain up to date with events.

"Will Group Captain Smithers see us do you think?" Jack was keen to be getting on with things.

"Oh, didn't you realise, he's also been promoted. You're looking for General Smithers. He would normally be very amiable, but the war has been going very badly. He's less inclined to permit distractions to his planning. We've suffered a number of heavy losses, in skirmishes with the Blade General and his troops."

"Would you take us to him anyway? We do desperately need to brief him of our situation." Jaden was very persuasive.

The Captain agreed and led them through a myriad of paths and caverns. The chambers of the General were guarded by two burly Resistance fighters. The Captain spoke quickly to both of them and one went inside to enquire if they would be permitted some of the General's precious time. Surprisingly, the man returned almost immediately.

"The General will see you right away young Sage."

Captain Johnson was most impressed. "You certainly have the Boss's favour, that's for sure. I'll see you all later; I've other duties to attend to. Good Luck."

They waved the Captain goodbye and were led into the offices of the General.

"Hello you four, it's been some time since we last spoke my young friends, what important tales do you have for me? I'm sure you know things aren't going so well, we've lost many good and honourable fighters during the past few months. Both the Blades and those dreaded Blues have been moving inextricably towards us. We'll not be able to hide out here for much longer."

Jaden quickly took the lead and filled the General in on most of the details. His eyes visibly widened as the young Sage described some of their adventures and meetings.

"Are you pulling my leg young man?" he said in disbelief. "Most of what you're describing is fable and fairy story."

Jaden turned to Jack and Cathy. "It's time for a demonstration Jack. You must show the General some of your Guardianship powers. He needs to understand and more importantly to believe us."

Jack nodded and held Cathy's hand. "Let's open the bridge up onto the hilltop; we'll take the General for a little jaunt."

Before they began, the General called out to his guards. "Wilson, no-one is to enter my chambers for the next hour; and, I mean no-one, do you understand."

"Aye-aye Sir," the guard replied.

The General dropped a heavy curtain across the entrance and led them through a low tunnel to another chamber. The space was small but private.

"Now young man, what is it you're going to show me?"

"Sit down General; this may come as a bit of a shock. Please understand, what you're going to see is a strongly guarded secret."

Jack raised his new staff; immediately it burst into the brightest white light and spiralled out across the wall in front of them. A gaping hole materialised in the wall and the brilliant beams of the bridge appeared. They were coloured differently from before and seemed to be more rainbow like rather than silvery.

"Make it exit on the hilltop Cathy"

"Take his hand Tina-Lu." Jaden directed.

General Smithers just sat with his mouth wide open. He'd never seen anything like this, and these kids treated it like it was perfectly normal.

Jaden and Tina-Lu had to physically lift the General onto his feet. "Let's go for a ride," they laughed.

They led the dumbstruck soldier onto the bridge and instantly stepped out onto the hilltop. The sun was setting over the savannah; the chilled air caught them by surprise. Another few seconds and all five stood together watching the bridge fade from view.

"What was that?" the General finally found his tongue. "How did we?" he stammered.

"That was the MoonBridge General. Jack and Cathy are the Guardians, just as I was describing."

Jaden turned back to Jack. "Would you also please demonstrate the light?"

Jack grinned at his friend and took several paces backwards. "You might want to shield your eyes a little," he warned.

Grasping his new staff, Jack concentrated for a moment and then burst into brilliant white and silvery light. He lit up the entire peak of the hill like a giant beacon.

The General stumbled backwards holding his hand in front of his face. "Okay, okay. I believe you now."

The others giggled as Jack shut down his illumination display.

"Let's get back shall we?" Jack and Cathy reopened the bridge and they all stepped back into the inner chambers.

"This is how the Blues move around so swiftly General. You see, there's also one other Guardian, a very dangerous and very ancient man who's been reborn as a young person by the leader of the Blue army. He's very dangerous indeed." Jaden knew every word, he now spoke, carried an almost mystical importance in the eyes of the General.

"What are we to do young Sage? Can this bridge permit my army to travel across the lands like we've just done?"

"We never intended to use the MoonBridge for anything except good. I think that helping you rid the lands of the Blue and Blade armies will be a very good thing. However, this can only be on a limited basis, the MoonBridge is a secret."

"Of course Sage, we need to find some way to hide it from the common soldier."

"If your men are to use it then we must make every effort to disguise its presence. I suggest we open the bridge in a suitably darkened tunnel and have your troops march through to their destination without fully appreciating how they have traversed the distances."

"An excellent idea Sage; is it possible to guide the bridge to any location?"

Jack took over the discussions from Jaden. "No Sir, we cannot open the bridge just anywhere, Cathy and I need to know the location that we're trying to find."

"That limits its usefulness considerably Jack. How can you know the places I would like to send my troops; without going there first?"

"Well Sir, I'm able to see places that are far off, even though I've never actually visited them in person. As long as I'm given directions, I'll be able to 'see' the place before we traverse the bridge."

General Smithers was even more impressed with these amazing young people. He decided Jaden and his friends should be fully briefed in the battle plans. Jack would then be invited to seek out the exit point for the troops. A test run would be conducted with a hand-picked small group of the Generals crack troops. Only then would the main force be unleashed.

Over the next few days, Jaden and Jack spent many hours with the soldiers. They learned of the plans being drawn up. Practice runs were completed and the soldiers had several very useful and extremely effective reconnaissance runs to spy on the enemy. Each trip was timed to last exactly three hours. The team proposed each mission would begin and end at the stroke of the clock. Only at that moment was the MoonBridge opened, the soldiers were to be given precisely one minute in which to cross the bridge. If they didn't show during that time then the MoonBridge wouldn't be opened again and they would have to fend for themselves.

After several days the Special Resistance Force (SRF) missions became very slick. The soldiers had never had so much information or knowledge and the General felt very much happier about releasing his army. Detailed plans for skirmishes were prepared. The General wanted to send his SRF troops to conduct exacting attacks on the enemy - he wanted to destroy their food, water and weaponry, and especially, to hunt down and kill the officers.

Jaden and the others became an integral part of the Generals plans for retribution. As each day completed; the pendulum, of hope, swung in favour of the Resistance fighters. Each mission became faster, more effective and incredibly efficient. One hundred specialist troops conducted several sorties per day. As the supply lines of the enemy's army were severed, so the effectiveness of those soldiers was strangled.

Two weeks of missions had been completed and not one of the General's soldiers had been harmed.

"You four young people are the greatest asset I've ever known." The General praised Jaden and his friends.

"We can't spend much more time in preparations General; we've other priorities to address." Jaden had become the spokesperson for the four.

"Just another week of this and we should be ready to move against the armies of the Blades and root out their leaders. Once they fall: the common soldier will desert, die or surrender to us? This war with the Blades could end in the next few days thanks to you four."

Jack and Jaden had been happy, and willing, to help resolve the predicament of the Blade soldiers, but they knew these were only a small part of the problem. Dealing with the Blues and the Elder would prove much more dangerous.

"I'm concerned the other Guardian will be nearing his preparations for his own offensive. When that happens, we must be ready. There's little time left, I'm certain of it." Jaden said. "The General is manipulating us. We must beware we don't become trapped by our own helpfulness Jack. He's already beginning to see us as his only way forward. That could become dangerous."

The days rolled on and one morning, whilst the four friends ate a very early breakfast, they were approached by an old acquaintance.

"Hello; you four." Captain Johnson greeted them with a broad smile and a very welcoming demeanour.

"I've heard on the grapevine that you guys are the reason for our recent successes." His smile was sickly sweet and patronising.

Tina-Lu didn't know why, but she suddenly felt a cold shiver run right down her spine. She looked at the Captain and just couldn't seem to see him in the same light as before. Something was wrong she was sure of it.

The Captain engaged the four in conversation; only three cheerfully chatted back. He was smiling, happy and very friendly; however, Tina-Lu sat silently shaking with fear and apprehension.

"What is it about you?" she thought to herself. Surreptitiously, she kicked Jack's foot under the table. He looked across at her bemused. "Could you come and help with something for a minute."

Jack looked even more puzzled at his sister. Tina-Lu stood up and grabbed him by the arm. "We'll be back in a minute, I've forgotten to do something, sorry."

They hurried out of the restaurant area and into one of the many tunnels.

"What on earth are you up to Sis?" Jack sounded a little cross.

"He's a spy, I know it."

"What?"

"Captain Johnson is an enemy spy, I'm certain of it. As soon as he came across to us I felt it. I can't explain how I know, I just know."

"But he's one of the General's most trusted officer's Sis, how can he possibly be a spy."

"Don't ask me how, he just is," Tina-Lu was insistent and squeezed Jack's arm as if to emphasise her concern.

"Okay Sis I get the point. If he really is a spy then we're in terrible trouble. First, he knows all the plans; second he has the ear of the General and third, he's extremely well respected by the soldiers. If we're to accuse him of this then we need a hell of a lot more than you just knowing it. I'm afraid your gut feelings won't do, we need hard evidence."

The two paused for a moment to think.

"Let's get the others together and tell them how you feel. We'll have to come up with some plan to catch him out; something to show if he really is a spy. Anyway, who would he be spying for - surely not the Blades? The Captain's been on too many missions. All of them have proceeded with his full commitment and cooperation. "

"What about the Blues? He could be a spy for them."

"I don't think so Sis. They only seem to deal with the Elder and anyway, they're too busy destroying everything."

Jack contemplated again before continuing. "That only leaves the other Guardian. Perhaps he's been taken over by Alanthian; he can be very persuasive when he sets his mind to it. We know that first hand, don't we?"

Tina-Lu nodded and shuddered at the memory of the Elder. "That's it, I'm positive. He's spying for the Elder and he's being visited via the MoonBridge; which is why he can stay here unhindered. The Elder has coerced him into being his puppet somehow."

They both knew these were very serious accusations.

"We've got to get back to the others. Let's find out if he's gone yet."

Jack and his sister returned to find Jaden and Cathy sitting quietly together - the Captain had left.

Tina-Lu quickly brought them up to date with her theory. Jaden's face was a picture. He was horrified he may have just helped an enemy spy. "I've only just finished telling him about the plans the General has made."

"So what do we do now?" Cathy held Jack's hand fearfully.

"We follow our spy of course, then, we tell the General." Tina-Lu spoke in hushed excitement.

Chapter 29 - Retribution

Alanthian used his most beguiling and subservient persona to win over the foul underworlders. He'd finally convinced the fools to return his precious canes as a necessity to progress their own schemes. "Yes my great Lords, I'll fulfil all of your wishes. But first I must call upon the powers, buried in these Guardian staffs, if I'm to defeat the Shumiat devils." The Elder kneeled, acting out his role perfectly. His damaged hands and arms shook with anticipation and a little fear. The power from the Guardianship flowed through his veins repairing his injuries and making him feel stronger than he'd ever felt. "Open!" his simple, emphatic, command brought forth the MoonBridge.

The Council of Speakers could do nothing to prevent the Elder from springing from his crouched position. Nimbly and accurately he fired a glancing blast of electrical energy straight at Lord Shadenor. Alanthian didn't wait for the response from his captors. He leapt head first into the rapidly fading MoonBridge and made a faultless getaway. "Now to deal with that fool Pen-D'anatè," the Elder sniggered. He drove the exit of the MoonBridge right next door to the central offices of the General. A slurping plop signalled the fading of the silvery beams.

The General was far too busy, planning his next move to chase down the Resistance, to hear the Elder arrive. He was singularly focussed on his Captain and aide, Spike Williams. "Still no word Spike, why has there been no word from the front. How long has it been? How long since we had any positive sightings?"

From the far door a soldier came running towards the Captain and jumped smartly to attention. "Communiqué for the General, Captain Sir."

"Right on cue Tomkins, from the front is it? Good news I hope, the General isn't happy today."

The man nodded and scurried away; he was dismissed. The Captain gave the General the news report, hoping the word was good. The rustle of papers saw the General's face light up.

"At last," he bellowed with a loud grunt. "They've finally found the viper's nest. The cowards are hiding across the southern wasteland in some honeycombed cave complex. Now we've got the scum, after all this time, we've really got them cornered."

Spike had rarely seen the General so excited or upbeat.

"Call everyone to arms, we march immediately Spike, let's go get them." The General paced around rapidly deciding the plan of attack. "Get the Elder in here, we need that MoonBridge of his, we need to send the troops across it to the Resistance hideout."

Spike rushed out of the chamber and bumped unexpectedly into the hiding Elder. "Ooophh," was all he was able to say as Alanthian slapped his hand across the Captain's mouth.

The Elder dragged the man into the shadows and out of earshot of the General. "Look at me Williams, look deep into my eyes. You know what you must do, it's time, and you'll do it now."

The Captain's eyes immediately glazed over. The hypnotic power of the Elder's voice triggered a deeply buried hidden response inside the man's mind. He was instantly transformed from the friend and confidant of the General, to the secretive spy for the devious Elder. In that single moment, his world switched over from one master to another. Williams knew what to do; his special commanded task required speed and stealth. The Captain turned, without a second glance, and headed straight into the General's office.

"Back already Spike, what've you forgotten?" Pen-D'anatè was still elated at the prospect of finishing off the Resistance. For the briefest second, the General caught the look on his Captain's face. "What's the matter with you…" was all he managed to say. Seeing the grinning Elder, appear in the doorway; his eyes widened visibly in disbelief.

Williams sprang, right at the General's throat with the renowned, spike, blade drawn. The force of the attack silenced the shocked leader of the Blades. Simian Pen-D'anatè never even had time to react; the weapon stole the life from him. Falling dead on the floor, of his office; he vaguely registered the Elder mouthing something. "Worthless fool…"

Alanthian looked on, grinning happily; his operative dragged the body into a side room. "Williams," he commanded. "Get some elite troops ready, I'll organise the Shumiat Lord and his Protectors. We'll cross the MoonBridge immediately and destroy this Resistance annoyance once and for all." Alanthian turned to leave, the grin still firmly across his face; he called back over his shoulder. "Congratulations General Williams, the army is yours now…"

***

Jack and Jaden decided it was best to just speak to General Smithers of the Resistance first, and try to explain their fears of a spy in their midst. They agreed it was far better the truth was spoken rather than scrabble around for proof that may never appear. The four friends made their way across to the General's chambers, but he was nowhere to be found. The guards couldn't help them and even the other officers, who they knew, hadn't seen him.

"This is looking very bad; he might've been kidnapped or worse." Cathy was feeling very vulnerable all of a sudden.

"Captain Johnson may have locked him up, or even killed him or something." Tina-Lu whispered in a hushed voice.

The four decided to go to the main entrance of the caves and check if the General had left to go anywhere. On the way they caught sight of Captain Johnson talking quietly to several burley soldiers.

"In here quick before he sees us." Jack dragged the others into a passageway that slid into the side of the tunnel.

"Can you project over to watch him Jack?" Cathy asked.

Jack sat down and tried, unsuccessfully, to concentrate. All the hustle and bustle of the passageways made it impossible to focus.

"I need somewhere quieter. This is too noisy."

They all ducked back into the shadows; the imposing figure of the Captain crossed the passageway. He carried on without even a sideways glance.

"Let's follow him Jaden." Cathy now accepted the idea that Johnson was a spy.

"Come on, he's getting away." Tina-Lu was already after the traitor.

Walking quickly towards the soldier's quarters; the four followed the Captain.

"What's he up to?" Cathy and Tina-Lu were really enjoying this.

"Hey Sis, wait up." Jack caught up with the girls. "Look, you two follow Johnson; we'll carry on searching for the General."

The four parted company with Jack and Jaden heading back towards the main entrance. The girls broke into a run to catch up with the fast moving Captain.

"Can you still see him Cathy? He's really in a hurry." Tina-Lu bobbed and weaved trying to keep the Captain in her sights. "Over there look, he's met some more soldiers."

"I know that man; he's the one who hurt Jack, what was his name, Jess or something? I bet he's a spy too."

"Wasn't it Jed?" Cathy suggested. "He wanted to kill Jack. He said he was a Blade collaborator and the General nearly packed him off to be a prisoner."

The Captain led several soldiers towards the armoury where all the weapons were stored for safe keeping.

"Get as much as you can carry and then burn the rest. Be quick about it, we need to leave before the Blue army wipes this nest, of vipers, clean."

Tina-Lu was horrified to hear the orders being given. There was no doubting it now, they'd been betrayed.

"What shall we do Cathy? We can hardly fight them."

Cathy slipped quietly into a semi-trance. She visualised Jack in her mind and called out to him. "Jack, can you hear me?"

Stopping suddenly in his tracks, Jaden bumped heavily into Jack's back. "What the…" he exclaimed.

"Shhh. Cathy is speaking to me," Jack whispered. He listened for a few moments and then said, "Things are getting really bad Jaden. Cathy and Tina-Lu have followed Johnson to the Armoury and he now has other soldiers also working for him. One is that awful Jed who tried to kill me. I never liked him. The girls say they're about to burn the place down and we're to be attacked by the Blues."

Jaden assessed this new information and came rapidly to a decision. "You need to open the Bridge and get us to the girls; we'll all go and get the help of the guard. You should be able to send them right to these traitors and you may even catch them in the act."

Before Jack could do anything; a huge explosion rocked the foundations of the cave walls. Choking dust billowed everywhere.

"What was that? It wasn't near the girls was it?" Jaden spluttered.

"No, I think it came from the entrance direction."

The quantity of dust in the air made it almost impossible to see anything. People began panicking and running everywhere. Mothers and children screamed hysterically in fear for their lives. Soldiers hurried to face the enemy.

"The Blues are attacking; we're all going to die," a petrified woman shouted; dragging her young daughter after her.

"Run for your lives." One of the soldiers ordered. He pushed Jaden to the floor and ran towards the main passageway.

"Let's get out of here." Jack picked up his friend and commanded the MoonBridge to open. With a single step they both leapt across to join the girls.

Smoke filled the area where the MoonBridge exited. Jack and Jaden ducked down low and shouted for the girls.

"Over here Jack." Cathy could just see their feet. She and Tina-Lu lay flat on their stomachs crawling away from the smoke.

Jack reopened the bridge and pushed the exit to the top of the hill. Together, he and Jaden pulled the girls out of the smoke and into the cold fresh air.

Bright Blue flashes split the darkness as the Shumiat smashed through the defences of the Resistance.

"Do we go back and help them?" Jack asked the others.

"It's too late for that now Jack. We need to get to the Lost Room and stop the Elder. This is the full blown attack we've dreaded. The Resistance fighters will have to fend for themselves. Anyway, I reckon the General has been killed by Johnson and they're leaderless. We have to take care of ourselves."

"What about Aunt Beth and the Doctor?" Cathy was distraught.

Jack looked at Cathy and grabbed her hand. "You two stay here and hide, we'll be back in two ticks." With that, he opened the MoonBridge once again and pointed it at the Infirmary. The two jumped across and came out screaming as loudly as they could.

"Aunt Beth..." shouted Cathy.

Explosions could be heard loud and very close. The Blues destroyed everything in their path. Brilliant blue rays mercilessly evaporated everything they touched. Deep rumbling humming floated down the passageway leading out of the sick quarters.

The pair checked every room, as rapidly as they could, but still couldn't find Aunt Beth.

A blue flash burst between them melting the rock; it sliced through the wall as easily as a hot knife through butter.

Jack fell backwards bashing his head and groaned loudly.

Cathy thought she heard something from across the cavern to their right. "It's them Jack, they're through there. I can see Aunt Beth."

Another white-hot poker pierced the walls opening a perfectly smooth hole about a metre wide. The ceiling crumbled. "The whole place is going to collapse on us if we don't move now." Jack dragged Cathy across the cavern floor and dived for cover as three further beams nearly split them in half. The rock was being evaporated at an alarming rate.

"We must get out of here now or we're dead for sure."

They made one more effort and skidded into the shins of the Doctor who was hugging Aunt Beth tightly.

"We must go now," Jack called the MoonBridge and helped the Doctor to his feet.

Cathy grabbed Aunt Beth's hand and they pushed the two bewildered adults onto the sparkling bridge.

An intense flue flash ripped through the opening and disappeared into infinity. Jack pulled the Doctor downwards to avoid the ray and then pushed him forwards with all his strength. The pair fell head over heals out of the exit.

"That was way too close," he puffed.

They scrambled to their feet and saw the enemy already closing in on them. The Blues were everywhere, hundreds attacked the base and the ground was peppered with holes where the creatures had fired their energy beams.

"Let's get out of here; quick!" Jack rapidly opened the MoonBridge, setting the exit for Searlan's cellar. They all rushed to escape as five Blues blasted the area they'd just been standing on. The earth melted around them; they'd barely missed being evaporated by a fraction of a second.

Doctor Frank Baker sat on the cold stone floor of Searlan's cellar and gulped a few times. "I've never met the likes of you four ever. Mystery, disaster and intrigue stalks you like the wolf and his prey?"

Cathy explained the situation to her Aunt as best she could. The others went to briefly explore upstairs. When they returned the

Doctor and his wife sat fearfully, having listening to the tales Cathy recited.

"There are scorch marks everywhere up top from the last Blues attack. The cottage is okay though and it should be fairly safe for now. Aunt Beth; you and the Doctor are going to have to remain here I think. We've some unfinished business with Alanthian."

Tina-Lu looked admiringly at Jaden who sounded so very powerful and commanding. He continued. "Jack, we'll sleep here tonight and first thing tomorrow we should get some supplies together and then head off to the fortress again. Alanthian is definitely going to make another attempt at the Lost Room and the great key. We've got to be ready this time."

Jack nodded in agreement.

"What about us?" Cathy wasn't about to be left out.

"The four of us must stay together Cathy. Lu had a premonition, we all form part of a unit, which will enable us to find the key."

Tina-Lu told Cathy of the strange message she'd received.

"Oh, that feels exactly right Tina-Lu, somehow I know it too. We must become one mind; merge our powers so to speak. The conduit remains hidden because the Allfather made it impossible for anyone to find. Maybe he didn't contemplate a melding of four minds together to seek it out? Maybe that's the point, we have to become more than our individual personalities. Only by developing into something bigger, something wiser can we hope to solve this riddle."

Jack was most impressed. "You're one smart cookie you know Cathy."

The girl's cheeks flushed bright red at the heartfelt compliment from her friend.

Aunt Beth put her arm around Cathy's shoulder and announced. "Of course she is; she's my niece after all."

Everyone decided it would be safer to remain together in the cellar, just in case the Blues attacked. Blankets and pillows were brought down from upstairs and the six weary travellers enjoyed a restful night of peace. At first light they all rose and the plans were laid. Jaden ensured they were stocked up with supplies.

"We don't know how long we're going to have to be prepared for."

Jaden showed the Doctor and Aunt Beth around his grandfather's cottage.

"We'll take good care of it for you Jaden. Don't you worry?" The Doctor was very impressed with the little house.

Finally it was time for the four to say their goodbyes.

"Be very careful all of you and look after my niece." Hugging each one in turn; Aunt Beth had tears in her eyes. When she reached Jack she held him especially tightly and whispered. "She's in love with you Jack Ferns. Take good care of her."

Jack grinned privately to himself and replied. "I know Aunt Beth, I will."

Chapter 30 - Unexpected Allies?

The damaged fortress was completely empty. The shattered roof of the tower looked like a splintered finger pointing to the sky. Cold winds whistled around the courtyard and threw autumn leaves scattering into the air forming spirals of dancing columns. A light, depressing, drizzle accompanied the dark and overcast sky.

"Let's get inside, this wind is freezing." Tina-Lu didn't want to spend any more time, than necessary, in this chilling place.

A large, heavy oak door blocked their path. Enormous spikes of iron protruded in a menacing and defiant manner; wide rusting hinges stained the dark wood. The surrounding stone work added to the overpowering immensity of the structure and sent an imposing message of invulnerability.

"Quite some entrance eh? Doesn't seem as though anyone one has been here for some time though, we should be okay." Jaden observed.

The metal hinges creaked as Jaden tugged at one of the huge door handles.

"Needs some oil I think." Cathy giggled nervously. She looked around fully expecting the Blade army to descend on them at any second.

The squeaking door echoed around the empty hall. A dank and putrid smell wafted out from the opening.

"Yugh, what is that?" Tina-Lu screwed her nose up at the foul stench.

Bats flapped their long contorted wings as they clung so cleverly to the ceiling high above.

"There's your answer Lu. Now look down at your feet." Jaden grinned, pinching his nose.

A thin layer of grey and white droppings covered the floor. The muck was several centimetres deep in places and indicated a large number of visitors occupying the rafters.

"Oh this is so gross. What on earth are we doing here?" Tina-Lu complained, trying desperately to avoid treading in the piles of waste. "I think I'm going to throw up."

One of the bats must have heard her complain, because, at that very moment a loud squishy splat accompanied the soggy, package, that hit Tina-Lu directly on the head. "Aghhhhh; that's sooooo disgusting," she screamed. The others burst out laughing. Tina-Lu frantically tried to wipe the filth from her hair. She jumped around waving her arms in the air and caused a real commotion.

"Stop it Lu, you'll frighten them all…" Jaden's warning was too late; hundreds of bats, clinging to the ceiling, decided to take to flight in a cloud of seething motion. Several dozen suddenly lightened their weight by relieving themselves. A bombardment of bat waste pelted to the floor and also covered the poor unfortunate onlookers.

"Yughhhh, run for it," screamed Cathy.

The creatures launched themselves into a melee of aerobatic delight all around the hall. Large and fearsome black monsters swirled in all directions.

Tina-Lu screamed even louder and ran, across the room, into the adjoining chamber. The others followed.

Jack slammed the inner door closed behind them and looked at his dishevelled sister. They were all splattered with stinking grey white mess, but poor Tina-Lu was covered. He reached into his pocket and fished out a tissue to help clean the droppings from his sister's hair.

"It's okay Sis, in some places that's considered good luck. Anyway; we're safe now, no bats here. You certainly shook them up didn't you?"

Jaden left his friends to clean up; he explored the room - high up on the wall was a carving of a fearsome looking figure. The ancient king held a broad sword aloft and looked as though he was about to execute some poor soul crouched at his feet.

"Who's that?" Jack asked.

"I think he's the original builder of the fortress, one of the great ancient leaders who fought against the aggressors from the North. King Mahoris was his name - he proved himself in battle on many occasions killing enemies in single-handed combat; hence the picture of the person at his feet."

"He certainly looks fearsome," Cathy agreed.

Tina-Lu cleaned herself up as best she could. The four walked through the hall and found the stairs that led up into the tower.

"We need to find an anti-chamber several floors up. Look for a room with a mural of a sun god painted on one of the walls. This is where our quest starts."

The search didn't take long, with no-one in the fortress it was easy to just throw open each door and make a quick check.

"Look here, is this the room?" Cathy called. She'd opened a small, unassuming, side door leading off a narrow passage.

Jaden agreed. They marvelled at the painted mural on the far wall. The picture depicted a god of the sun shining brightly over the lands and feeding the thousands of worshippers gazing upwards in wonderment.

"Is that the Allfather do you think?" Tina-Lu asked Jack.

"Guess so Sis; doesn't look much like him though, does it?" he giggled.

Jaden busily pressed and felt around the edges of the painting.

"What're you doing Jaden?" Jack stepped alongside his friend and smiled at the intensity on his face.

"Somewhere here should be a special lever to open the inner chamber. That's what we need to find."

"How do you know?" Jack cut himself off mid sentence. "Silly question, I know; one of your ancients telling you eh?"

Jaden nodded without being distracted from his task. "Ah, here it is." He pressed the nose on the face of one of the onlookers and a whole section of the wall opened outwards a metre or so.

"This is where we need to go." Jaden led them inside.

"This kid's so good," Jack acknowledged; following his friend into the dimly lit chamber.

"Here, let me help." Jack held out his hand and made the Lujnima light flood the darkened room with a silvery, shadowy glow.

The girls pushed close behind the two boys and entered the room. Disappointingly, it was more like an oversized cupboard rather than another chamber.

"Are you sure this is not just the closet?" Tina-Lu asked sarcastically.

"Shut up Lu and watch." Jaden was very serious. "Behold the secret chamber," he waved his arm in triumph at the receding walls.

The door closed behind them. Walls, which had seemed so tightly squeezed together, moved apart. The ceiling raised high above their heads.

"Wow, what's going on here?" asked Jack; bewildered at the expanding room.

"I think the room's the same, it's us who are shrinking." Cathy shook her head disbelievingly. "Aren't we Jaden?"

A distant echoing rumble drowned any possible response. The floor shook violently and dust filled the air peppering them with oversized lumps of dirty mush.

"What was that?" squealed Tina-Lu.

Another huge boom rattled their teeth and shook every bone in their bodies.

"It must be the Blues and the other Guardian. They've followed us again, we must hurry."

Jaden ran forward and beckoned the others to follow. "DOWN HERE YOU LOT. QUICK," he shouted loudly, as a third explosion rocked them sideways.

A small shaft appeared in the floor close to the far wall.

"Jump in before we're all smashed to pieces." Jaden was doing his best to hurry them and dived head first into the opening. The sound of his voice was totally overpowered by the destruction of the entrance.

"Run Cathy." Jack shoved his sister down the hole and grabbed Cathy's hand. The two leapt into the opening together as bits of wood, stone and dust smashed all around them. A blinding blue light filled the entire space, but disappeared from view as the two friends hurtled down the winding tunnel. They writhed helplessly as they plummeted.

"Lay still Cathy." Jack was unable to keep his balance and was conscious he was rolling all over her. He didn't quite know where to place his hands.

Cathy took charge of the situation and just grabbed him by the arm and slid herself close to his left hand side. "Just hang on you silly idiot," she yelled sensing his embarrassment.

They slid faster and faster along the polished surface until they flew out of the bottom and scuttled onto a flattened floor where Jaden and Tina-Lu picked themselves up. Jack flipped sideways and rolled, several times, over Cathy. Clinging frantically to her; they came to a halt with Cathy lying right on top of the extremely embarrassed boy. She had her face a few centimetres from his and couldn't resist the moment of unexpected intimacy; she quickly stole a cheeky little kiss by pecking him on the lips.

"No time for that now," Tina-Lu laughed; mocking her brother's obvious predicament.

Jack hurriedly clambered up and dusted himself off. His face was bright red and he couldn't bring himself to look at Cathy or his sister.

The tunnel they'd travelled down disappeared melting back into solid rock.

"Wwwhere are wwweee?" Jack stammered trying desperately to change the subject from his close encounter with Cathy. "Have we changed back to our normal size or are we still shrunk?"

"This is where we should have been the first time we wanted to find the lost room. I think we've changed back to normal size again, weird isn't it," Jaden explained. "This is the path of the Unnamed. Only a handful of people have ever been here. We must now find the portal to the gods if we are to reach the entranceway."

The room seemed devoid of any openings. The walls were completely unblemished grey and black polished rock surface.

"Where's the light coming from Jaden? There aren't any doors or windows and I can't see any form of lighting." Tina-Lu busily rubbed her hand over the point where the tunnel had been moments before. "It's disappeared; there's no sign of the tunnel."

"You're right Lu, we're trapped. I think the illumination just seems to be in the air." Jaden had no idea how they could see.

Jack and Cathy were attracted to a small orange glow filtering through the opposite wall.

"Can you see that Jack or is it my eyes playing tricks on me?"

He examined the spot closely. "It seems like the rock is being lit from behind, almost as though there is something or someone hidden behind this wall." He rubbed his hand on the spot where the glow was brightest. "Woooo," his hand sank up to his wrist into the solid rock.

"What's happened? Can you feel anything inside Jack?" Cathy turned to the others. "Hey, you two, look at this?"

Tina-Lu and Jaden rushed across to find Jack with his hand stuck in the rock.

"I can't get it out." Jack said panicking. "Someone has hold of me."

A loud slurping sound belched all around the room as Jack's forearm was sucked into the wall and made him jump with fear.

"Don't muck around Jack. Pull your arm out." Tina-Lu was convinced her brother was playing games.

Another loud gulp and Jack was tugged up to his shoulder. The look of horror on his face showed his sister that this was no trick.

"Grab him quick."

Jaden grasped Jack by the waist and tried to wrench his friend free. They others joined in and pulled as hard as they could without effect. An even louder slurp sucked Jack and the others deep inside the rock. No-one could move; they were all trapped in a heavy, jelly-like, substance that clung to every part of their bodies.

The pressure mounted against their skin and Jack had visions of being trapped in the rock by the underworld creatures. The noose tightened, squeezing them until they all felt like they were going to be squashed or strangled. They couldn't breathe; Tina-Lu had already slipped into semi-consciousness. Cathy soon followed and even Jack fainted.

"Jaden, use your powers. Think boy." The voice of Searlan floated to the front of the Sage's mind.

"What do you want me to do Grandfather?" He was at a loss and couldn't think straight.

"Command this rock to release you boy. Be the Sage."

Fighting to remain alert; stars spun around Jaden's head. "Listen to my voice, oh ancient creature of the deep. You don't want to eat us; we mean you no harm and seek only safe passage. Free us now." His demand was less than convincing.

"Oh this is ridiculous." Searlan's voice took on a commanding and powerful stance. "Step aside boy. I'll handle this."

Jaden was in no condition to argue with his grandfather and just seemed to slip into the background as his mind was taken over by his elder. "Back off foul creature, I'm not your supper. You'll suffer an eternity of pain if you don't release me NOW," Searlan smashed his way deep into the heart of the rock creature. The power and light blinded the stinking presence and immediately alleviated the crushing force.

"Sssssssssss." The loud hiss was quickly followed by a spitting sound as the four were dumped in a heap on the floor of the chamber. They were covered in a sticky gooey mess that smelt even worse than the bat droppings. No one moved for several minutes.

Jaden was the first to react to the smell of burning filling the chamber. A needle-sized pinprick of bright blue penetrated the far wall at an angle of about sixty degrees. The brilliant, iridescent, light melted the surrounding rock.

"They've found us again. That's the Blue's weapon." Jaden sounded very concerned; the pursuers had caught up with them.

"What shall we do now Jaden we've nowhere else to run?" Cathy shook in fear at the sight of the growing beam.

"We must find the gateway. These things don't know the word, give-up." Jack was already searching the walls again.

"No, let's try something else. Quickly, hold hands; hurry." Jaden grabbed Cathy's hand and then Tina-Lu's. "Jack, form the circle. Quick, they're almost here."

Jack dived across to the other three and took the girls hands.

"Remember what Lu said, we all form part of the key. We have to become one mind - think hard." Jaden had no idea how they were supposed to form one mind.

The metre-wide beam of light burned brightly; smoke filled the chamber.

"Sis, think; what was the message you received? How do we do this?" Jack was sceptical, but tried desperately to relax his mind. He thought about Cathy and the way he managed to speak to her through his thoughts.

Cathy looked back at Jack. She sunk into his eyes and imagined him slipping and sliding alongside her. She remembered the way he called to her and how she saw him from afar. "I hear you Jack, we are one."

Tina-Lu didn't know why, even though she closed her eyes, she still seemed to be looking at the other three. She imagined her voice calling out into the darkness and asking for help. "Allfather, hear us, we've returned and need your guidance; protect us please."

Jaden watched Cathy and Jack; he felt their connection and joined with it steering their Guardianship powers and sending it in a large protective circle around them all. "Guard us well Guardians of the MoonBridge, by the powers of Lujnima, surround us with your strength."

Smoke billowed into the chamber filling the space with a choking dense fog. The blue beam disappeared as the air started to vibrate with an ominous hum.

"We are one being, one mind and one Guardian. Join now and become the key to the hidden places and the passage to the lost room. Hear us powers of the day and night, we seek your council." Tina-Lu wasn't even sure where the words came from.

The first Blue creature appeared from the melted tunnel followed rapidly by four others. The leader carried Alanthian lying flat upon its upper surface surrounded by a thin protective sleeve. As the creature levelled out, above the floor of the chamber, the sleeve reformed into a perfectly fitting open seat.

"Can you clear this smoke my Lord?" the Elder requested.

An obligatory resonating hum emanated from four of the Shumiat and the smoke instantly evaporated.

"There you all are, so we meet again. Only this time you'll not be so lucky." Alanthian used his most condescending voice. The words crossed the chamber like a hail of bullets.

The four had subconsciously huddled together. Within the blink of an eye they reformed into an outward facing circle, each looking towards

North, South, East and West. They linked their hands and stared directly ahead.

Tina-Lu looked straight at the Elder; she squinted as if trying to refocus onto his face. He'd stood up and spread his arms wide apart. In each hand he proudly displayed the two stolen Guardian staffs. "Elder, leave now whilst you still have the chance. You've no powers over us here. These creatures you've brought with you will not be permitted to cause any further destruction. This is your only chance to leave."

Alanthian didn't quite know whether to laugh or not. He saw and heard the sincerity in Tina-Lu's voice but felt insulted at the threat. "You're even more beautiful, Lu, than I remembered."

Alanthian's words cut into Tina-Lu's heart like a sharpened Blade sword. She could neither repel nor ignore his powerful words. Unwillingly, she actually believed him and found herself looking interestingly at this handsome, fit young man before her.

"I'll spare you and your friends if you come to me and give me the key I desire."

Tina-Lu's resolve weakened; she almost let go from both Jack and Jaden.

"Don't listen to him Sis." Jack tightened his grip and shook her arm, calling to her. "His words are poisoning you. He's using his powers to make you break our circle. Stay focussed."

Jaden spun the four around so he was facing the Elder. "You're powerless against us Elder. We will destroy you if you persist. Leave at once or face the consequences. You've no idea of the forces at our command."

Alanthian turned bright red with rage. "Oppose me and you'll all be evaporated. You'll be the ones to perish fools, not me." The words spat out of the Elder with such venom that Cathy buckled under the attack.

"Don't give in." Jack held her very tightly and lifted her up again. "We're one, remember."

Cathy managed a half smile at the words of encouragement.

"Show them my Lord. Show them what we can do." Alanthian screamed, pointing directly at the face of Jaden.

A blinding blue flash pierced the air and instantaneously smashed into an invisible barrier a few centimetres from Jaden's face. The light splashed harmlessly in all directions.

"Again, my Lord; all of you fire together." The Elder jumped up and down in a terrible fury.

The leader of the blues hummed loudly calling the others to join him, they came together to form a single large unit. Alanthian grinned broadly as they generated a brightly glowing, oscillating mass.

"Yes my Lords, destroy them now." Alanthian hysterically urged the Shumiat creatures on.

The leader directed a metre wide beam of impossible intensity at the four. The air surrounding the field of force immediately fluoresced in the brightest blue glow; popping and crackling wildly. Jaden squeezed his eyes tightly closed, fully expecting to be turned to ash. The bolt of raw power smashed into them but didn't penetrate the guardianship barrier.

Jaden opened one eye, cautiously, and realised they weren't being evaporated.

Cathy stiffened and grasped Jack and Jaden's hands so tightly the blood almost stopped flowing. She seemed to be growing and expanding with each passing second. "Guide me Lujnima," she screamed.

The beam of energy swirled around like a raging vortex. The four were swathed in seething blue illumination. Cathy gripped her friend's hands more tightly than ever, she lent her head backwards and opened her mouth widely. Breathing inwards, she sucked every drop of the raw power from the Blue creatures until the light around them was extinguished. She effortlessly spun the other three around until she faced Alanthian. His face was a picture of pure anger.

"Prepare to meet your maker fool," her words carried as much ferocity as the beam she'd just swallowed.

Cathy filled her lungs with a great gulp of air. Her chest felt like bursting; directing her breath at Alanthian, she blew as hard as she could. The energy beam exploded out of her mouth and was refocused into a spear of purest power. The conflagration emitted from her was transformed into a clean silvery blue-white colour shimmering with multifaceted brilliance. The light hit the Elder hard on the chest.

Absorbing the blast; Alanthian screamed momentarily, "Aghhhhhhh." The pair of staffs attracted the raw power, of the beam, for a briefest second. Gripping them tightly he sneered contemptuously at his attacker, he threw his arms wide open in defiance and distain for the girl. "I am the guardian by right; your powers are pathetic and insignificant." The Elder smiled sickeningly at Cathy; he seemed to cope with the onslaught.

Cathy was outraged and redoubled her efforts sending even more force racing across the chamber.

Jack shook violently, "Go for it Cathy, give them everything you've got."

Alanthian's grin turned to horror as Tel-Vah-Nar and Tel-Vah-Ney tugged at his grasp. Within an instant they burst into a million, needle sharp, splinters sending their deadly arrows in every conceivable direction. The force of the explosion embedded the shards deeply into rock, stone and flesh. Alanthian screamed in agony as his entire body was punctured by a thousand lethal darts. With his protection lost and mind overcome by pain he fell to his knees and was instantly vaporised by the unprecedented heat and power of the ray. Not one single molecule was left of the Elder.

"Nooooooo," screeched the Blue Lord who'd been supporting Alanthian. He then took the brunt of the continuing onslaught. His body shell reflected much of the energy and seemed also to expand as it burned into him.

"Finish them Cathy." Jack screamed uncontrollably.

The beam from Cathy's mouth continued relentlessly for many more seconds, each moment brighter than the last. The other Blues, surrounding their leader, dragged him backwards and up towards the hole in the rock. They retreated as fast as they could but not before a perfectly formed cylindrical hole carved its way right through the heart of the Shumiat Lord. The humming stopped from the creature and the other's simultaneously dropped him and exited at breathtaking speed through the opening.

The dead Shumiat Lord crashed loudly to the floor of the chamber and crumbled into a myriad of tiny blue cubes. The energy beam ceased. Cathy's head dropped forward in complete exhaustion from her efforts; she released her grip on the boys and fell limply to the floor.

No-one spoke a word.

Jack tumbled to his knees in shock. Jaden stood completely motionless with his arms hanging loosely by his sides, the blood drained from his gaunt face. Tina-Lu looked down at her friend lying crumpled on the floor and swallowed deeply not really sure if she was alive or dead.

They were alone again in the darkened chamber. No sound could be heard; no-one felt capable of moving. Jack eventually reached over to Cathy and shook her gently on the arm. She didn't initially stir.

"Oh my head hurts," complained Tina-Lu.

"Mine too," agreed Jaden.

They all looked around in surprise as a familiar voice floated across to them.

"You must hurry my children if you're to find that which was lost. You've far less time than you think. These evil creatures are wounded but not defeated. Even now they're calling for their colleagues to support them. Many thousands will be gathering to rise up against you. Even your new found ability will not defend against the combined might of the Shumiat." The calming, yet insistent, voice of Searlan filled each of the minds of Jack, Jaden and Tina-Lu.

Jaden was the first to reply. "Grandfather is that really you?"

Across the room an apparition of hazy gossamer writhed up from the floor. Swirling rapidly for a few seconds, the shape coalesced into the form of Jaden's Grandfather. "I cannot maintain this shape for long my children. I've been granted this one opportunity, by the Allfather, to directly assist you in your quest." The old man walked over to Cathy and knelt down beside her. "You've done well my child; the Allfather sends this gift of healing to you." He placed both hands gently across her cheeks and blew a sprinkling of glittering effervescent stars onto her face. The stars crackled and popped as they coated and then entered her skin. Cathy opened her eyes and focussed on her benefactor.

"Thank you Allfather, we owe you a great debt. Oh, it's you Searlan I thought…"

"Be not afraid little one, your body is healed and your wounds will fade. Step up now." He lifted her as if she were made of feathers and placed her carefully on her feet.

"We still don't know how to find the lost room or the key Grandfather. Have you come to show us the way?" Jaden had just realised how much he'd missed his Grandfather's company. Even though he'd spoken to him in his mind several times, it wasn't the same.

"I cannot guide you as I do not know the way. Only you, Guardian, can do that." The old man stepped closer to Jack and took his right hand. "You have it within you to do this Guardian. You, Jack Ferns are the path and the light. Search within yourself and you'll know the route you must take."

Jack thought for a moment and tried to delve inside himself for the knowledge the old man insisted he had. He smiled at the apparition and nodded solemnly. "You're right as ever dear Searlan, I do know the way." Jack walked confidently over to the far wall. But this time, instead of touching it, he stopped about an arms length from the surface. Without glancing back to his friends he spoke quietly. "Vinkef protector, hear my voice. I'm Jack Ferns, Guardian of the

MoonBridge and master of the hidden key by right. Rise up from your loneliness and come before me, I release you from your imprisonment and relinquish your eternal oath."

The others were drawn towards Jack's commandment. They waited expectantly, but nothing seemed to be happening.

Jack placed his hand firmly on the wall without it sinking into the trap. "You are lost Korbynithus, I'm your light and your path, come to me NOW."

The wall shrunk away to reveal an endless tunnel stretching off farther than the eye could see. In the distance a ball of light glowed dimly, it moved, at great speed, towards Jack.

"Welcome voice of the Vinkef, we meet again." Standing before him was a young man of about eight years. He looked quite like Jaden, as a boy; the same broad smile and friendly air.

"Thank you Guardian, I'm forever in your debt. You truly are a powerful and great force. The Vinkef will honour any request you make of us, we serve you now."

"No, my dear friend, you don't serve me, or anyone else for that matter. You're free of your oath and free to do your own will. I ask only one thing of you, show me the path that I seek."

Korbynithus hugged Jack tightly in his grasp. Tears rolled down his face. An eternity of devotion and duty had been lifted from the Vinkef's collective shoulders and the relief was more than he could bear.

"As you desire Jack Ferns, the path is already revealed to you. Take your step and you'll reach your goal."

The tunnel, before them, changed subtly in colour from grey to white; the distant end seemed to foreshorten and the path widen.

"Know this all of you; I'm forever at your command. If you ever need my services you've only to call. I'll always hear you. Thank you, farewell and good fortune." Korbynithus bowed low to the ground and then just faded from their view.

"You never cease to amaze me little brother. Where did all that speech come from eh?" Tina-Lu grasped Jack around the waist and tugged him fondly several times in appreciation.

"Well, shall we go find this key or what Sis?" Jack stepped headlong into the tunnel pulling his sister with him. His friends jumped smartly after him with huge grins of anticipation on their faces.

A brief flash of silvery light signalled the shrinking of the passageway behind them; they disappeared from sight. The chamber silently collapsed back into hidden nothingness and the rock reformed as if it had never been burned or moved by any Blue destructive beam.

The intrepid friends had taken the greatest step of their lives and their adventures were only just beginning.

Glossary and Characters

Alanthian 'The Elder'	The last of the elders and the secret Guardian.
Aunt Beth Wilde.	Cathy's Aunt and surrogate parental Guardian.
Belandron	An ancient ancestor of Jaden and the first of the Sages.
Bellaberry	The place where the peoples destroyed by the Unnamed came from.
Brandy	Jack and Tina-Lu's pet dog.
Captain 'Sandy' Connors	One of the Resistance leaders.
Captain 'Spike' Williams	The General's right-hand henchman.
Cathy	The fifteen year old heroine. She is the officially recognised Guardian.
Chaos	The Underworld spokesman.
Crossley	General Simian Pen-D'anatè's personal orderly.
Danthienne	The Land of the Sun and the Moon.
Digger	One of the very nasty Blade Soldiers.
Doctor Frank Baker	The doctor who nursed Aunt Beth back to health.
Epheron the Younger	One of the peoples of Bellaberry.

General Simian Pen-D'anatè	The cruel and wicked head of The Blades army.
Greg	One of the Resistance fighters who thinks that Jack is a Blade.
Group Captain Smithers	One of the Resistance leaders.
Jack Ferns	The fourteen and a half year old hero. He is the off world Guardian of the MoonBridge.
Jaden	The eleven year old Sageling / Sage steward and keeper of the ancient knowledge.
Jed	One of the Resistance fighters who thinks that Jack is a Blade.
Korbynithus	The face of the Vinkef.
Lancaria	The General's name for the conquered lands.
Layette the Decider	A mythical creature that now lives in the jewel of the brooch.
Lieutenant Johnson	One of the Resistance officers in command of Jed and Greg.
Lord Granstone	A member of the Underworld Council of Speakers.
Lord Shadenor	The Underworld Council of Speakers Leader.
Lord Shalewort	A member of the Underworld Council of Speakers.
Lord Tzerach (*Serrash*)	The head of the Blues.

Lujnima (*Loon-hee-ma*)	The Goddess of the night and the manifestation of the moon powers. She is also the twin sister of Tarre-Hare.
Lutharim (*Loo-thar-rim*)	An ancient evil spirit who imprisoned Layette.
Marwearsort	The town where The Blade fortress houses the Lost Room and the conduit.
Mr 'Jonno' Johnsonby	One of the Resistance fighters that Brandy became acquainted with.
Mrs Hadley	The Resistance Fighters cook.
Protector Beharim	The Blues second in command.
Searlan	Jaden's grandfather and Sage of Sages.
Searlanelle	Searlan's only daughter and Jaden's mother. (Elle)
Searlanlay	Searlan's captured and tortured son. Jaden's Uncle.
Sergeant-at-Arms Healworth	One of the Resistance leaders.
Tarre-Hare (*Tah Hair*)	The goddess of the day and the manifestation of the sun powers. She is also the twin sister of Lujnima.
Tel-Rew-Hay	The staff that was given to Searlan the sage of sages by Tarre-Hare to open the portal.
Tel-Vah-Let	The conduit parent of the twins. When joined with the two Guardian staff the conduit forms the MoonBridge key.
Tel-Vah-Nar	The feminine twin staff that is carried by the Male Guardian.

Tel-Vah-Ney	The masculine twin staff that is carried by the Female Guardian.
The Blades	An army of conquerors who wish to take over all of the peaceful lands.
The Blues	Off world creatures who wish to strip the land of all of its resources to feed their own kind.
The Shumiat	The Blues true name.
The Unnamed	The father of Lujnima and Tarre-Hare.
Tina-Lu	Jack's fifteen and three quarter year old sister.
Trevor	One of the Resistance fighters who find Brandy and cares for him.
Vinkef	An ancient invisible protector of the Elders.
Warrior	General Pen-D'anatè's pie-bald horse.